I0671302

CROSSLINE

RUSS COLCHAMIRO

CRAZY 8 PRESS

THE WARP ENGINES were ready for the first of six return blasts it would take to get him back to Earth, when a blip came across the screen. Powell shifted toward the incoming message, but his short-range sensor interrupted him. Something in the Saturn rings. Video amplification revealed that among a cluster of particles was an odd-shaped fragment, with sharper, more reflective edges than he would expect. But he supposed that after debris crashed around over millions if not billions of years, who knew what was really out there? He looked again. Probably nothing of consequence. Just some lagging hallucination from the multiple warps.

As suspected. Just ice particles swirling around the planet. Billions of frozen blue ice particles floating in space that—

Powell focused his monitor on the third ring layer. Studying it more carefully, his sensors revealed that the particle cluster wasn't in the Saturn ring, but among it. The fragment wasn't random, a collection of dust, or some anomalous asteroid fragment.

It was another ship. Looking just like *Crossline*. And headed his way.

Copyright © 2012 by Russ Colchamiro
Cover by Richard Ellis
Interior design by Aaron Rosenberg
ISBN 978-0615777313
All rights reserved. No part of this book may be used or reproduced in any
manner whatsoever without written permission except in the case of brief
quotations embodied in critical articles and reviews. For information address
Crazy 8 Press at the official Crazy 8 website:
www.crazy8press.com

First edition

To MQR—
Soooooo…

PART I

BLAST OFF

"Copy, Tower. Let's drop this rock and get some flyin' done."
—Captain Marcus Powell

"The ship's fine, you idiot. It's the pilot I'm worried about."
—Dale Aranuke

CHAPTER ONE

Houston, Texas
Present Day

Marcus Powell felt like the most powerful man in the world—and in a way, he was. Powell was tipped back within *Crossline*, the most advanced, elegant, and sophisticated spacecraft known to man. And though he was sheltered from view, he still felt like the eyes of the world were upon him.

Out on the launch pad, at the Taurus Enterprises Space Center in Houston, *Crossline* was encased within the windowless cone of *Taurus IX*. The sleek, silver rocket was equipped with three massive external tanks, each containing enough explosive liquid propellant to blast all the polygamist cult leaders in North America back to the mother comet.

After reaching the proper altitude, the rocket would open, unleashing the smaller, sleeker craft within. Until then, Powell took it on faith that the images on his monitor—blue skies, sunshine, white clouds shaped like a humpback turtle—were actually what lay ahead.

Looking through *Crossline's* canopy, all he could make out against the rocket cone's underside were the blue and green lights projected from his cockpit—and an elongated helmet shadow. The distortion revealed the true nature of his journey. How big it all was.

There was a *click* and *crackle* when a familiar female voice came through the communicator in Powell's helmet. It set off a sickening blast of queasiness and adrenaline, snapping him into full alert. *"Taurus, this is Tower. You copy?"*

"Roger that, Tower." Powell straightened up, rolled his shoulders within the one-man spacecraft. "Just wiping down the dash. Don't want tequila shooters gumming up the works."

"Funny, Powell. Funny."

"You gotta relax, Chang. Like my dad always said—if you don't got the juice, it's tough to stay loose."

"Huh. Whenever I was being a jackass, my dad told me to jam a cork in my cakehole and pay attention."

"Well," Powell said. "If you're going to be that way about it…"

"Thanks. You're a peach. Start systems check now."

Crossline's design was similar to that of an Air Force fighter jet, but upgraded to sustain the brutal, unforgiving forces of deep space—due in no small part to the vessel's state-of-the-art Tritanium shielding. Tritanium was only one one-hundredth the weight of titanium, but more than ten times as strong, and was malleable enough for aerodynamic designs.

The ship was also equipped with the soon-to-be-tested warp thrusters. Based on Hunsucker's relative isolation theory of quantum physics, they would propel him through space at a velocity seven times the speed of light. Although in the case of *Crossline*, for just fifty-four-second intervals. The engineers were still working on a sustainable energy source, but they considered any light speed travel pretty freakin' awesome nonetheless. Assuming, of course, that it would work.

Snug in the cockpit, Powell closed his eyes. He felt a surge— *I'm really doing this!*—and then steadied himself. The thoughts may have only lasted a few seconds, but faced with the grandest opportunity of his lifetime, he was suddenly drawn to a series of tasks he left unfinished throughout the years: the model train by the side of his bed, after his father died; a Philly cheese steak he left unattended at his cousin's bachelor party in Seattle; an awful love poem he started for his wife, Chandra ("I love you more than daisies love the sun; what fun!); the guitar lessons he quit in the fourth grade. But now it was time to complete what he started.

"Roger," he said finally. "Beginning systems check now."

Switches ran along the console. Above each switch was the system's name. "Fuel line...check." With a *click* he pressed a square button, turning it from clear to red, setting it to the *ON* position. He read aloud each additional system and pressed the corresponding buttons, preparing *Crossline* for launch.

"Boosters...check. Auxiliary power...check. Weapons... check." Powell confirmed the remaining systems—propulsion, hydraulics, avionics, communications, landing, computer relay, caution sensors, terrain, approach, bioinstrumentation, dosimeters, digital recorder, thermal shielding, heading and vector, weather, vertical displays, jamming, infra-red, medical, autopilot, backup generator, and navigation—until there was just one remaining.

Powell took a breath, held it, and then let it pass through his pursed lips. "Life support...check." Surrounded by mechanics and darkness he thought of his father just then. Had he lived to see it, Thomas Powell would have been proud of his only living son, on this day of days, despite frustration over Marcus's life-long obsession with flight.

I'm coming, Dad. Watch me.

The rocket sat alone on the launch pad. It pointed toward the heavens. Noon approached. Earth's six billion residents tuned in to all manner of Web-, television- and podcasts. They held their collective breath to see if a successful test of *Crossline*'s warp thrusters would revolutionize space travel, ushering mankind into a golden age of exploration. With Powell leading the way.

Come on, he thought. *Whisper those sweet words. You know the ones.*

"*Taurus*, this is Tower. Outer boosters confirmed and integrity intact. All systems are go. We are cleared for launch."

Bingo.

Absorbing the rocket's intensifying vibrations—and the immense gravity of the launch—Powell stared at a picture taped to the upper left corner of the top console. Chandra and their five-year-old daughter, Jesse, leaned against the short adobe wall that lined their yard. Eight miles from the restored Buffalo Bayou, theirs was the only house in the valley. They were smiling, as if anticipating a moment that had not yet arrived. Powell felt like he should have remembered what was happening outside the frame, or who took the picture, but the specifics eluded him.

He reached for the instrument panel, and smiled. Something in his jumpsuit pressed against his chest. Jesse made him promise. Passed down from her Grandma Feather, the doll was *Nan'yehi*, the greatest Cherokee Beloved Woman. Her spirit would look after him, because there was a secret power deep in her heart. Jesse said that when he figured out what it was, he would know for sure that he was in good hands.

Cynthia Chang's voice crackled through the headset. "Powell...you ready?"

"Are you kidding? I'm gonna fly this sucker like it's stolen."

"Just bring it back when you're done. My sunglasses are on the dashboard." They were. A joke between them. And then Powell heard three words that echoed all across the globe. "Prepare for launch."

The rocket's boosters awakened. "We have T-minus ten..."

...*RUMBLERUMBLERUMBLERUMBLERUMBLERUMBLERUMB-LERUMBLE*...

In his mind's eye Powell saw Chandra and Jesse smiling in their yard. Four days earlier, Chandra started to tell him something important. She never quite got the words out, but he knew what she wanted to say. *Don't go. Don't do this. I'm scared.* But she wouldn't. He knew Chandra loved him, but that didn't mean she loved everything about him. Not everything.

"...nine...eight...

...*RUMBLERUMBLERUMBLERUMBLERUMBLE*...

In his mind's eye Powell saw the faces of people he'd never met, in Mumbai and Rome. In Budapest and Seoul. In Nairobi and Oslo. In Auckland and Cincinnati.

"…seven…six…"

…RUMBLERUMBLERUMBLERUMBLERUMBLE…

In his mind's eye Powell saw the long, sleek rocket that concealed him, a missile-shaped tower pointing into the unknown.

"…five…four…"

…RUMBLERUMBLERUMBLERUMBLERUMBLE…

In his mind's eye Powell saw the rocket boosters, ready to propel him off the Earth, away from everything—and everyone—he had ever known. He saw little Jesse. Her fine hair danced in the breeze.

"…three…two…"

…RUMBLERUMBLERUMBLERUMBLERUMBLE…

In his mind's eye Powell saw himself—as both a stranger and companion. And then he went perfectly still. There were no jitters, fears, or apprehensions. No sounds or interruptions. Powell drifted into utter, soothing peace. Just black. And nothing else.

…RUMBLERUMBLERUMBLERUMBLERUMBLERUMB-LERUMBLERUMBLERUMBLERUMBLERUMBLE-RUMBLERUMBLERUMBLERUMBLERUMBLE…

…KKKKKRRRRRBBBBLLLLAAAAAAMMMMMMMM!

A twenty-acre mushroom cloud of fire and smoke and chemical thunder erupted from the boosters, launching *Taurus IX*. Powell felt every morsel of it. "*Whoa-ho-ho-ho-ho,* oh yeah! God damn, oh *man!* The pool's in but the patio ain't dry!"

"Confirm, *Crossline,* this is Tower. We have liftoff."

"*Ohh, yyy-yes www-we d-dddo.*" Even though Powell was a passenger only at this point, he gripped the flight stick anyway. His entire body vibrated like it might completely break apart. His heart lodged in his throat. "*O-ohhh…y-yyyyeeesss…w-wweee…. d-dddoooo.*"

With the rocket boosters almost ninety percent extinguished, Powell no longer felt propelled as much as drifting upward. He took a deep breath, waiting for the mouth of the rocket to open.

Tower Command announced the rocket's ascension. "*Taurus

nine is approaching forty-eight thousand feet. Twenty seconds until Phase Two."

Chang prepped him for the next phase. "You get that, Powell? Twenty seconds until disengagement."

"Copy, Tower. Let's drop this rock and get some flyin' done."

"*Crossline*, this is Tower. Disengage outer casing."

Powell heard a metal *CLANK-RONK*. From the cone of *Taurus IX* he saw the first sunbeam, and as the rocket casing dropped away, the glorious, energizing light finally engulfed him. His heart swelled. His breaths grew tight. *Crossline* was free.

"*Crossline*, you are confirmed for ignition sequence."

In succession Powell ignited the thrusters. One—*blam!* Two—*blam!* Three—*blam!* His ship scorched with such ferocity the sky seemed to melt around him. At almost twenty-five thousand miles per hour, he was being propelled as fast as anyone had ever flown before—yet still at only an infinitesimal fraction of the rate he would soon achieve.

"*Crossline*, you are approaching three hundred twenty-seven thousand three hundred sixty feet. Know what that means?"

Powell took a moment, surprised at his own sense of being literally starstruck. Billions of stars twinkled in the great, black distance. "Outer space."

"Don't get all gooey on me," Chang said. "This is just foreplay."

With a haunting silence Powell just stared at Earth—awesome, breathtaking, triumphant. A thin, blue halo clung to the planet's rim; the mysterious, black forever of space beyond it. The Earth was an elegant marble, cool and slick, glossed with a sheen of perfection. Continents set against the deep blue oceans. Immense white weather swirls. Never before did he truly consider just how magnificent the planet was. How the atmosphere around it had just the right mixture of gases to sustain life. How the Sun kept it warm. How the Moon influenced the tides. How stars inspired dreams. How our place in the Universe—our very origin—was still unknown to us.

He swelled with a symphony of sadness, awe, and inspiration. The sheer beauty brought tears to his eyes. *Maybe there's a God after all. How large his hands must be. Because I'm so small.* And somewhere down there, Chandra and Jesse were waiting for him. The next time he touched down he would not just be a man—but a man of history.

"Time to do your thing, Powell. Initiate warp."

"Copy, Tower. Commencing in five...four...three...two..."

Powell bent his knuckle in what seemed like ultra-slow motion. He then found himself shifting in that great chasm where life and time and space end and some new dimension of consciousness begins. He licked his lips. Whatever his existence had been up until that moment, he knew it would never be the same again. There simply was no such equivalent experience that could have truly prepared him for the amplitude of his next few words.

"Initiating warp...now."

With a *click,* the button was red. And Powell was gone.

CHAPTER TWO

"...Ron Bowlerman here with Margaret Danillo, coming to you live from just outside the Taurus Enterprises Command Center. Today is a history-altering moment in mankind's long and storied journey. The Taurus IX rocket has successfully launched and is hurtling toward space. But it's the Crossline warp thrusters we're all waiting for. Only then will we discover once and for all if the vision of Taurus Enterprises CEO Harlan "Buddy" Rheams Jr. and his highly controversial warp thrusters will work, transporting mankind into a new era of space exploration.

"Buddy Rheams arrived in 1957 as a young upstart from Sacramento, who transformed a small oil drilling company in Kinsey, Texas, into what is arguably the world's most influential corporation. In addition to the oil and Tritanium divisions, Taurus Enterprises also contracts with various police departments, and the United States military, and, of course, is lead sponsor in the Space Program.

"Will Buddy Rheams top even that? I'm not sure how you folks are doing at home, but I can tell you it's simply electric out here. Right, Margaret...?"

Chandra Powell muted the launch broadcast from the notebook computer she left on the patio table. She told Jesse that they were watching the launch from home, from their backyard, because they'd have a better view, but really Chandra just couldn't be that close to it all and still feel so far away. At a moment she was most vulnerable, she didn't want to be confined in a room full of strangers at the Command Center. But when it was time for him to land, she would be there. She would always be there.

"Daddy's gonna bwast into space, righty Mommy?"

"Yep," Chandra said, and though she swore to herself that

she would stay calm, her heart pounded away in her chest. "Any minute now."

"Daddy's speshew to do that, right, Mommy? He's frying the bestest spaceship ever."

Chandra sighed. "Yes, honey. The best ever." She faced the Sun then, following the great trail of white smoke, knowing that her husband was at the other end. They'd fought just days before the launch, and though they were intimate afterward, neither her heart nor mind was at ease. She admired Marcus, was deeply proud of his ability and commitment, but she resented in these moments having to live with the agonizing fear and torment that the wives of firefighters, soldiers, and law enforcement officers share.

Yet Jesse, as always, seemed unconcerned. Not indifferent. She cared deeply. But she knew in the way only children know that her daddy was coming home.

And now that the moment finally arrived—Marcus hurtling through the solar system into the vast unknown—what Chandra wanted most was to close her eyes tight, squeeze hard and open them again, and have Marcus appear before her. The family together.

If only she could, Chandra would have gladly missed the whole thing.

The Tower Command staff flipped switches, spoke urgently into headsets, and scuttled between rows of long consoles. Sunshine beamed through the ceiling-to-floor windows. They wrapped across three sides of the fifth-floor operations center, a quarter-mile from the launch pad.

Monitors were set into the consoles of every technician and then mounted again atop the various support beams. The largest screen was set in place of the center window so that it was visible from every vantage point in Tower Command. And on each individual monitor was the same image—a trail of white smoke and the *Taurus IX* outer casing falling away.

Emblazoned on the wall and above the breast on every company-issued Polo shirt was the Taurus Enterprises logo—the head of a bull, with horns and a nose ring, encased in a crest. The name *Taurus Enterprises* was spelled out, curving along the crest's outer edge.

Chang was at her console. Her hands were practically shaking. At five months pregnant she was beginning to show. "I never thought we'd get this far. It's amazing."

Dale Aranuke, Tower Command's Director of Operations, was unimpressed. "That's why you're a technician…and I'm your boss. If it wasn't today it would be tomorrow, and if not, then next week, next month, or next year. Advancement is simply part of our DNA, Chang. It's embedded in who we are. We're engineered to move forward. Wishing doesn't make it so. *Doing* it does."

Chang was sympathetic to the pressures that came with Aranuke's position, but it was *Show Time*. "No offense there, chuckles, but we trained a lot of pilots, and it came down to Powell. He was selected because he was the best, not because he's lucky."

"Screw Powell. He's just a monkey in a billion-dollar cage. My cage. Feed him a banana and he'll push all the buttons we want." Aranuke leaned forward, setting his hand next to a large, red button—protected by a flip cover. And it wasn't just any button. It was *the* button. Above it was a label: *Crossline – Destruct*. Just in case. He glanced at the back of Tower Command. Up in the high tower was Buddy Rheams Jr., Taurus Enterprises' founder and CEO.

Behind glass, in his private viewing station, the Old Man watched them all. He had white, receding hair, liver spots on his forehead and right cheek, and sagging jowls.

He won't live forever, Aranuke thought. *Not forever.*

"And if Powell won't flip the right god damn switches," he said, and then flipped up the casing to fully expose the console's big red button, "then I will."

Chang sighed, when a red light blinked on the console. The Old Man. "Dale. It's him."

Aranuke reached for the phone. "I told you. It's *Mr.* Aranuke, or Sir. I don't care if we started here together. You work for *me.*"

"*Tsch.* Oh. You're so adorable when you're all Big Bad Boss Dude. It totally turns me on. What are you doing after?"

Aranuke shifted his eyes ruefully. "Yes, Buddy." He listened, nodded. "Yes, I mean, Mr. Rheams, sir, of course, sir. Yes, yes. No, you're right, you're right. *Crossline* is on target." He nodded again, then once more. "Understood. I know. He will. I'm pos—" The Old Man hung up.

"Fucking Powell. Only thing I hate worse than a monkey in a cage is a monkey with a bad attitude."

"Actually," Chang said, "for someone who's basically sitting on a nuclear bomb, I'd say his attitude is pretty good."

Aranuke clenched his fists, grit his teeth. He leaned in, furrowing his brow. He would never accept this much smack talk from anyone. But Chang was a special case, with almost unlimited cover. And from his eyes, she milked it for all it was worth. "We all know how you got this post," he shot back with the little restraint as he could muster, "and why the Old Man keeps you here, but once this flight's done and that fucking ship's on the ground, I'm transferring you to the medical waste department… in Detroit."

Chang offered a fake shudder. "How Motor City badass of you. But before you huff and puff and blow your itty bitty brains out, you gonna let me get this warp test under way or what?"

CHAPTER THREE

Crossline careened across the Universe at seven times the speed of light. The black canvas of space appeared cylindrical. Peppered with stars, it rotated clockwise, melded into a charcoal coil. It picked up fragments of space—the purples and pinks of errant gases, the blues and yellows of streaking comets—so that rather than gazing through a kaleidoscope Powell could swirl at his command, he was traveling through the heart of one that he couldn't.

Powell heard his heart booming in heavy, elongated beats, as if the mighty organ was all but paralyzed under ketamine sedation.

...KOONG-KUNG...KOONG-KUNG...KOONG-KUNG...

Conscious of his actually being conscious and participating in this flight, yet unable to formulate his words, Powell felt dissociated from himself. Though traveling in a nanosecond, the electrical signals from his brain—directing his body to act—seemed to be on delay. He was echoing throughout the Universe, among planets and moons, among asteroids and comets. Between time past and time future, between now and not yet, between then and just gone. His eyes glazed over. His mouth was like taffy.

As Powell scanned the console—the screens and readouts, the controls and switches—all he could make out was a blur, a separate, multicolored swirl rotating counterclockwise against the clockwise, charcoal swirl of space. He was dizzy and confused, lost in the shadowy ether of creation itself.

Only within the cockpit, in his very seat, Powell knew that he hadn't moved, that he was stationary. But what he experienced was swimming in a thick, creamy sea of milk and raspberry, of blueberry and orange. And smeared within that milky white swirl were the faces of Chandra and Jesse, as if the picture of them had been dropped into the cosmic blender.

...*KOONG-KUNG...KOONG-KUNG...KOONG-KUNG...*

His eyelids were heavy...heavy...heavy...fighting their way down in millimeters, as if chained to cinder blocks, struggling along his eyeballs, pulling, inching over his pupil. And finally, once closed, for what seemed like forever, his eyelids...heavy... heavy...heavy...started their ascent.

...*KOONG-KUNG...KOONG-KUNG...KOONG-KUNG...*

Slowly...slowly...slowly...they began to pull...and inch... back...open.

...*KOONG-KUNG...KOONG-KUNG...KOONG-KUNG...*

In that otherwise imperceptible passing of time, during that individual blink—three tenths of one second—Powell had traveled 942,356 miles. And again with the next blink...

...*KOONG-KUNG...KOONG-KUNG...KOONG-KUNG...*

And the next...

...*KOONG-KUNG...KOONG-KUNG...KOONG-KUNG...*

And the next....

Still under the paralyzing warp sedation, Powell felt like the hand of God had reached into his chest, penetrating far more than flesh and bone and tendon and nerve and organ—but to something deeper, more essential. As if this mighty hand, this embodied grip of fate and time and space, had wrapped its fingers around his soul, tearing it away one strand at a time. And in doing so it released the divine molecules of his spirit—his essence—which shot from his chest like a canister of sparkling fireworks, spewing innumerable fragments of his illustrious white light.

...*KOONG-KUNG...KOONG-KUNG...KOONG-KUNG...*

Anesthetized by warp, blurred by a long white streak of stars, Powell couldn't read his monitors until the thick, creamy swirl of milk and raspberry, of blueberry and orange, fused together and slowly dissolved, easing his console back into focus. His monitor read:

WARP ACTIVATED...
END WARP SEQUENCE 5...4...3...2...
SEQUENCE COMPLETE
As quickly as *Crossline* had entered warp it cut to its non-warp propulsion; in comparison the ship seemed to be stationary. And yet Powell huffed and heaved as if pulling himself aboard a capsized boat. The console readouts showed his heart roaring at 220 beats per minute—the maximum rate it could temporarily sustain before exploding.

"*Hh hh hh hh hh hhh...holy...whoo...whoo...whoo...hoh... hoh...wow...*"

His lips were dry and cracked; his mouth was like sandpaper. He had no idea warp travel would make him so thirsty. With his disorientation faded, he glanced to his right. Hanging out in the distance, in its rust-colored glory, was Mars—the God of War, son of Juno—floating in a sea of black. Powell then heard a faint beep. The second monitor on the console read:

DISTANCE FROM LAUNCH: 92.367 MILLION MILES

A transmission from Tower Command shot between satellites, piggybacking on the warp signal—traveling as fast as *Crossline*—enabling almost real time communications despite the remarkable distance between them. "*Crossline*, this is Tower. Do you read?...Are you okay?"

Powell didn't answer straight away. He wanted to look at his hand, to survey the cockpit, to make sure it was really him they were talking to. Much had transpired in fifty-four seconds. He then laughed a silly, inexplicable laugh of relief and thrill, of jitters and joy. Powell had never taken drugs, but he knew then and there that he could become a warp junkie, no problem.

Through his headset Powell heard thunderous applause, and while the cheers originated within Tower Command, he imagined they were from around the world. And that the adulation from Chandra and Jesse was loudest of all. He could almost see his daughter bouncing up and down in that manic clap she did when she would practically pee herself, overwhelmed with the kind of unfettered excitement only children, dogs, and untreated schizophrenics are capable of experiencing.

"So, Powell," Chang said. "How does it feel to be the first man through warp?"

Powell looked through the canopy, at Mars—that amazing red planet—confronted by just how utterly small he was in the scheme of the Universe, just a speck against the infinite landscape of forever. And why he should always strive for greatness, bound only by the limitations of his imagination. He sighed in humble recognition. "Like I'm on top of the world."

"Copy, *Crossline*. Great job. You look fantastic from here. Now let's bring you home and get this party started."

"Copy, Tower." Powell tightened his gloves. "Just one thing first."

"Oh, yeah?" The smile came through Chang's voice. "What's that?"

Powell couldn't help but shake his head, letting a mischievous little grin stretch across his face. *Hmm*, he thought. *Should I?*

After all, Buddy Rheams came to him unexpectedly a few nights before the launch, in the *Crossline* hangar, one of only two times they were ever alone together.

"They say you should shoot for the Moon, my boy, and if you miss, you'll still be among the stars." Buddy nodded to the twinkling sky. His enthusiasm belied his advanced years. "If I was a younger man, such as yourself, out there on my own, in the far reaches of the cosmos—face to face with the gods— I might just have to *accidentally on purpose* chase those stars as far as they go. *If* I was that kind of man. Which, let's face it,"—the Old Man offered a sly grin—"I am. But that's just me. Right, Powell?"

At the time, Powell didn't know what to think about Buddy's visit. Just the ruminations of an aging trailblazer, about to see his life-long dream become a reality—and living vicariously through a much younger and able-bodied man who also shared his cosmic sense of wonderment and adventure. But now that Powell was finally out there, all alone, among the stars, he knew exactly what to do.

"Oh, yeah," he announced. "Absolutely. I'm going again."

CHAPTER FOUR

DALE ARANUKE HAD long accepted that in response to a nuclear attack, fleeing the city or retreating to a bunker was about as safe as hiding at the bottom of his tropical fish tank. If a nuke was ever on its way to Houston, he preferred not that it explode somewhere *above* the city, but rather that it literally crack his skull open and *then* explode, vaporizing him instantly. If civilization was getting blown to smithereens, leaving an apocalyptic wasteland, he didn't want even a one in one hundred billion trillion gazillion chance of survival. Just kill him real quick like.

There were no bombs on the way, but Aranuke was beginning to feel that the end of the world would have been a more desirable alternative to what Powell had just announced. Aranuke kicked Chang's chair, which got her to chime back in.

"Negative, Powell, negative. You are not cleared for a second warp. Reset coordinates—"

Aranuke grabbed a headset. "Don't fuck with me, Powell. Prepare for return warp—"

But it was too late. Powell was already gone.

Tower Command fell silent. Buddy Rheams stood behind the window of his upper office. The Old Man's expression did not change. He just stood there. Waiting. His eyes simmered.

The *Crossline* warp thrusters may have succeeded, but until Powell returned the ship to Earth fully intact, the mission was far from over. Buddy Rheams was ready to put an entire fleet into production, but those ships sure didn't come cheap.

Chang spoke for everyone. "What do we do now?"

Aranuke let out a short sigh. Despite an intricate satellite network Taurus Enterprises deployed over several decades, there was no sign of Powell or the expensive merchandise he was operating—and with it, the fate of the corporation. "Well," he said, "if you've got stock in the company, you might want to sell. And deal with that god damn radio broadcast. This isn't good."

*"The energy is remarkable just outside the Taurus Enterprises Command Center. Not since the **Medallion IV** sent satellite photos from Jupiter has there been such anticipation in the space program. But for those of you unfamiliar with the history of the **Crossline** project, I'll turn you over to Margaret Danillo. Margaret...?"*

*"Thanks, Ron. Taurus Enterprises founder and CEO Harlan 'Buddy' Rheams Jr. said that he had been inspired by the stories of Norwegian sailor Roald Amundsen. A century ago, he was the first person to successfully navigate the Northwest Passage in the Arctic, linking the Atlantic Ocean to the Pacific Ocean. Conventional wisdom at the time was that large vessels were needed to physically smash through the polar ice. But the massive, bulky ships could never make it through. Exposed to the Arctic's sub-zero temperatures, the ships either got stuck in the ice forever, or sank, or were forced to return from whence they came. But then Amundsen reasoned that a smaller, more navigable ship, the **Gjøa**, would be able to maneuver around the chunks of ice, rather than barge through them. As history proved...Amundsen was correct.*

*"Enter Buddy Rheams. Taking a cue from our Arctic explorer, Buddy theorized that a sleeker craft would be better suited than the older space shuttles to test the warp capabilities in deep space, and put the **Crossline** model into production.*

"Buddy Rheams certainly had the right people—the New Einsteins—to make this all happen. Making use of Elena Smith's Tritanium for the reactor's casing fuselage and Terrance Abercrombie's Fractronic memory chip capability, Vernon Doyle was able to trigger a nuclear explosion large enough to power a city, but small and efficient enough to be contained safely. These three core elements have resulted in the remarkable new craft we've all been dying to see in action.

"And in just a few moments, the Crossline project, with

*Marcus Powell at the controls, will either verify Buddy Rheams'
warp drive theories, or mark the failure of the firm's $671 billion
investment..."*

Pulled out of his second warp, Powell heard Aranuke's voice
crackle through the headset. "What the fuck are you doing? Get
your ass back here."

But Powell was too busy following the advice of Buddy
Rheams—chasing the stars as far as they would go. The warp
deactivated another fifty-four seconds and seventy-one million miles from Earth, and yet Powell wasn't even close to being
done. As soon as the warp recharged, he hit the switch again.
Zooming beyond Mars, the warp sensation was less disorienting
this time—not so gooey. He was getting used to it. Powell did
this four more times, until he was able to function within warp
haze—like an acid junkie acclimating to the trip. After each
warp he would hear Chang plead, Aranuke scream, tune them
both out, wait for the warp engines to reset, and then blast off.

When the computer relayed that *Crossline* was about to come
out of warp again, Powell blinked twice, and found himself
cruising just beyond the great rings of Saturn. The yellowish-
brown planet was humongous—more than nine times the size of
Earth. Known by the ancient Greeks as *Kronos*, father of *Zeus*,
and by the Romans as the God of Harvest, Saturn took more
than twenty-nine years to orbit the sun. Its beautiful blue rings,
nine in all, were astonishing. Immense. Spectacular.

Each ring was subdivided into thousands of individual ring-
lets, which again consisted of billions of particles, themselves
composed of ice and contaminated dust.

Powell was breathless. Never before did he truly appreciate the
depth of the Universe and its awesome and dazzling mysteries.
That the molecules of his soul—if there was such a thing—
were engulfed by the incredible expanse. That he was somehow
connected to the particles in the rings, to the enormous planet,
and, perhaps, to the very fiber of the cosmos.

Church wasn't exactly his *thang*, but for him, this was a holy moment. He gazed once more at Saturn and the shimmering ice particles circling it. So tiny, so alone, he basked in the power of the galaxy. "Fuuuuuuuck me," he said. "Whoaoaoaoaoa."

His eyes drifted then from the massive rings to the photograph—a moment of sobriety. Inexplicably, compared to Chandra's soft and loving lips and Jesse hugging him close, wrapping her little arms around his neck, the incredible planet before him seemed insignificant. In the presence of mighty Saturn he truly understood that the vast solar system extended far beyond his capacity to appreciate its depth and magnitude. But if forced to choose, he would pass up eternal dreams of the Universe just to hold his baby girl once more.

"Still," he said, chuckling, and then commenced gawking. He wasn't ever getting another shot to be out that far again. "This is crazy."

In the distance, more than half of Saturn's sixty-two known moons visibly orbited the planet. He responded to Chang. "You can't believe what I'm looking at. There's nothing like it."

"Well, I'm pretty sure you know what I'm looking at here."

"Aranuke pissed?"

"Um...he's processing."

"Copy that, Tower. This is *Crossline*. Preparing to recalculate coordinates and commence return warp, over."

"Copy, *Crossline*. Awaiting your mark."

With the computer recalibrating, Powell contemplated his return to Earth and the mix of cheers and barbs that would greet him. Would he be treated as a hero? A criminal? Both? Would the Tower wonks "retire" him after his joyride? Would they jail him? Ruin him? Worse? Or would Buddy Rheams, a fellow maverick, give him a pass? Would they even celebrate together?

Once again, Powell took in the great ocean of space. He just gawked at Saturn.

Yep, he thought. *Totally worth it.*

CHAPTER FIVE

THE WARP ENGINES were ready for the first of six return blasts it would take to get him back to Earth, when a blip came across the screen. Powell shifted toward the incoming message, but his short-range sensor interrupted him. Something in the Saturn rings. Video amplification revealed that among a cluster of particles was an odd-shaped fragment, with sharper, more reflective edges than he would expect. But he supposed that after debris crashed around over millions if not billions of years, who knew what was really out there? He looked again. Probably nothing of consequence. Just some lagging hallucination from the multiple warps.

As suspected. Just ice particles swirling around the planet. Billions of frozen blue ice particles floating in space that—

Powell focused his monitor on the third ring layer. Studying it more carefully, his sensors revealed that the particle cluster wasn't in the Saturn ring, but *among* it. The fragment wasn't random, a collection of dust, or some anomalous asteroid fragment.

It was another ship. Looking just like *Crossline*. And headed his way.

"Son of a bitch," Powell said, amazed, excited, and a little bit freaked out. "I thought they were just messing with me."

One week before launch, Powell sat at a folding table in a small and otherwise empty room in the bowels of the Taurus Enterprises Space Center. Arms crossed beneath the dim overhead light, he was being briefed by Dale Aranuke, a pinhead for sure, but a pinhead with brains, authority, and something else he couldn't quite put his finger on.

Neither Powell nor Aranuke quite played by the rules—both instinctively knew it took a little jazz in their mojo to get to places they wanted to go—but even without words there was an immediate loathing between them. They would not agree to disagree. These two bitches would not hug it out. Beneath Aranuke's slick, corporate veneer, Powell sensed something intrinsically dangerous. Yet posturing aside, Powell was honest with himself about just how badly he wanted to pilot the first warp engines in space. And the higher powers deemed him the best man for the job—which gave him leverage.

Aranuke reached down for his KATI, and checked his message. KATI was short for KT-5, Taurus Enterprises' best-selling multi-format smart phone. He refocused on Powell. "There's a lot more riding on this flight than the warp drive. It's…we tested thirty-two pilots. Only six could handle the simulation."

"I know. Hicks was a good pilot." Powell hated to bring it up—he liked Gloria Hicks and grieved when she died—but he needed Aranuke on edge. "She just pushed herself too hard."

The corporate chief exhaled, then dragged his chair until the metal edge scraped along the floor. Powell knew it was just Aranuke's way of trying to make him uncomfortable, but mostly it gave away his seething rage, resentment—and desperation.

"Yes, well…of the six, two had nervous breakdowns in the isolation pod, Dolingo's liver exploded in the re-entry phase, Draper got so drunk that he fell out of the cockpit…Hicks…" Aranuke clenched when he said her name. "And you."

As much as Powell was meant to be feeling the heat, he was having a darn tootin' time. Aranuke was a snaky little turd. It was good to see him squirm.

"You're the…" Aranuke expelled a sigh of bitter capitulation, "…you're the only one who can fly the ship out that far and get it back in one piece. And our sensors indicate there might be… something out there. And whatever it is, it can't reach Earth."

The briefing had been kept all priority code Alpha Tango Niner Charlie Bravo double-secret-probation didn't-officially-exist nuh-uh Oreo-cookie-promise pinky-swear hush-hush, but Powell hadn't expected all this cloak and dagger.

Aranuke clarified. "We *are* testing the warp engines. We need them to work. More than ever. But this is a Search and Destroy, Powell. If you find something—and I'm not saying you will—but if you do, take it down, salvage what you can, and get the hell out of there."

This was news to Powell, who was now anxious and even a little bit upset. "But—"

"I'm giving you a direct order, Powell. Do you understand?"

"Do you understand?" Chang was insistent. "*Crossline*, repeat. We are reading an unidentified object in motion. Do you understand?"

Despite his flying solo almost seven hundred fifty million miles from Earth—with no backup—Powell's instincts were to keep the Tower wonks in the dark, if for only a little while longer. He needed to think. "Uh...not picking anything up on my visuals. Are you sure it's not a space rock? There's tons of 'em out here."

"Negative, *Crossline*, negative. Its velocity is increasing."

It sure is.

Powell couldn't hide it any longer. "Confirmed, Tower. Will investigate."

"Affirmative, *Crossline*. But proceed with extreme caution. Arm all weapons."

Not a real blood and guts man, Powell nevertheless felt his combat training—and survivor's reflex—kick in. Fear shot through him. His heart raced. He clenched his fingers around the stick, his thumb a millimeter to the trigger's side. He reduced speed, then flew in small, tight arcs. Plus he had no idea who was piloting the ship. A man? A beast? An alien?

Chang broke in. "*Crossline*, this is Tower. Do you read? We're picking up—"

Powell silenced the com. He needed to focus.

The ship mimicked Powell's movements—two panthers

squaring off in the jungle. Each waiting for the other to strike first.

The aft thrusters kept *Crossline* hovering in place, allowing the unidentified craft to slowly draw closer. Finally, the ships had their noses pointed at one another, separated by less than five hundred feet—cosmically speaking, they were practically touching. The outer rings of Saturn swirled in the near distance.

Powell enjoyed a round of Deep Space Chicken as much as the next guy, but something told him they weren't going to laugh about it later over beers. He couldn't make out a face, but seeing the pilot's outline reassured him somehow, knowing that a person—not some slimy, six-eyed, tentacled space freak, as he had imagined—was maneuvering the other ship.

The readouts on his control panel were supplying data, pinpointing SpaceFreak's location in relation to *Crossline*. But what most confused him was that, as far as the Fractronic computer was concerned, Powell was facing off against the unlikeliest of spacecrafts—his own.

SpaceFreak shifted its nose up and to the left—once, twice, and then again.

"What the...?" And as Powell contemplated the answer to his own question, SpaceFreak repeated the gesture, but signifying what? Fight? Follow? Powell didn't know what SpaceFreak was up to, but while his own weapons were armed, he was also a stationary target, and the alien ship—this supposed threat—hadn't fired upon *him*. Powell was a pilot first, second, and third, and a soldier way, way down the line. But if he had to unleash a can of Saturn-fried whoopass on SpaceFreak, that's how it was going down. SpaceFreak banked hard right and took off in a blast.

"Hell, no," Powell said. "You ain't gettin' away like that."

SpaceFreak accelerated again, leaving the enormous planet behind, as if daring Powell to keep up. In tight pursuit, Powell turned his com back on. "Tower, this is *Crossline*. I have—"

"*Crossline*. Did not receive last transmission. Repeat. Did not receive trans—"

Even Aranuke was tight in the chest. Tower Command froze, waiting for his instructions, struck by the news of an alien craft and, in this one case at least, Powell's reluctance to follow orders. Aranuke grimaced as he looked to the Old Man, hovering from his glassed-in perch, watching. Judging. Aranuke struggled for the words, when Powell came through the com.

"Tower, this is *Crossline*. Weapons armed."

Chang responded. "Copy that." Then to Aranuke. "Dale. Seriously. Can the ship handle it? He's so far out."

"The ship's fine, you idiot. It's the pilot I'm worried about." The adrenaline raged so hard Aranuke clenched his fist to keep it from shaking. He flipped up the casing on the big red button. He inserted his key above it, leaving it in the *disarmed* position. Aranuke resented that Powell had advanced on talent and charm while he'd had to fight and plot and a few other things he would never repeat to anyone to get where he was. Plus, he had other reasons to hate the man. "I said he was trouble from the beginning, but no-ho-ho…nobody listened. I knew it. I fucking knew it."

"We have to tell him."

"That won't be necessary."

"But, Dale—"

"I said…that *won't* be necessary. But if you know something the rest of us don't that'll guarantee the safety of the entire planet and everybody on it, then by all means…"

Aranuke and Chang both turned back to glance up at the high tower office, where Buddy Rheams was overlooking Tower Command.

"Good. Now talk to your fucking boyfriend up there. He's in a shitload of trouble."

The two ships were heading even deeper into space. Powell had SpaceFreak in his sights. Chang came through the com.

"Powell, this is Tower. What is your pursuit?"

"I'm not sure. There's a lot of debris out here."

"Debris from what?"

"It's difficult to say."

"Try."

Powell's sensors alerted him to concentrated radiation, beyond SpaceFreak, although his instruments could not identify the source. His screen read: *UNKNOWN*. Looking through his canopy, he could make out a faint blur, like a tiny blue smudge in space. "What the hell…?"

"Say again, Powell. Say again. What's going on?"

"Nothing, Tower, nothing. It's just…a little strange up here." But the closer he pursued SpaceFreak the larger the smudge appeared. And then he could see it wasn't so much a smudge as a ripple—a pocket of dense blue light, with a brilliant white light at its center. The entire blue pocket shimmied. With SpaceFreak headed not so much toward it, but into it.

Aranuke gave specific orders. "Powell. Engage the alien ship."

"Sir?"

"We read the ship on our scope. You know what to do."

Even Powell was at odds. *How'd I get myself into this? What am I doing?*

"And Powell…?"

"Yes…?"

"I'd hate to see you make a bad decision out there…you being a family man and all."

Powell would be the first to admit just how oblivious he often was to the fibrous political machinations embedded in corporate America, and to the many heart-wrenching slights incurred by family and friends, stemming from forgotten anniversaries, faulty memory, unreturned phone calls, a roll of the eyes, unacknowledged accomplishments, or unspectacular birthday gifts. He just wanted to fly his ships, kiss his girls, and call it a day.

But he damn sure knew a threat when he heard one. Drawn to the photograph of Chandra and Jesse—his everything—for the first time since he set foot in *Crossline*, he felt like he might never see them again. With little subtlety, Aranuke made clear that Powell was in no position, figuratively or literally, to protect his family from any manner of misdeed other than to do exactly what he was told. Do it...or else.

Powell placed his thumb on the trigger, ready to unleash a swarm of Tritanium bullets—powerful enough to rip through a concrete building. He set his targeting scope on SpaceFreak. A yellow crosshair appeared on screen. SpaceFreak was drifting toward the center. The instrument panel read: *TARGETING ENGAGED.*

Chang was back. "Powell, this is Tower. We read the ship. Prepare to fire."

Powell was about to comply. SpaceFreak scorched the path before him in a sharp jutting trajectory, closing toward that glowing blue amoeba—what now appeared to be a crater in space.

Aranuke was barking orders. "Powell. Fire on the enemy ship."

SpaceFreak crossed his immediate path, perfectly centered. Bullseye. The console read: *TARGETING LOCKED.*

"What are you waiting for?!"

Powell felt the trigger against his gloved hand. A single thumb depression would destroy SpaceFreak. But whatever he was, wherever he came from...whatever he wanted...Powell just knew in his heart of hearts that SpaceFreak wasn't the enemy. He was something else. Until an outraged Aranuke commanded otherwise.

"God damn it, Powell! I said fire!"

CHAPTER SIX

ONE SQUEEZE. THAT'S all it would take. Powell's finger hovered above the trigger, in that netherworld between life and death. Just a quick *blam-blam-blam* and SpaceFreak would be no more. Powell had the power to kill him. To *kill* him.

At current speed, SpaceFreak would enter the rippling blue amoeba in less than three minutes. Where it led, Powell had no idea, but they were closing in quick, and whatever was waiting on the other side, SpaceFreak wanted him to follow. But why? To what end?

Powell's gut seized up. He didn't want to fire the first shot—he never wanted to fire *any* shot, ever, unless his life depended on it, and what he saw on the photo in front of him *was* his life, one that increasingly seemed to depend on such a pre-emptive strike. SpaceFreak had appeared mysteriously, was taunting him to enter an uncharted ripple in space, and wasn't providing any reasons for doing so. Yet as desperately as Powell wanted to know what SpaceFreak was up to, he sure as hell wasn't flying through that shimmering crater to find out. No way, no how.

Until SpaceFreak altered the rules of engagement.

Aranuke stared at the screen. "What's he doing? What's he waiting for?!"

"Unlike you, Dale, he's never acquired the taste for blood."

If Aranuke had the ability to shoot flames through his eye sockets, Chang would have been nothing but a pile of dust and a trail of black smoke. He leaned in to the console so that his face was inches from hers. "Listen," he said.

"Back off, Dale. I'm tel—"

"*Lis-sen.* I don't care whose unholy love child you're carrying." Aranuke shifted his eyes to the Old Man's glassed-in office, and then back at Chang. The rest of Tower Command flipped switches and otherwise carried on with effect. "I will disappear you—permanently—if you don't shut the fuck up...*right now.*"

Chang did as instructed.

"I may not always agree with the Old Man, but there is an alien craft that appears heavily armed facing off against our one and only ship. We've got enough nukes to wipe out every planet in the Milky Way...*down here.* But *out there* we have a fleet of *one.* Look, Chang. I know he's your friend. I'm not looking to kill the man. I'm not." Aranuke knew that was only partly true. "Taking out Powell may be the only way to destroy the enemy."

Aranuke straightened his coat. "I'd prefer to spare the ship—and the pilot—but if Powell won't comply...that's his problem."

He turned his key one position clockwise. The big red button was right there.

"*Crossline,* this is Tower." Chang cleared her throat. "...En-un... engage the craft. It's...an order."

There was silence before Powell responded. "Tower, this is *Crossline.* Am in pursuit."

"Powell! You have the ship in your sights. Fire! What are you waiting for?" Again, there was no response. "Powell! POWELL!" Aranuke felt sweat-glazed anxiety flood his armpits until finally he picked up the console phone and turned to the Old Man perched upstairs.

Two words came through the receiver. "Do it."

"Dale..." Chang said.

Aranuke stared at the button. Even he knew the decision wasn't as simple as whether or not to proceed. Pressing that button meant leaving a certain part of himself behind forever, smothering the edges of his soul. If Powell died by his hand, Aranuke would have to live with the consequences. Tower Command was silent. They waited for him to choose. And finally, with two fingers on the red button, Aranuke determined their destiny.

With a *click*, *Crossline* disappeared from the screen.

Outside, in their yard, the sun was warm. Chester was lying in the shadow of the adobe wall, stalking a bird. It flew away. Chandra Powell studied the summer red maples in the gorge, and then closed her eyes, searching for an old American Indian prayer, passed down from her mother and her mother before that. After a quiet moment, the words came from within.

...Oh Great Spirit...

...Make me wise, so that I understand...

And then Jesse started jumping up and down. Much like her Grandma Feather, she had an uncanny intuition, one that had been kicking in more and more, as if looking through a window to their past, present, and future. "Daddy's going fast, Mommy."

...the things you have taught my people...

...Let me learn the lessons you have hidden in every leaf and rock...

"Daddy's going fast."

Chandra opened one eye. She squinted at the sun. "I know, Baby."

...I seek strength...not to be greater than my brother...

...but—

"No, Mommy. Daddy's going fast fast. *Weely* fast."

...to fight my greatest enemy—

Chandra opened her other eye just then and turned to Jesse, realizing that she was saying something important. "What is it, Jess? What do you see?"

—myself.

"I told you. Daddy's going weely *weely* fast. He broke the wules." Jesse giggled and did a little dance, lifting one leg, then the other. She twirled clumsily. "Daddy's always doing that. He's gotta chill out, Mommy. Daddy needs to chill."

Oh god oh god oh god. Marcus? What've you done?

Not one to panic easily, Chandra was a mix of fierce independence and ritual calm. She was the offspring of Feather, a Native American woman of the Cherokee Nation who, much to the chagrin of both families, married entrepreneurial Brooklynite Irving Finkelbaum. Together they opened the first Jewish delicatessen in Houston, *Finkelbaum's*, becoming both a mainstay of the community and the center of gossip and kvetching.

"But Daddy's okay. He's playing *chase me* with the other spaceman."

Chandra, who had been half-ignoring Jesse up until then, was now giving her undivided attention. "*What* other spaceman?"

Jesse let out a stretch, reaching for the Sun. "In the spaceship. Just like Daddy's."

Chandra turned the sound back up on the radio.

"*...Ron Bowlerman here with Margaret Danillo coming to you live from just outside the Taurus Enterprises Command Center. And just this very moment we've gotten word, ladies and gentlemen, that* **Crossline***...is a GO! Warp engines are a go! Can you believe it? Warp engines are a go! This is a moment for the ages! After twenty-three years of struggle, expense, and experimentation, Buddy Rheams has finally brought us warp speed! They said it couldn't be done, and now we have the ability to travel far—*"

The broadcasters shifted storylines.

"*Well, hiya there, folks. We just need to make a few adjustments in the booth and then we'll get right back to it. But as we await this historic moment, another space-related story broke today. Right, Margaret?*"

"*It sure did, Ron. After decades of wild speculation, the truth about Area Fifty-One has finally been put to rest.*"

"Daddy's hurt, Mommy. Daddy's hurt."

"*Since the 1950s, outlandish stories and conspiracy theories have run amok that the secret Nevada facility stored remains from an alien spacecraft that allegedly had crashed in 1947 in Roswell, New Mexico.*"

Chandra's eye went wide as she saw worry lines spread across Jesse's face. "What? How do you know that? What do you mean hurt? How's he hurt?"

"Fanatics have long insisted that the United States government captured the alien crew, experimented on them, and then harvested the crashed ship's advanced technology to develop applications for military weapons."

Jesse rubbed her little hands over her ribs and face, then shut her eyes and shook her head back and forth.

"Well...the stories have been confirmed. Area Fifty-One is indeed a secret underground facility...for gambling!"

"All over, Mommy. All over. We hafta find Meaty."

"The brainchild of our very own Buddy Rheams Jr., Area Fifty-One is an audacious, Las Vegas-style casino and resort with an aliens-and-flying saucers theme."

Before Chandra could think of what to say next, Jesse stared out toward the horizon, as she often did, lost in thought, as if communing with the spirits—and Grandma Feather. When Jesse first started to drift off, as far back as the crib, Chandra knew then that Jesse was her father's girl—a dreamer. But when Feather died and Chandra and Jesse were the only women left in their Cherokee bloodline, Chandra hated herself for feeling jealous of her own daughter, because Jesse had this innate ability to connect with Feather in a way Chandra never could.

"It started as a joke by army generals who tired of the persistent rumors, and started a poker room, calling it Area Fifty-One—the most single-day calls they received about the rumored spacecraft."

Jesse had been talking a lot lately about a boy she had never the opportunity to meet, her Uncle Meaty—Marcus's younger brother, Peter...Petey—who died of leukemia almost thirty years before she was born. They had pictures of him as a small boy. Jesse stared at them again and again and again, like he wasn't really gone.

"Over time, the poker room became so popular that Buddy

Rheams was approached for funding and development."

Yet Chandra took comfort and pride knowing that her little girl was the embodiment of Feather. That while Chandra could pass down the family name and their traditions, Jesse carried Feather's spirit. Maybe someday, Chandra would carry it too.

"It has since become one of the most popular getaways serving high-level executives, government officials, and foreign nationals. The V.I.P. suite—Hangar Eighteen—is reserved for the top eighteen biggest spenders."

And suddenly the tension was gone. With a renewed smile, Jesse hopped down from the adobe wall and waddled over to Chester, who was curled up in the shade. "It's okay, Mommy. Daddy's all rested. He's better now. He's chillin' out. Daddy's funny, Mommy. Daddy's funny."

"Discussions are now under way to expand Area Fifty-One for the public, including an entire wing devoted to families. Talk about conspiracies. Right, Ron?

"You said it, Margaret."

The radio spoke volumes. Chandra had enough. "That's it, honey. Get in the truck. We're checking on Daddy. Now."

CHAPTER SEVEN

In the solar system's outer reaches, with the Saturn rings in sight, Powell was ready to break off course and let SpaceFreak return from where it came. And then he saw the back of the alien craft light up. Followed by the launch of three back-loaded missiles.

Powell may have had reservations about firing first, but he sure as hell had no qualms about returning fire!

In immediate response Powell broke off several rounds of Tritanium-coated bullets and two of his own front-loaded missiles, which SpaceFreak easily outmaneuvered. But rather than SpaceFreak's explosives closing in for impact, the missiles crisscrossed in front of *Crossline* in an elliptical pattern—and then passed beyond it—as if forming the guide wires for a net around Powell's ship.

Which is exactly what happened. SpaceFreak's missiles looped under, above, and around *Crossline*, and in an arc, accelerated toward Powell, from behind, chasing him. The missiles' elliptical formation boxed him in on all sides, preventing evasive maneuvers.

Powell reached for his com to signal Tower Command. But the missile warheads lit up—about to detonate. Given the urgency of his predicament—he was going to be dead, real soon—counterattack was out. He had no other tactical option. Rather than warp his way to safety or else blast his counterpart to dust, Powell was forced to follow SpaceFreak through the ripple in space, that shimmering radiation patch of unknown origin, substance, and consequence.

And take his chances.

SpaceFreak entered the cosmic ectoplasm. Then the missiles erupted.

Powell didn't know if it was the ripple effect or his death, but the dense blue light before him gave way to a gleaming center, unfolding, revealing itself. Followed by a great white flash. Brilliant. Pulsing. And another flash, then another, like passing through an electrical storm. It crackled all around him. His skin pulled taut. His bones ached on a molecular level; an incredible force extracted the fabric of his being. Pain beyond words.

Another electrical surge followed—that crackling:

...In a flash, he saw Chandra sitting on the edge of their aqua blue bathtub, draped in her white, silk robe. It was undone, barely covering her naked body. On the yellow windowsill, four candles were lit—one for each of the four seasons—to balance the forces of nature. Her legs were brown and smooth. She curled her finger, drawing him near. She smiled. Unbuttoning his shirt, Powell shut the door behind him.

...In a flash, Powell saw Jesse running her fingertips along the adobe wall that lined their yard while gazing off into the horizon. She was searching for her grandmother's spirit, which she said came to her in dreams. A spirit hawk, circling in the distance. Watching over them.

...In a flash, Powell was thirteen again, on his bicycle. He rode up the driveway of his childhood home, only to find his father, ravaged by a stroke. Thomas Powell was slumped across the front seat of his car—no longer a man, just a body with no force. Powell had already lost his brother, and now his dad. Forever burned in his heart was the grief of his mother, looking from behind the drapes. It rained later that afternoon, but he remembered a blistering sun. Burning.

...In a flash, Powell was nine years old, in the woods, with a rifle in his hands.

...In a flash, Powell sat on the edge of the hospital bed in the maternity ward. Chandra held tiny Jesse in her arms. They smiled at each other.

...In a flash, Powell saw the *Taurus IX* rocket set on the Houston launch pad.

...And in a flash, Powell was in a cloud bank. There was little visibility except for the tip of a wing. But as the cloud cover thinned out, the skies brightened until they were clear and blue. With SpaceFreak in his sights.

The *Crossline* sensors, which had momentarily gone offline, were functioning again. The readouts put Powell somewhere in northern Arizona, even though he had been almost a billion miles from Earth just seconds before, passing the outer rings of Saturn.

Disoriented, Powell looked from side to side to confirm his surroundings. Was it another flash phase? Hallucination? The passage into death? His sensors verified land below. His eyes told him the same. He wasn't sure if he could trust either.

And then his screen read: *INCOMING MESSAGE*. The square icon flashed, stopped, and then began: *D-E-S*...until the panel overloaded. The cockpit filled with the singe of smoke and sulfur and melting wires. *Crossline* plummeted. It spun like a gyroscope. SpaceFreak dashed in and out of view. There and gone, there and gone, there and gone.

The stick fought like a seizing cobra. The tendons in Powell's wrist trembled. Finally he reached down to the base of the seat, gripped the *Eject* lever. But as quickly as the controls cut out on him, they came back online. He took command of the stick and leveled out *Crossline*. In control again, he depressed the trigger to fire at SpaceFreak. No luck. Like his communication system, the weapons were inoperable.

Unarmed, alone, and under attack, Powell again had no choice but to follow SpaceFreak, who was on a clear path toward rocky terrain below.

At four thousand feet Powell could finally make out where he was: over the Grand Canyon. The ridges were deep and spectacular, embedded with millennia of glacial deposits and erosion. Formation. The remnants of time, memories of the world. Shadows spread along the beige and red grooves. The Colorado

River snaked throughout the jagged nooks.

SpaceFreak directed him south, over and beyond the canyons, until they descended upon what Powell's scanners identified as the city of Sedona, in the northern Verde Valley region of Arizona. Chandra had often suggested that they visit, to experience its unique beauty. Powell had resisted, ironically, because he said they lived in dry lands already. Taking in the majesty of the Red Rock mountains, he could see that he'd make a mistake.

Called by some immense power. Powell felt an immeasurable connection, as if the winds of time and space and nature were blowing through his chest, tugging on him, running flush through his limbs. He had spent a great deal of his lifetime outdoors, but he'd never before experienced anything like it.

The ships flew over three ridges and into a valley, reduced speed, and finally set down on a runway carved from red rock. Waiting there were a dozen armed soldiers, in uniforms Powell didn't recognize. He figured it was the Auxiliary Air Force, or more likely an undisclosed division of Taurus Enterprises, come to arrest him for his unauthorized jolt across the cosmos. But his gut told him maybe it was something else. He checked his sidearm, just in case.

Knowing exhaustion might soon overtake him, Powell gave himself an adrenaline spike to the thigh. With the booster, he was fully alert.

Down and exited from his own ship, Powell saw SpaceFreak approaching with a firm stride. But after removing his helmet, it was evident that SpaceFreak wasn't a *he* at all. She had long, red hair and blue eyes, and was taut, fit, and curved in all the right places. It was suddenly apparent that the uniformed squad was at this woman's command. She looked over at Powell, and then engaged her team in delighted, conspiratorial whispers.

Finally, she made first contact. "You're not much of a pilot, now are you?"

"You take a shot at me and now you're making jokes? Nice."

"Don't be so sensitive, flyboy. I just needed you to follow."

"I could have killed you."

Like her comrades, the redhead laughed. "Uh…I don't think so. Besides, I'm a lot more fun, once you get to know me." She turned to her uniformed buddies. "You think he's ready?"

"*Through the valley,*" they said in unison.

"Through the valley." She took a step closer. "My husband's been gone nearly two years. I kinda miss the guy.... Where is he?"

"No offense, lady. But what are you talking about? What *valley*? What *husband*?"

Her chuckle exuded playful frustration. "Mitri? Amos? You're flying his ship. Well, not his ship exactly, but one just like it." She introduced herself as Keela Amos, wife of Mitri Amos, whoever the hell that was. "Did he send you? He sent you? Is he coming? Is he next?"

Since Powell had spent a good portion of the last day purging through various forms of space and time, and wasn't anywhere close to having all of his wits about him, he figured it best to stay cool, giving himself time to assess what was what. And her words to the contrary, Keela's vibe conveyed to him that one more test of her patience and he would be on the receiving end of a stiff right cross to the windpipe.

He thus took his cue from Keela and followed her small team from the landing strip and through a cave entrance, which led to an intricate tunnel system inside the mountains. After a stretch they crossed beneath a subterranean waterfall and around a small lake that glowed a crystalline blue—a remarkable contrast to the jagged red rock. The path dipped and rose around the lake, taking them past more underground cave mouths, which led this way and that.

They finally climbed a small embankment, which took them back outdoors, into open air. They emerged onto a narrow ridge with a ravine at its base. They were surrounded by mountain peaks. At the ridge's back edge was a giant red rock, hollowed out by nature, in the shape of a heart, tilted on its side. The early evening sky was a soft violet.

"Welcome to Tilted Heart," Keela said. "The center of Grinroad." She brought Powell out front while her fellow Grinroadians—almost a thousand in all—filled the ravine just below.

There was a palpable silence. Anticipation. Powell could feel their wanting, their focus. With these strangers before him, he glanced over his shoulder. There was nothing but mountain peaks and sky. Directly behind him was a long, precipitous drop onto jagged rocks.

Powell shifted to face front, toward the ravine, where townsfolk stood in loose formation. A steady drumbeat echoed through the canyon:

Buhm bum buhm bum buhm bum buhm.

Buhm bum buhm bum buhm bum buhm.

Behind the crowd, an orange and black flag waved to the drumbeat.

Keela saluted her comrades, then dropped her hand. The drum *buhm-bummed* once more, then stopped. A breeze rolled through the ravine. The tiny hairs on Powell's neck stood up. Taurus Enterprises had never been entirely truthful with him, so skepticism was part of the drill. And yet this display had him particularly off balance. "What uh…what's going on here?"

There was an odd silence, as if late one night he'd stumbled home drunk and started to undress, awakening a stranger, only to then realize that the half-naked woman sprawled across the mattress wasn't actually in his bed, but that Powell himself was in the wrong house.

Keela gestured to her people. "What do you mean, flyboy? We're at war."

CHAPTER EIGHT

POWELL STOOD at the rim of Tilted Heart. Opposite him, the setting sun dipped below the horizon, turning the sky purple. Cool breeze. He stared out at the narrow ravine as it filled with townsfolk. Peaked mountains were in the near distance. Like the canyon, they were red.

Among the desert mountain range, he needed clarification. "Uh…say what now? We're at what with who?"

Keela yelled out. "The Gods sent us a trickster. He asks whom we battle." Laughter echoed through the ravine. "Tell him."

The townspeople chanted. Again, their voices echoed through the mountains:

"*SCRA-PERS DIE!*"

"*SCRA-PERS DIE!*"

"*SCRA-PERS DIE!*"

Powell hunched slightly at the power of their collective voice, which reverberated off his molars. He exhaled, nodded. "Okay, thanks. Good talk." He shook his head. "…W-what?"

Keela gestured to the cave. In a slow stumble, a figure emerged from shadow. The crowd resumed its silence.

With just a slight limp, a middle-aged black man approached. A thin braid descended from the back of his head to the middle of his shoulder blades. He was dressed in green corduroy pants, a beige collared shirt, and a maroon and brown corduroy vest. He reeked of marijuana. His eyes were glossy and bloodshot.

"My name is Malcolm Quincy Reneau." His grin revealed a missing tooth on the left side of his mouth. "But everyone calls me Chill."

Powell eyed him closely. He'd seen that look before. "Are you…are you stoned?"

Chill gave a slight shrug, grinned.

Powell slapped his own forehead. "Oh, for the love of Aunt Margaret."

Chill reached out to Powell, offered his hand, but poked him in the eye instead.

"Ow. Watch it." Powell's eye swelled from weed-coated finger skank. "That hurt."

"Sorry. I meant to do this." Chill placed a hand on Powell's forehead.

Squinting from that poke in the eye, Powell was running out of patience, as if summoned from the audience at a child's party, where the magician pulls a large coin from behind his ear. "Look," he said, "are we doing something here or are we—"

Blackness. A pulsing strobe light. *Flash-flash-flash*. Instantly, Powell was a thousand feet above, soaring. He looked down on the ravine. From the freedom of the skies he saw himself and these strangers as nothing but tiny specks in the heart of the Red Rock mountains. The *whoosh* of the wind against his face. Through his lungs.

The screech of a hawk echoed through the canyon. The shrill, high-pitched call rang out, echoed for miles. After a moment, Powell realized where the call came from. It came from *him*.

And then Powell was back, panting, eyes open wide. Chill's hand was still on his head. "What the...what the hell was that? What was—?"

Another strobe light. *Flash-flash-flash*. And then blackness, and then another *flash-flash-flash*. Powell was soaring. First over one mountain peak. *Wingbeat*. Then another. *Wingbeat*. Another. Ripple of fluttering wind. Through the canyons, hugging the mountain ridges, Powell felt like he could reach out and grab the shrubs from the soil; a gopher ducked into its hole. His sight was intense, amplified. He could pick out fibers in the gopher's fur. Grains of sand in the rock beads. A single dewdrop settled on a cactus leaf.

The force of the air funneled around his flesh, catching the updrafts. *Flash-flash-flash.* Beyond the mountains. Crystal blue river. *Wingbeat.* Shadow on the water. *Wingbeat.* Shadow of a hawk. *Wingbeat.* Beyond a green field. Swoop through a small ravine. *Wingbeat.* Rise. *Wingbeat.* Rise.

Powell was gaining speed. He was soaring…but without his ship. In control yet without a cockpit. No electronics. No helmet or parachute, no thruster or targeting system. No computer readout or Tower voice in his ear. It was Powell and Powell alone. But not quite Powell either. It was a part of him, set free. And he was soaring. He was *soaring.*

Embracing flight, Powell felt himself smile through his soul, and with the slightest glance to his side he saw the tip of a hawk's wing come into view. It held, until another wingbeat, and then a thrust and an undulating path through the sky. And then there was another wingbeat, and another, until finally Powell understood that the wingbeat was his wingbeat. The wing was *his.*

And as he opened his mouth in awe, another shrill screech echoed throughout the canyon, stretching on for miles.

I'm flying! My God! I'm flying, I'm really flying. I'm—

Powell was back. Panting, he looked at Chill, who removed his hand.

Chill flicked his eyebrows. "*Sooooo.* Cool, huh?" He nodded, smiled, and turned to Keela. "He has visions, but not the sight."

Keela responded in annoyed mock sing-song. "Chiiiill, don't start with the spirit world of my left ass cheek mumbo jumbo. I'm not in the mood. Is he the one or what?"

Chill squinted, then held out his hand, tilted it side to side. "Meh. He's a bit of a tightass. But give it time. He'll come around."

Keela shrugged. "Good enough for me." She faced the ravine, raised her hand in victory. "We rise!" The crowd responded in kind: "*WE RISE!*"

After an acknowledging nod, Chill and Keela started down toward the ravine and into the crowd, which dispersed. More than just a little bit confused, Powell reached for Keela. "Good enough for what? Good enough for *what*?"

Keela slapped Powell on the back. "To save us all, flyboy. What else?"

CHAPTER NINE

WHEN POWELL WOKE late the next morning he wondered if his journey into the Red Rock mountains had been nothing but a dream. He sat up on the side of the bed, put his feet to the smooth rock floor. Sunlight sprayed the cave, converted to living quarters. The mattress and pillows were soft, draped in white linens and a blue comforter, which were strewn about. On the dark wood nightstand was a fat, yellow candle, set on a silver tray.

Nope. Not a dream.

Opposite the sleeping quarters was a separate, open room, aglow from the morning sun. It had windows on three sides, with small glass panes surrounded by wood frames. Against the far wall, beneath the windows, was a rock couch with a blue cushion. Powell started toward the windows, toward the sun, when a voice pulled him away.

"You sleep okay?"

Powell stared at the young man, strong and fit, about twenty-five, yet seeming far older somehow. "What? Sorry. Could use a cup of coffee."

"I would think. I'm Sean. Keela sent me. We met yesterday. You probably don't remember. Don't worry about it. This is my... *was*...my sister's room."

As Powell was clad only in yellow boxers with laughing monkeys on them, each one holding a banana, he reached for his jumpsuit, which had already been cleaned and folded, draped over a chair. "Where are we? Arizona? Colorado?...I don't get this."

Sean tried to hold back a laugh. "Sorry. It's just...never mind. Let's get you some food and we'll go for a hike. We'll talk then." He bit his lip. "Nice boxers."

Powell felt exposed, in more ways than one. "My wife picked them out. She loves buying me underwear. Not sure why." He zipped his jumpsuit. "Look, where's my ship? I want to call my wife. I need to tell her that I'm—"

"Listen, uh...Powell? It's Powell, right? Look. Your ship is wrecked. You had wiring issues in the belly. It shorted out your systems. The guys are working on it. It'll be a while."

"What do you mean wrecked? Where's Taurus? Where's Buddy Rheams? Where the hell are we?"

"Come. I'll show you."

Powell reluctantly followed Sean through the cave system. It was lit like an atrium, giving the red and brown rock a soft metallic glow. "It's bright down here."

"Yeah. We've got hair-thin optic wires embedded in the walls. They're invisible to the naked eye, but harness natural sunlight. Works pretty good."

They came to a winding corridor. It dipped a few times before banking left, and then to a wide berth, before it finally opened into a massive cave with an underground lake large enough to house a fleet of submarines. Crystalline blue water flowed throughout, leading to the mouth of two smaller caves, side by side.

"The Tosca Waterfall is right on top of us." Sunlight shone down from an opening above. Reflecting off the red rock, the water glowed like a river of gold. The waterfall's *ssshhhhh* grew louder. "It's all part of the irrigation system. Feeds the entire region." Sean picked up a stone and skimmed it. *Fipp-fipp-fipp.* Rings rippled along the water. "I can normally get it five, maybe six times. Must be off my game." He pointed to the left cave. "Keela's waiting. But seriously, though...try to stay calm. She's intense."

Powell ran his hand along the contours of the cave. "I noticed. She always that way?"

"Nah. Not always." The *ssshhhhh* echoed throughout the caves. "Rarely. Sometimes." He nodded. "Mostly. Hey...check it out." Sean opened his stance, pulled his arm back and cocked his wrist. He slung another rock. In a low-angled trajectory, it hit the water on a perfect slant.... *fipp-fipp-fipp...fipp......* *fipp.........fipp.* "Oh, man. I almost had seven. So close." Sean turned to Powell. "But seriously, when Keela gets going...don't freak out."

Cold spring water splashed down as they climbed behind the waterfall, and then ascended the cave wall, making use of odd-shaped nooks as steps. Powell reached forward, one nook at a time. Waterfall mist coated his face. "On my first trip through space using an experimental warp drive, almost a billion miles from Earth, I was engaged by another ship, which I was supposed to attack, and when I didn't, I was threatened by my own people."

Powell stuck his hand into the fresh water, rubbed it on his face. "*Whooh. Man.* Then you blast missiles at me, forcing me through some ripple in space and landing me here, only to find that you guys—*whoever* you are—are at war with the Scrapers, or...whatever you call them."

Before taking the next nook, Powell adjusted his hand, making sure his grip was secure. That *he* was secure. "Then you have a stoned-out hippie freak poke me in the eye and drug me into some kind of acid trip, and when I come out of it, you tell me that I'm your savior. And now we're in the Batcave, behind a waterfall, on the way to see Little Red Riding Hood, who seems hellbent on revolution." The golden sunlight was more intense now. They were approaching the surface. The *sssshhhhh* grew faint. "Why would I freak out?"

Sean gave a half shrug. "You wouldn't. But...wait. What's a Batcave?"

Achy from the tremendous journey through space, Powell was relieved to be out from the caves, to feel the sun on his skin, to smell the pines. Seeing the sky, the possibility of flight, reassured him. Calmed him. He followed Sean along an inclined path, and then over a small waterfall, until they entered a pine forest.

To the east was a freshwater pond, with tree cover, that flowed along the hillside. There was a constant, hushed rumble not far away. Sean pulled a pine cone off a low branch and rolled it in his hands. "Where did you say you're from? A hundred million miles from *where*?"

Powell looked at Sean like he'd been sucking on Chill's bong. "Houston? Earth?"

Sean looked at him with equal measure. "Uhrr...oh...you mean Aretha?"

Generally a patient man, Powell was struggling to stay composed "...Aretha?"

"You know? Big blue and green orb in space? The planet we're on? Aretha."

There was no sense fighting it. Either they were testing him (likely), he was actually still in space, lost in some form of warp drive delirium (more likely) or they were all off their meds (most likely). Powell was also keenly aware that Taurus Enterprises engaged in mind games, so he blinked hard, and then exhaled a baffled sigh. "Sure. Why not? Aretha."

They came to a small clearing with a long drop. Keela was there waiting with Chill and a young girl with a look that strongly implied *I hope you drown in a bucket of your own whizz*. They directed Powell so that he was backed near the edge, with the largest waterfall yet over the side. At the bottom were rocks. Water crashed on them. If the goal was to make him uncomfortable, it worked.

"Feeling better, flyboy? You were a little shaky out there."

Powell squinted as the sun caught his face. "Peachy. Thanks for asking. But I've had a heckuva day and I just want to get home. Tell me—"

Keela interjected. "Let me explain how this works. I ask, you tell. *Then* we see what's what. I'm not here to answer you. You're here to help *us*."

"Whoa. Hang on, there, Red. First off...who the hell are you?

And second…why would I help you? You took a *shot* at me."

"That again? Yikes. I told you. That was *mo-ti-va-tion.*"

"To do *what?*"

Keela rolled her eyes. "To follow me through the wormhole. Duh. It's not like you were in any real danger. Well…I suppose one of the missiles could have detonated and then set off the others…but that hardly ever happens."

"Wait. That ripple out there? With the blue light? That *was* a wormhole. Son of a bitch. I thought maybe…"

"Maybe? Look, flyboy. You knew just where to find me. So let's have it."

"*Find* you? It was an accident. A mistake. I was…"

Buddy Rheams told me to push the limits. To chase the stars. Well, he didn't tell me to, exactly, but…

"No," he said. "No. Who are you? Really? What's all this? What do you want?"

Keela shook her head with a look of amused frustration "What do I want? What we all want. Peace. But if I can't get that, then to blast those techno bastards straight to hell. Right, Olivia?"

Looking barely on the cusp of her teenage years, Olivia snarled. "Too right, those techno wanker bastard asshole scumwad dickheads."

Chill put a hand to his face. "Oy. Forgive them, oh mighty gods. They have fire in their veins. Help them find their path to chill."

"Look. I don't know who you think I am or what magic powers you think I've got, but I'm not looking to kill anyone. Although you're pretty high on my list."

Laughter. "Oh," Keela said. "You had no chance."

"You were locked in!"

"Yeah, well…your ship is a bit of an…older model. And while I'm sure you find the weapons quite effective for shooting… squirrels or…chipmunks or…some really ferocious gophers… it's a little outdated, no?"

"Outdated? It's a prototype! It's brand new."

"Flyboy," she said. "Shut up. Listen."

Powell was speechless as Keela revealed the history of the Aretha clan, and how they settled in that part of the country.

When he first came out of that intense flash, his sensors displayed that he was somewhere on the edge of the Grand Canyon. But he was suddenly less certain. "Show me a map."

Keela looked at him quizzically.

Powell re-mocked her. "Humor me. Me dumb. Need map. Show."

Offering a touché nod of recognition, Keela produced a small, hand-held device—much like his KATI—which projected into the forest air a 3-D map with topography. "See here?" She pointed to what Powell knew as the northwest corner of the Grand Canyon. In particular, to a town nestled between deep canyons to the north and east, fertile valleys to the west, and a basin to the south. They had access to all the food, water, and minerals they would ever need. "That's us. Grinroad. We settled here generations ago. We're very well protected."

Only it wasn't the Grand Canyon, or even North America. At least according to Keela's 3-D map. There was no such region marked *Oklahoma*. There was no *Missouri*, no *Iowa*. Or any recognizable cities or states, for that matter. And a portion of the Midwest was gone. In its place was Lake Abandarro— what Powell knew as the Mississippi River—expanded five-fold through a combination of natural erosion and man-made demolition.

Sean also explained that treacherous currents and radioactive mineral deposits rendered the lake—the predominant physical barrier separating East and West—virtually impossible to navigate by boat. "These," he said, pointing to the land masses on both sides of Lake Abandarro, "are the last two major regions on Aretha. A hundred years ago, the planet was ten billion strong. Now we're down to eight million, maybe less."

"We don't know for sure," Keela said. "It's impossible to keep track."

Powell shook his head. He pored over the 3-D map, and just knew he was staring at the United States. What else could it be? There was the Florida peninsula in the southeast, and the hat of Northern Texas he knew so well, and the unmistakable ridges of the California coastline. But according to the map's notation, it *wasn't* the United States. It wasn't the country he knew. The one he left only yesterday. It was the same, only...different.

"It's a fake," he said. "It's a trick. It's bullshit. You totally faked this."

"Did we?"

Their silence notwithstanding, they didn't really expect him to believe that they were on another...planet? Did they? Common sense alone made it easy to dismiss their claims.

An alternate Earth? An alternate reality? Oh, come on.

But, still...Powell launched into space. He really did that. He chased another ship outside the Saturn rings. He did that, too. And he passed through a ripple with a glowing blue light. But how did he know it was an actual *wormhole*? Because they said so? And even if it was, which he doubted, didn't it make more sense that Aranuke or Buddy Rheams staged this little scene to mess with him? That they drugged him within *Crossline* and were now feeding him more lies?

But what if, he thought, what if, for argument's sake, he *had* flown through a wormhole? And what if, as remote as it seemed, it wasn't just a wormhole of space, but of time or dimension or some combination of them all? Transporting him from one reality to another?

Keela continued. "We lived in a state of bloat—vapid, lazy, and self-indulgent—until we finally broke apart. Riots erupted about whether we were cannibalizing the planet, and knowing that if we didn't change our ways, we would destroy it—and each other." She gestured to Sean, Chill, and Olivia. Through the forest, behind them, was a gorge with a flowing river below.

Beyond it, in the distance, were snow-peaked mountains. "This is what's left."

Powell was suddenly attuned to the rushing water below, growing louder, louder, louder. He shook his head. "I don't...It doesn't make sense. I..."

"Come," Chill said. "Let's take him from the edge. He hears us." They moved to an open patch surrounded by forest. Powell sat on a large rock. Chill offered him a water pouch. "When the war finally ended, more from exhaustion than conclusion, the survivors settled into two main camps, on opposite ends of the continent. The Westies, as we are called..." Chill gave a regal bow, "...we took to the caves and mountains, to reconnect with the land. To chill."

"We embraced a communal life," Sean said. "Our foundation is family, mediation, study, physical endurance, and feast. But our enemy—the Scrapers—compacted themselves into highrise towers in just a few dense cities. Prado City—their center of operations—is the worst of all. Their culture is based on virtual game worlds, orgy palaces, opium dens, and shopping. The Scrapers embrace an unashamed philosophy of indulgence and practicality. Why do more—and have less—when you can do less and have more?"

Keela adjusted her gun holster. "They are pleasure seekers. They're aggressive. They're vain. And they want *us* to be like *them*."

"We just don't believe in commerce as a value system," Sean said. "The Scrapers don't want to hear it. They think if they slow down, if they let the noise settle—if they allow quiet and calm— we'll infect their souls with weakness."

"After decades of war," Chill explained, "we reached a state of collective chill, with nary a bomb exploding on either side. And for more than fifteen years we chilled on our side, and they chilled on theirs. The Scrapers carried on in their cities, engaging in commerce, while we've been out here, cultivating the land, communing with the gods, meditating, finding our innermost chill as it reached into the kingdom of—"

Sean interrupted. "They did their thing while we did ours. Lasting peace actually seemed possible. And then, about seven years ago—"

"Eight," Chill corrected.

"Right. Sorry, Chill. Eight years ago, bombs went off on both sides of Lake Abandarro, in their cities, and in our caves. The Battle of Lightwind. It's been back and forth ever since. It just takes a small band of zealots to keep us at war. We try to lock them down, but sometimes…they live among you, and you don't. Even. Know it."

As those words hung in the air—*they live among you*—Powell had the distinct feeling, as he did in the caves, that Sean was accusing him of something. Something sinister. And with each second of passing silence, the weight seemed to amplify, settling on his shoulders.

"The violence affects us all," Sean said. "The pressure. It gets to you. But you adjust. You deal with it. Unless you don't."

Olivia spoke, but they all had the same thought. "Riva. Unmerciful death."

Sean bounced his shotgun in his hands. "There's a madman out there, Powell. A lunatic. He burns people alive. He slits their throats. We think he was from Grinroad, if you believe that. I knew him from our school, as a boy. His family died in the Battle of Lightwind. They said he snapped after that. But he was already disturbed. It was only a matter of time." Sean looked to Chill, and then took a step closer, staring right at Powell. "And now he's with the Scrapers. Their savage on the loose. *That's* what war does to people. *That's* what we face."

His heart thundering, Powell thought of Chandra and Jesse just then. They never seemed farther away. The hole in his center felt even wider, like a pebble falling down a canyon. Falling. Falling. *Sploosh*. Without his girls, his life had no meaning.

"Wait," he said, standing up. "Hold on a sec."

Sean responded by asserting his shotgun. *Chk-chack.*

"Whoa. Take it easy. What the hell?"

"Back off, Powell. I'm telling you." Sean gestured his shotgun. "Back off."

Olivia lunged at Powell with a raised fist, gun in the other. "You heard him, dickbag! Back. Off!"

Keela grabbed her, like yanking the leash on a snarling pit bull. "You can't be this stupid, Powell. You just can't. Don't you get it? Don't you see?"

Powell breathed deliberately through his nose. It burned. His eyes shifted back and forth, plotting his escape. Over the cliff? Through the forest? Near his feet was a fallen branch the size of a baseball bat. He was quick and strong and could hold his own in a scrape. But he was outmanned and outgunned. Yet coursing adrenaline instigated a fantasy in which he was capable of moving faster and with greater precision than the laws of physics would actually permit.

"Whooaoaoaoa," Chill said, perhaps sensing Powell's ill-advised contemplation. "Sean, Olivia. Ease off a bit. Chill. The man is still hearing. Now let him listen."

Sean wasn't having it. "Chill, do you really think—?"

"Remember the day, Sean. Remember the night."

Finger coiled around the trigger, there was tense deliberation behind Sean's eyes. Powell wasn't entirely sure, but he had the very real sense that were it not for Chill's intervention, Sean would have emptied both barrels—and still might.

In his mind's eye, Powell saw Jesse then—evolving through the phases of her life, at five, at fifteen, and as a grown woman. Yet right in front of him, in the moment, there was nothing but Sean's two deliberate eyes. And then, finally, after a prolonged silence where Powell dangled over the precipice between life and death, Sean eased his shotgun grip, and finished reciting Grinroad's oath to their fallen comrades, and the future.

"Remember the day, remember the night. Remember the howl…remember the rite. Remember the dreams, remember the plight. Remember us all…remember the light."

Chill looked to Keela and Olivia, who both nodded, and then at Sean, who did the same.

Powell exhaled. He felt safe…*ish*, at least for the moment.

"Better," Chill said. "Better. Now Marcus. I know you're anxious. You have questions of your own. But, please. Bear with me. There's more to know."

Powell had heard enough from them to take their stories more seriously. But was he convinced? Could he really know for sure? Either way, all he wanted was to rush home to his girls, hold them close, and never let go.

Three birds flew overhead. Keela watched them pass, then continued. "Those years ago, during the Battle of Lightwind?… We know why it came. We were testing a new propulsion system. We achieved advanced warp. It changed our lives."

Powell found that eerily familiar.

"The Scrapers have their own air fleet, but nothing that can match us. So they waged war. They attack at night. They want our designs. They want to even the skies, to take them over. We could launch our own offensive. With the warp drive, we could enter their airspace in minutes. But they have superior ground-to-air defenses. It's a magnified pulse. They react so quickly. They can pick us off with ease. We just can't win this war, flyboy. No one can. So we made a choice. Fight the Scrapers off until we can find a new planet. Start over. We were going to leave Aretha. Just leave the Scrapers behind."

Keela wandered off a bit, shaking her head. "I love this land. The thought of leaving…it rips my fucking heart out. But the propulsion system worked brilliantly. And then, by accident…we found it was the key to something else. Something…unexpected. We were trying to amplify the warp thrusters, but the adjustments we made…had a different result. We were able to cut a hole through space. The wormhole."

Sean rubbed her shoulder. "But the technology is still new. It's not something we can just slap into a fleet of ships. The circuitry is complex, dangerous, and difficult to replicate."

"It takes careful installation and testing," Keela said. "It takes time. Time we don't have. The Scrapers know what we have. And they'll do anything to get it, too. Ironic. The wormhole just might be the key to our salvation. Unless our enemy destroys us over if first. About two years ago we got word of a major offensive, so we had to move quickly. My husband volunteered. Mitri flew a solo mission using the wormhole to find us a new planet." Keela turned red; her eyes nearly welled up. "He never came back."

"But after he took off," Sean said, "we found glitches in the system. Real problems. It took all this time to resolve them and install a second ship. It wasn't easy to wait. But the minute it was ready, Keela went looking for him. And after a few weeks...she found you."

Keela came closer. "Wherever you're from, my husband is stranded there, alone. You're my only link to him. You're going to get him back."

A woman without her husband. A family torn apart. Chandra. My god. What have I done?

"I don't know him," Powell said. "I swear..."

"Now *that* I believe. But your prototype? It's his. Has to be. You stole my husband's ship and then used it to build your own. Your engineering sucks, but the design is unmistakable."

"Whoa. Hang on. It took more than fifty years to build that ship. It's not some—"

"It's not what? A forgery. A copy?"

Powell wanted to defend his position, but felt the tent poles in his conviction fall away.

"What do you think, huh? That by sheer coincidence you arrive here, on *this* planet, in a replica of our ship...and there's no connection?" Keela shook her head. "Really? That's what you're saying? Come on, flyboy. Think. Use your brain. Where did that ship really come from?"

"I...uh," he said. "It must've..."

It was slow at first, but in succession the dominoes toppled over in his mind. How *did* an obscure oil drilling company become the most powerful corporation in the world? How *did* a poor, uneducated gas attendant elevate himself to a global icon? Was he really just the great rags-to-riches story, the American Dream? Or like many before him, had Buddy Rheams built an empire on the pilfered genius of others?

"You stole it. You get that? You fucking stole it. And let me tell you one more thing. My husband better still be alive...because if *he's* not...*you're* dead." Keela patted him on the face. "How's that for magic powers?"

Sean leaned over. He offered Powell a shrug. "...Told you."

Dazed as he was, Powell still had some fight in him. "That's it. Enough. You say I don't belong here. Right back 'atcha. And you know what? Maybe they did steal your husband's ship. Who knows? Those...what did you call them? Techno wanker what-holes?"

Olivia clarified. "Techno wanker bastard asshole scumwad dickheads."

"Right. That. I know just the techno wanker bastard asshole scumwad dickheads you mean. But now you listen to *me*. I honestly don't know if your husband is captured or buried, dead or alive or just a figment of your imagination. The only thing I care about is getting my ass out of here and back to my girls. So unless you've got some secret solution I don't know about, it's time to stop your clucking and send me home."

Not sure if he impressed them, scared them, or if they were convinced that he cracked, Keela, Sean, Olivia, and Chill all suddenly broke into smiles.

Keela extended a hand. "I think he's finally ready. Agreed?"

They nodded, and responded in unison. "Agreed."

Powell's band of interrogators started away. "Whoa, whoa, whoa." He jogged after them. "Agree to what? Agree to *what*?"

Keela stopped before a massive pine, and threw him a strange smile. "Oh. Plenty of time for that, flyboy. But now...it's time to feast."

CHAPTER TEN

NOt the first night, the second, or even the third. Riva needed to wait for the crescent moon. Eric Osgood sent him to Grinroad. To find the one. The one with answers. About warp drives. About wormhole emitters. Riva would do as instructed. But he didn't care about politics, commerce, or war. He had plans of his own.

I failed once before, he thought, approaching Maria's window. *But not again.*

Riva hadn't returned to Grinroad since the Battle of Lightwind, when he was just Carlos Guerra, a teenage boy already losing his grip on reality. And then his family died in the bombing. Buried alive. Lost in the horror of violence and war, Carlos journeyed into the mountains. Where he found his true self. And his maker as well.

I will come for you, too, Chill. We will talk again. But not yet. Not now.

Riva approached the back door. Fear coursed through him. He couldn't breathe. It had been so long. He removed the blade from his pocket, slid it through the crack in the locked door. He unbolted it, snuck inside the red rock apartment. He saw shadows on the wall. His shadow.

Easy, Riva thought. *Easy.*

First the parents' room. The wife was face down, while the father snored, loud, then soft, and then loud again. The cycle repeated. Riva thought about killing them, too. *But, no,* he told himself. *Maria first. I'm here for Maria.* And then Riva pulled the bedroom door closed so that he was alone again in the hallway. The silence unleashed his memories. Explosions. Rubble. Severed limbs.

Katie. Enrique. Mother. Father.

And then a cloud of bloody dust in his mind wiped away the memory, leaving Riva with a strange calm and then a savage need to kill.

He stood outside Maria's door. His body tingled.

Be patient. Slit her throat. Last time you struck too fast. You missed. And then she ran away. So did you. Then you were a wolf cub who snapped at his prey. But now you are a beast with the power of the night. And your purpose is pure.

Inside her room, she laid asleep, face up—a woman now, still living with her parents. Riva watched her chest rise and fall, as the air entered and left her body. Candlelight flickered. He opened his free hand, and once upon her, gripped her throat. He squeezed. Soft at first and then tight, tighter, tightest. With his other hand, he held the blade to her closed eye.

Just as Maria had once stolen teenaged moments with his sister Katie—designed, he was certain, to exclude him, to humiliate him, to intentionally shut him out—he was now sharing a moment with the gods—with Maria's life in his hand—that even she did not yet recognize.

"You are the cursed and the divine," he said. "The temptress and the thief."

Maria's eyes snapped open. She thrashed about, but Riva held her down. Immobilized her. He had no interest in her breasts, nipples, or ports of entry. He was not there to rape her. He wanted something else.

Riva felt the contact of his subdued victim. The thrill only intensified as Maria struggled and fought, to save herself.

She could barely speak. "C-Carlos?...Is that y-y-you? What are you doing?"

"Your tongue is like a snake that spits in the grass. But you don't die from a snakebite, do you? No. You die from the venom."

Riva released his grip just enough to let her speak, to invite false hope—that she might somehow survive. That her life wasn't already over.

"We're your people, Carlos. Where did you go?"

"There are only gods and fools and the wrath of the sun. I went to the East, to be with the one. I live in the towers, and use my blade. And now I am here. For you, for Chill. I dreamed of this night. Or it dreamed of me."

"My god. You're Riva. Unmerciful death. I heard stories from the East…"

"Stories are tales that linger in the night. But I am real…. And so are you."

Maria squirmed, exposing the long, jagged scar on her arm. Before he was Riva, when he was still Carlos Guerra, he attacked her once before. A teenager then. A monster now.

"Please, Carlos. I'm sorry. Why do you do this? What have I done?"

"You poisoned my Katie. You took her soul."

"No, Carlos. Don't. I…I loved her."

"Our bond was profound, like the gods who created us. But you are a demon who hides in the light. You tempted her with flesh and whispered lies. She was not yours to take…. She was mine."

"No, Carlos. I loved her. I LOVED her."

"She was MINE!"

"She was your sister."

"My twin. You poisoned her very spirit. And now she is dead. As you will be. And your family down the hall."

"N-no! Mom—!"

Riva stifled her words. "You are worst of all," he said. "You are yellow moonlight in the great, dark night. I will cut the head off the snake. I will kill you."

Maria's face filled with water. Riva looked upon her eyes, saw past her irises. Before him was the realm beyond terror. The infinite blackness.

"You are the daughter of life," he said. "The goddess of sun."

"C-Carlos. I don't…"

Riva raised the knife. Candlelight struck the blade. It glistened. "You know the sacred oath. Or has it no meaning for you?"

-Remember the day, remember the night-
-Remember the howl...remember the rite-
-Remember the dreams, remember the plight-
-Remember us all...remember the light.

Maria dove forward, but fell to the floor. Though standing just five feet, two inches tall—a skinny twerp when viewed from a distance—Riva had trim, hardened muscles, powerful hands and unflappable determination. He grabbed Maria by the throat again, eased her down. The panic turned to fury that screamed in his head. But like a tornado that blacks out the sky, he was consumed by the unquenchable need to kill Maria. His vision was colored red, so that all before him was streaked. Streaked with blood.

"You breathe with the night," he said, and angled his blade. "You sleep with the Moon. And as the starlight fades to black... so will you."

Riva thought killing Maria would ease the screaming in his soul. It didn't. Then one at a time he dragged her mother and father to witness. To see her slit throat, her lips sliced off. To experience his power. "She will whisper no more," he said. But after he killed the parents, too, as their blood oozed into the rug, all he felt was emptiness. A void.

Though Riva was the only living soul in that bloodied room, he spoke to Eric Osgood, who was somehow there with him in Grinroad, in Maria's bedroom, as witness.

Riva understood that Osgood directed their efforts from his Prado City office—on the other side of the divided continent, the Scraper side, more than 2,000 miles away—and had not physically materialized before him. But in his mind's eye, Riva's surrogate father was there with him nonetheless. It had become Riva's ritual. He needed to share the moment with someone

"People think I'm a monster," he said. "They are right."

Osgood's apparition responded. "I know," he said.

"It was my destiny. I have no choice."

"I know that, too."

Riva sat on Maria's bed, triangulated among the three dead bodies. Daughter. Mother. Father. He then posed a question that required no answer. "Do you fear me?" Riva hoped on the one hand that Osgood did not, and on the other hand, that he very much did. "Scrapers, Westies. They all bleed the same. But I know you have a plan. I have one, too."

Osgood answered in the manner the monster had come to expect—with a gentle tone, an offer of compassionate resignation. "I know you do, Carlos. I know you do."

Riva ran his finger along the edge of his blade. It was right for the task, as it had just been, and would be again. "Thank you," he said, upholding the social contract.

Light from the crescent moon seeped in through the window. Riva held up his fingers. He reached out, to gut Eric Osgood, but the blade simply sliced the air. "I know you're not here. But I feel you with me. I held your hand. I saw pieces of your mind. I've seen what you see. I swam in your soul."

It was then that the strobe light went off in his mind again. That *flash-flash-flash*. Linked to Chill's visions—their eternal connection, their communal bond—Riva had his own. *Flash-flash-flash*. Of a congregation. Of pain. He saw a journeyman, a stranger he had not yet met, but one he remembered most. And another *flash-flash-flash*. He saw a truck at the corner. Soldiers. A massacre. An inferno. *Flash-flash-flash*.

"Carlos," Osgood said. "Do you remember your quest?"

"Yes. I remember. I know where to go."

"The St. Brewer's Day Feast is under way. In the great hall."

"Your friends left the note," Riva said. "As you said they would."

"Yes. They are loyal to the cause."

Riva let out a curious smile. And then as he did with all of his victims, he carved a small, crescent moon under Maria's chin. The same again to her parents.

"There is no peace, just a breath of the light. You can travel the stars and the worlds in the sky, but there is no greater force

than the will of your mind. In these hands of mine. You can follow the gods or follow your lies. But you still have to choose."

"Just one more night, Carlos, and you are forever free. Your
knowledge of Grinroad has proved invaluable. Our friends will
do the rest. Your team is in place. They will meet you."

*You cling to the notion of friends and foes, of wrong and right.
But we are none of us the same. We are watched by the gods.
Judged by their might. We can search for our place in their deep,
dark eyes, but each of us is alone. Each of us is alone.*

As Riva looked down upon the bodies before him, he knew
that he could wait no longer. Osgood wanted to shift the balance
of power between East and West. To take the skies. But for Riva
it was the power of one. He needed to draw out the shaman of
Grinroad. To purge his soul. To complete the cycle. The time, at
last, had finally come. Riva recited aloud, as it was foretold:

-When the one who comes to save us all-
-The man of peace will rise and fall-
-And those who see will grab the light-
-To start anew-
-To end the night-

The winds of change howled. Whether anyone but Riva
could hear them, he didn't know. He also didn't care. Grinroad
was preparing a feast. He dreamt of it often. And when Chill
finally arrived, they would have little to discuss, but the words
they shared would mean everything that still mattered.

CHAPTER ELEVEN

LIKE THE REST of the Westie towns, Grinroad—the smallest, but also one of seven strategic centers in the region—was preparing for its annual celebration. "Today is the grandest of days," Chill said. "It's the St. Brewer's Day Feast. Eat, drink, and beat cherry."

"Be merry," Powell corrected.

"Whoaoaoa." Chill stopped in the underground corridor and furrowed his brow. "I know you didn't get a hero's welcome, but that's done now. No reason to get cruddy with me."

Keela and her band of rebels had given Powell quite an interrogation, but could he really blame them? It's not every day that a man from another...planet?...time?...dimension?...falls from the sky, and with a ship stolen from one of their beloved members. Would he have been any less suspicious had the situation been reversed?

But as he began to more richly digest the implications of his predicament—*good, god, I might really be in another dimension*—he fell into a panic attack.

Jesse. Candy. I'm out here, my god. Please don't worry. I'm okay, I'm alive. I'm lost and confused and a little messed up right now but I'll find my way back. I have to. I have to! I don't know when or how, but soon. I'll find a way. I'll find it! Don't let your heart sink because I'm a fool. Don't lose faith in me. I'm coming, I'm...

They came to arched, wooden doors. A low vibration rumbled through the caves. Chill offered the lead. "*Soooo*...I think you're going to enjoy this."

"You know...I'm not really in the mood for any more surpri..." As the doors opened, Powell faced a banquet hall lined with long, wooden tables and benches. Musicians plucked joyous tunes. The wire-thin lighting fixtures kept the hall festively lit. Oil lamps and candles hung from black chandeliers; others were set on the tabletops. Laughter swelled. Hungry, smiling faces of all ages. The entire town ate and drank. Danced and hugged. Grinroad had come to feast.

And how could they not? The aroma was warm, sweet butter. On the tables were heaping plates of barbecue ribs, corn on the cob, buttermilk biscuits, and fried chicken. Baked beans with maple syrup glaze. Green beans. In one alcove, a happy-looking fellow, sharpening two large knives, stood over a roast boar turning on a spit with a candied apple in its mouth.

Hungry with a vengeance, Powell surveyed the hall, drooling over plates of salmon fillets and grilled shrimp. Buckets of crabs. Mounds of mixed green salads with plump, red tomatoes, carrots, cucumbers, and radishes. Butternut squash. Grilled chicken. Sausages. Steaks.

Along the back wall was a setting of pies the length of the room. The scent of hot fruits. Apple and blueberry. Pumpkin. Cherry. Peach. Pecan.

And, of course, along every table were pitchers of wine and ale.

Chill brought Powell to a few empty seats at the end of an otherwise full table. Olivia and Sean sat opposite him. "Go on, then," Olivia said. "Get your grub on."

Taking a nod from Chill, who wandered off into the crowd, Powell nibbled on a honey-glazed rib. He was hesitant, but when the marinade hit his taste buds his inner caveman went all *hooba hooba gimme. Bunk off. Eating.* It had been days since his last proper meal. "*Mmm...good...I'm* starving...*mmm...oh, yeah.*" Drawing stares, he offered a sheepish wince, stoned on barbecue. Rib meat hung from his mouth. "*Wha?*"

"You got some guank on your face, there, mate. There. On your cheek." Olivia wiped his face clean with a napkin. She rubbed pretty hard. "You need a woman, mate. You're a mess."

"Just so long as Little Red Riding Hood keeps her

distance…I'll be fine." Powell looked around. He shrunk a little. "She's not here, is she?"

Sean chuckled. "She's over there. And don't worry, she feels kinda bad about before. We had to make sure you weren't one of them. The Scrapers. You know. You can never be too sure."

Powell nodded, then devoured another rib.

"Well, she doesn't blame you for her husband, per sé…but look at it from our eyes. You showed up like you did, playing dumb as a post."

"Too right," Olivia interjected. "I guess they don't grow them too bright on Uuu-rrth." Then, as if a bell went off, she looked at Sean, and wide-eyed they smiled at each other, looked at Powell, back at each other, and in unison broke into a chant:

"*Ooooh-oooh, Uuuu-rrth. How pretty does he look?*"

"*Ooooh-oooh, Uuuu-rrth. For genius he mistook.*"

"*Ooooh-oooh, Uuuu-rrth. How glorious may he be?*"

"*Ooooh-oooh, Uuuu-rrth. He's all the guank, you'll see!*"

They laughed and high-fived across the table.

Powell had enough. "This is bull! I didn't know what she was talking about!"

"We know that *now*," Olivia said. "You can't fake that kind of stupid." She gave a quick shake of the head. "You really are a bonehead."

Powell wiped his face, and then downed an entire stein of ale. Cold. Frosty. It dribbled down his chest. He exhaled deeply, then sat back down, still chewing rib meat. "Thanks. You really know how to apologize."

Olivia nodded, gave a wink. "Sure thing."

"You remind me of Jesse. My daughter. She's a smartass, too."

"I like her already. If she's got your wife's brains and looks, she'll probably go places."

Almost falling into a trance, Powell thought of his little girl just then, running through the gorge back home, with her arms out, airplane style. "She does. And she will."

Sean gestured to Olivia. "Your brother's coming. Terry. With you-know-who. He's got his guitar with him. Looks like we're in for another mopey dopey song set."

Powell turned toward Terry—tall, wiry, unshaven—who looked like he just came off the wrong side of a four-day bender.

"Meal time with the brown-eyed hoebag," Olivia said. "Fuck it all."

Terrified that his own daughter might someday hit this level of pubescent rage, Powell felt the need to speak up. "Aren't you kinda young to be so...you know...vulgar?"

Olivia posed a question of her own. "Why don't I shove that rib plate up your ass?"

"I stand corrected. My bad."

Sean chuckled. "Don't mind her. She's just protective of her brother. And Faye's a bit..."

"She's a grunge-eyed skankwad."

"Maybe. But Terry's in love."

With the banquet hall in a state of revelry, music, and mirth, Olivia jolted up with such force that the bench scraped back. She pointed a fork at Sean—and seemed committed to using it on him. "Terry is not, repeat NOT in fucking love. *Got* that? She's just a slut of the month with no lock on her box."

"Okay, Liv. Take it easy. It's all good. Maybe he'll write another love song about her. '*Oh, Faye, my babe. I wuuuuv you. Kiss-kiss-kiss. Mwah-mwah-mwah.*'"

"He's a musician, jerkwad. Not a moron. He's beautiful."

"Well...," Sean said playfully.

"I swear to the ten flags, Sean. Another word and you'll fucking eat that guitar."

Powell didn't know the family history—it was obviously intense—but he saw fire behind the young girl's eyes, eyes that revealed far more than any twelve-year-old should ever know. What had she experienced living beneath the dueling tyrannies of puberty and war? But with no sight or even mention of her parents, Powell assumed that whatever happened in the preceding years, they were stories best left untold.

Powell then saw himself, with Chandra by his side, caught between the joys and grief of parenthood, watching their little girl become her own woman before their very eyes. Much to his own surprise he felt a compulsion to protect Olivia, who in a very real way was still a child, yet assuming responsibility for her wayward big brother.

And then a wild, red blur broke his concentration. Keela sat down. Once again tense and uneasy, Powell started in on a hunk of corn, slowly—a dog showing his teeth.

"Easy, flyboy. I came to make nice." She handed him a plate of baked goods. "Strudel?"

He put down the corn, wiped his hands. "No, thanks. I'm good."

"Oh…don't be like that, flyboy. It's a peace offering. Apple-blueberry. Dolores baked it herself. Best in the valley."

"Powell," he said.

"What's that?"

"Not *flyboy*." Powell stared right at her. His father said he should never hit a woman, but in this one case, he might have made an exception. He wasn't over the whole *you shot missiles at me and forced me through the wormhole* thing. "It's Powell. Captain. Marcus Powell."

Keela ran her tongue along her teeth. She clenched her fist, and gestured toward him, but Sean put a hand on her thigh. "Keela." Sean opened his eyes wide, held them, and then removed his hand, which he left on her leg just a second or two longer than one might expect. "Keela."

She sighed with aggressive frustration, grit her teeth. "Okay. Puh…*grrr*…Powell."

Chill strolled by, his eyes as glazed as the barbecue ribs. "Everyone getting along? Nice and chill? Anyhoosey…if I might borrow our guest. I'd like to show him the Cake."

The table came to a sudden hush, then turned to Powell, who couldn't help but notice that everyone within earshot was staring at him. "Uh, no, thanks, Chill. I'm full." The many eyes on him went wide. Feeling very much on display, Powell got the feeling that his cake refusal was akin to urinating in the pew during Sunday church. "I mean…I'm just not a cake guy."

Fork in hand, Keela made a move across the table before Sean pulled her back again.

Olivia presented Powell with the facts of life. "You are just the biggest nimrod alive. Go with Chill before Keela stomps your balls—and I join her."

Two dozen townsfolk danced in a circle as the fiddlers plucked away. Following Chill toward the music, Powell received a range of stares and winks—some nasty, some curious, and others with what appeared to be invitations for orgy-style sex. He whispered to Chill. "What's up with them? I'm just not a cake guy. I don't like sweets."

Chill patted his shoulder. "I think it's safe to assume you don't know what *Cake* is."

"Flower and eggs? Chocolate frosting? Goes with a glass of milk? You know? Cake."

"Ah." Chill brought him to a cave hallway opposite the musicians. They were alone. "Do you understand the concept of divine prophecy?"

Powell stared for a moment. Though not to the same degree as his father, he had limited patience for any spirit-walking molecule talk. It pleased him that Chandra passed stories down to Jesse—mother-and-daughter bonding. But for him? Not so much. "Yeah. Like…the serpent god of a thousand lakes will lead its people to the benevolent church of the purple iguana?"

Chill looked at Powell oddly, blinked a few times. Then a few more. "Close enough."

Powell was still struggling to connect the dots. "*Okaaaaay.* So…?"

Chill held out one hand. "Divine prophecy." Then the other. "Cake." He repeated the gesture, switching between hands. "Divine prophecy…. Cake. Divine prophecy…. Cake. Are you embracing the flow? Divine prophecy means *Cake*. Or the other way around. However you like."

"Oh. Okay. Gotcha. Where I come from, cake just means, you know…cake."

Chill simultaneously sighed, dropped his head, and shook it. "I really need to smoke this." He took four quick tokes on a joint, held his breath for what seemed like an awfully long time, and then expelled a massive cloud. His eyes re-glazed. "Better." His shoulders drooped. He smiled. "Want?"

"No, thanks." Powell's voice held a hint of contempt. "That's my wife's bag."

"Yes. You have a wife and daughter. Indeed…a gift from the gods."

Powell nodded. "I have to get home. They need me."

"As I'm sure you need them. The Cake, I mean, divine prophecy, says that you will see them again. It's a chill."

"Oh, for the love of Aunt Margaret. Look…Chill. Don't take this the wrong way, but a divine cake prophecy doesn't mean anything to me. No offense."

"That's actually redundant, you know. 'Cake' and 'prophecy' mean the same thing." Chill did the one-hand-other-hand thing again. "But I suppose that's not your concern right now."

"Chill. There's no cake prophecy about me. I think you hit the bong too hard."

"My boy, first…" Chill stared at Powell until his eyes drifted off. He smacked his lips, swallowed. "Thirsty. I could use some ale." He chuckled. "A little cotton mouth."

"Chill!"

"One of our oldest Cake prophecies…Oh, see? Now you've got me doing it. The Cake says that on St. Brewer's Day Eve, 'the one who soars will come,' and when 'the skies are open and true' he will 'find the child.' And upon doing so, he will return from whence he came. The family reunited."

"Look, Chill. That's a great…er, Cake and all. Really. But you're starting to annoy me. What's that got to do with *me*?"

"Ask Jesse. She knows."

Powell instantly saw red. "What did you say?" He grabbed Chill by the collar, forced him against the wall. "How do you know her name? How do you know that?!"

Chill let out a low mumble. "Whoaoa. You said it before. In the woods. Chandra. Jesse."

"No, way, Chill. No way. Don't mess with me. I never said their names. Never!"

"Are you certain?"

"What do you mean, *am I certain*? Of course I am. What the hell? I would never…"

The rage extinguished from Powell as quickly as it erupted. Given his recent experiences, was he absolutely sure about what he had or had not said under duress? Could he testify to it with assuredness? Was it possible that he had uttered their names, out there in the woods, like Chill said, but in his confused and agitated state had not realized it?

"Perhaps in our first meeting, then? During our flight through the valley."

Though only inches from Grinroad's shaman, close enough to smell Chill's dirty tobacco breath, Powell couldn't see his face. Not the ridge of his left nostril or the stubble on his chin. Rather, he fell back into their trippy dream flight together. The strobe light went off in his head. That *flash-flash-flash*. Like a hawk he soared above the ravine and into open skies, flapping those powerful wings. And whether in his mind's eye he was only now seeing what had existed there all along or she appeared through suggestion, his daughter was there, on a mountaintop. She waved. Powell reached out to her. His heart swelled. "Jesse," he said.

The strobe light went off again. That *flash-flash-flash*. He then saw a city street in flames, and a young man whose eyes burned raw with hate. And in the sky, turned to blackest night, he saw a face in the crescent moon. It winced with agony and despair. It dripped with blood.

Another *flash-flash-flash*. Without realizing he did so, Powell released Chill, and then fell back on his heels.

"The dream flight is sacred," Chill said. "It binds the two of us. Connects us. No matter what you see, it remains between just you and me."

Powell rubbed his hand over his eyes, nodded.

"Much has been asked of you, I realize. And I apologize. We have no desire to upset you. It's not our way. But you have stirred the passions in us. Our zeal."

"Yeah," Powell whispered. "Zeal."

Chill offered Powell a friendly rub on the back. "Come, now. It's time."

Already feeling Grinroad grip his every move, Powell let out a sigh. "Just not the eyes, okay? I can't take any more."

Chill let out a soft chuckle. "Not to worry. Your eyes are safe and sound."

"Thanks. Sounds good." Powell dusted off his clothes, feeling the need to control at least one part of his present moment. "But what about the rest of me?"

Chill whispered to the lead fiddle player, who smiled, and with a definitive nod instructed the band to wrap it up. Powell took a step to the left and behind, out of harm's way.

The crowd applauded, giving its full attention. Chill gestured to Olivia, who joined them up front and kept everyone focused. "All right, you wankers! Let Chill do his thing."

Laughter.

"Thank you, Olivia. As always, it is wonderful to have us together, in celebration." The hall filled with cheers. "And tonight, as you all know, is an occasion we've dreamed of since our earliest days."

Powell looked on as the crowd drew quiet. Respectful.

"And as we are gathered here, in a state of chill, let me bring to you now, someone who, in his own way, has been here longer than us all. Since before we first walked the lands."

Brought to the front, Powell grew squeamish. Yet again he found himself at the center of attention, when what he wanted most was to hold Chandra and Jesse and let the rest fade away.

"This man came to us yesterday, of all days. And while in our deepest hearts we desired him to be the one we see...we needed confirmation. Keela style." The crowd offered a knowing laugh, and looked back at Keela, who blushed. "But now that we know... this man needs to know it himself."

Chill nodded to Olivia, who pulled on a long tassel. It drew back a maroon curtain on the cave wall. The hall went silent. Revealed was a painting, old and faded. It was of a man with his wife and daughter. Big, smaller, smallest. They were in a valley, with a house, and a short wall. A hawk circled above. It clutched a white feather.

Despite himself, Powell stared at the painting. He couldn't help it. *Man. Woman. Child.* Their faces were clear. Distinct. His time on Aretha seemed like an ongoing hallucination, one that morphed and twisted and reconfigured—a waking dream. After a pause, as if seeing the ghost of a friend who died years ago, he finally reached out to touch the ink. To feel it. *That's me,* he thought. *That's...*He shook his head slightly, in protest. His mouth opened, but no words came out. His knees buckled. His chest deflated.

Olivia spoke softly. "That's no joke, flyboy. It's Cake."

Powell blinked quickly, then turned to face Chill, and then the townsfolk. "But that's...I mean..." He shook his head. "You did that today, right? It's new."

Chill offered a calm reply. "You don't really believe that... do you?"

With just a slight gesture, Powell answered. "No," he said. "I guess not."

Grinning like a sea otter, Chill nodded to Olivia, who then slapped the lead fiddle player. "Get going, you wankers. He's the bloody one!"

The Grinroadians roared as music played again. Chill

grabbed Powell's arm, and raised it high. "The Cake has finally come! The Cake! Has! Come!"

The hall erupted with hugs and kisses, barbecue sauce, and butter, music and dancing. All except Powell, who stood there, dumbstruck, feeling ever so much that he had been the victim of a lifelong farce and was only now beginning to appreciate just how obvious it had been all along.

And while among the cheers, he saw Keela and Sean, Olivia and Chill, thinking that Aretha wasn't some distant version of Earth, but perhaps the other way around. Or maybe his mind just snapped. Powell wasn't sure what the hell to believe anymore, but he felt in his gut that whatever they were telling him was at least as true as the life he had left behind—

Piercing light.

Deafening silence.

A million little daggers in his brain.

Oh, God.

Blown against the wall, against the painting of him, Powell's head jerked back violently. There was blood and smoke. Fire. Voiceless screams. Demolished tables and benches. Rubble. Food smeared across the hall.

I can't move. I can't move. I can't...

Paralyzed with fear, Powell felt like the room had just exploded. Which, of course, it had.

Townsfolk scrambled through the fog of pulverized stone. Survivors were trapped in the rubble. Next to him, amid the wreckage, were two legs without a torso, and a severed hand. Nearby, a woman was slumped over. Twitching, she stared down at her arm, at the elbow. Bone penetrated skin, cracked at a violent angle, revealing the marrow. Shock rendered her silent.

A wind tunnel caused the double wooden doors to swing open and slam against the wall. Powell took a gunshot of air to the chest. Sand and debris whipped his face.

Sean was screaming at Terry. Powell could see lips moving, but still there was deafening silence. "COME ON! COME...

ON!" Keela lunged forward as a chunk of cave ceiling crashed down. Bloodied, Olivia was before Powell, on her back, trapped beneath two dead fiddlers. Head throbbing, dazed, the roar inside his own head was like a jet engine. Powell pulled himself to his feet. He lumbered toward Olivia, to pull her out, when someone grabbed him from behind. Powell yanked one arm forward, threw his other elbow back, catching someone—

Another explosion. Blown to the ground. Rubble. Blood. Mangled bodies. Dust from the blast clogged the air. He had to reach Olivia, had to make sure that...

...

...

There was a soft white glow. Faces drew fuzzy. Distant. He felt that hazy drift of warp travel. Slow. Blurred. As if trapped by a great, immovable force. And then his eyes began to close. Until finally...finally—just as Powell began to contemplate his purpose in all the cosmos—there was nothing to see at all.

PART II

THE GASMAN COMETH

"I ain't never pried into what you been up to these years 'cuz I don't really wanna know. I figgered you had yer reasons, and that was enough fer me. But whatever they are, I hope it's all worth it, 'cuz I got nothing left of the old me to give, except an old me. The man I was is dead and gone. I'm just wearin' his clothes."

—Doc Anson

"You don't have to believe in the magic pipe, but it wouldn't kill you to believe in something."

—Chandra Powell

CHAPTER TWELVE

MITRI AMOS FELT like the most powerful man in the world. And in a way, he was. Strapped inside the *Kosono*, he was equipped with the kind of history-altering technology spawned not only by experimentation, but also, perhaps, from an act of divine intervention, where the gods reached down to save humanity from its own idiocy.

In addition to the ship's newly augmented warp thrusters—permitting travel at more than seven times the speed of light—the *Kosono* was equipped with a one-of-its-kind wormhole pulse emitter, or WHPE (Whippee, as the pilots called it). This latest technological advancement would enable Mitri Amos to slice through the fabric of space-time and then travel from his star system to another sector of the Universe altogether. Distances that would otherwise take hundreds, thousands, or even millions of years to pass through, even at maximum warp, would be bounded in a matter of seconds.

Test probes sent through the wormhole indicated that the new technology was safe and reliable, but no one yet knew with specificity where Mitri would emerge on the other side, how the experience would affect him—or if he would ever make it back.

Lucky for Mitri Amos, he was not burdened by the stress of self-doubt when it came to spaceflight. Once he decided to do something, he was all in. He had no death wish, but he often found that the mere doing of things was far better, and more fun, than the endless debates *about* them. Besides, as dubious as the endeavor may have been, leaping across the Universe was just too juicy an opportunity to pass up. And if not him, then who?

Someone had to take the leap of faith that might end Aretha's civil war and the centuries-long destruction of mankind. And the way things were going, the possible extinction of human life on Aretha seemed to be coming sooner rather than later.

Mitri had only one mission—to find another habitable planet to which his people could relocate. This would not only end the war, but allow the Westies to heal, to let the pain and sorrow of the generations slowly fade away. If that wasn't motivation enough to plot a new course in human history, then nothing would be.

And yet it almost didn't matter. Mitri would have done it anyway, if only for Keela. His wife was the most beautiful, dynamic woman he had ever known, and the one person who more so than any other pushed his clan of survivors to accept nothing less than their rightful destiny in the Universe.

Keela had forced herself into a role as one of the fiercest warriors in her community, but she had done so reluctantly. It wasn't that she thirsted for her enemies' blood or craved the glory of victory, no matter what others said. She only wanted to see her people survive, and be free. Nothing less was acceptable.

If Mitri could help accomplish that, if he could find the Westies a new home, give them a new life, then maybe the gods would find it in their ultimate wisdom to finally relent and let Mitri and Keela finally conceive the child they so desperately desired. Keela's infertility left her feeling like less than a woman. Barren. Damaged.

Mitri told her time and again that he loved her exactly how the gods envisioned, but he knew that his words only pacified her in the moment. He needed to *do* something to prove his commitment to her, to demonstrate that their fates were intertwined, and that he considered their marriage a privilege, not a burden.

Yet he wasn't delusional. Mitri understood that finding a new planet was at best a crazy long shot and that he very well could be flying a suicide mission that would end almost as soon as it started. But if the Westies could hold off the enemy long enough to upload the WHPE to a few more ships, thereby increasing their odds of success, then his efforts, whether or not he lived long enough to see the outcome, would be worth it. He wasn't looking to get himself killed—he absolutely wasn't—but Mitri figured that without an intervening miracle or two, he wasn't going to live much longer anyway, so blindly leaping across the Universe didn't seem like so much of a risk, all things considered.

Far beyond Aretha's atmosphere, Mitri activated the WHPE. Before him was a pocket of dense blue radiation, with a brilliant white light at its center—the mouth of a wormhole. Without hesitation he flew through the cosmic ectoplasm.

Mitri didn't know if it was the ripple effect or his death, but the radiation before him gave way to a gleaming core, unfolding, revealing itself. Then a great white flash. Brilliant. Pulsing. And another flash, then another, like passing through an electrical storm. It crackled all around him. Another electrical surge followed—that crackling:

...In a flash he saw Keela stripping down beneath the Tosca Waterfall, diving beneath the water. She surfaced with her red hair slicked back as the water coated her smooth, white skin. She curled her finger at him, drawing him near.

...In a flash, Mitri was thirteen years old, staring down the long canyon at Daydem Point. Forever burned in his heart was the grief his mother felt upon hearing the news. Mitri found his father laying there in the canyon, paralyzed, his spine crushed in a rockslide—a dynamic man reduced to a living ghost. The sky was blue and clear that day, but all Mitri could remember was a brutal snowstorm. So cold.

...In a flash, Mitri was nine years old, in the underground caves with his father, with a safety line in his hand.

"Listen," his father had said, sensitive to just how terrified Mitri was. That he was about to loose his grip. That his footing was no good. "I know you think I just the love the thrill, and I do. That I need to be first. But when you take the cliffs, you respect the fall. There's no bluffing with terrain like this. When you hit a rough patch, you trust your gear, you keep your cool. And sometimes...the smart play is to just turn around." Mitri's father looked at the long drop below. "But if you're not willing to go all the way when you start, it's better not to go at all. There are times in life when, once you've taken that first step, there's no going back. Even when you have no idea what's ahead. Today, we have a choice, so we'll turn back. But sometimes...we don't. And we can't. Understand?"

And in a flash, Mitri arrived. The readout on the *Kosono* console said the entire trip through the wormhole lasted only 4.6 seconds, but that somehow just didn't seem possible. And yet it didn't matter. He made it. He fucking made it. With a heaping smile on his face—just pure elation—he thought of his dad. "First one through." The pride he knew his father would've felt washed over him. "First one."

Mitri took in the vastness of space. That infinite sea of darkness and light, one filled with possibility, the unknown. Planets and moons. Stars. There was a freshness about it, a vitality that seeped in through his pores, conveying to him, in a way only the Universe could, that he was on the verge of something spectacular. A new day was upon him.

According to his sensors, the nearest planet was 13.317 million miles away, a quickie at maximum warp. With the flip of a switch, Mitri sent a signal back through the wormhole that he was a-okay, and that based on his initial readings—confirming those of the earlier probes—there were eight planets for him to survey. The *Kosono*'s 3-D readout displayed their orbits around the Sun. Mitri chuckled. "Eight," he said. "I can work with that."

And for the first time since he volunteered to leap through the Universe, he thought that maybe this wormhole thingy wasn't such a bad idea after all.

Mitri powered up the *Kosono*'s warp engines, cracked his knuckles, and paused to note that he was taking the first leap toward the rest of his life. He then ripped through the unknown star system, which refracted around him—a smear of space and light and color. His sensors finally alerted him to an upcoming planet that, under ideal circumstances, would be the new landing spot for the Westies—a peaceful home far, far away from the madness of war.

But quick inspection revealed that said dwarf planet was pretty much just a gigantic hydrogen and helium ice ball, with an average temperature of -213 degrees Bolston Randor Percentage (BRP). The atmosphere was almost frozen solid. Not quite what he was looking for.

Another warp trip brought him to a red planet with a thin atmosphere and devoid of liquid water, rendering it inhospitable. Mitri didn't want to get all mopey-dopey out there, alone on his first day in a strange part of the Universe and all. But after several hours, so far, not so good. The initial adrenaline rush had worn off, leaving him strung out. Even with a catnap and some energy bars, wormhole travel was losing its charm. He did feel the explorer's awesomeness of warping through an uncharted star system, but Mitri wasn't out there to look about. He had a job to do.

The next planet he came to was yet another ginormous, uninhabitable ice ball, this one far less blue but even greater than the first one. Yet its awesomeness triggered a strange glimmer of déjà vu, of distant familiarity. It also unleashed in him a distinct feeling that the payoff for negotiating the Universe through a wormhole wouldn't come close to matching the collective genius, timing, luck, stupidity, haste, recklessness, arrogance, desperation, courage, ego, and, well, balls it took for him to actualize such an endeavor.

Still, Mitri took solace that there were five more planets to go, and as he made his way closer to the Sun—the star system's brilliant source of heat and light—his chances might improve for finding a winner. In fact, the more he thought about it, the more re-energized he became.

Mitri envisioned his fellow Grinroadians just then, gathered in the Red Rock canyons, with laughter and cheers. He saw the stress leave their bodies, replaced with utter joy. He felt the presence of the gods, like the sun on his face. Warm. Life affirming. And amidst the celebration he saw Keela aglow, rubbing her round belly, with a healthy baby growing inside her—their first of many. The greatest gift for a new life. A life without war. Without savage violence. Without the agony of surviving simply to ward off extermination. It would be a life of peace. A second chance.

Could be, he thought, smiling, out there, alone in space. Could be.

And then he warped again, bounding space-time in incredible increments, finally reducing speed as yet another planet came within reach. He approached the massive body with awe.

Mitri felt emboldened with possibility. He felt hopeful.

He felt the power of fate. He felt—

Like road kill. His heart sank. His body slumped. He knew what he saw before him, but it just couldn't be so.

No way, he thought. No. Humping. Way.

The Kosono's sensors were programmed to identify the thousands of known elements and particles in the Universe, alerting Mitri if the planets he came upon were viable for settlement. He didn't need a computer this time. He gazed out through his canopy, stunned at the gargantuan gas planet. And the massive rings encircling it.

What became sickeningly clear to him was that the celestial body before him wasn't some uncharted planet in some uncharted galaxy. The wormhole hadn't facilitated his leapfrog between separate star systems, bridging what at first seemed an almost immeasurable distance. Instead it transported him from one end of his own star system to the other. It had taken an extraordinary effort to travel what seemed such a long, long way, but as Mitri now realized, he never really left at all.

The Kosono sensors confirmed his shock. At least one part of his brain could appreciate that the distance he instantaneously negotiated—and the method for doing so—was incredible. And perhaps the Westies would devise a strategic tactical advantage utilizing the technology. But for the time, at least, he had to face that there would be no new home. No fresh start, no end to war. The cruelty and toil would continue.

As much as he knew that finding a new planet was just some crazy, desperate dream and that maybe his hero fantasy was always going to outshine the brutal fabric of his reality, he still let himself embrace the possibility of their salvation because he wanted so badly to believe it. And he wanted to do something that really mattered—a purpose beyond mere survival.

But liberator of the human race? Uh, yeah. Sure.

Mitri stared at those massive rings, and shook his head. He was tempted to lash out, to unleash his pain, anger, frustration, and sorrow so that the mighty forces and fibrous tissue of the Universe would remember him. But to what end? He understood that even at his finest moment he would never be more than just the tiniest grain of sand in the desert of time and space, so why should now be any different? What did his efforts, his plight, really mean to the gods? Did they even know his name? Did they even care?

Singularly trapped with his own heartbreak, Mitri nonetheless signaled the Westies that the wormhole emitter did in fact, work, but that the mission had failed. And that he was coming home. In no hurry to hear the devastation in their voices, he just couldn't bring himself to explain that he had never even left their own star system, and that despite the remarkable technology, it wasn't going to provide the immediate solution they hoped for.

But he also felt a sense of safety and comfort, knowing that his people...Keela...were close. And for all the anxiety and pain that would be waiting for him upon his return, Grinroad was still his home, as much as he tried to convince himself that no longer mattered to him as much as it really did.

CHAPTER THIRTEEN

After warping once more, Aretha—that beautiful blue and green orb in space—came into view.

"Hey, gorgeous. Maybe next time." Within direct communications range, Mitri flipped the switch. "Grinroad, this is *Kosono*. Am entering…"

The red light above the wormhole emitter started to flash. "Hang on…" Mitri tapped the console, waited suspiciously. He reached again, when the light went off. *Huh. Probably nothing. Yeah, nothing to wor—.*

The light flickered repeatedly, followed by a *ffffp, ffffp-ffffp-ffffp*. His monitor went blank. Mitri tapped his helmet. "Grinroad, this is *Kosono*. Come in. Do you—?"

They didn't. Communications were down. Mitri hoped it was just a loose wire mucking up the works, or maybe the *Kosono* was reacting to wormhole radiation he couldn't account for. But either way, he was on his own. He shifted in his seat.

Just get me home, girl. Just get me home.

Mitri sweated out passage through the planet's atmosphere—he was cocooned within a scorching fireball—but the ship responded appropriately as he re-entered what was hopefully Westie airspace. There was little visibility except for the *Kosono's* wingtip, but as cloud cover gradually thinned out, the skies began to brighten. With Mitri's first glimpse of solid land below—a suitable landing strip was in visual range—he was starting to feel more confident about the ship's electronics.

Ffffp…ffffp-ffffp-ffffp…ffffp…

His monitor repeatedly flickered on and off. *Ffffp-ffffp-ffffp-ffffp*.

The monitor came back up. The little square icon flashed several times, stopped, and then scrolled across the screen:

INCOMING MESSAGE
And then the control panel completely overloaded.
ZZZZZZ! KKKKRRRRKRKKK! ZZZZZZ!
The cockpit filled with the singe of smoke and the rubber/copper fusion of melted wiring. Mitri donned his oxygen mask. He adjusted the controls. Engine No. 1 flamed out. The *Kosono* rolled and yawed violently. The left rudder did not respond. And then engine No. 2 flamed out. Mitri immediately pitched down to maintain airspeed, but the *Kosono* buckled and swirled. With Aretha jutting in and out of his sightline, he tried to restart the engines. No go. The ship was now eating up airspace with increasing velocity—plummeting toward the ground—until there was only one option. He flipped down his visor and gripped the ejection lever. He gave it a hard pull.

The cockpit depressurized, followed by a roar of wind. In seconds, the ejection seat—powered by a rocket motor and fire blast—catapulted Mitri from the swirling ship. His parachute deployed. Gripping the straps, he followed the *Kosono* as it plunged toward the flatlands—and its inevitable demise. There was a distant thud, fireball, and cloud of black smoke. The *Kosono* and its wormhole emitter were done.

Although unsure of his exact location, Mitri did recognize his imminent good news/bad news scenario as he drifted downward. The good news was that he was still alive.

The bad news was that he would touch down in the desert and, according to his portable sensor, at least a thousand miles from Grinroad—on the wrong side of Lake Abandarro—in the desolate, westernmost region of Scraper territory. He was further limited to the supplies he had on him, which at most would last him three days. Maybe.

Mitri was also keenly aware that a squad of Scraper soldiers had likely mobilized to meet his position. And if they got to him or the *Kosono's* wormhole technology—if either survived the crash—life as he knew it would end, and much sooner and far less pleasantly than he would wish on his worst enemy, who it so happened was coming to bang him up big style.

His only chance was to arm his weapon and then search for a cave, rock, or gopher hole to hide behind. Which is exactly what he planned. But then a violent gust of wind corkscrewed him several times and collapsed his chute, blowing him from the sky.

Blackness. Brightness. Blackness. Brightness.

Mitri struggled to open his eyes. His head throbbed. The sunlight blinded him. He rolled over, facedown, wondering if he was dead, alive, or something else altogether. But, no, he was definitely alive. The shooting pain in his knee told him so. He rolled back over, winced, then removed his helmet and unclasped the parachute harness.

The flatlands were dry and coarse and the yellow haze of the Sun beat down on him like he messed with its sister. Mitri barely got to his feet, his knee throbbing and useless. He tried to spit dust from his mouth, but made no saliva. He pulled a narcotic syringe from his aid pouch. The injection eased the pain but made him even woozier, which was itself a problem, because he had to focus. Focus *now*.

Even though the crash was sure to draw attention he surely didn't want, Mitri couldn't risk any portion of the wormhole emitter or its coordinates remaining intact. He had to make sure the *Kosono* was completely destroyed, assuming he could even hobble there. With dry nothing for miles in every direction, he followed the trail of smoke to the west, hoping he got there before the Scrapers. If there was one tactical advantage for the Westies, it was that they had the wormhole technology, and the Scrapers didn't. It had to remain that way. Absolutely had to.

Mitri fashioned a cane out of a dead, white branch lying in the desert dust. After a time the sharp, intense pain came roaring back, as if hot steel was being jabbed into his knee. Even with a narcotic booster and water he drank from packets in his vest, the throbbing dropped him again and again. But still he pushed on, struggling beneath the brutal heat. He had to get there before the Scrapers, who were surely close behind and gaining ground. His firearm held forty rounds, enough for a short assault. But he was more likely to shoot a mirage than the enemy.

By the position of the Sun, Mitri figured he'd been out in the desert at least an hour now—or was it two hours? Or even three?—when he finally had the *Kosono* in sight. By then his throat was like sandpaper; his lips were cracked. He was bleary-eyed and his back and calf muscles seized from dehydration. He barely had the strength to lift one foot in front of the other. But at least he got to the wreckage first. At least he did that much.

Like it was an aging stallion, Mitri reached out to pat the nose of the *Kosono*—what was left of it, anyway—to let his faithful ship know that he had come back, to see her off to her final resting place. But his hand never made it. He fell on his face, in the dust, with no hope of standing back up. The dead, white branch lay beside him. Mitri gasped for breath, fumbled for a water packet. And then he heard a faint motor. He turned his head so that his left cheek was caked in the dust. He cracked one eye open. In the near distance he saw a vehicle shimmering, shimmering, drawing closer. Like angels of death, the Scrapers had come.

With one last grasp he wriggled his dust-dried fingers. Inside his thigh pocket was a small grenade. He just had to flip the trigger guard, press down, and then roll the explosive beneath the *Kosono* remains. Blow them all to hell. Mitri's fingers crept into his pocket. He could feel the trigger guard. But was it the grenade? A stone? Was it his own finger, broken beneath him? All he could do was press down and hope that he hadn't failed everyone yet again when it mattered most.

The vehicle stopped. The engine pinged, rattled. The door opened and closed. With just his one eye open, Mitri saw a black boot. It crunched in the dust. Saw another. He tried to raise his head, but there was nothing before him. Just the shadow of a figure caught in the midday sun. Struggling with consciousness, Mitri reached for the grenade. His pinkie grazed the side, felt the edge of the trigger guard. He could reach it. He could almost reach it.

Lying in the salt desert, broken, defeated, and clinging to the grains of his insignificance, Mitri took solace in all he had left. *I got here first. At least I did that.*

And as his eyes fell and the strain of daylight finally faded to black, he heard the *clack* of a pistol trigger. A single gunshot rang out. Mitri smelled the gunpowder. It was bitter. And then the thoughts of his life dropped away like figs from a tree, until he felt absolutely nothing.

CHAPTER FOURTEEN

ONE EYE OPEN, then the other. Mitri found himself lying on a cot, in the back room of a beat-up gas station. Out front were two dusty pumps, an air hose, a dented gas can, and a tire with worn treads. A rusted lawn chair was tipped over on its side. The front door sign drooped from a chain. The sign read: *Open.* The gas station windows needed washing.

Mitri hobbled into the connecting general store. A quick look around confirmed that he really was dead, or at least suffering from an infection-triggered fever dream—cars hadn't run on gasoline in at least eighty years. But he shrugged it off, figuring that he should just make the best of it, wherever he was. He soaked his head in the washroom sink, re-wrapped his damaged knee, then loaded up on fluids he found in the cooler (he never heard of Dr. Pepper; it wasn't bad).

There was a heavy, thumb-press cash register on the counter, near the window. Behind it was a stool. Mitri sat down. As he leaned back, his eyes fell upon a calendar tacked next to spark plug coupons. The calendar girl featured a saucy redhead in blue jean shorts, bright red lipstick, and a red-and-white checkered top, knotted above her exposed navel. Though the title said *Marilyn Monroe*, in his half-conscious state, Mitri thought she looked an awful lot like Keela. So he smiled at her, then took note of the date printed on the page's upper left corner. And figuring he'd gone truly, completely mental, he passed out again from the pain.

Two slaps to the face jostled Mitri awake. He sniffed hard, grimaced, then swatted at the slapping hands like someone snapped a medic's ammonia stick under his nose. He was covered in sweat. The infection was getting worse.

"No. Wait. Where am I? Keela. What time is it? Am I late?"

"Easy, fella. Easy. There ain't no Keela here. You're hurt, son. Your plane crashed."

Mitri was on the floor behind the counter. Standing over him was a scraggly young man in dirty overalls and a baseball cap. An *H.R. Gas* logo was sewed into the brim. The gas attendant's look was such that he spent many Saturday nights alone.

"You okay, son? Rattler almost gotcha out there, but I took care of that for ya. One shot. Plus that knee's a fine mess. We better get Doc Anson out here to fix you up. Looks busted, but what the hell do I know? I'm just a gas man."

Remembering where he was—deep behind enemy lines—Mitri's fear center adrenalized. Maybe he really was alive. "Are you a Scraper? What do you want? Where—?"

"Whoa, whoa, whoa. Easy there, fella. Easy. I got some scrapers over there. Gets ice off them wind'ahs. Not too cold right now, but it's good to have when the frost comes rollin' in. All in good time."

Hearing that word—*time*—Mitri felt it hang in the air. The date on the calendar burned in his brain. *It's April 17, 1956. It's 1956. It's—* "That can't be. What's the time? When's the time? When's—?"

"It's half past ten, fella. You were out near sixteen hours."

"No. I mean…where am I? Where are we? What do you want from me?"

The gas attendant chuckled. He tipped up his cap. "I don't want nuthin' from ya. We're in my shop. It was my pop's before he passed a few months back. It's the last stop outta Kinsey."

Mitri pulled himself up. "Map. You got a map? I need a map. I have to—"

"You're all riled up. Got a fever goin'. Just settle down. I'll show ya." The gas attendant pulled a map from a drawer beneath the register. He unfolded the pages, then drew his oil-stained finger across the road lines. In block letters was the region's moniker: *TEXAS.* "Here's Odessa…here's Waco." He tapped on Kinsey. "We're right plumb in the middle. Nuthin' but open road in every direction."

Mitri didn't recognize the landmarks. "Where's Grinroad? Where's Djoza?"

The gas attendant lifted his eyes. "What are you on about, son? You ain't some commie pinko are ya?"

"Give me a bigger map. Of the whole territory! All of it!"

There was a moment of awkward hesitation, but the gas attendant reached back into the drawer, then laid out another map.

Mitri read the header: *THE UNITED STATES OF AMERICA* "America? What the hell's America?"

"Whoa there, fella. You musta' hit your head harder'n I thought. It's the god damn U.S. of A., son. America. The good ole red, white, and blue."

"Red, white, and…?" Mitri stared at the map. There was no Westie territory, no Scraper territory. And Lake Abandarro—dividing the two regions—was nowhere to be found. In its place was the Mississippi River and boxed-off territories with names like *Arkansas* and *Kansas* and *Nebraska.*

Mitri stumbled back against a shelf of spark plugs, knocking some to the floor. This had to be a mistake, just a great, big joke that wasn't the least bit funny. *It's a fake,* he thought. *Gotta be. Just a Scraper lie. Yeah, a damn Scraper lie. Or maybe I'm hallucinating or—Yes. That's it. That's it! I'm hallucinating. I'm hallucinating. I'm…* To confirm that he was not of right mind, that he wasn't wherever the gods were trying to convince him he was, Mitri reached for the map. He threaded the corner through his finger tips. He felt the paper's coarseness. It crinkled. "I'm really here," he said.

And if I'm really here, if I'm alive, that means this time, this place, this…Kinsey…this Texas…this…United States of America, wherever…isn't on Aretha. It can't be. It's someplace like Aretha, only…the planets were all the same. The scanners confirmed. They confirmed! The wormhole must have crossed me up, crossed me over. I'm someplace that shouldn't be, that shouldn't exist. I'm cut off, I'm gone, I'm out here on my own and...

The gas attendant waved a hand in front of Mitri's eyes, which were locked in a trance. "You okay, son? You with me? Hell." He chuckled. "You got a name?"

Mitri snapped awake, confronted by the fact that he was stranded, trapped in some distant corner of time or space—or maybe even his own mind. But wherever he was, *whenever* he was, he needed protection. A cover. He scanned the general store to get his thoughts churning. On the racks were comic books, newspapers, Twinkies, motor oil cans, chewing gum packs, combs, nail clippers, and jars of licorice, beef jerky, and pickled pig's knuckles. He had to say something.

"It's uh..." A flyer was sticking out from beneath a carton of Marlboro's. It read: *That'll Be the Day - Buddy Holly on KWLR.* "Buddy Holly," he blurted out.

The gas attendant laughed again, tipped up his cap. "Code name, huh? Well...I suppose a military man's gotta be careful. Rank and serial number, I thought. But okay, then. Buddy it is. I'm Harlan Rheams Jr., but everybody just calls me H.R." He reached out his dirty hand. Though reluctantly for sure, Mitri shook it. "Glad to have you aboard...Buddy. Now why don't we get that knee looked at and see if there ain't somebody to come pick you up."

CHAPTER FIFTEEN

THREE DAYS INTO his Kinsey stay and Mitri thought, *my people will come for me. Just a matter of time.* Bunked up at H.R.'s place, he told himself the same thing after two weeks, three weeks, then four. By the second month in the desert, he still said it to himself, but not every day, and by the third month he accepted the necessity of a longer view, figuring it could be a year, maybe longer before he got word. And if it happened tomorrow, then all the better. Yet however long it took, he was going to have to pace himself. *But they'll come for me,* he thought. *They'll come.*

Until then, staying out of sight was simple enough. *H.R. Gas* never got more than a half dozen trucks a day coming through, and sometimes none for an entire week. But Mitri, whose knee had healed well, needed something to occupy his time. Most days he spent in the garage, tinkering with the *Kosono* debris, cleaning off the wires and chips and polishing any other pieces that survived the crash. The telecom system was demolished; only fragments of the wormhole emitter were still intact.

"That sucker's plum busted," H.R. said, surveying what was essentially a junk pile.

But the wreckage fascinated H.R., which was one of the reasons he let Mitri stay on with him at the gas station. It also became clear that H.R. needed assistance. Despite his diminutive and humble stature, Harlan was a man with big dreams. Plus, he wanted someone to talk to.

"I'm gonna be rich, ya see. Famous, too. And that's when the girls'll come runnin'. I got the double hex on me. Broke as a spoke and ugly as a goat. I ain't got them good looks like you. But once the cash starts rollin' in...*whooo-eee!* Ask me how many women I'll have on my arm. Go ahead. Ask me."

Mitri chuckled. For a man with no legitimate prospects beyond his middle-of-nowhere gas station, H.R. was always cheery, as if he felt each and every day that the rising sun was going to shepherd the day that God finally smiled upon him. Surveying the endless dust that stretched out in every direction from the station, Mitri couldn't come up with even a single reason H.R. would feel that way. But trapped more than his scruffy host could imagine, Mitri understood the need to believe in a future that looked better than his present. H.R. had a childlike enthusiasm that still embraced the magic of hope and possibility. That dreamer's mojo was also alive somewhere in Mitri; he wouldn't have leapt across the Universe without it. So if H.R. was convinced that their fortunes were about to change, then Mitri was going to believe it, too. It was better than thinking anything else.

"Okay," Mitri said. "How many women?"

They had the same conversation almost every day.

"Depends on how much oil's down there. I know most folks think it's just good fer nuthin' dust, but my pops figured there's ten thousand barrels worth. Me? Hell. I figger there's at least double that much. And at three dollars, and say, three girls a barrel, I'll be so rich and looked after I can hire some smart boy like you to do the countin' fer me. And with the way you been helpin' out with the riggin' and such, I'm gonna cut you in fer a big ole slice. I know it's my land and all and it's like givin' away free money, but I can't operate them suckers alone. You got a right instinct for it, Buddy. I'd be nowhere withoutcha."

Mitri—who stuck to his codename "Buddy"—stared out into the vast nothing. The sun was strong and hazy. All he could see was dry desert dust choked under the blistering heat. No Red Rock canyons. No flowing waterfalls. No fertile valleys. A ridge of low mountains stretched out in the distance like an old mutt stifled by the sun. Kinsey was a leftover pit. A wasteland. Just a place between places.

As difficult as it was, Mitri tried not to think about the time gone by, because the way he looked at it, his months on Earth weren't truly lost, but spent differently, trying to figure out a way back home. *But until then, until I get it worked out, I'm still me and everyone on Aretha is still them.* With few distractions other than Harlan's quest for oil, Buddy grew to appreciate just how long, slow, and cruel a single day—and even that crawling bitch of a second hand—could be. The desert flatlands were filled with so much lifeless nothing—just a decaying will to exist—that unless you found a way to pass the time, you were left with nothing but your dried-up soul.

And on those days when he slipped into dark places, he told himself that *a day is a day is a day and it's just one day strung after another and nothing's really changed for any of us except that for right now, for just this one moment, I'm here and they're there, but I'm still me and they're still them. Aretha is still my home. It's still my home.*

Mitri looked over at Harlan, and then out toward the desert. That place between places. It was filled with just so much nothing—and nowhere to go.

"Well, I'll tell you what, H.R. As an old friend of mine often says…if you just take a breath and chill, and really listen to the wind, you're bound to find what you need, even if it's not exactly what you're looking for."

"Huh. I ain't never heard it quite said like that b'fore, but I think I know whatcha' mean."

Staring through the front windshield, Mitri wanted nothing more than to be back home on Aretha, in his wife's arms, soothing each other amid the pressures of war. "Good," he said. "Good. Then maybe one day you can explain it to me."

CHAPTER SIXTEEN

THE FIRST THREE drilling sites were dead ends. Even though Mitri helped build the rigging for the first nothing, the failure came as no surprise, because what the heck did H.R. really think he was going to find out there, digging holes in the middle of the desert? The region was ruined—devastated by droughts, wind erosion, and dust storms laying waste to everything in their path. But there the two of them were, ripping through tons of useless topsoil, battered into fine sand.

And yet after the second failure Mitri was slightly more invested, if only because he hated to put the time and effort into a project with no results. But by the third go he was actually disappointed. He was starting to believe, as much as it defied his own logic, that there really was oil down there, that H.R. had a big payday coming and that euphoria would encompass them once the drill bit broke through the right swath of desert.

The sun peered down as Mitri handed H.R. a sledgehammer to pound in a wooden stake. As with the other drilling sites, the desert nothing surrounded them.

H.R. wiped his forehead with a dirty rag. "You been out here, almost, what, plum near six months? Mm. And you still ain't heard nuthin' from your people?"

Separated from his homelands by more than time and distance, Mitri smiled, appreciative of the familiar. H.R. asked at least once a week, and every week Mitri answered the same way. He oversold it the first few times, but he eventually got his story down pat, even picking up local affectations as part of his dialect. Being in a place does that to a person. It changes you, whether you notice it or not. Even Mitri was starting to believe his own b.s. story, as if it really happened the way he said. And he needed to believe it.

Because as much as it made him ill, there was a part of himself that felt: *I deserve the peace. I deserve the quiet. I'm free.* And then guilt would consume him until he shamed himself into a depression for having those thoughts at all.

"Nah. They said if my plane went down to just cover up and sit tight. They'll come for me when they do."

"Well, I sure ain't wish that crash on you, Buddy, and I ain't sayin' the Air Force done you right...but I'm glad it happened. If you take my meanin'. I ain't had me a friend in a long time." H.R. went quiet, let the hammer's head drop to the dust. The old acne scars pockmarking his face seemed to deepen just then, boring through more than flesh. "Heck, other than my momma, yer pretty much the only one ever believed I was better'n a goat. That right there's a heapin' pile of somethin' in my book. I only came out this way 'cuz pop's heart was startin' to give. Just didn't feel right letting him pass without seein' him one last time. He didn't want me none as a tyke on account of my momma bein' a whore and me being too...well...anyway. I didn't even know about this here drillin' until a month b'fore you showed up. Can't let old grudges hold ya down."

H.R. took a swig from a can of beer. That was his limit. One a day. "It's like my momma told me before the cancer. She said if we're real lucky, the Lord's gonna make it up to us for the rough years gone. 'He's gonna show us the light. By then you'll be big and strong like Taurus the Bull, and everything'll change.' Well, you know what, Buddy? Now that you showed up, I think momma was right."

Time and again Mitri had wanted to tell H.R. who he really was, where he came from—he wanted to tell *somebody*—but as sweet and trusting as H.R. seemed to be, revealing that, *Hey, I'm from a parallel dimension on a mission to save my people from extinction* might have thrown a wrinkle in their friendship. Besides, as he learned from the tabloids H.R. stocked on the news racks, alien talk in 1956 America had a tendency to raise eyebrows.

Supported by the derrick, the drill string was suspended from above, on the drill line, through a pulley system. Shaped like a giant, hinged arm, the hoist raised and lowered the drill string, and controlled the force applied by the drill bit. The metal cutting piece, with sharp, spiraled ridges, rotated into the earth, creating the borehole. With the rigging all set, it was time to break ground once again.

"Whaddaya say there, H.R.?" Mitri gave a smile. "This the one?"

H.R. took the dirty rag to his forehead. "Can't say, though I reckon it might be. Why don't you do the honors. I ain't had much luck so far. Maybe you got the touch."

With noon almost upon them, they endeavored to find black gold where everyone said only fools would look. Reminded of the *Kosono*, Mitri patted the rig and smiled. The depression of a big red button broke a silence brimming with possibility. The two watched the rigging as it powered and chugged, that massive, mechanical arm driving the drill bit into the earth.

Rocks and dirt and dust kicked about. Still nothing. They drilled deeper, waiting for oil to spurt out. They knew to be patient, to allow enough time for the drill to make its way through the dry earth. But with every drill site there comes a point when doubt seeps in, fearing another dead end. Staring into the borehole, Mitri suggested they shut the drill, clear the debris, and try again. H.R. agreed. He reached down to the broken earth, to push away the rubble, when a sudden and distinct shift arrived, in a manner that has no equal. They felt a buzzing, a vibration, a tremor—a knocking together of molecules—and then a bitter, salty breeze. They smelled a storm coming.

And finally, from just below the earth, came a sound they would never forget:

RUMBLERUMBLERUMBLERUMBLERUMBLE...

Eyes wide, Mitri and H.R. looked at each other. And as a

singular question dangled in the air—*is there treasure beneath our feet?*—the answer became as clear and dazzling as the noon sun: *Yes...there...is!*

An exploding black river erupted from the borehole. The spewing treasure fountained at its glorious peak and then rained down on them—baptism by oil. H.R. jumped into Mitri's arms, wrapped his legs around his waist, tackling them to the ground. Drenched in that oil, even Mitri let out a holler. "Oooo-eeeee! Ooo-eee-ooo-eee!"

"Damn, Buddy. I think you're finally gettin' the hang of this place."

The two men danced and laughed and reached their hands up to the glory of the gods. But watching their newfound riches going to waste, they shut the rigging, and with a metal cap sealed the borehole. Mitri then climbed up on the derrick—just stood there—and took in the contraption and all it brought them. He leaned on the railing, offered a smile of relief. Below, covered in oil, H.R. removed his cap, and raised his hands in a victorious V. He smiled back.

Mitri shook his head with delightful disbelief when a pulse of optimism slapped him in the berries. If beyond all reasonable expectations H.R. could strike it rich, there, in a desert no man's land, then he could do it, too. His fortune would follow.

They're coming for me, he thought. *Darn tootin', they are.*

He hadn't realized it until then, but over time the desert emptiness institutionalized him, convinced him that the vast nothing—the miles he could ascertain with his own two eyes—was all that there was. That his memories were just illusions, just false ideas. Brittle, half-constructed dreams that would crumble into dust by applying even the slightest pressure.

Staring at an oil-covered H.R., Mitri concluded that he had been overlooking the obvious all along. The desert wasn't convincing him of an endless nothing. It only seemed empty if he focused on what *wasn't* there, instead of what was *actually* there. He had a friend. He had peace. He had room to move and time to think.

There wasn't much left of the *Kosono*'s telecom or WHPE to get either of them working. But if he could mine their individual computer chips, there was always the chance of there being enough data left to rig up a new piece of equipment, to send a signal home. He knew it wasn't much to work with—maybe just a grand delusion—but in his wildest dreams he never would have imagined ending up where he was anyway. He needed to drill for his own kind of oil. And with H.R.'s help, there would be enough money to buy all the equipment he would need to make it happen. He would figure out what to tell H.R. later.

After a few heart palpitations, Mitri chuckled, straightened up, and turned to come off the derrick. He wanted to get back to the *Kosono* remains immediately. *They're coming for me. I'm going home.*

Ready to reclaim his life, Mitri took an eager step forward. And then, as if on cue, the heel of his boot caught on an oil-slickened two-by-four seam in the flooring. In an attempt to stabilize his foothold, his hip jerked to the side, twisting his body, which came out from under him. Mitri went down on his chest.

With a violent *crack* he broke at least one rib, and probably more. He was wheezing more so than breathing. He lay there for a moment. Shooting from torso to temples, the pain was so debilitating that he bit down and sliced open his tongue. When he opened his eyes, the left side of his face was flush against the drill bit, so that his eyelash practically grazed the metal ridges. Had the gods nudged him just an inch closer, Mitri's face would have been sliced clean off.

"Buddy! Hang on! I gotcha." H.R. dove up on the derrick. He pulled Mitri away from the drill bit, sliding him on the oil, unaware that excruciating pain shot through Mitri's chest as his bruised ribs found every imperfection in the unstable floor. "Damn, boy. You ain't supposed to getchaself killed now. We're rich! Just like I told ya. Come on, son. We're gonna—"

SNAP! KER-ACK! BAM!

The flooring gave way. Mitri and H.R. crashed to the ground.

They were twisted and battered, covered in wood and oil and dust. With an almost endless supply of liquid gold beneath the surface, the two men responsible for its discovery were buried alive.

H.R. was facedown. His arms were flat and limp, with two long beams crisscrossed on his back. There was a gash in his forehead. Mitri was next to him, on his side, pinned beneath a section of flooring. His right leg felt broken. His nose was smashed. His belly was punctured and leaking blood. In desperate need of medical attention, it would be more than half a day before anyone knew they were even missing.

Of the few who even knew him, no one expected much from the rough and lonely life of Harlan Rheams Jr. The son of a California whore and a dead-broke gas man, he had been tossed away by life, with but one friend in all the world.

And before losing consciousness, the stranger from another land, who only moments before believed with all his might that some way, somehow, his people would come for him, now feared that he would never be found. That along with the name Mitri Amos, the flesh and blood man would die out there, in the desert, just as he had found a way to save himself, once and for all.

CHAPTER SEVENTEEN

THE BEDROOM WAS dark save moonlight creeping in through the window. Doc Anson sat on the edge of his bed, in red long johns. He slugged down the last of his bourbon. His wife had been dead six years now, and while a sip of liquor wasn't the same as her kiss, it helped him feel a little bit woozy and just a little bit horny. Not so bad considering Doc Jr. down there was long overdue for his physical.

Barely under the covers, Doc's heart pounded when the phone woke him from a dream. In it, he was on the deck of an ocean liner, baptized with raindrops as thick as scrambled eggs and blacker than Cyril Horton's cancerous lung.

When Doc pressed his ear to the receiver and heard what he thought he heard, he sat up and turned on the light. He scratched his gravelly white scruff. Though only 46 years old, he had the liver of a man at least ten years his senior, and was not up for jokes. But this was no joke. He thought for a moment, then uttered a phrase that had left his lips at least a thousand times before. "On my way."

At the going rate of his own physical decline, Doc figured he might have another five years before the drink finally caught up with him. Maybe less. But now that oil was flowing from H.R.'s well, Doc saw opportunity. If he did what needed doing and in the time and manner in which it needed to be done, he would be able to kick back and retire—tomorrow—and as a very rich man at that.

The room was still. Doc turned to face the ghost of his widow, his Laura Anne, who often said that God would take care of him, in this life or the next, so long as he was a good Christian and helped tend to the flock in his own special way—as a man of medicine, and a kind heart. A car accident took her far too young, but at least she was with the Lord. At least that's what Doc told himself.

Which is why he hesitated and then slugged down another full glass of bourbon before deciding that the flock, for all his wife's good intentions, could up and flock itself. It was time to cash in. All he had to do was get rid of the body.

When Doc arrived at H.R.'s shop, in the dead of night, he found the man he knew only as Buddy, in very much the same condition as upon their first encounter—barely conscious, on the floor, and concealing a secret—although Doc sensed it was more out of caution than duplicity.

"You got a knack for banging yourself up, son. How you feelin'?"

"Busted a couple of ribs, broke my leg. Nose is busted. Gut's a mess, too."

Doc helped Buddy shift so that he was leaning against the front counter, then with a small flashlight, inspected his pupils, and then his belly, which had finally stopped bleeding. "You drove yourself back from the site? That's not a bad splint you gave yourself. Musta' hurt like hell. You're a tough sonuvabitch."

"I've been through worse. You should've seen the flight here." Buddy reached for his leg. "You got something for the pain?"

Doc removed a bottle from his black bag. He gave Buddy two white pills and a cup of water to wash them down. "Not too much, now. Just sips. There you go. Like that."

Buddy nodded, took another swig. He sighed. "Thanks."

After almost a quarter century treating Kinsey's bodies, hearts, and minds, Doc had come to learn that very little distinguished folks from one another, proclivities aside. And yet Buddy, or whatever he truly called himself, was a different kind of man altogether. Whether he was a stranded Air Force pilot, as he claimed, a private contractor, a con man, or just a fugitive on the run, Doc still couldn't be sure.

"So," he said finally, "it seems we got ourselves a situation."

Buddy grimaced in pain. "I'd say."

Doc produced a thin cigar. He chewed it. The medical man in him wanted to rush Buddy to a hospital, but a life-changing proposition had been made that needed resolution, and until an agreement came to pass, the injuries would have to wait.

"Harlan came out this way a few months back, so I can't say I knew the man all that well. But I helped with the service when his father passed. Harlan Sr. was a...well...he had ideas about what he deserved, and what people owed him, always talkin' 'bout how he was gonna make it big in the oil game. We were friends, I suppose. He never did feel too good about leavin' H.R. back when he did, but Harlan wasn't really the parenting sort. Too bad. H.R. had a good heart. A steady hand could'a made a big difference."

"He was just lonely, and I was...*aahhh*, damn that hurts..." He shifted his good leg to relieve pressure from the broken one. "...an extra set of hands. But he did right by me. He treated me like a brother."

Doc spit on the floor. "And now you want his oil."

Buddy went silent. There was a glint in his eye, a hint of judgment, before he answered. He gently poked at his eye, swelling from the broken nose. "I'd say *we* want his oil. Right, Doc? If we're really talking...let's talk."

H.R. was barely twelve hours dead and gone, and there Doc was, looking to pick the boy clean. "Just don't seem right, is all."

"No, it doesn't," Buddy said. "But it'll be a matter of days, if not hours, before somebody finds that rig. And when that happens, it's all over."

"And you reckon it oughta be us?"

"Look, Doc. I'm in bad shape. And you barely know me. I know that. Believe me when I say I'd be a whole lot happier if H.R. had lived to see it through. But that didn't happen, and now we have to move quick. There's a lot at stake out there."

"You mean for you an me?"

"Among others...yes. I can't speak for H.R., but if not us... then who?"

"Still don't make it right."

"Doesn't make it wrong, either. If the gods have taught me anything, it's that no matter where you are or what you're up against, you make the best of what's in front of you. Because if you waste the moments you have, they'll be gone before you know it. And then it's too late."

H.R. had no family to speak of, and that vast supply of oil, as Buddy said, was going to *someone*. In a region ripe with chugging wells, Doc had seen fortunes made by men far less worthy. "My Laura Anne, before she passed...she would'n approved. Not the Christian thing to do." Doc transferred his cigar from one corner of his mouth to the other. He bit down. Hard. "But me an the Lord, well...we ain't never really seen eye to eye. If you take my meanin'."

Buddy grimaced, took more water. "That mean yer in?"

Doc surveyed the gas station, knowing that he had spent far too long watching sunsets pass him by. "Yes," he said. "I reckon I am. But let's get one thing straight. I ain't gonna ask you yer business and you ain't gonna judge mine. The less I know about you, the better. So if we're gonna do this thing here, I got me some conditions. And you're gonna say yes to each an every one of 'em. 'Cuz if not, yer on your own."

"I don't have much of a choice, now do I?"

"Oh, we always have a choice, son. Trick is findin' a way to live with 'em."

As his words hung in the air, Doc waited for Buddy to acknowledge either that they were going to forge a pact that would redefine the scope and purpose of their lives, or that they were about to have an extremely awkward exchange. Buddy looked at his fingers as if he'd seen them for the first time, and then curled them in and out of a fist once, twice, and again.

"Maybe it don't affect you none, but I need to make it right with my Laura Anne...Lord rest her soul. Clean slate fer us both."

With an odd smile, Buddy looked up at Doc, who nodded in agreement. Doc then spat in his own hand, reached over, and offered it to Buddy. They shook.

"Deal," Doc said.

"Deal," Buddy said.

Whether or not he truly appreciated the magnitude of his decision, Doc at least knew that his desert town life, which had lost its meaning years ago, was finally coming to an end.

"Let's patch you up," he said. "I need my partner up and at 'em. We got work to do."

Buddy smiled through his pain. "You have no idea, my friend. You have no idea."

The first few hours were critical. Doc gave Buddy a sedative, and while he was unconscious, reset his broken leg. Doc still had to take Buddy to the hospital for x-rays and a proper cast, but first thing first. He left Buddy to rest, then drove out to the derrick site. Doc had spent many nights along unlit roads and desolate fields. Such was life in Kinsey. And yet part of him felt like he was in one of those darn horror movies the kids all went crazy for, where the body snatchers lurk in the darkness.

What will I find out there? What am I really doin'?

Not a paranoid man by nature, Doc nonetheless parked his truck, flipped the headlights on, and grabbed his shotgun. It took a little effort, but he managed to finally reach H.R. beneath the wreckage, and shone a flashlight on him. As sad as it was to see his lifeless body there, mangled and alone, Doc took comfort believing that H.R.'s last moments were more ecstatic than most people would ever experience. H.R. left this world at the height of his promise.

There are worse ways to go. Much worse.

He then secured one end of a chain and hook around H.R.'s leg, the other to his truck, and dragged H.R. to flat ground. But Doc still had a problem. Despite the overall condition of H.R.'s body, his face—unappealing as it was even under ideal circumstances—had come away from the accident with only a few scratches and bruises. So Doc took a healthy swig from his flask, wiped his mouth on his sleeve, and let out a short sigh.

Doc had encountered plenty of dead bodies throughout the years. Occupational hazard. But he became nauseated just then. He threw up. With H.R. laying there motionless beneath the headlights, Doc doused him in whiskey, picked up a busted two-by-four, and smashed his face beyond recognition.

CHAPTER EIGHTEEN

Mitri Amos, Henceforth known to the world as Harlan "Buddy" Rheams Jr., had survived civil war, interdimensional space travel, a near fatal crash, and a derrick collapse. But just minutes from his first press conference as the founder of Taurus Enterprises, Texas' newest oil company, and he was slightly rattled.

"I don't know what I was thinking," he said in his downtown Houston office. For a man who had fought against extinction to live in a communal setting free from the blistering vapidity of urban egoism and chest thumping, he was now prominently positioned in a gleaming high-rise tower with all the indulgent trappings of financial success. "I can't pull it off."

"Sure you can, Buddy. You're Harlan Rheams Jr. Anybody says you don't seem like the ole H.R. they remember, you just stand up straight, smile, and say, 'It's amazing what a haircut, new suit, an a million bucks'll do for yer complexion.' Then you laugh—a real warm laugh with a gentle pat on the back—to make folks feel at ease."

"I don't know. It makes me nervous. They'll know I'm not him."

"Listen, Buddy. If you wanna take faith in anything…it's this: Americans ain't stupid. But people? They're as dumb as an ox gone kicked itself in the head. You and H.R. had similar builds and were roughly the same age. Nobody knew squat about H.R. and there ain't nuthin' left to find. And now with yer looks, our money, and these medical records sayin' you are who we say you are, we'll be right as rain. You just keep pumpin' out them sound bites. And don't forget to smile."

After Buddy's public appearance, there would be no turning back. But he and Doc agreed that the best way to own the persona of Harlan Rheams Jr. was to go all in, and welcome the scrutiny. "It's like a game of cat and mouse," Doc said. "The more you hide, the more they chase. So let's give 'em a show they can make their own."

The name Mitri Amos may have died out in the Texas desert, but the man was very much alive. He let out a nervous sigh. "Thanks. You're really earning your twenty percent."

"Twenty-five, son. Twenty-five. Plus a lifetime guaranteed contract at seven hundred fifty thousand bucks a year...with five percent annual bumps."

"Hmm. If I didn't know better, I'd say you're the best paid doctor in the world."

Doc took a sip of bourbon from a thick glass. "And fer good reason."

Buddy couldn't argue. Getting back to Aretha was the end game, but to get *there* he had to focus *here*. And to do both, he needed Doc far more than Doc needed him. Not that Buddy would ever concede as such or explain why it was true. But as part of his on-the-job education, Buddy was learning, quickly, that the revenues his company generated—his personal net worth was already in the tens of millions—carried far more currency than just its exchange for goods and services. It was a conduit for power, influence, and respect.

Yet putting his energies into his Earth endeavors made it more difficult to feel connected to the people he left behind on Aretha. Almost overnight Taurus Enterprises had surpassed 700 employees and was expected to at least triple in size within five years, if not sooner. Beyond the scope and size of the company, no one on Earth had even the slightest idea as to what truly motivated him. And how could they? They naturally assumed that Buddy Rheams Jr., like all big Texas oil men, was interested in the four biggies—money, land, women, and power, although not necessarily in that order—when all he really wanted was to go home.

To ground himself, Buddy kept a private, hand-written log, locked in a wall safe behind a framed Taurus Enterprises logo—the head of a bull, with horns and a nose ring, encased in a crest; the name *Taurus Enterprises* was spelled out, curving along the crest's outer edge—to remind himself that *this isn't my home. I'm a soldier behind enemy lines. A day is a day is a day and it's just one day strung after another and nothing's really changed for any of us except that for right now, for this one moment, I'm here and they're there. But I'm still me and they're still them. Keela is the love of my life. Aretha is still my home. Aretha is my home.*

Buddy didn't dare consider that his fellow Grinroadians were all dead and that he was trapped on Earth forever. He insisted to himself that his comrades…Keela…were still alive and thinking of him, and that they were doing all they could to bring him back. But he couldn't wait for them. He had to take action.

"Listen, Buddy. Yer gonna get questions. I mean…puttin' one third of the profits into science and technology? I get diversification, but *this*?"

"You got your pet projects, I got mine. Remember what you said. To honor your Laura Anne, you insisted that we fund the Taurus Enterprises Medical Division. I said, 'Great. You pick the city and we'll build the hospital. First-rate all the way.' We got one in St. Louis, Atlanta, and San Diego, and another on the way. I think Cincinnati is next. I lost track after that."

If there was even the teeniest tiniest itsiest bitsiest morsel of a scrap of a chance in all the cosmos that Buddy could rebuild the *Kosono*, that was enough for him. His people needed him. And he missed his wife. He felt empty without her.

"But it's the stars, Doc. It's outer space. The future. If you only think about what's in front of you—right here, right now, on the ground—that's as far as you go. If you want to reach your true potential, you gotta look beyond yourself. H.R. taught me that. He helped me realize that if you let other people decide your worth, you'll trap yourself inside the cage they're trying to lock you in. And you'll hate yourself—and them—while it happens. No, my friend. You've got to stare up into the sky once in a while and know that the Universe is vast and remarkable.

And that it's always waiting for you."

Doc stood with his drink. "That's good, Buddy. Nice. Add that to yer speech. It'll fly...pardon the pun. But remember, we're in Texas, son. If you don't say the word 'oil' at least ten times in the first two minutes, you're gonna lose 'em."

Buddy straightened his tie, then shot his cuffs. He had it. He was ready. "Don't worry, Doc. I will. But know something.... Now that I see just how big we can really be, I won't settle for less. Hold on tight. It's gonna be one helluva ride."

CHAPTER NINETEEN

BY October 1963 Buddy Rheams Jr. was considered an arrogant, bleeding-hearted corporate rebel, with his three largest competitors lined up to put him out of business. Beyond the financial implications, Buddy aroused their ire by hiring and promoting more female executives, and providing paid maternity leave and on-site daycare centers, far in excess of what any other company did in America at the time.

Buddy also had plans to someday establish the Taurus Elementary School System, first in Downtown Houston, and then throughout the country, with attendance free to all residents who qualified. He also was planning a massive, ongoing investment into equipment, training, salaries, and benefits for America's teachers, doctors, nurses, physical therapists, and social workers.

And still he was ashamed of just how little he did to protect his people compared to what Keela would have insisted upon if she had been there with him. But that didn't hold him back.

"What do you think, Doc? The Taurus Enterprises Cultural and Space Center. I might change the name. Maybe the Taurus Academy of Scientific Excellence. Not sure just yet. But when it's done, it will be—and pardon my Frenchy-vu—spec-humpin-tacular." Buddy pointed to the massive undeveloped lot. The sun shone upon them, giving the dusty terrain a golden glow. "When it's all done, I'm figuring two-and-a-half million square feet of the most immaculately designed real estate in the world. Maybe bigger. Just depends on how a few projects unfold."

"It's hard to imagine."

"Not for me. I see it clear as day. Where we're standing, right here, on this very spot, will be Tower Command. This will be the lifeblood of the entire Space Division. We'll have a launch pad, about a half mile out. I like the President. We had lunch last week. But forget just going to the Moon. That's like saying we should try real hard not to hit the toilet seat when we take a whizz. We need to aim a little higher."

Doc sighed knowingly. "The stars?"

"You got it, Doc. The stars. As far as they go."

But what Buddy didn't share, and wouldn't—not even with Doc—was that he had finally assembled a team of sophisticated engineers who were mining the *Kosono* debris for usable parts that, if the gods were smiling, could be replicated. He hadn't lost faith in Grinroad, but when it came to wormhole travel it was clear to Buddy just how much was simply unknowable. Besides, there was always a very real possibility that war on Aretha had erupted, rendering a rescue mission impossible.

So Buddy put his faith in those currently around him. There was Doc, whom he still kept in dark about his pre-Kinsey days. There was Communications Director Larry Cahill, whose strategic messaging and poised managerial skills were increasingly crucial to all Buddy had set out to accomplish. And, of course, there were the individual researchers themselves.

The engineers had no idea where the damaged technology came from or how it found its way into Buddy's possession. Appealing to their national pride, he would hint that it had been part of a joint experiment with disgruntled Russian and German scientists and it was their duty as Americans to beat them all in the race to the Moon. His engineering team was also being compensated far beyond what they could earn anywhere else, and he informed them—despite its total fabrication—that they were working in contract with the United States government. As such they were required to sign nondisclosure forms that would result in treason—with the penalties of lifetime imprisonment or even death—if they leaked even the slightest information about what they were working on, the location of their lab, or who they worked for or with.

Doc picked a pebble from the sand. He tossed it up, and then caught it. "You know I hate to be the one…," he began.

"I know, you do." Buddy winked. "Out with it."

"Latest count, revenues are down seventy percent."

"Seventy-one. I checked this morning."

"Right. Seventy-one. Dextron, Link2. Surge. It's gotta be the most open case'a collusion in history. The government's been turnin' a blind eye and the courts won't back ya. The big three are just eatin' their own profits, waiting to drive us outta business. And it's workin'. I don't mean to rain on yer parade, Buddy, I really don't. But unless we play ball with them, there ain't gonna *be* a Space Center. We ain't gonna have space at all. They're gonna buy up the wells at seventy cents on the dollar, fire most of the gals we got on staff and then drive up oil prices higher'n ever. Word is…your time is up."

But Buddy was counting on his competitors' greed. Like Taurus, they were hemorrhaging funds, and Buddy figured that he had an ace up his sleeve no one could match, so he would just wait them out. If nothing else, Buddy had learned to be extremely patient. "Sit tight," he said. "I got the boys working on something that's gonna make all the difference. And when it does, there won't be a big three. It'll be Taurus Enterprises…and everyone else."

Doc tossed the rock aside. He squared up. "Buddy. We are months, if not weeks away from goin' under. Unless we do somethin'—and I mean right now, as in…today—this company is done. You get that? Out. Of. Bid'ness."

Buddy wasn't used to this much pushback from Doc. He liked it.

"We can't blow it now. You know what it took to get us this far, better'n anybody."

Indeed, Buddy thought, smiling. *Even more than you know.*

"Oh, I'm glad yer so amused. I don't get you, Buddy. Never have. I promised I wouldn't ask questions"—he pointed right at him—"and I don't. But you gotta help me out here. Help me understand." Doc threw up his arms. "Space divisions, cultural centers. Are you outta yer God fersakin' mind?! What's wrong with you?"

As Doc wandered off, muttering to himself, Buddy wanted to reassure his friend. Wanted to let him know that, despite how their predicament looked, they were actually going to not only survive this onslaught, but thrive. He wanted to say those things with conviction. He really did. And so he offered Doc those words. But in his heart of hearts, Buddy was genuinely worried that he had overreached. That very much like Aretha's ancestors who set civil war in motion, he had run roughshod over the culture he had worked so hard to build as it crumbled around him.

Buddy knew he had backed himself into a corner. If he shut down funding to his off-the-grid project, Taurus Enterprises might weather the storm. Maybe. But he feared that if he stopped operations on the *Kosono* retrieval now, when they were *thisclose* to a breakthrough, he'd never have the power and influence to start it up again. His dreams of reuniting on Aretha, with Keela, would have been smashed forever. Besides, right or wrong, Buddy wasn't one to sit back and hope that his situation improved. He recognized the dangers of getting in his own way. But he also wasn't going to put his future in the hands of his enemies.

"I need you to take a leap of faith with me, Doc. I need you to chill. Because even if we go under—which ain't gonna happen—you're still set for life. It's not about money for you. Not anymore. It's about something else, ain't it? Deep in your heart, you believe in what we're doing. You believe in *me.*"

Buddy could see the glint in Doc's eyes, could see just how much he wanted to relent, but couldn't do so without a fight. Intrigue dueling logic. Dreams dueling the known.

"So what do you say, Doc? You willing to ride it out? Are you willing to see it through?" Buddy offered his hands, palms up. He raised his eyebrows. His smile widened. He was prepared to stand there all day, if that was what it would take. And knowing Doc, it just might.

Doc looked up into the afternoon sky, scanned the distance.

Buddy wasn't sure what he was thinking, but he saw a brimming of possibility, a shared twinkle of mischief.

"Oh, what the hell. I ain't never met anybody like you, and doubt I ever will. So, yeah, Buddy. I'm in. I still don't know what yer up to, but I'm in."

Buddy let out a wide-eyed chuckle. "Thank God. I didn't want to beg."

"Yeah, well, just promise me one thing, will ya?"

Buddy smiled again. "Sure thing. Name it."

"B'fore you push us over a cliff, just wait 'til I see Hawaii first. I promised my Laura Anne, and I wanna live long enough to get there."

CHAPTER TWENTY

THE INTERCOM WENT off in Buddy's office. He was poring over financial reports. The latest figures were worse than he thought. Buddy's assistant was on the line.

"Yes, Helen. I thought I told you. Hold my calls."

"I know. I'm sorry, sir. But Doctor Anson insisted."

"I'll call him back."

"He seemed pretty upset."

"I'll call him back."

There was a pause before she spoke again. "Um…I'm not really sure what it means, but he said it's *gas station bad*. He said to come now. It's Mr. Cahill. I think something's wrong."

While difficult to prove, consensus was that a young staffer named Millie Holmes was the firm's mole regarding the oil collusion power play. Just twenty-three, Millie started at Taurus Enterprises as an intern in the public relations department, and under Larry Cahill's supervision, was promoted to associate communications director within a year.

"It's Cahill," Doc said. "He's dead."

"Dead? What do you mean *dead*? When? How?"

"He stopped on the Southlake Bridge, left the motor runnin', climbed over the railin'…and jumped. Seems he had an affair with Millie Holmes. It went bad."

Buddy's hand began to shake. With his enemies out to destroy him it was taking all of his willpower and concentration to keep Taurus Enterprises alive, and now he had a multilayered tragedy on his hands at a time when he could least afford one. "Call his wife. Call Dana…"

"Darren and Janie are on their way to the house. They're draftin' a statement for you, too. Jack and Theresa are at the bridge. Beat the news crew there. But only for so long." Doc poured them both a drink. "You know them jackals. They're gonna crucify us."

"I know."

"Gonna say we're done."

"I know."

"We need to ask fast."

"I said I fucking KNOW! Jesus H. Christ, Doc! Larry was my friend, too, you know? We all made decisions together right here in this room. He was the most solid guy I knew. And now he's dead!"

Buddy slumped in his chair. He dropped his head in his hand.

"Come on, Buddy. It's not yer fault. You couldn'a known."

"But that's just it. I *did* know. Millie always had a darkness in her. A danger. I remember years back, when I was in...," and he almost said *Grinroad*, "...when I was back home, there was this young boy, name of Carlos. He tried to kill a girl he was in love with. Snuck into her room, used a knife. It's in the eyes, Doc. You feel a coldness. Millie has it, too. I don't know how we let her through."

"She's a smart, beautiful girl, Buddy. She's so sweet. So charming."

"And devious. I knew in my gut. I needed to pay attention."

"You can't be all things. Nobody saw this. Larry was good people."

"Then how did he let this happen? How did I?" Buddy rarely drank, but he slugged down a scotch. And another. "Where is she? Where's Millie?"

"In Human Resources. She's shaken up."

"I'll talk to her."

"No, no, Buddy. Bad idea."

"I have to."

"Not yet. Angela's with 'er. She'll handle it. You and me need to get with legal. Know where we stand. *Then* Millie."

Buddy didn't know exactly what he was watching, but he caught Doc take a drink, stare out the window, and then slink away into an odd gaze.

"Thing is...I can see how Larry might'a fallen for her, an just got in too deep. You get to a certain age, reach a certain point... you start thinkin' about times gone by and people long gone. We gotta remember. It's tragic for Larry. And his family. But Millie's a victim here, too. She's just a girl. She made a mistake."

While Buddy and Doc huddled with the lawyers, Angela Johnson, the head of Human Resources, did her best to calm Millie, who leaned back on a leather couch.

Millie had fair skin and a slight build. Her voice was soft. Her eyes were small, brown, and yearning. To look at her was to think of a baby's breath. She clutched a cup of water. "You're all bein' so nice to me. I know I don't deserve it. I'm the worst."

"Oh, don't say that. This is all very upsetting. It's hard for all of us."

Millie sniffled. "I knew it was wrong, being with Larry, I mean...Mr. Cahill. But he was such a wonderful man. He was my mentor, my boss. I was just so selfish..."

Angela offered her a box of tissues.

"And then I kept thinkin' about his children. Little Barney, Amanda. I felt so guilty. So I told him we had to stop. It wasn't right. But then he started callin' me at home, followin' me to the store. I didn't want to say anything." Her eyes went wide. "I didn't want trouble. But he started to scare me, Angela. I was afraid. So I called his wife. What did I do? Oh, God."

"There's no easy way to handle this, Millie. But we're family here. We'll work it out."

Millie took Angela's hand. "Thank you so much. I never thought I'd be in a situation like this. This is such a great company and Mr. Rheams is such a legend..."

"It's okay, Millie. Really. Just one step at a time...okay?"

Millie nodded, wiped her nose. "So, um, I wasn't really sure when to bring it up...you know, it's such a hard time, like you said...but Larry promoted me a few days ago and...I'm afraid people are gonna think the worst. You know…because we were together….”

“Oh, yes. I saw the request. But promotions take time, Millie. Larry knew that. We were going to discuss it next month.”

“What?” Millie stopped crying. Her resolve instantly returned. “He said it was done.”

“No, I’m sorry. It’s not.”

Millie stood up. For a woman barely five feet tall, she seemed to suddenly fill the room. “What do you mean it’s not done? That’s my promotion. That’s my job.”

“I know you’re upset, Millie. But we should discuss it later. You’ve had a rough day. We all have.”

“Don’t give me that flower-lovin’, hippie-crap talk.”

“Millie. I really think—”

“No. You listen to me.” Millie drew into a steely-eyed stare. “I sixty-nined that dirty old pig, right on his desk. His wife’s picture starin’ at me. Have you seen that slob? So don’t tell me it’s not official. That fucking job is mine. And I want it now.”

Blinded by rage, Millie was surrounded by a dozen Taurus employees who had gathered around the glassed-in office to check on the commotion. Whatever sympathy—and leverage—she had, evaporated instantly. She immediately transformed herself from the sympathetic victim of a colleague’s tragic, midlife crisis to a duplicitous, home-wrecking bitch. She subsequently agreed to a year’s severance and a sealed file in exchange for a permanent gag order and waiving all rights to sue the company, its subsidiaries, or any of its employees.

Within the office walls, the name Larry Cahill lived on with a mixture of sadness, joy, and regret. And for the years that followed, Millie Holmes seemed to just disappear.

CHAPTER TWENTY-ONE

It was a day of infamy: March 9, 1964. Barely three months after JFK's assassination in Dallas, Buddy Rheams' fellow oil barons celebrated with all manner of degree and perversion when the following headline was emblazoned across the front page of every major newspaper in America:

TAURUS ENTERPRISES TO FILE FOR BANKRUPTCY

The victory, however, was short-lived. Just four days after the Chapter 11 notification, an otherwise unknown Taurus Enterprises scientist named Terrance Abercrombie announced that he finally perfected the compound for Tritanium, a metal alloy ten times stronger than steel yet at a fraction its weight. In just the first year alone, Taurus Enterprises' Tritanium revenues equaled the firm's highest single-year oil revenues. And after just three years, the burgeoning corporation overtook the steel industry, becoming the country's largest metal supplier.

Thanks to its malleable properties, Tritanium was utilized in all sorts of items, including refrigerators, toasters, coffee pots, watches, and computer casings, as well as in motor vehicles, airplanes, nautical ships, and commercial and residential buildings. It also had medical, military, and industrial applications, among countless other uses.

With the company's resulting might and solvency restored, the oil division reclaimed its market, crushing the collusion against Taurus Enterprises and Buddy Rheams forever.

Rumors persisted that Buddy Rheams held back the Tritanium announcement until after the bankruptcy notice as a special *How ya like me now, bitch?* to his competitors. But Taurus executives repeatedly stated in interviews, subpoenas, and drunken conversation that they had never seen Buddy so fearful that the firm was legitimately going out of business, and that his unswerving faith in the research department was what ultimately saved them.

Buddy's commitment to science and technology only magnified his celebrity. He became one of the richest and most famous men in the world. His status further intensified as fellow Taurus Enterprises researcher Vernon Doyle developed cold fusion—a clean, safe, and inexpensive power supply—followed by Elena Smith's perfection of the Fractronic memory chip, which became the core mechanism for all computer programming. The combined force and influence of these three new technologies set the Techno-Industrial Revolution in motion.

The movement was so large that it would take more than twenty years before the effects would reach into every American home and then stretch throughout the world. But the nation's infrastructure would advance in that short time more than it had in the previous two centuries. Humanity, of course, could not keep up.

Which is why Buddy Rheams gave Abercrombie, Smith, and Doyle—whom the media dubbed "The New Einsteins"—explicit instructions when the time came to unveil each of their respective technologies. Still, he knew that as much as he meditated and prayed and reminded himself of who he was and where he came from, that every day he pretended to be the legend of Buddy Rheams Jr., the more he *became* that legend. He hated keeping this part of himself from Doc, who had been loyal to the man, even if he never truly knew the cause.

With Taurus Enterprises itself being one of the larger world economies and progress mounting on the *Kosono*, Buddy had much to feel good about. And he did. But the success came at a price. While mostly forgotten in the company's expanding dominance, Larry Cahill's suicide shook Buddy to the core. It changed him, infiltrated his psychological and spiritual DNA. More and more he was becoming a stranger even to himself, falling into the void filled by a fabricated persona. A living disguise. A lie.

How many sacrifices had been made to service Buddy's quest? How many more would come? Larry Cahill burdened his family, left them to forever carry the disgrace and ruin of his choices. Fearing he had inflicted the same on those he loved most back on Aretha, Buddy would look in the mirror some nights and feel his very essence recoil.

Is this what I've become? Was it meant to be? Do I know this man? Is it even me?

And while Buddy told himself that all he had done, and would still do, was to get back to Aretha, to his wife, he wondered if the price he was paying, and forcing others to pay, was really worth it. And if the gods would ever forgive him.

CHAPTER TWENTY-TWO

BUDDY, DOC ANSON, and each of the New Einsteins—Abercrombie, Smith, and Doyle—each downed a porterhouse steak and red wine. They sat around a marble table with the Taurus Enterprises logo carved into the top. Armed security officers in suits, sunglasses, and earpieces manned various balconies and entranceways. The veranda of Buddy's ranch overlooked the south end of his private lake.

In their many years together, Doc had been willing to perpetuate the charade because the money was just so damn good, the original lie had been easy enough to sell, and despite the bamboozle, Buddy had done right by their vast employees, honored his commitments to America with the firm's medical, educational, and scientific programs, and, for a man with no past to speak of, had been quite a good friend.

But Doc also saw that with the scientific advancements reshaping America—and Taurus Enterprises' power and influence growing daily—Buddy was more driven than ever, and not for the better. Whether Buddy recognized it or not, he was overlooking the abyss, about to make a fateful decision. And Doc feared that unless he cut ties with Buddy right then, right there, his soul would be just as damned, and he would have no one to blame but himself.

Just walk away, you damn fool. One foot in front of the other. Just walk aw—

Buddy raised his glass. "A toast to our success. We couldn't have done it without you. You three are a credit to mankind in ways you will never fully comprehend. Just last week we started construction on the Taurus Atlantic Riverside Dam, in New York City. Who would have ever thought? But fortune favors the bold, does it not?"

The New Einsteins forced out uncomfortable smiles.

"Come on. Why the tense faces? We're here to celebrate, and to discuss the future. Relax. Enjoy. Look where we are." Buddy gestured to the vast estate, gaudy even for Texas oilmen. He gave an impressed shake of the head. "Amazing. Now think back to just ten years ago. What was your life like then? Hah. I know where I was—and it sure wasn't here."

The New Einsteins nodded without blinking.

"My father used to say that a good meal was a way to commune with the gods, but that getting fat insulted their generosity. Come. Walk with me. We'll burn off this red meat. I want to show you something."

Last chance, old man. Just cash out and wash your hands of Buddy Rheams forever.

Doc's knees went weak as Buddy directed them around the kidney-shaped pool, beyond the tennis courts, and strolled onto his private golf course. The thirteenth green had sand traps at the upper and lower slopes. The group stood at the edge of the lower trap. From their position, they could no longer see—or be seen from—the mansion. They were isolated. Alone. Buddy started them off, as much as Doc wished he wouldn't have.

"Go ahead, Doc. Show 'em."

But you're not going to, are you? You're just slidin' down the well.

The New Einsteins looked curious, confused, and more than a little bit petrified. With an internal sigh, Doc removed three white golf balls from his jacket pocket.

"Three," Buddy said, and gave a slight nod.

Don't do this, don't do this, don't—

"One for each of you."

Oh, sweet Jesus.

As if they were thirds of his own soul, Doc tossed the three golf balls into the sand trap—*blunk, blunk, blunk.* They made small dents in the sand, and began to sink. Lower. Lower. *Bloop.*

"Quicksand," Buddy said.

Lord, have mercy on me.

Abercrombie, Smith, and Doyle barely moved. Their confusion morphed to unadulterated terror. The slightest step and they would have gone in, too.

But you won't. And you shouldn't.

Buddy looked to the quicksand, smirked, and then once again focused on his guests. "The three of you are in a remarkable position. The New Einsteins. You are rich, famous. You lecture around the world. You've each won the Nobel Prize. You are treated like royalty. And God bless. You deserve it." A long rake lay next to the green. Buddy picked it up, flicked the metal spikes. "*Ow.*" He shook his hand, sucked the blood droplet from his finger. "Sharp."

Doyle's face was covered in sweat. He gulped.

"But even with these rewards," Buddy continued, "we need to cement our confidentiality agreements. To recommit our bond. And it goes something like this: You will forever embrace your role as the New Einsteins. You will enjoy all the trappings that come with it. You will live long and die wealthy. For my part, I will continually sing your praises for being the geniuses the world considers you to be. I will fund any research you wish, within reason, and will continue to compensate you at a level I think you will all agree is far more than generous. Your great, great grandkids can already start shopping for housekeepers."

Doc smiled despite himself. He liked that one. The smile quickly faded.

You're drunk on power. You're lost. You used to have a moral compass, a center. You used to fight for people. You cared.... What the hell happened to you? What have you done?

Buddy dragged the forked end of the rake along the quicksand, then flipped the handle so that the rake was standing upright, held in place.

"But this part's particularly important. So pay attention. We also agree that you will never ever ever ever ever never ever

ever…never…ever…EVER…for even one molecule of one nano-second, forget that you invented…nothing. You discovered *nothing*. Of course, you are all intelligent and competent scientists in your own right. But I *gave* you your discoveries. I *let* you claim them as your own. Your role, now and forever, is to keep saying your lines. Do so, and your lives will be joyful."

The rake fell over just then, laying flat in the quicksand.

"You should have obvious incentives to honor the agreement. No one wants to be labeled a fraud. I sympathize. But beyond that, it's essential you understand—without the slightest doubt or confusion—that if you ever decide to speak out of turn, write a book, text a reporter, look for more money…or impress a bimbo…well, very much like those golf balls…you will be with us in the world one minute…and gone the next."

Doc crumbled inside, but it was Buddy's next few words that seemed to manifest from somewhere far blacker and insidious than ever before, like puss leaking from an infection site. A cancer of the soul.

"Your families, too."

There was a slight slurping sound, and then a bubble. After a few seconds, the quicksand settled so that the surface was smooth again, like the rake had simply never existed. Buddy shook the sand off his hands. "We're going to spend the weekend out here, by ourselves, away from distraction, getting to know each other. So let's head back, go for a swim, and I'll have Douglas pour us another drink."

Vernon Doyle collapsed into the quicksand. His fellow Einsteins pulled him out, knowing they very well could be next.

On the way back across the golf course, Buddy forced out a confident smirk. "I can't believe that worked," he said to Doc. "I went a little overboard, but the words came rolling out."

There was much Doc wanted to say, much he should have said. But it was too late. "You can't mess with folks like that and expect the Good Lord to forgive you, Buddy. This ain't no joke, or maybe it's the biggest joke of all, I don't know." Doc shook his head. "I knew we've been livin' on borrowed time, but we just damned ourselves to hell. You and me both. Right there, on the thirteenth green. My wife was the true believer, God rest her soul, and I guess I just ain't the man I used to be. Hell…there ain't no guessin' about it." He turned back to The New Einsteins, who looked in no rush to join them. "I ain't never pried into what you been up to these years 'cuz I don't really wanna know. I figgered you had yer reasons, and that was enough fer me. But whatever they are, I hope it's all worth it, 'cuz I got nothing left of the old me to give, except an *old me*. The man I was is dead and gone. I'm just wearin' his clothes."

Buddy had an odd look about him. Doc could see the struggle behind those eyes, that the man he'd helped create hadn't started out taking delight in cruel manipulations, but maybe it was just too late to reclaim his humanity. Or was it? Either way, Buddy was going to have to figure it out on his own.

"Come on," Buddy said. "Don't be so dramatic. There's only four inches of watery mud beneath the sand trap. It couldn't drown a gopher. I'm not that guy. You know that. It's all an act. It's for show."

Doc wiped his forehead with a handkerchief as they came upon the veranda. He let out a defeated sigh. "If you say so." Because he knew from there on out he would just be running out the clock. "Let's get that drink," he said. "Lord knows I need it."

CHAPTER TWENTY-THREE

THE MONTHLY BOARD meeting at Taurus Enterprises drew a packed room. The pending acquisition of Loredo Orthopedics Inc. was being finalized. Once it went through, Taurus would officially control the largest orthopedics group in the Southwest, paving the way for its eventual expansion into advanced spinal surgery, medical robotics, and the emerging field of nanotechnology. But Doc Anson, who made the introductions and set the sale in motion, was a no-show yet again. And Buddy, who was becoming increasingly worried about his partner, was now forced to lead the negotiations.

"So you'll see here," Buddy said, using a laser pointer on the projection screen, "today it's mid-year nineteen sixty-eight, and we are conservatively projecting a four hundred percent return by the same time nineteen seventy-five, if not before. And if our hospital group continues on its current path of growth, profits will be even greater. Unless there are any other questions, I think we're ready to close."

As the meeting dispersed, Loredo's fifty-eight-year-old CEO Robert Elizondo Loredo had a question for Buddy, one he'd been hearing more and more, and one to which he had no answer.

"I don't know how ya do it, Buddy. Do you just grind yer cash up into paste and rub it on yer face? The rest of us just keep getting' older and you look as spry as the day we met."

From the outside looking in, Buddy wasn't aging at quite the same rate as everyone else, which, it turns out, he wasn't. It required a nuanced solution that he finally had to resolve.

"Oh, I don't know about that, Bob. My bones ache pretty good."

"Ache, hell. Yer makin' us look bad. Probably why Doc ain't

been around. Compared to you he looks a hun'red years old."

"You know better than that. He's got more energy than the two of us combined. I don't think I've slept more than six hours a night over the last ten years. But he just keeps on going."

"Well...whatever yer doin'...God bless ya. And share, ya greedy basterd!" Loredo slapped Buddy's shoulder. "Anything that keeps you lookin' this good's gotta be worth it...or totally illegal!"

Unfortunately for Buddy, his partner's absence was trumping all other problems. Taurus Enterprises was about to make a major commitment to aeronautics, but with Doc having essentially checked out, Buddy had to assume an even greater role day-to-day at a time when he needed to focus more on his private team of engineers. They had finally reverse-engineered the *Kosono* to a point where warp propulsion at least seemed plausible within their lifetime.

Yet Buddy was finally facing the reality that he had no clearcut successor for Doc. From an operational standpoint, Buddy could subdivide Doc's responsibilities into various roles, which he probably needed to do, regardless. But because of the numerous lies and deceptions that went into forming Taurus Enterprises, Buddy was in some ways more vulnerable than ever. While he now ran one of the most powerful companies in America, if not the world, he didn't have an inner sanctum he could trust—or one motivated to protect him anywhere near to the degree that Doc would, and certainly had. Buddy knew that it was just a matter of time before Doc could no longer be a true partner, leaving him to fend for himself.

Over the following days Buddy left messages for Doc—all unreturned. Which is why it came as a surprise when he showed up unannounced in Buddy's office late Friday morning, and with a huge smile on his face.

"I'm in love," Doc said. "I'm a scruffy old fart and a fool on the hill. But I'm in love, my boy. Can you believe it?" He shrugged. "I'm in love."

Buddy leaned back in his chair, smiled, and let out a relieved sigh, although it was more acute and revealing than he intended. But if Doc was looking to escape the pressures of running what was now a global operation, better to the arms of a good woman than the inside of a bottle.

Doc helped himself to the liquor cabinet. They clinked glasses. Buddy sipped his Scotch. Doc gulped his down in one throw. "I know what you're gonna say, Buddy, but b'fore ya go on with the speeches...just hear me out."

"Well, okay then, you dirty old stud muffin. Details. It's good to see you. Let's have it. Who is she?" Had Buddy known the answer he was about to receive, he may not have even asked the question.

"It's Millie Holmes. I ran into her playing craps at casino night for the scoliosis research group I chair. It's crazy, I know. But she ain't who you think. She's amazing. We ran the table for an hour, and next thing you know we're two peas in a pod. I just can't leave her side. Don't want to, neither."

Buddy wasn't sure if he passed out, went blind, or broke out in a rash of penetrating brain tumors, but the mere utterance of the name *Millie Holmes* sent him tumbling into a pit of heart-thumping hysteria. Buddy's jaw hung open. *No no no no no no no no no no no no no.*

"I know she caused a ruckus back when, but she went home to St. Louie after that and got right with the Lord. You know me and the Big Man upstairs ain't never really been on the same page an all, but if he can bring a sweet young thing like Millie to my doorstep, then I'm willing to give him another try."

Buddy's instinct was to pitch Doc out the window and blow-torch his corpse to burn out the evil that had seeped into his DNA. No matter how insane the choice might appear, when a man is infected by tainted love, there's no reasoning with him. It's the most dangerous, insidious drug ever known. The user defends that corrupted emotion—poorly defined as love—with delirium, and, ironically, rage in his heart. Buddy had to say something. "Doc. Hold on. She almost ruined us."

There was conviction in Doc's eyes, a serious, dedicated calm Buddy had never seen in him before. "No. *We* almost ruined us. You and me. T'gether. So don't blame our sins on her. She was young and foolish and got caught up in the glamour of it all. This…monstrosity. This lie." Doc gestured to Buddy's office, the vastness of Taurus Enterprises. "We set things in motion. We poisoned the well."

"I know," Buddy said. "That's what I've wanted to tell you. You were right about me. I lost my way. Remember that day? On the golf course? With the New Einsteins? When you left after that weekend, when I was all alone in that godforsaken house, that…hideous mansion I had constructed…I finally saw myself then the way you saw me. And it made me sick. So I pulled myself back. I rededicated myself to doing things right. Like we started out. But you disappeared after that. You vanished."

"I told you as much. But you didn't listen."

"I know, I didn't. I'm sorry. I…Doc. Look what we've built. Look where we're headed. I owe you my life. Twice over at least. And I get that you're in love. I know how that feels…. But, Millie?" He let out a controlled sigh, a pleading for reason. "Really?"

"You can have all the 'pinions you want, Buddy. I really don't care. Millie's put the past behind her. And I have, too."

"But—"

"Enough, Buddy. Enough. You want me to see things like you do? Follow wherever you lead?…I don't even know yer real name! I don't know who you are. And the thing is…I just don't care. Not anymore. I'm done. You run this place however you want. I just ain't got the strength. But Millie? She does. She's smart as a whip and knows how ta' get things done. She's got more brains 'n I ever had. She's gonna take my place. I gave her my proxy on the board."

"Doc," Buddy said, trying to restrain himself, because there was no way he could ever let that happen. "I know she's your lady friend, but—"

"Watch yerself, Buddy. She ain't my lady friend. She's my wife. It's official. Saw the judge last week."

Buddy blinked several times. The *Kosono's* warp design was still at least a decade away, and very likely even farther off, but he finally...finally...felt that his ultimate goal was within reach. And now that he needed Doc more than ever, his closest friend and advisor had invited a deadly asp into their midst. No matter what Doc said, now that Mille Holmes had returned and with her hooks deeply embedded in him, Buddy knew she would be far more dangerous, ruthless, and cunning than before.

"Millie wanted to wait, the sweet thing, but I told 'er that an old fart like me ain't got enough breaths to take any of 'em fer granted. Well, don't just stand there like an idiot. Pour us a drink. Congratulate me. It's the least you can do."

The founding members of Taurus Enterprises stood in Buddy's office. Sunshine careened off his desk. They shared a drink in heavy, awkward silence. Whether Doc aligned with Millie out of spite, depression, or as penance for his sins, Buddy never found out. But no matter what else passed between those two men—architects of an enterprise built on perseverance, death, and the dreams of a fallen comrade—Buddy did know this: the toast would be their last.

CHAPTER TWENTY-FOUR

It was not a meeting Buddy wanted to take. It was one he had to. Doc had only just laid the news on him a day earlier, and yet there she was already, in his office, like she owned the place.

"Don't worry, Buddy. I know you don't like me. I stole your friend away. I get it." Millie Anson, formerly Millie Holmes, batted her eyes. "But he adores me, and I adore what he can do for me." She shook her head in a way that let Buddy know she considered both him and Doc just silly little boys getting in the way of her more significant endeavors. "The older they are, the harder they're not. Just a whiff of my perfume," Millie said, and then craned her head, exposing her young nape, "and Doc can barely see straight. He's tired, you know. You pushed him way past his expiration date. He's just a dopey old mutt who needs a daily walk and a tinkle. And I'm holding the leash."

"What do you want, Millie?"

"Ooooh. Getting right to it. I like that." Millie wrinkled her nose and then sauntered over to the couch, running her finger along the leather. She sat down, crossed her legs; one bounced easily on her knee. Her skin was smooth. She left a button undone of her silk blouse. Her breasts were small. Her seductive poses were in direct contrast to Buddy's reserved posture. His true face still looked young and vibrant, but he'd had some touches done to age him appropriately so that he looked every bit of the forty-nine he claimed to be. "I left something on your desk," she said. "Take a peek."

Had it been almost anyone else, Buddy would have handled this confrontation differently, but Millie was an insidious breed of malignancy that demanded his attention. He unspooled the red tie string, opened the manila envelope, and then scanned the documents. He looked up.

"Don't get me wrong...*Buddy.* I'm a great believer in remaking yourself. Tell your story first and often until finally it becomes the truth. Your truth. Everyone's truth. But stealing a man's identity? Faking medical records? *Tt-tt-tt.* My, oh my. If I had known you were so devious...I might've gone for you instead."

Buddy had long expected a day of reckoning. But now he had more to lose than ever.

"Of course, you'll make me a rich woman to keep quiet, but I'm already rich. You've paid Doc a king's ransom. Now I know why. What I want," Millie said, re-crossing her legs, "is something money *can't* buy. I know you've got an underground facility. I want to see what's going on down there."

Doc doesn't even know about that. Oh, god.

"That's right. I've known about it for years. But *how* I know is another matter. We need to focus on the present. And here's how it's going to play out: You are going to give me access—to whatever I want, whenever I want—or these medical records will be pumped through the news cycle until we both die of old age. You, obviously, long before me. Now don't get me wrong. You are worth far more to me where you are than if I ruin you. And don't think I'm not tempted. You were very mean to me last time. I'm very sensitive, you know." Millie offered a fake pout with a tinge of *go fuck yourself.* "So think about it, handsome. You play nice with me...maybe I do the same. You don't play nice, well...you know the drill. You're publicly humiliated, convicted of fraud, bribery, and embezzlement, you die in jail, blah blah blah."

Taurus the Bull was raging inside Buddy's chest, its razor-sharp horns ripping at rib and breastplate to burst out. He forced a smile nonetheless.

"Take a few days," Millie said, "and in the meantime, I'll run off some more copies."

Unbeknownst to Millie, Buddy wasn't the least bit worried about those medical records. Fearful that Doc would die suddenly or fall victim to dementia, bribe, or blackmail, he long ago brought in his own medical team to create new, customized records that Doc himself didn't even know existed, and had them embedded in the healthcare database, replacing the original forgeries. Buddy was safe in that regard. Millie could leak all the medical records she wanted. They would just come across as sour grapes.

But he had also gone to enormous lengths to keep the underground facility secure and off the grid. That Millie knew about it sent him into a free fall. He'd come too far and been through too much to let anyone get in the way now.

On his way back from the underground facility, Buddy stopped dead in his tracks. A jolt of fear shot straight though him—intense, unbridled panic that gave him lung-scorching palpitations. He reached for his chest. His face went flush, burning. Sweat broke out. His heart was struck with a thunderclap. He couldn't breathe.

Oh god oh god oh god oh god...

So when Buddy nodded mechanically at the female security guard in the laser-shielded, bullet-proof barricade protecting the lab's entrance, he noticed a bracelet on her wrist. It was a modest piece of jewelry that he normally would have overlooked. Except Buddy knew that bracelet. He knew it well. The guard, Janice Calder, a former soldier and dedicated professional, had been a loyal and trusted associate for eight years. She passed every background check and her twice-yearly reviews, covered shifts for her fellow guards, and never asked questions that were not for her to ask.

Yet around her left wrist dangled a piece of jewelry that might as well have been a mafia boss' smooch on the cheek—the Kiss of Death. A bracelet Doc Anson gave once to his first wife, when they were just teenage sweethearts. The bracelet Doc then gave to Millie Holmes. The bracelet Millie must have given to Janice. She was probably the last person on Earth Buddy would have thought susceptible to Millie's corruption.

"Are you all right, sir? You don't look well. Do you need a doctor?"

Buddy looked upon Janice, this tough, faithful colleague who had proven her worth time and again. His hand began to shake. He leaned forward to catch his breath, wondering if Janice had any idea just how dangerously she had been manipulated. "No. I'm…I'm okay. Something I ate. I'm nauseous."

"Understood, sir. How can I help?"

Though Janice Calder was ever present, the same reliable Janice he had known all those years, all Buddy could see was that bracelet—like a stalker leaving an exposed razor blade on his front stoop. It was a message from Millie, one so subtle no one but Buddy would even recognize it as the very real threat that it was: as long as Millie Holmes, the wife of his former best friend, business partner, and in a very real way, co-conspirator, was in Buddy's life, nothing he knew or had was safe.

Millie Holmes was coming. And if she could get this close, there was just no telling how much closer she would get. Or what she would find out once she got there.

Buddy pressed the *BRS* button, his code for Buddy Rheams' Suite. The elevator doors shut. He checked his watch and then eked out a sad smile. The retinal scan was set to corroborate that he was definitively who he claimed to be.

But deep down a part of him still hoped that one day, maybe even that day, maybe even right then, the scan would expose him as the fraud that he actually was. That the metal gates would slam shut, trapping him in place while a deafening siren whirred and an automated voice announced: *INTRUDER ALERT! INTRUDER ALERT! INTRUDER ALERT!* The jig would be up, once and for all, and he could go back to just being Mitri Amos from Aretha, whoever that guy was.

The elevator's breathy female voice confirmed his identity. "Welcome, Mr. Rheams."

When the elevator stopped again, it opened to a foyer with

hardwood floors and a gentle glow of overhead lighting. The foyer flowed into a plush-carpeted den with two beige couches, matching massage chair, and a coffee table. Flat-panel TVs—far in advance of the technology the rest of the world had to endure at the time—were mounted on the opposite wall leading to a small kitchen. To the foyer's left, a long hallway led to Buddy's bedroom. And to the foyer's immediate right was Buddy's viewing station, the perch from which he spent much of his time overseeing construction of Tower Command, the first building in the Space Center to go up. It would still be several years before the complex was fully operational, but he was on the work site as often as possible. He didn't want to leave anything to chance. Like the rest of his suite, the viewing station was soundproof and bugproof. And bulletproof.

Buddy kicked off his shoes, unfastened his tie, and then tossed it on the bed. His jacket, too. He rolled up his sleeves, turned his music to shuffle, and flipped on the bathroom light. He stared into the mirror, not entirely sure who was staring back.

Through the speakers, Sam & Dave growled about a *Soul Man*.

Buddy peeled the synthetic mask from his hands and face. The material allowed his skin to breathe well, but it was always a relief to be free of the fabricated coating. With every day he hid behind the mask he felt just a little bit more that he would never be able to really take it off.

"...I'm a soul man..."

Whether it was the result of wormhole radiation all those years ago or the effect of being in an alternate corner of time and space, he just didn't know. But other than the emotional and psychological toll, he looked virtually the same as when he first arrived on Earth. Whatever the reason, he'd had to employ a team of specialists to create the synthetics, aging him appropriately, and paid them a mind-numbing sum for their discretion. Though pushing fifty, without the appropriate touch-ups he didn't look a day over thirty-five.

"...I'm a soul man..."

After a shower, shave, and the music running through *Buddy Holly's Greatest Hits*, Buddy changed into cargo shorts and a plain white t-shirt, laid on his bed, and drank a cold Belgian ale. By the time his namesake and the Crickets rocked through *Oh, Boy!* and *Peggy Sue* and insisted that he go and *Rave On* with his bad self, Buddy' stress started to wash away. But he still couldn't relax. Not really. Millie Anson was a cold, sadistic mongoose, with Taurus Enterprises in her sights, leaving Buddy with fewer and fewer options to deal with her in a rational manner.

Rather than force a decision he did not want to make, Buddy dimmed the lights, shut the music, and then stepped into the hall closet outside the foyer. He closed the door behind him. And as was often the case, it was several hours before he came back out.

CHAPTER TWENTY-FIVE

IN TULSA, OKLAHOMA, almost four thousand townsfolk gathered for the ribbon-cutting ceremonies. It was a cool September afternoon of 1968, but the sun was bright. There was electricity in the air. Buddy Rheams stood at attention. The media was in full effect. The mayor spoke:

"Tulsa has always been a proud city, caring for its people, and especially its children." The crowd cheered. "But we are not just a city," the mayor said, "but a community. It has been a longstanding commitment of my administration to bring children's healthcare to a new level of excellence, and thanks to Harlan 'Buddy' Rheams Jr., the president of Taurus Enterprises, that dream becomes a reality. So without further ado... Mr. Buddy Rheams."

The crowd roared.

On Wakimi Road in Oahu, on a winding, two-lane highway overlooking the Pacific Ocean, Doc Anson and his new bride sped toward the distant Sun. It was early morning. Hawaii. The water below was deep and blue. Cold. Foam-peaked waves broke toward the shore. Millie Anson reached over to her husband. She threaded her fingers through the back of his hair. It was white. "I love you," she said.

Doc's heart nearly skipped a beat. He grabbed the wheel tighter, and smiled. "I love you, too."

In Tulsa, Buddy Rheams addressed the crowd.

"Thank you for such a kind welcome. People tell me I'm a natural showman. That I bring the circus." The crowd laughed and smiled. "Well, it sure does seem to follow me, although I can assure you, none of this comes naturally." More laughter. "But the Children's Hospital isn't about me. We are here today because my oldest and dearest friend, Doctor Arthur Anson, told me years ago that he would only be part of the Taurus family if we were committed to doing what was right...what was needed. That we put the American people—our friends, our families, our neighbors...each other—ahead of everything else."

Along a winding, two-lane highway in Oahu overlooking the Pacific Ocean, Millie Anson—formerly Millie Holmes—stunned her husband. "I'm pregnant," she said. The thought of it so overwhelmed Doc that he almost drove their rented Porsche off the cliff.

In Tulsa, Buddy Rheams clarified his position. " 'I'm all for making a profit,' Doc told me, 'but if it only goes in your pocket, then count me out.' " Buddy ran his thumb and forefinger down his suit lapel. "Well, I'm not going to lie. My pockets are full." Laughter. "But the money only has value if, as Doc said, we put it to good use. And that's why we're here. Doc asked that I speak for him today because that lucky son of a gun is on his honeymoon right now."

Along a winding, two-lane highway in Oahu overlooking the Pacific Ocean, Doc Anson turned to his beautiful young bride, whom he'd known intimately for all of four months. "Are ya sure? Don't toy with an old man."
Millie curled her arm through his, leaned into him. "I'm sure."

In Tulsa, Buddy Rheams Jr., the president of Taurus Enterprises, concluded unfinished business. "So in Doc's honor, and with his guiding hand, I hope this marvelous building behind me—the Children's Hospital of Tulsa—does right by you, your families, your neighbors. Each other." The Mayor handed Buddy Rheams the ceremonial scissors. They posed for photographs.

Along a winding, two-lane highway in Oahu overlooking the Pacific Ocean, Doc Anson once again discovered that his life was about to change forever, and in a manner that far exceeded his expectations. "I'm gonna be a father?"

In Tulsa, a red ribbon was clipped.

Along a winding, two-lane highway in Oahu overlooking the Pacific Ocean, a car approaching from the opposite direction closed in on Doc and Millie Anson. The driver depressed the clutch and shifted into fifth gear. The engine revved. The speedometer approached one hundred twenty miles per hour.

In Tulsa, balloons went up.

Along a tight curve in Oahu, seemingly designed to feed any passing prey to the Pacific Ocean below, an oncoming car accelerated into the wrong lane. Doc Anson swerved. The Ansons' rented Porsche crashed through the guardrail, went over a cliff. The other car kept right on driving. Below, there was nothing but the sound of waves breaking on the rocks.

In Tulsa, a marching band broke into a brassy version of *Good Day Sunshine,* by The Beatles.

On a rocky shore, in Oahu, the Porsche that Doc and Millie Anson rented for their honeymoon exploded. It took the EMTs and rescue workers seven hours to reach their charred bodies. Both newlyweds were pronounced DOA, and placed in black bags.

In Tulsa, Buddy Rheams leaned against the very hospital he dedicated to Doc Anson, his oldest friend. Even though the atmosphere was filled with revelry, his heart sank. Alone in a way very few people would ever truly understand, he saw himself then only as Buddy Rheams Jr., president of Taurus Enterprises.

Because Mitri Amos, the husband of Keela Amos, the long lost son of Grinroad, would never have done what he did. That man—after believing he had reclaimed himself from the edge of darkness—was finally, truly gone.

CHAPTER TWENTY-SIX

SUGAR TREE MEDICAL was a misnomer if ever there was one. Dale Aranuke almost punched out the desk clerk when he saw a discarded gauze pad on the hallway floor and a soiled gown hanging out of a laundry bin. Aranuke had just been promoted to Associate Research Director in the Taurus Enterprises Nanotechnology Division in Boston, but his savings were meager, leaving his mother to rely on Medicare, which didn't come close to paying for what she needed.

Even as a Taurus employee, Aranuke couldn't get her into the newly opened hospice care facility in Houston. Although a wonderful program, there simply weren't enough beds to meet the demands of 1996, which saw an influx of aging Americans move into specialized healthcare facilities. Instead his mother was stuck at Sugar Tree.

"You. Asshole," he said to the clerk. "Get my mother a blanket. It's freezing in there."

The clerk stared down at the *Houston Chronicle*. It was open to a two-page article in the travel section about seasoned noodle dishes served at a luxury resort in Bali.

"Hey. I'm talking to you. I said, get my mother a blanket."

Whether stoned, asleep, or simply indifferent, the clerk barely lifted his head. "I called an orderly, bro. Should be here soon."

"Fuck the orderly. You do it."

"Can't."

"What do you mean *can't*? She's right down the hall."

"Can't leave the desk." Without looking up, the clerk tapped a sign taped to the counter. *DESK TO REMAIN ATTENDED AT ALL TIMES.* "The rules."

Although Aranuke tried to emulate his father by remaining

calm in the face of morons, bullies, and clerks, he felt his composure slip away. "You listen to me...*bro*. My dad's company embezzled his entire pension while he suffocated from emphysema. And now my mom's down the hall just praying for death. And you're telling me you can't leave this desk...because the fucking RULES say so?! Are you kidding me?! Get her a blanket! NOW! There's no one here but us."

The clerk barely looked up. "Like I said, bro. Orderly's coming."

Aranuke stormed off and riled through an open hallway closet. He took two blankets for his mother, who was barely ninety pounds. The pancreatic cancer moved fast.

"Here, Mom." He kissed her forehead. "This'll keep you warm."

She smiled meekly, too weak to raise her head.

Aranuke sat by her bed, took her hand. It was cold, frail. Watching her waste away he felt the insidious river of depression encroach on his soul. He had horrific, violent fantasies. But who was he angriest with? His father, for trusting the wrong people? The company's chief financial officer, for being an unscrupulous, criminal pig? God?

Or himself, for being self-absorbed with his career while his parents fell into a precarious state, as if their fate had ever been his to control. And because he'd been so single-minded, often ignoring the family, his mother was now penniless and alone, spending her final days in what to Aranuke was no better than a kennel.

"How did this happen, Mom? You were going to travel, to see the world. Tuscany and Paris? Then Australia and New Zealand. I was going to visit you and Dad...remember? We were going to toast each other at the Sydney Opera House. It can't end like this. It's not the life you planned. Not the life I promised."

His mother opened her eyes. "I know it's not, honey. But it's the life I've got."

The fight in her was gone. Aranuke had watery eyes, and fury in his heart. "What can I do for you, Mom? Before it's too late? Let me take you home with me. It's small, but it'll do."

"You're such a good boy, Dale, but I think I'll stay here. It's nice."

"No, Mom. You can't. It's a *hell*hole. A dump." Tears streamed down his face. "You're moving out. You'll stay with me."

"Dale—"

"Mom, I can't let you…"…*die like this. I just can't.*

"Kiss your mother," she said, barely above a whisper. "I'm tired."

Dale Aranuke did as he was told, then sat by her side until morning. She was pronounced dead at 6:24 a.m.

The whisky bottle was unopened. Aranuke left it on the table opposite his bed. A reminder. To stay strong. To fight for his survival, no matter what. His mother had been dead almost thirteen years. His father longer than that.

Routine was the key. Repetition. Aranuke read a study once that said the average person, rather than planning to succeed, spends up to four hours daily obsessing over at least one of the following: minor squabbles; problems that have not occurred, but are assumed inevitable; past slights; sex.

To keep his mind focused, every morning before stepping into the shower stall, Aranuke laid out his clothes—suit, shirt, tie, cufflinks, briefs, undershirt, socks, shoes, belt—and then, as he showered, in his mind, reviewed his *To Do* list. Same as his father. *Plan to get ahead, Dale. Implement that plan, adjust as necessary.*

The year ahead was poised to be the grandest in the history of Taurus Enterprises, and with Buddy Rheams Jr. turning ninety, the end of 2009 was being treated as a glorious milestone if ever there was one. By everyone except Aranuke.

He was almost nauseous just thinking about attending the annual holiday party that night, but as the chief executive overseeing the company's forthcoming *Crossline* pilot selections, he had to be front and center as the Old Man made his speech—an annual company tradition.

Hot beads of water cascaded down Aranuke's skin. He ran

his fingers through his hair. It wasn't too gray. Not yet. Brush teeth. Rinse. Shampoo. Rinse. Conditioner. Body lather. Rinse. Routine. Repetition. *Adjust as necessary. Plan to get ahead. Implement that plan.* Depression. That's what Aranuke remembered. Depression. Hospitals. And whisky.

When his father went broke, and then his health deteriorated, he tried to numb his pain, but only made it worse. A sober man, he only took to drink, at the end.

On the local news, as Aranuke dressed for the party, a panel of scholars said that Buddy Rheams Jr., the CEO of Taurus Enterprises, was either a madman or a genius, and possibly both.

Joy Delaporte, the Taurus Enterprises' associate communications director, was being interviewed about the enigmatic executive's workforce philosophy and his dedication to the arts. "... as Buddy Rheams always says, 'train 'em, pay 'em and stay 'em, and America can do anything.'" She continued, "The firm's economic success, going strong more than forty years, also spawned a cultural wave considered to have eclipsed even the Renaissance. Through Taurus Enterprises' generous donations to the patron arts, we have seen the Uhrgman Fountain in San Francisco, the Mozart Statue in Denver, the Pablo Picasso Park in Baltimore, and Pietro Carmona's vast underwater coral sculptures in Lake Tahoe, among many other wonderful works. It even launched the career of world-renowned artist Mary Ibner, who was on with Conan last week..."

Looking in the mirror, Aranuke straightened his cuffs. Left, right. Routine. Repetition. *If they only knew,* he thought.

Delaporte continued. "Buddy Rheams has also been one of the most influential spiritual forces in American history. He founded the Taurus Meditation Center right here in our corporate headquarters, and with a branch in every Taurus Enterprises building, and throughout the firm's hospitals, school systems, and children's recreation centers. As I'm sure you know, Buddy believes in making peace with whatever forces you think oversee the Universe. I'm more of a Jesus gal myself, but as Buddy says, just so long as every man, woman, and child is free to pray to whoever they want…let 'em pray, let 'em pray, let 'em pray-pray pray."

On Aranuke's bureau was a printout from Taurus Enterprises. It took almost eight months to obtain. They showed funds, not large individual sums, but enough that added up over time. Funds diverted from several departments to the Auxiliary Research Department.

Only there was no Auxiliary Research Department. Nothing he could find, anyway. But there *was* a lockdown bunker far beneath Taurus Enterprises. Not even Aranuke had access. It didn't officially exist. An ambitious young woman named Millie Holmes found out once. It was almost a very big problem. *But the Old Man took care of that, too, didn't he?* Aranuke brushed a strand of lint from his shoulder.

If they only knew the real you. If they only knew.

CHAPTER TWENTY-SEVEN

More than seven thousand Taurus Enterprises employees and their significant others gathered for the holiday party at the Cultural Center, which included the Waldencroft Art Museum. On display were a fully restored saber-toothed tiger and woolly mammoth, on separate mounts, as well as an open-mouthed pterodactyl, secured on the wall.

The soirée also included a feast large and diverse enough to put the combined efforts of the Fourth of July, Cinco de Mayo, and Mardi Gras to shame, more colored lights than in Santa's psychedelic fantasy, and Cirque du Soleil in the counter round. And as a topper many joked that only Buddy himself could have arranged, a full moon hovered in the night sky, shining through the massive glass ceiling.

Here we go, Aranuke thought, as he helped his boss to the stage. *Let the lies begin.*

Shaky at times, Buddy's voice was amplified by the tiny microphone secured to his lapel. His hands and face were wrinkled and worn. He had large liver spots on his neck and forehead. His hair was thinning and white.

"We may have begun with oil," the nonagenarian said, "but science is the key. And yet it won't get us traversing the solar system unless we have the conviction it can be done, and that it's worth doing. Some *p-p-p,*" he stuttered, cleared his throat, "s-sorry folks…some people say I'm running this company into the g-g-ground, that I'll ruin us with my c-crazy d-dreams. Of reaching the stars." As part of the CEO's annual holiday celebration, each Taurus employee had been awarded a healthy bonus, plus a choice of toys for their children or a family voucher to be used at one of the sixteen full-service vacation resorts the company owned and operated throughout the world. Supporting himself with a cane, Buddy raised his free hand. It shook. "You tell me. Do you think we're on the right t-track?"

The party erupted with cheers and applause.

"I couldn't agree more. To get ahead in this world—and reach all the others—you've got to have vision, d-d-drive...and a stomach for humble p-pie if the gods prove us wrong. I don't think we are, but that's what makes it fun. Enjoy the party, f-folks. Big days ahead."

The festivities resumed. Aranuke helped Buddy, who hobbled, even with the cane.

"What's the matter, Dale? It's a party. It's Christmas. You don't seem happy."

"I'm happy. Just a little tired. Been a long year."

"Oh, I think we both know better. Grab a drink. Let's talk."

Aranuke took a champagne flute from a waiter and begrudgingly followed Buddy into a small hallway behind the stage.

Go ahead, old man. Make another speech. I know your lies. I've heard them all. And now I know yours. You bastard.

"You're not like most men," Buddy said. "You don't want presents, money, or fame. We're surrounded by people who believe in the dream, even if it's not their own. They want to be a part of history. Of the future. But yet you feel isolated. Cut off." With a silk handkerchief, Buddy wiped dried saliva from the corner of his mouth. "The problem, Dale, is that my time on this Earth is limited, and you want my post when I'm gone. Everyone sees that. You're in charge, but that's not why they hate you. It's not why you're alone."

For someone who rose from unpaid intern to one of the most prominent executives in the Taurus Enterprises empire, Aranuke was probably the last person who would consider himself a company man. He didn't believe in the global monstrosity that Taurus Enterprises had become or what Buddy Rheams Jr. claimed he stood for. Aranuke found something he was loath to uncover, because with men like Buddy Rheams, there's always something to find. It's how they get to be who they are.

"It's that you're not in charge *enough*. You've got one eye focused on today and the other on tomorrow. You act like the staff is beneath you, like you're wasting your time with them. And maybe you are. I really don't know. You've always had the drive to help shepherd the Space Program. That's why I brought you here. You know how to block out the noise. But as of this moment, you have no chance to succeed me, Dale. None. You are not on the short list. You're not on any list. So make a decision, because you're in between worlds. You demand their loyalty, but give none in return."

Although he didn't show it, a snare drum of anxiety beat in Aranuke's chest. He forced himself to blink so he wouldn't just stand there, paralyzed with fear, embarrassment, and rage.

He's testing you, pushing you. He wants you to doubt yourself. Don't listen to him. Don't believe his lies....

"I never had the pleasure," Buddy said, "but an associate of mine...he knew your father. He offered many compliments. I was sorry to hear about his final years. He didn't deserve that. From what I understand, he was a fine executive. Knew how to keep things moving. And knew his limits."

I hope you fucking die right now you god damn son of a—

"You got the right amount of bastard in you, Dale, but not enough killer. Being in charge, with the enemies we've made... it's like living in a shark tank that's also filled with piranhas. Dealing with the people inside these walls is only half the battle. Your teeth are sharp, Dale, but you need fangs...the will to use them...and most important, the discipline to hold back, even when you can taste their blood. Leadership requires being a bastard *and* having a heart, whether anyone sees it or not. A real leader doesn't seek credit. He just does, because it needs doing."

Aranuke stumbled back into the party, fighting through the crowd, so he could just get the hell out of there. And then he literally ran into a woman half his age who nicely filled out a slinky black dress with a slit exposing her right thigh. She had an arresting presence, a confidence, he couldn't ignore.

"Whoa," she said. "Hang on there, cowboy. You got a full head of steam."

"What? Huh? No. It's nothing. It's…" The band's horn section was in full swing mode. "Who the hell are you?"

"Now that's the holiday spirit. We met last month. I'm Hicks. Gloria Hicks." She pointed her beer bottle like a pistol, then blew on the lip. "License to kill."

Aranuke was in no mood for flirting and not easily won over by women, even when they made it easy. And yet with just a single look from her he somehow knew that he was in good hands, even if he didn't quite know why. In a moment where he seemed least likely to pause, to slow down even a little, he just focused on the woman in front of him, and began to let his angst slide away. She was almost as tall as he was.

"Yeah," he said. "Fair enough. Okay. Maybe I'm a bit Grinchy."

"A bit? Pal. You'd need to kick a puppy in the balls before you mellow out to *Grinchy*."

He raised his hands. "Okay, okay, okay. You win. It's a party. I surrender."

"Hmm," she said. "That was easy. So…wanna make out?"

Aranuke chuckled, shook his head playfully. "Seriously. Who *are* you?"

"I'm Gloria H—"

"Yeah, you said." Almost despite himself, Aranuke smiled. He couldn't stop staring. "Okay, then, Hicks, Gloria Hicks, license to kill. I'll play. What's your story?"

"I'm just a chick at a party talking to some dude I met."

"Technically…to the boss dude."

The band erupted into Simon and Garfunkel's *A Hazy Shade of Winter*.

"Yeah, I know who you are. Everyone does."

"And you talked to me anyway? You're brave. Most people run the other way."

"Yeah, well...I'm not other people."

Aranuke let out another smile just then, one that, of all things, felt *good*.

"No," he said, and finally took full notice of just how sexy she was. "No, you're not."

Hicks polished off her beer, gave him a soft kiss on the lips, then led him by the hand.

"Um...Hicks, uh, Gloria...where are we going?"

Hicks looked over her shoulder, and then gave him a wink. "Don't worry about that, boss dude. It's gonna be a good night."

CHAPTER TWENTY-EIGHT

Aranuke was completely on edge. The *Crossline* selections were coming and he'd put himself in a position he couldn't resolve. Gloria Hicks was one of the best pilots Taurus Enterprises had, and a worthy selection. But she was also the woman he loved. At minimum, their relationship presented him with a conflict of interest. It was impossible for him to remain unbiased. He had only been in love once before, as a teenager, and at his age, didn't expect it to ever happen again.

Hicks was a pilot and he knew that from the beginning, and his brain told him he had no business deciding now, after eight months together, that he didn't want her taking risks. His heart said something else. They had also agreed to keep their relationship secret. They would otherwise have had to break up, which they considered unacceptable, or see Hicks disqualified from *Crossline* consideration—also unacceptable.

They fell back on his bed, breathing heavy, and craving pepperoni and pineapple pizza.

"You are so cute," Hicks said.

Still unaccustomed to silly bedroom talk, Aranuke was embarrassed. "Come on. Stop."

"You are. You're so cute. You're like a box of puppies. You're like a toddler speaking French." Hicks thought a moment. "You're like puppies barking French."

"*Barking* French?"

"You know. Le woof. Le arf. Le pant-pant. Le *arrooooooohhh*."

Aranuke chuckled. "You're such a dork."

Hicks shrugged, drank from a water bottle. "Dale. Can I ask you something?"

"Le ask, my little baguette. Le ask."

"Why does everybody think you're such a...well...you know...?"

"A ten-gallon a-hole?"

"Well...yeah. Kinda."

"Because I am. I make it that way."

"Not with me. I don't get it."

Aranuke ran the back of his hand along Hicks' exposed thigh. "I love you because I don't have to be that guy. With you, I don't think about policy or rules or Buddy Rheams or where I work and what the things we do mean to the people around us. I don't worry that the world might collapse around me."

Hicks took another swig of water. "Whoa. Dude. Intense much?"

"That's what I mean. I've had plenty of reasons to hate Taurus Enterprises. You work for any place long enough...you're going to get burned, deserved or not. But whether through fate, dumb luck—or just that the Universe loves to hate me—I learned something about Buddy Rheams I wish I didn't know."

"Don't get all evil corporate pissy. Tell me. You just licked my nipples raw. You owe me good gossip. If you won't take me to Vegas, you gotta tell me this. Spill."

"Trust me. You don't want to know."

"Ooh. Now you *have* to tell me!"

Aranuke shook his head.

"Oh, come on..."

"I said *no*. Leave it."

"But—"

"Gloria. Enough." He looked over at Hicks, laying there, naked in his bed. She could have had any number of men, but she chose him. Because she loved him. She didn't understand the pressures he faced, but how could she? He had operated independently for so long and with such purpose that he almost forgot how to trust anyone. But he wanted to trust her. He needed to. "You're a pilot in the Space Program for Taurus Enterprises. You get here on luck?"

"No."

"Me neither. When I first showed up here I had these big ideas of where I would fit in, and how my life would go. How *life* would go. And when it didn't happen that way, I figured I had two choices: sulk at the mercy of others, or make my own destiny. I saw what happened to my dad—thirty-six years and then his pension embezzled. Emphysema after that. Then he died. Then my mom died. Broken. Ruined." Aranuke shook his head. "Not happening to me. No way. I've had to do some things I didn't want to do. I'm not proud of it all. But I'm not entirely ashamed of it, either. I've been with Taurus for twenty-three years in various divisions all across the country. And once I saw Buddy Rheams Jr. for who he really is, I finally understood something I had rejected on principle. Sell the right lie…and the world is yours."

She whispered. "Dale. I'm sorry. I didn't know. If it's so bad, why don't you leave? You don't need him."

"Isn't it obvious?" Aranuke fell into a stare, envisioning a scene he'd played in his mind time and again. His father got flushed out of his corporate position because he hadn't culti-vated the strategic relationships and didn't have the leverage or resolve to overcome the greedy, scheming bastards in charge. Instead of retiring in style, his parents' lives were ruined. Ara-nuke refused to suffer the same fate. "Because when the time is right, I'm gonna jam this company right up his ass."

CHAPTER TWENTY-NINE

ARANUKE COULD SEE the strain on Hicks, intimidated by the tremendous skill of her fellow pilots and the responsibility that came with it. *Crossline* selections were just three months away and the scrutiny was growing ever more intense. Aranuke visited her in the pilots' quarters after a rough day of simulations.

"I can do this, right? I'm good enough?"

"Of course you are. Don't be ridiculous," Aranuke said, although her insecurity told him that she really *wasn't* prepared. And he would never confess to anyone that he manipulated the medical results of Benchetrit and Beetham, two pilots who probably would have been phased out anyway, but at the time had ranked ahead of Hicks. Aranuke helped her make it to the final four, but that was as much as he could do. He assumed that simply advancing that far would have been a confidence booster for sure, and a feat she could carry with her forever. But he underestimated just how much the temptation of victory would infect her.

"I admit," she said. "I never thought I'd get this far. But now that I have, I want this. Bad. Do you know what it's like to see what's right in front of you? To know you're so close, and yet you just can't reach?"

He did.

Hicks worked her hair roughly then slammed the brush down in her open locker. "I know I'm good. Better than most. But this is fucking *Crossline*, you know? Warp engines. It's incredible." She brushed a strand of hair from her face. "And now that I can almost touch it…it's all I think about."

Despite her ability, Hicks had often displayed a rigidity under pressure that limited her potential. Yet her approach became more fluid as she made her way deeper through the *Crossline* process. Aranuke had remained silent on the matter during internal selection committee discussions, so as not to be accused of favoritism.

"Just keep at it," he said, but what he really wanted was for Hicks to develop a physical ailment—a broken wrist, a dislocated knee—that would remove her from the competition. Rarely one to back down from confrontation, Aranuke prayed almost daily to be spared from making an excruciating decision. "The Old Man looks for resolve. He's a rebel himself. He admires people willing to break the rules. Don't get me wrong, he demands that you master your craft, but if you aren't willing to play in the margins now and then, he probably won't select you. It's just the way he is."

"Like Powell does?"

Yeah, Aranuke thought. *Exactly like Powell.*

"Don't worry about him. You can't control what he does. Just focus on you. A lot can happen between now and the selection date, and for now, it's anybody's game."

Hicks looked up at him with pleading eyes. "Really?"

Aranuke took gentle hold of her shoulders. "Really," he said.

"Yeah, you're right. Just pre-game jitters. We all get it."

"Look, babe. I can't promise who will or won't be chosen, but I can say this: don't hold back. Buddy Rheams has proven to be determined, focused,…and unpredictable. He rarely plays it safe. But however far you're willing to go, make sure it's worth it. Because he has a way of sucking you into his dreams. And if they don't come true, it can feel like a nightmare."

Even after hitting three buckets of golf balls, Hicks still wasn't calm. Aranuke could see her body tense up, stressing over it. The *Crossline* pilot selections were still down to the final four. He knew that getting involved with a pilot was a bad idea—especially this pilot—but for the first time in his adult life, when it came to a woman, he just couldn't help himself.

Hicks loosened her golf glove. "I'm sick to my stomach. No matter how hard I train, no matter how many simulations I nail...I'll never be as good as Powell. Ever. It's like he knows something we don't. I fucking hate that guy." She squeezed her eyes tight, shook her head. There was the *zjip* of metal drivers whacking golf balls down the range. "Listen to me. I'm a wreck. I never wanted anything so bad in my life, and I know it's not gonna happen. Don't lie to me, Dale. Powell's getting *Crossline*, and I know you know it."

"Nothing will be announced for two weeks," Aranuke said, careful to say *announced*, and not *decided*, because that way he wasn't technically lying, although Powell's selection had been confirmed. Buddy Rheams himself made the choice. "What I do know is that it's between you, Powell, DuBois, and Fox." What Aranuke left out was that while Powell ranked dead last as a team player, he was first across the board when it came to in-flight proficiency and creative problem solving, except by Aranuke, who wanted him banished from the solar system. Hicks ranked third overall. "You deserve to be the first *Crossline* pilot as much as any of them. Maybe more so. You're my choice far and away."

Before she had the chance to object, Hicks dropped her head and then let out a smile she just couldn't hold back. She put her golf-gloved hand on his chest. "Stop. I am not."

Aranuke took her face in his hand, and caressed her chin. He looked her in the eye. "You are," he said, and even if he didn't completely believe it, he absolutely meant it. "You are. And that's no bullshit." He kissed her, in that moment realizing that the pangs in his gut he'd had for weeks weren't guilt, but love. Almost in unison came the *zjip zjip zjip* of three different drivers.

"See?" Hicks said. "I told you that you were cute."

Aranuke raised a slight hand. "Don't start that again." He had to make a decision then and there. Tell Gloria Hicks—his lover—that as long as Powell held his course, she would never get the nod to pilot *Crossline*, or let her believe she was still under consideration. Hicks was a legitimate alternate, and until the

Taurus IX rocket blasted off the Earth, Powell could drop out or be disqualified for any number of reasons.

She needs her confidence. Let her fight for what she wants.

And yet Aranuke could hear his father's disapproval, that if he cared about Hicks as much as he claimed—if he loved her— then he should be honest, and let her pride take whatever fall it needed. But he just couldn't do it, as much as he knew he should. If she was going to get bad news, he didn't want to be the one to give it.

"Well, you *are* cute," Hicks said, "whether you admit it or not."

Aranuke tipped back against a golf cart. *Admit that you're lying. Just tell her the truth.*

About this, at least, he never did.

Aranuke had the dream again. In a speedboat, his heart pounding; a man with a flat, featureless face at the wheel. In the middle of a sun shower; a rainbow cutting through it. And his father, pale, gaunt, and dying of emphysema, water skiing behind the speedboat, laughing in a way that said *oh yes oh yes I see my death so bring it on, bitches! Wooo yeah!* In the dream, Aranuke felt so puny and powerless—and yet somehow responsible for all their fates—that when the speedboat's front end literally lifted off the water and flew off to the side, about to crash into the boardwalk, he jolted up from the covers. His eyes opened just before impact.

Only when he woke, the dread remained. He turned on the light. There was a note taped to the bedroom TV: *Extra simulator training. Gotta rock it!*

Underneath it was a tilted heart drawn in red lipstick, with her name—*Gloria*—written in the middle.

Still feeling sick and puny and powerless—and responsible for all their fates—Aranuke went to *Ralph's Diner* and ordered what he always ordered when he couldn't sleep and needed a sense of control: two fried eggs sunny-side-up, rye toast with butter, home fries, side of extra crispy bacon, black coffee. Milk, no creamer.

When the food hit the table Aranuke let out a slight, uneasy chuckle. He was forty-nine, had worked in the Space Division for five of those years, and never before did he think that his eggs looked like, of all things, flying saucers. From outer space. The arc of the yellow yolks on top of the flat, white base. Two flying saucers. Two. Flying. Saucers.

He hooked his fingers through the handle of the porcelain mug. And just as the hot coffee fell down his throat he felt his KATI vibrate. His heart leapt; his stomach tightened. He didn't need to read the text message because in his gut, he already knew. But when he saw the actual words typed out across the screen, he dropped the mug. It didn't break. It just rattled on the floor with a high-pitched *clankety-clank-clank-clank*. Each *clank* pinged his soul, until finally the mug swirled and rolled under the bench. Coffee spilled out on the floor.

There was an accident in the flight simulator, off hours. Gloria Hicks uploaded the wrong program by mistake—a panic sequence triggered by enemy attack—and set the difficulty level to maximum stress, initiating a systems overload. With no one on site to shut it down, the fight simulator—which unbeknownst to Hicks was scheduled for maintenance—short-circuited, and caught fire, causing an explosion. The doctors said she died almost instantly. *Almost.* Aranuke could never let go of that image, of her laying there, in the wreckage, alone, her life slipping away, all because she chased a dream she had little chance of catching as long as Marcus Powell was in the picture.

CHAPTER THIRTY

THE HANGAR WAS open with just a month before the *Crossline* launch. With Grade Four security clearance, Cynthia Chang made her way there whenever she could. It was important for her to make the connection, to have physical contact with the machinery she would help guide into space. The engineers were at work, ratcheting and drilling, screwing and unscrewing. Sparks. Hoses. Wires.

Marcus Powell was going to sit inside *that* ship. And then *that* ship would be hoisted into a giant rocket. And that rocket would blast into space. And through it all, it would be *her* voice in *his* ear. She climbed the ladder, leaned over the cockpit. Before anyone could see, she placed her sunglasses on the dashboard. Powell dared her to do it. Said she didn't have the guts, which of course, they both knew she did.

And when my son is born, Chang thought, *he'll know for all his days that his mother was a part of history. Part of something incredible. And he'll grow up a believer.*

Chang looked the ship over, feeling diminutive in comparison, and yet somehow like she tamed a wild stallion. She ran a hand along *Crossline's* Tritanium wing. The hairs on the back of her neck stood up. And then, with the same hand, she rubbed her belly.

My son will grow up in a world where space travel is possible. My son will look at his mother and know she helped change the course of human history. His mother. Me.

Chang got extremely tired all of a sudden. It happened now and again. The pregnancy.

I just don't want him to know it all.

She was about to climb inside the cockpit. It was a thrill. Daryl, the security chief, said it would be okay. Only morning sickness had her on the verge of upchucking what she assumed would be the remainder of her spleen and maybe a section of her pancreas, and the last thing she needed was to vomit inside the most famous craft in the world, especially with Dale Aranuke on the warpath.

Startled, Chang took a step back as she emerged from the ladies' room. Texting with age-defying dexterity, Buddy Rheams Jr. was leaning against the wall, between a water fountain and a glassed-in fire extinguisher. He spoke without looking up. "How ya doing, Chang?"

Constipated, nauseous, and stinking of the second-trimester troika of mint Listerine, arm pit sweat, and pregnancy puke, Chang wiped her brow. "Peachy, sir. You?"

"Just trying not to ruin the world. You know...Tuesday."

Rather than try to subtly fix the front tail of her blouse, Chang yanked it out from her waistline and re-tucked the corners. No sense trying to hide what a total mess she was. "Tell me about it."

The Old Man looked up from his KATI. "Jesus, Chang. You're a wreck. The baby?"

"I think I'm carrying a Tasmanian devil. But that's not it."

The Old Man offered an odd smile. "Let me guess. Dale?"

Chang could handle the pressure that came from being a woman, a lesbian, pregnant, and a Tech One on the main console in Tower Command for the Crossline project, one that would bankrupt the firm—and possibly send the world into a global depression—if it failed. And she could deal with half the Tower Command staff thinking she was a skanked-out, double-dyking ménage o' slut, which was only half right. But the Old Man made her nervous, and not because he was a larger-than-life icon who had grown increasingly reclusive in the last several years and seemed more unknowable than ever. It was that she always sensed he was far more, or perhaps far less, than his image projected, and that if the world ever found out who he really was, life as they knew it would disintegrate beneath their feet. And now he knew her by name, and wanted to chat. About her boss. Always a bad move. But then she figured, *fuck it.*

"Something like that, sir. Pretty much."

Buddy Rheams was giving Chang his full attention now. Despite the years, his voice still held its power. "Listen, Chang. Dale can be rough, I know, but he's vital to what we do here. I owe him a lot. And he's had a rough patch, which…," he turned away slightly, "…is mostly my fault."

There was a sudden shift. With those two words—*my fault*—Buddy Rheams dropped his head, revealing a man Chang never thought to consider. Sure, they *called* him the Old Man, but he was an *actual* old man—childless, unmarried, with brittle bones, slumped shoulders, white, thinning hair, and liver spots on his hands and face. And even though he still stood over six feet tall and carried himself like someone half his age, he had almost a century of life behind him, carrying the weight of mankind's past, present, and future. Just a fraction of his responsibilities would have sent her to the loony bin in a pink bunny suit.

Chang searched those eyes, those old, old eyes, and when she finally found them peeking up at her, cautious and distant, reaching out for a sign of forgiveness, she didn't see this modern-day emperor whose legend had surpassed the man. Instead there was a stranger hiding behind an old man shell. Chang wanted to comfort him, to reach beyond that wrinkled facade he wore and find the real Harlan Rheams Jr., who seemed to have long since forgotten how he got there in the first place.

"Go easy on him, Chang. It's hard to lose someone. Ambition's a tricky beast. It can drive you to win…or drive you mad. Miss by just a little and you're down the rabbit hole—lonely, lost, and disillusioned—with no clear, easy, or obvious way out. Grief can really undermine you. It can get anyone, anytime. No one's immune."

Of course, she knew what he meant. At least she thought she

did. "Hicks, sir? She was a friend of mine."

"I guess you heard about them."

"Everyone knows. It was impossible not to. Especially after Gloria, well...you know. Dale shut down after that."

Buddy nodded. "Sometimes we just get so attached to a person, a place...even an idea...that we construct our world view around it. It shapes the way we see ourselves, the way we see everyone. And if that...person, place, idea...suddenly goes away—especially if it's taken—that through-line is shattered." Buddy offered a reassuring look. "You can get over it...in time. But when you put yourself back together, you're never quite the same. If you're open to it, you might find a way to be a better person. A more peaceful person, anyway. If you're not...life's a bit tougher to swallow."

CHAPTER THIRTY-ONE

THE OLD MAN'S KATI vibrated twice. He stared at the tiny screen, let out a bemused sigh, then returned the text. Back to business, the Old Man pointed. "But don't take any crap from him. Got that? I need you doing what you do best. He gets all alpha cock knocker on you, you keep kicking his ass." He raised a hand to clarify. "Metaphorically speaking."

Chang raised her hand in kind, feeling like after years in obscurity she might finally be in a corporate position that wasn't quite so perilous. "Will do, sir. Metaphorically speaking."

Buddy Rheams returned another text, and then took a sip from the water fountain. As he leaned over, Chang noticed that his neck looked surprisingly smooth—youthful. *Must have had work done.*

"While we're being all BFF here," he said, and then wiped a droplet from his mouth, "I…heard a rumor about why you were promoted to Tech One."

Of all the conversations that could have possibly arisen between them, Chang couldn't think of a more embarrassing alternative. And yet there they were. "Because you popped a little blue pill, plowed me reverse cowgirl, and now I'm your baby momma?"

The Old Man's mouth hung open, then composed himself. "Huh. You heard that?"

All Chang had discussed about her pregnancy was that she planned to raise the baby with her girlfriend, and was otherwise keeping the details confidential. Even the father didn't know.

"No offense, sir. But it's old news. I don't know if you remember, but a few months back you came by the simulator room to observe training. You stepped out into the hallway to take a call, and I ran into the bathroom, to, well…puke. The baby. You know. The morning sickness. It's relentless…. On my way back, you were hunched over, searching for your contact lens. I helped you look."

"That was you? Sorry. Didn't notice. A lot on my mind."

"Me too, sir." Chang rubbed her belly. The baby kicked just then. "When I leaned over to find your lens, well, I guess someone saw, and thought it didn't look too, you know…kosher. Me in a skirt, bent over in front of you." What Chang left out was that over the years she had been sorta, kinda…stalking him…in a non-creepy way, figuring that if she was in his sight line often enough, he'd remember her when it came time for promotions.

Buddy raised an eyebrow. "You and I both know that's not it. You're on my team because people like Dale are often needed to get the toughest jobs done, and people like you—smart, competent, can roll with the punches—are needed to deal with people like *him*. If life has taught me anything, Chang, it's that the Universe has a funny way of balancing itself out."

Feeling a bizarre mixture of empowered gossip slut and badass technician, Chang had another question. "Since we're sharing, sir. I've been here seven years and you've barely spoken to me. I mean, I know you're the CEO and all, but…do I smell?" Since the pregnancy, her b.o. had gotten a bit ripe. She got a whiff of herself just then. *Yikes.* "I mean…other than now?"

"Chang. More than three thousand people work in this building alone. I just don't have time for everyone."

I figured that…

"Plus, you're easy on the eyes and carrying my bastard love child." He tilted his head. "I figured I should keep my distance."

…But I didn't see that coming.

"Are you…flirting with me, sir?"

"Chang. I'm ninety. I'm a bit old for you, no?"

She offered a nod. "Well, if it's any consolation…you seem much younger."

"I get that a lot. My doctors tell me ninety is the new

eighty-nine. Old enough, but not so old that I don't notice. I ain't dead yet."

"Don't sell yourself short, sir. I bet the nursing home grannies think you're a stud muffin. Those ankle-length nighties are hot."

"Funny, Chang. Funny. You know what's also funny? You cleaning out your desk if you don't get back to work."

Okay. Play time's over.

But she had to know. "Just one more thing, sir.... Do you really think I'm a Tech One?"

The Old Man took a step toward her, and as he stood closer to her than he ever had, she couldn't miss his vitality. He was feared and respected for a reason. "Think about where you are, Chang. Nobody's in that room that doesn't deserve to be. You are where you are because I need you there. Got it?"

The preggers combination of full-body chill and wicked hot flash hit Chang hard. Rank sweat came roaring through her pores. "Yes, sir. Loud and clear."

"Good. Now go clean up. You actually do smell pretty bad."

CHAPTER THIRTY-TWO

CHANDRA POWELL HAD already taken the tour of the Taurus Enterprises Cultural Center, Buddy Rheams' $17.4 billion art deco masterpiece. But with Marcus going up into space in just a few weeks, she wanted Jesse to experience the interactive session herself, even if she wouldn't totally understand it.

Marcus had Jesse on his shoulders, dangling upside down. "What do you think, there, Jess? You ready to come in for a landing? It's tour time."

Jesse giggled. "Tour-tour-tour. Down, Daddy, down."

In front of the marble complex was tree-lined green space, with flowers, benches, and sculptures. On each side of the grass were freshwater ponds stocked with angelfish, gouramis, and tinfoil barbs. A translucent canopy shielded the park. The forecast called for temperatures just above one hundred five degrees.

The Powells picked up their tickets at the service counter—the lines moved swiftly given the crowds—and walked down a long, white corridor leading to the Cultural Center.

Nancy Childress and Marla Mayhew, respectively the mothers of Douglas and Arlene—two fifth-graders Chandra knew from the school where she taught—were off to the side. They were in the crowd, not exactly whispering.

"There's that weirdo from school," Nancy said. "She's always pushing that Indian Earth gobbledygook on our kids. Why can't she go to a regular church?…I wonder if her coyote spirit is eating from the garbage cans."

Marla snickered. "She's probably howling at the moon right now."

Chandra debated whether she should just let the comments go, especially as she was with her family. In public. Her decision was predictable. *Nah.* "Actually," she said, and with a firm smile, turned to face the gossiping wenches. "I prefer Crazy Spirit Woman. Weirdo is just so…I don't know…," she bopped her head back and forth as if listening to music, "like a bag lady, who I have nothing against, by the way. Crazy Spirit Woman is more…eccentric. Life-affirming. So if you're thinking about what to call me, go with Crazy Spirit Woman. You know. For future reference."

Standing side by side, Nancy and Marla were speechless.

Chandra continued. "It's a funny thing. My mother taught me to think of other people. That we are all children of the land the gods blessed us with, that we should share it with a sense of balance and harmony, and that we should respect each other's point of view, especially when we disagree." Chandra put her open hand against the side of her mouth, in mock hide. "Between you and me," she said, almost whispering, "it's kind of a bad habit. And you know how tough it can be to break a habit. You start thinking a certain way, and next thing you know, that's the person you've become. In my case, it's always trying to be considerate of others and the world we live in." She shrugged. "Oh, well. My bad. We all have our crosses to bear. Enjoy the tour, girls. My daughter loves this part." Chandra left the stunned pair to their own devices.

"See," Nancy said after the Powells moved up a bit. "Weird-ohhhhh." Marla nodded in agreement.

Marcus had a steady hand in flight, but Chandra knew that social awkwardness made him uncomfortable.

"Was that really necessary?"

"Well…" Chandra closed her eyes, smiled, and then hugged herself like she just slipped on her favorite sweater on a cool morning. "I wouldn't say it was necessary, but it sure was tasty. Yum-yum-yum."

"I thought your mother taught you to overlook the foolishness of others, and…what did she say?…Keep a silent tongue and the gods will set them straight?"

"She did. But she also said that if a bunch of twitty skank-wads gossip about me within earshot, the gods call for me to stick my moccasin up their bungholes."

"Candy! Not in front of the kid. Besides, your mom did not say to stick your moccasin up their...well, you know..."

"Bungholes?"

"Yeah. That. She never said that. When did she say that?"

Chandra shook her hand in the *so-so* motion. "It's a loose interpretation of an old Indian prayer, but that's the gist of it."

Marcus sighed, shook his head. "And people say I'm a cowboy."

"Don't worry, honey." Chandra flashed her big, round eyes. "You're all bronco to me."

Jesse tugged on his shirt. "Daddy? Is Mommy going to stick her moccasin up those ladies' bungholes?"

Marcus sighed again. "No. She's not. Your mother's... being silly."

"Bungholes." Jesse giggled. "Mommy *is* silly. Bung-*holes*! Bung-*holes*! Bung-*holes*!"

Jesse's chant drew a chorus of stares and whispers.

Born on a late spring night, during a full moon, Chandra had rolled on her stomach, showing her naked, golden-brown butt, and giggled. Her father joked that she already had his sense of humor. "Hemachandra," her mother said in the delivery room, although it was typically a boy's name. "Golden moon."

Chandra's attitude carried over three decades later. "Well," she said as the tour was about to commence. "My work here is done."

CHAPTER THIRTY-THREE

THE FOLLOWING TUESDAY Chandra's fifth-grade students spilled into the hallway. Barney Cahill lumbered by. A gentle giant with a beer belly, Barney had been a friend to Chandra and a stand-up principal, although he had once confessed that he wanted to quit the teaching racket and open a toddler's clothing store in Austin.

"Oh, hi Barney. Swizzle stick? I confiscated it from Frozeman."

"Uh...sure. Thanks." Barney took the candy. "Listen, Chan. Um...just as a reminder, the bake sale is Thursday. If you can stay after school for an hour, that would be supa dupa."

Chandra threw Barney a goofy wink. "Ten-four, good buddy."

Barney smiled uneasily. "Yeah," he said. "Ten-four. Ten-four." He drummed the swizzle stick in his hand, looked down at his shoelaces, then back up at Chandra. "Um...oh yeah, so, about your, you know, your lesson plan on comparative cultures. It's uh...great, really. Quality stuff." Barney chomped on the sickly sweet candy. "It's just that, well...I kinda need you to...you know...," he shuffled his feet, and then shrugged, "...stop."

Chandra was half expecting this. "Uh...huh. And why's that, exactly?"

The Taurus Elementary Charter School, or TECS, was considered an across-the-board success. In just its fifth year, test scores were among the highest in the state, discipline problems were minimal, and since Chandra joined the faculty, the school was drawing increasing praise for its cultural awareness program. But once TECS became the administration's darling despite initial protests of the school's loose, liberal, corrupting practices, parents from across the county wanted their children transferred there, and pronto. With the increased attention and demands came the influx of voices breathing in Barney's ear. As fond as Chandra was of Barney for being the big lovable lunk that he was, she knew that sooner or later he would bend to the will of the people, because that's what principals do.

"It's just a little, uh…you know…outside the lines of the curriculum and—"

"It's about ethics, Barney. Being honest and truthful? Living up to your responsibilities? Participating in the community for the greater good? It's modeled after the Founding Fathers. But that's only if you care about those things."

"Oh, no, hey-hey-hey. Whoa-ho. Like I said. Quality stuff, absolutely. Ethics all the way. Can't get enough ethics. Goooo ethics." He raised a fist in meek cheer. "Ethics."

Chandra raised an eyebrow. "But you want me to stop teaching it."

Barney squinted before answering. "Yeah," he said. "Could ya?"

Barney tended to buckle against confrontation—especially when he knew he was wrong. Chandra straightened her back. "Barney, are you instructing me to cancel a student lesson on responsibility and ethics? That doesn't sound quite right."

"Oh, no-no-no. No-no. No. Uh-uh. Don't misunderstand. Of course we want our faculty to pass along only the most honorable messages to our students. It's just that—"

"You don't want *me* to do it."

Barney looked away. Marla Mayhew, Arlene's anorexic, bulging-eyed mother, was down the hall, chatting conspiratorially with Douglas Find, the Assistant Principal and second cousin to Assemblyman Goldie Jenkins.

"Chandra. Come on. Of course not. It's just that…you know… if you could just maybe…tone down the Indian fairy tales—just a smidge—so there's more…balance. Yeah, that's it. More balance. I think we'd be right as rain."

Chandra was not convinced. "What kind of smidge?"

Barney squinted, instinctively protecting his crotch. "Completely?"

"Is Marla Mayhew spewing her bile again? If anyone could use a little knowledge, it'd be that hag. She'd back over Gandhi if she knew how to work the stick shift. It's amazing her kid is so sweet."

Sneakers chirped against the hallway floor. Student chatter echoed. And then her gentle giant of a principal stepped forward, suddenly not so gentle. Chandra never felt even the least bit intimidated by Barney. Until now.

"I've had your back since day one," he said, his voice deeper and more forceful, "and I'll never get into how much I've fought for you since you got here. You're a great teacher, Chandra. Great. If it was up to me, you could teach whatever you wanted and I'd flush those jackals for good. But I can't do it anymore."

"What? You don't have to—"

"At the beginning, when everybody said we'd crash and burn, we could pretty much do what we wanted. But now they're watching, so we have to pull it in. There's no reason for anyone, not even me, to put up with the grief. The superintendent knows me by name. Not good. As much as it makes me want to puke, these people own me. I got four kids. That's four sets of karate lessons, four sets of art classes, four college tuitions. Money in, money out. I'm just the middle man. I can't fight these people, and I'm too old, broke, and tired to start over. If anyone's outta here, it's you."

Chandra felt the string of her life unspool. The carefully crafted knot was coming undone. "I'm not fighting you, Barney. We're doing great here. Why are they after you?"

"Because you go out of your way to remind them—through what *you* teach *their* kids—that you, Chandra Powell, daughter of Irving and Feather Finkelbaum, are the superior, open-minded cornerstone of society, and they're the bigoted morons who need to be bitch-slapped out of their ignorance."

"They are!"

"I know! But so what? I've given you plenty of room until now, but it's your job to teach the curriculum we agreed upon.

Not what *you* decide. Make no mistake. Buddy Rheams might be the most progressive CEO we've ever seen, but that doesn't mean he's won people over. Some folks love what he does. Others? Not so much. He runs this city, but he's pushed us way too far, way too fast. You're just like him, only…you have no power. You can't force people to accept the way you think, Chandra. So they nod and smile at him, but underneath they hate him. And they hate you, too. And it's not because you're liberal, eccentric, or wrong. I happen to agree with most of your points. You know I do. But they don't want their morality preached to them."

"Except in church."

"Exactly. They…Hey! Don't get snarky. If you want to teach your daddy's East Coast values, then you should teach on the East Coast. You're in Texas, Chandra. Texas. I may be more socially flexible than most of the flock, but I live in this world. We're not backwoods hicks, but we're not ready to have you wrapping every lesson into the Indian spirit world. I know you've been ramping that up since your mom died last year. I know how much she meant to you and the influence she had. But these are our kids, Chan, and parents don't have a sense of humor about them. You should know that."

Chandra raised a satisfied eyebrow. "My kid's a riot."

Barney took and then exhaled an angry, frustrated sigh. "Make all the jokes you want. But unless you get on board, right here, right now—in this room—this will not end well. Because even if you get tenure, which at this point is remote, my guess is that you don't last another year. If the *Crossline* flight goes well and your husband's still a star by then, the spotlight will own you. And we all know how well you respond to public pressure. But if his flight goes south for any reason, you'll have no cover, and it'll get rough for you. Really. Really. Rough. So either you change—*immediately*—or you're done."

The starting bell for the next class rang out. Chandra long expected that she would get a talking to, but this had her legitimately rattled.

A daughter of two worlds, Chandra was part of both yet the whole of neither. It wasn't that her parents intentionally pulled her in either direction at the expense of the other, but they were both confused rebels themselves, taught to be fiercely independent and then chastised for it.

On his way out of the classroom, Barney turned back. He closed his eyes, sighed. His shoulders slumped. "Just…lay off the fairy tales…okay?"

Chandra corrected him. "Folklore. They're not fairy tales."

"Just make it work, will ya?…For me?" Barney smiled. It was hopeful.

Returning the smile, Chandra nodded.

"Good. You've got a science lesson in two minutes. What's it on?"

Chandra squinted at the Sun. She didn't want to give him any more grief, but as much as she loved Barney, she couldn't let the corporate jackals—and their pea-brained groupies—get the last word. She just couldn't.

"The Four Sacred Colors of the American Indian Medicine Wheel."

CHAPTER THIRTY-FOUR

In Desperate need of a day off, Chandra hoped to once and for all make peace with the *Crossline* flight, which was only four days off. To the side of their house, she sat cross-legged on the swept dirt floor of her sweat lodge.

The small, domed hut was made of slender withes of willow, lashed together with buffalo hide. In the center of the sweat lodge was a sacred fire pit for the sacred stones, the eternal light of the world. The entrance to the sweat lodge faced the East, where each new day began, with the rising of Father Sun—the source of life and power, dawn of wisdom. Entering the sweat lodge was to seek a new day of spiritual beginning.

Outside the sweat lodge was an altar barrier, beyond which permission was required. To warn of the danger, a buffalo skull faced visitors atop a post. At the base was raised earth. On it were a hawk's feather, four candles (black, red, white, and yellow, one for each of the Four Directions), and a pipe rack for what the Sioux language calls the *Chanupa*, the sacred peace pipe.

Three paces beyond the altar barrier, Chandra had attempted to awaken the spirits in the sacred stones, by heating them in an outdoor fire, until they were red hot.

With a small pitchfork, she scooped the stones, one at a time, entered the sweat lodge, and laid them out in the pit—one each to the West, North, East, and South, and then, into the center. Chandra then sat before the pit, ladled from a bucket, and poured water onto each of the hot stones.

As steam rose off the rocks, penetrating her skin, she filled the Chanupa with her sacred tobacco (weed she grew herself a half mile from the house), lit the peace pipe, and inhaled. The smoke was warm in her lungs. Chandra held it, then closed her eyes. She exhaled slowly, inhaled again. Exhaled. Eyes closed, the tingling—like a million tiny legs grazing every nerve—crept down her spine, to her fingers and toes. And finally, once the forces co-mingled, the sweat came, and she smiled. Chandra smiled.

As her mother taught, in the clear of her mind, Chandra searched for the Four Balances, the Four Directions within each man and woman, the Four Levels of being and unfolding—they were the Four Colors she had mentioned to Barney: the Black West, where the Sun sets and the Creator may be asked for a spirit guide; the White North, for courage, strength, and endurance; the Red Road of the East, for daybreak and the rising Sun of wisdom; and the Yellow South, for spiritual growth and healing.

Chandra waited for the call of nature to reach out from the great beyond and connect with her, to find the answers, which were there for her to know. Mother Earth would come, if only Chandra would allow it. After many moments, anticipating, yearning, she felt adrift in the vast Universe. Still, she felt alone. She opened her eyes then. Marcus was right outside, to join her. Not to smoke, but to listen. Chandra wasn't quite sure what she would say, but in her deepest heart it all came pouring out.

My god, don't go. Don't go don't go don't go. I try to believe that you're untouchable, that the gods will look after you, that your charm and ability render you impervious to danger. But you're flying a machine, crafted by men, and just one loose wire, one miscalculation, and you could die, physically literally die in space a million miles from home, from us. From me and Jesse. And then we'll have to spend the rest of our days with broken hearts missing you and blaming ourselves for letting you go...

But I promised myself I would never be that woman. I promised myself that if I married the man, then I was marrying the pilot. You can't turn it off. It's who you are. And I choose you. I choose you.

But Chandra couldn't bring herself to speak the words aloud because once she said them she'd never be able to take them back. And she just couldn't bear the thought of Marcus carrying her doubts with him all the way into space. The Indian warrior had always been strong in her, but the Jewish guilt? Oy gevalt.

She chuckled when it occurred to her, that when Marcus was in flight, lost in his own world, he could get word that nine-legged aardvarks were falling from the sky and he would probably shrug, do a few loop-de-loops, and *then* try to find out what the heck was going on down there. Flight came first.

Concealing her doubts for the final four days before the *Crossline* flight would take more strength than she believed she had. So Chandra sat cross-legged in the sweat lodge. It filled with steam and heat and the call of the Four Directions, and her frustration that the answers remained elusive. Her whole life Chandra tried to be one with Mother Earth. Her whole life she failed. And with her needing that connection now more than ever, Marcus was right outside.

Her husband rarely entered the sweat lodge. It was her private sanctuary, a place to pray and feel connected to her culture, to her mother, but Chandra knew that Marcus accepted her smoke habit, even if he wasn't thrilled about it.

Chandra sat cross-legged on the ground. Marcus sat opposite her. She unrolled a leather pouch. Laid out before them was a small bowl made of red clay, and a long, hollowed-out stem. She assembled the pipe, filled the bowl with marijuana, and then puffed away. She offered him the pipe, knowing he would refuse. She released the smoke.

Marcus would never admit to being scared of flight, but there was a worry in him she'd never sensed before. But instead of talking about it, he acted out toward the one person most likely to treat him with kindness and understanding.

"You really want Jesse to become a pothead?"

Chandra's eyes glazed over. "No. But I don't want her thinking this is wrong."

"It's illegal."

"It's sacred."

"Oh, God. Here we go."

And as Chandra had done with him before, she recited the tale of the sacred pipe and the great warrior Arrow Woman who changed the Indian culture forever.

CHAPTER THIRTY-FIVE

"ARROW WOMAN WENT on a journey deep into the woods, until by accident or divine providence, she stumbled upon Atagahi."

Powell interjected. "The sacred lake of the animals."

Chandra offered him a surprised look.

"What?" he said. "...I listen."

Impressed, Chandra continued:

*After the long journey, Arrow Woman fell into a deep sleep. When she awoke, before her, high above the water, was **Uktena**. The great and powerful serpent had horns on its head and a blazing, arrow-shaped crest on its forehead. Arrow Woman jumped up and grabbed her spear. But Uktena just smiled. "I mean you no harm," he said.*

Uktena dipped his head into the sacred lake, and then came up with a crooked stick and a leather pouch in his mouth. He laid them out. "This is the sacred pipe of the Creator," he said, telling Arrow Woman to pick up the pipe. "The bowl is of the same red clay of Womankind, from the Earth.

"Just as woman bears children and brings life, the bowl bears the sacred tobacco and brings smoke. Rigid and strong, the stem is Mankind, from the plant kingdom, and like a man it supports the bowl, just as man supports his family."

It was then that Uktena showed Arrow Woman how to join the bowl and stem, place the sacred tobacco in the pipe, and light it with an ember. "The smoke is the breath of the Creator," he said. "When you draw the smoke into your body, you will be cleansed and made whole. And when the smoke leaves you, it rises to the Creator, bringing with it your prayers, your dreams, your hopes, and your desires—the truth in your soul."

As Chandra uttered those words—*the truth in your soul*—her

gut tightened, even though her calmer self urged her to exhale, to release the tension welling up inside. She knew Marcus loved her, considered her a true and genuine partner, but no matter how articulate she might be in any single moment, he resisted her deepest yearnings. Try as she might, she had never been able to absorb him so thoroughly and completely as to experience his thoughts, his feelings, his perceptions…his very essence…precisely, exactly—to the very last micro-detail—the way he experienced them himself. She couldn't, in effect, slip into his skin and occupy his emotional, psychological, and spiritual space.

Chandra had never reached this level of spiritual intimacy with anyone, not even herself. But Feather had the capacity. Jesse, too. Whether it was her head or heart, Chandra didn't know, but she considered her inability to connect on this plane her deepest failing. A weakness of faith.

Staring into her husband's eyes as he sat before her, she worried that he would always and forever truly be alone with himself in the Universe. It started for him as a child, after his brother died and then his father. He learned to become his own strength and refuge. And though he never acknowledged it, Chandra sensed in Marcus that his brother Petey had never really left him, that his spirit lingered, as they do. That perhaps Petey's essence, in a way, had fused with his own.

Jesse felt that presence, calling his name again and again. *Meaty-Meaty-Meaty*, she would say, mispronouncing it. *Meaty-Meaty-Meaty.*

Chandra let herself be with Marcus as much as she knew how. Her love for him was rich and layered. And yet she questioned whether it would ever be enough, knowing that his complete self was his and his alone. Or maybe she was just projecting her fears onto him—that Marcus would never know her as deeply and intimately as she desired. That the fabric of her purest self would float like a mist, but never truly seep into the hearts of those she loved most.

To cleanse her loneliness, Chandra finally closed and opened her eyes, to wash away her feeling so distant from Marcus right then, even though he was just inches away.

"The pipe is sacred, honey. The smoke binds me to you, and then together brings us to the Creator. And my dreams are that when you're so far away from us…he keeps you safe."

Chandra scoured his eyes in hopes that he would reveal his most inner self. She saw his fingers inch forward, as if to take her hand in his.

He hears me, she thought. *He finally hears me.*

Breaking the quiet, Marcus pulled a pebble from the dirt, and then looked away before saying something incredibly stupid. "You just like getting baked."

Though it pained her heart, that she had failed to reach him yet again, Chandra remained steadfast. Her eyes were slits. She smiled. "You betch'er cute butt. But it's an ancient tale my mother told me many, many times. It brings me comfort. Just because I don't judge the choices you make, doesn't mean I don't worry."

Chandra could see his mind at work, that he had something else to say.

I'm here, honey. It's okay. You can say it. I can't imagine how you must feel, but just know that I love you.

There was a long and meaningful silence. She held the moment as long as she could. And though the words never came, Chandra leaned over and kissed her husband on the mouth. She let her lips linger on his. She packed up her roll.

And then, finally, she acknowledged that the moment, as they do, had passed. "You don't have to believe in the magic pipe," she said, "but it wouldn't kill you to believe in something."

CHAPTER THIRTY-SIX

On the other side of town, Jesse's first-grade class dispersed for recess. But while the other five-year-olds claimed space in the sandbox, threw foam balls awkwardly, and took their places on swings and slides, Jesse sat, examining the giant DNA helix painted on the blacktop. With a yellow outline, the helix was divided into boxes. In each was a letter of the alphabet, in white paint. A, then B, then C, and so on. Each box was shaded. Red, blue, aquamarine. Red, blue, aquamarine. Nearby was a hopscotch board with a matching color sequence.

Daddy, Jesse thought. *He's going far away.*

And the idea of her Daddy blasting off into great big outer space made her sad, because they wouldn't be together for a while. But when Daddy got there, to the other place, with the red mountains and the caves, he would have a new friend. A nice friend. Mostly a nice friend. His name was Chill. He could talk to Meaty when no one else could.

With the DNA helix laid out before her, Jesse tapped each letter of Chill's name. His real name, before he changed it. Before his family went dead when the bombs fell. Malcolm Quincy Reneau. M, then Q, then R. She did this once, twice, then again.

"Watcha doin', Jesse?"

Teddy was always asking her that, whether she wanted him to or not. Mostly not. And with just four days before her Daddy had to leave, Jesse didn't want interruptions. It was time to focus. But she knew Teddy would keep on asking until she said something.

"Spelling Daddy's fend."

Teddy blinked many times. "What kinda fend?"

Unfortunately, Jesse also knew that answers to Teddy's questions invited more questions. She thought for a moment, deciding whether or not to respond. "He says fings. Wots of fings."

Again, Teddy blinked. "What kinda fings?"

Jesse sighed. "*Fings* fings. Speshew fings." She shook her head. "Oh, for the wuv of Anne Mawet. You ask too many questions."

Teddy ran off, crying.

Jesse shrugged. Daddy was going far away. To be with the new people, like the lady with the red hair. He was going to help find the girl who got lost, looking for her brother. But Daddy knew the way there—over the canyons, beyond the great lake. When he closed his eyes he could fly like a bird, and see the place, in the big city, in the building. It was scary, though. There was a bad man there. He was mean. Daddy had to meet him. They had a fight. She just couldn't see how it ended because it was so far away and there was so much noise and fire. Even when she closed her eyes and searched for Grandma Feather.

So Jesse looked again at the letters, to figure it out.

She searched for the only man who could help her Daddy. Searched for Chill.

Then she tapped the letters.

M, then Q, then R.

INTERLUDE

MY GOD!

The thrust of *Taurus IX*'s mighty boosters nearly yanked Powell out of his skin and...

Engine No. 1—*Blam!* Engine No. 2—*Blam!* And ...

What's that? Up ahead? Is that a ripple in space? A gateway? It's blue and shimmering and bright. I don't know where I'm going or what I'm doing, but...

*Floating. Yes. That's it. I'm floating. In the sky? In the sea? Ohh...I see. I'm floating. **I'm floating.** I understand now. I get it. I know where I am. I must be dea...*

Powell walked through the gorge back home, but was he really walking? He was moving for sure—the grass *whooshed* beneath his feet—but he couldn't feel his legs. He was definitely thinking about walking. His brain was telling his body that he should...No. He wasn't *thinking* about walking, he was *feeling* it. He was... floating? Drifting...? Gliding...?

Whoosh. Jesse was just a blur. Dashed behind a tree. "Meaty, Daddy, Meaty." The sing-song for her Uncle Petey lingered like fumes.

Whoosh. In a blur, she dashed behind another tree. "Meaty-Meaty-Meaty..."

Whoosh. And then another. "Meaty-Meaty-Meaty..."

Powell still couldn't quite make her out, just a whir, but he heard her giggle, Jesse's silly laughter, as if echoing from a radio tower. He turned to find her—*whoosh.*

Wait! I don't...Oh! There she is! She's right over there. She's ducking behind...

Their house was right there, with a porch. Only their house didn't have a porch. Or did it? Powell didn't remember a porch, but he also couldn't remember there *not* being a porch. But their house was right there, right in front of him. And then it wasn't.

But I just saw it. It was right there, it was...

There was a beautiful woman. *Whoosh.* A blur. *Whoosh.* Another blur. And then closer. *Whoosh.* And then right upon him. *Chandra? Is that you? Yes, oh, yes. Candy, I missed you, my god. I see it now, I see. Don't give up on me. Please! Don't let me drift away into the nothing. Don't let me disappear. Don't let me fade away until there's nothing left of me. Don't let me g—*

Chandra smiled, touched his face. Powell couldn't feel her palm on his cheek, and then...

Wait. I'm dreaming. That's it. That's IT! She's a dream that I'm dreaming and none of this is real but it's just so wonderful and warm and light that I could stay here in this dream that I'm dreaming forever and—

Pulsing strobe light. *Flash-flash-flash.*

Powell was nine years old again, with his father, just before dawn, deep in New York State's Mohawk Valley. Early April. Southern ridge of the Adirondack Mountains. The tinge of sugar maples and the bitter mint of white cedars. Nearby, a brook ran downhill. The rising Sun eased through a canopy of branches. The air was cool.

They strode softly over the hilly terrain, each with a rifle in hand. His father was a hunter, determined to make him one, too. But all young Powell wanted was to soar through the heavens at the speed of sound. He looked up, through the leaves, searching for a plane. Any plane.

"Marcus," his father whispered.

Still scanning the skyline, all young Powell could see was the enormity of the woods and an overwhelming notion that the view would be far more spectacular from a thousand feet above. From ten thousand. He would see everything from up there. His younger brother, Peter, died of leukemia two years earlier. His father, Thomas Powell, compensated by pushing him to be in control all the time. "Don't let anything get the jump on you. Ever." Even in youth Powell knew that cancer could get anyone, but grieving parents are unlike any others. It profoundly changes them. They never truly recover.

"I know you've got that streak in you," his father said. "God knows where you get it. But there's more to life than speeding jets and rocket ships." Thomas Powell had a black mustache, trimmed neat, with a few white whiskers. "You've got to focus on what you're doing—when you're doing it. Understand?"

"Yes, but—"

"Ah, ah. Are we deer hunting or aren't we?"

Young Powell sighed. "We are."

"Good. Then let's go." It wasn't more than an hour into the hunt when his father leaned down, took him by the shoulder. "*Shh...shh...shh.* There he is, right over the ridge. See it? It's drinking in the brook. Now's your chance."

Young Powell started to sweat. He was overcome with fear and adrenaline. With dread. He wanted to run through the woods and morph into an eagle. To fly away and be far from guns and violence and death. But his father was counting on him to do what real men do. To kill. So he raised his rifle. His small hands shook.

"Okay, son. Look through the scope. Find the target. Do you see him?" The deer was like a puppet. It just stood there, its eyes black and vacant. "Steady your legs. Take a breath." Though full of shame, young Powell followed his father's instructions. "Good. Now put your finger on the trigger...but don't squeeze yet. See the deer through your scope. See it...see it. And when you're steady...," his father whispered now, "...*fire.*"

Young Powell licked his lips. He felt queasy. Just one trigger squeeze and that deer, just standing there, looking at him blankly, would cease to exist forever. The bullet would rip through its flesh, extinguishing its life force. Even in Powell's small hands, he had the power to kill. But did he have the will? He held the rifle steady, his eye against the scope. And then a twig cracked in the distance. Startled, the deer ran off.

"Marcus. You let him get away. Why didn't you shoot? You had him."

Young Powell dropped his head, shrugged.

"This isn't a game, son. You take up a weapon, be prepared to use it. There's no bluffin' with guns. Use 'em or don't. But no in-betweens. Okay?"

Staring at the ground, young Powell's answer was faint. "Yes, Dad."

And then his father, with that amazing power, turned sour into sweet. "What's that?"

Young Powell looked up, smiled. "Yes, Dad."

"Atta boy. Now let's go home."

Pulsing strobe light. *Flash-flash-flash.*

Powell's eyes snapped open. Laying in bed, in the hospital, his chest heaved and rose. Electricity seemed to crackle all around him. Chandra held his hand. He could feel her warmth, see the worry on her face. And he thought, *thank God. It was all just a dream. It was really just a dream I was dreaming and...* Chandra's hair morphed from black to red, her skin from brown to white. And Jesse was no longer five, but twelve. She was taller and her face wasn't his little girl anymore and she had a look of sadness that had never been there before and...

Jesse. Look how you've grown! Where have I been? What's happened?! I missed you so much. I'm sorry, baby. I'm sorry. Please forgive me. Jesse, you've got to...

Flash-flash-flash.

Blackness.

The gentle calm of infinite nothing. *Easy...easy......easy.*

In the dark, a shrill, high-pitched screech rang out.

Flash-flash-flash.

The sky was soft and blue. Flapping wind. White clouds. Flapping wind.

Flash-flash-flash.

Hospital bed. Doctors. Sunshine beamed through a window.

Red rock walls. Chill leaned over. Olivia screamed. Keela howled
with rage.

Flash-flash-flash.

Wingbeat. Mountaintop. Wingbeat. Lake.

Flash-flash-flash.

Wingbeat. Skyscraper.

Flash-flash-flash.

Olivia leaned over the bed.

Flash-flash-flash.

Industrial shelves. Bodies everywhere. Blood. So much blood.

Flash-flash-flash.

Streetscape. Coldness. Chill was silent.

Flash-flash-flash.

Door slammed shut. Blazing fire.

Flash-flash-flash.

Wingbeat. Echoed screech of a hawk.

Flash-flash-flash.

Total, utter blackness.

And the quiet, gentle calm of infinite nothing.

PART III

ME AND MY SHADOW

"I've got that stranger-in-a-strange land kinda thing going on. The food was good, but the service…? Not so much."

—Marcus Powell

"It's like somebody broke our system into teeny tiny pieces, then put it back together with junked-out scraps. The engineer who worked on it is either a crafty son of a binka-dink and made the most of what he had…or he's kind of an idiot."

—Desmond Bachra

CHAPTER THIRTY-SEVEN

POWELL FINALLY HAD the strength to dress himself despite a clumsy left thumb splint, and his right ankle, which suffered a bone bruise from an exploded serving tray, was healing nicely. Dr. Doug removed most of his stitches—his chest and left thigh took the worst of it—and the ringing in his ears was gone. The concussion Powell suffered during the St. Brewer's Day bombing made him nauseous initially, and for a few days after, his skin had taken on a vomitty shade of green, which was also gone. And while he had a crick in his right shoulder, his body was otherwise on the mend.

But Powell still needed help getting around. It was an unsettling predicament, as he was not one to ask for assistance, no matter how much he secretly desired being looked after. His father acknowledged the weaknesses of men, but didn't dedicate any thought to the issue. Powell had a more forgiving instinct, more like his mother in that regard. And yet the pull of his father's stern, judgmental voice often overwhelmed his desire to behave according to his own nature. Powell needed to feel more solid, that he could hold his own again.

Chill approached. Powell put up a hand in protest. The trippy dippy hippy dude wasn't quite what he was looking for. "*Ep-peh-peh.* I'm finding my way back to a state of chillitude. My flux capacitor is fluxing. My eagle spirit is soaring through nature's glorious womb, yada-yada."

"Well *all right,*" Chill said. "Good to hear. Your color's looking good, too." He chuckled. "*Soooooo*...what else is going on?"

Powell raised his damaged thumb. He was a pilot without a craft or the appendage to operate one. "Dr. Doug said I can get the splint off tomorrow."

Chill nodded. "Dolores is preparing a hot meal for you. The bread is baking as we speak. Get your strength back. If anybody can fill your belly, it's Dolores. Anyhoosey…just wanted to see how you were feeling."

In Powell's limited experience with Chill, the resident shaman never just *stopped* by. And for a man who claimed dedication to peace, balance, and harmony, his presence only brought Powell increasing levels of agita. "That's all? No other reason?"

Chill opened his hands in a wide-eyed gesture. "You tell me."

As a boy, after his father died suddenly of a stroke and his mother retreated into the church, Powell no longer cared about toys, and had few friends. His escape from grief came as long as he could study the mighty air machines and later fly them at bristling speeds—able to outrun all the demons chasing him—and come home to his wife and daughter. And he believed that was all he would ever need. That because he had already lost so much, the gods wouldn't be so cruel as to punish him even further. But away from Chandra and Jesse, denied access to the skies—he was stripped bare. The mental and physical beating he'd been subjected to since he arrived on Aretha nearly demolished him. He couldn't allow himself to think there could be more or worse to come.

"I've got that stranger-in-a-strange land kinda thing going on. The food was good, but the service…?" Powell gestured to his many wounds. "Not so much."

"I understand the pain that reverberates from violence. We've all suffered." And then Chill's shoulders drew tight. His hand coiled into a fist. His eyes narrowed, focused, as if he had been transported to a time and place wherein the unfathomable unfolded. "Too much pain," he said. "Too much…"

"Uh…what's going on, Chill. You're freaking me out."

Chill informed Powell that Grinroad itself was still in shock from the bombing. Besides taking out several chunks of cave wall, eleven were killed in the explosions, while thirty-nine others suffered various injuries, ranging from minor cuts to broken bones, although a few amputations had been necessary. Fingers were still being pulled from the wreckage.

Powell shook his head slowly. "Jesus. I didn't realize. I don't remember that much."

"The battles are awful. But they're fought on many fronts."

"Chill. Seriously.... What's up?"

"During the feast, did you meet Olivia's brother, Terry? He has a girlfriend."

Powell struggled to recall. "Mmm…I saw them, but we didn't meet."

"They're gone."

"Dead?"

Chill shook his head. "Abducted. Kidnapped. The Scrapers…they've done this before. They attack during the night and snatch who they can…"

"What do you mean *kidnapped*? They just took them? *Why*?"

Powell could see anger in Chill—a deep, penetrating fury. The same desire for retribution Powell carried with him since his father's death. But who do you strike out against when your enemy has no face? Where do you put the hate?

"It instigates fear, turns brother against brother. The shame infects us, for not protecting our own. We weep for their souls— and ours."

Powell froze. The word *abduction* unnerved him. Until then his mere presence on Aretha had felt like a cruel cosmic joke. But immersed in their struggle and with the scars to verify it, he was coming to see that he hadn't been unlucky, punished, or a victim of circumstance. Nobody *forced* him to pilot *Crossline*. And nobody forced him to blast across the solar system. And when he was faced with an alien craft and the means to attack, he refused to enter combat until it was too late. His father tried to teach him an important lesson once, in the woods, with a rifle in his hands. But it didn't take.

As a young boy, Powell didn't understand that his father wasn't excited by the thrill of the kill, wasn't driven by bloodlust.

Maybe his father didn't have the words to articulate his sentiments or just assumed it was understood. But Powell could see now that his father tried to pass along to him that taking a life isn't a sport, but a grueling responsibility, and that if he were to pick up a gun there should be no joy in pulling the trigger, even when necessary. Killing isn't *supposed* to feel good.

His father hadn't considered that deer a target, a toy, or soulless fool. It was a sacrifice. A single deer to protect his only living son. Powell didn't understand it then. But he did now.

Walking with a slight limp, Powell made his way with Chill through the canyons, drawing all measure of looks. Some Grinroadians wished him well that he was up and around, while others were less forgiving, as if he had brought this latest wave of violence upon them, and had no right to have survived the St. Brewer's Day bombing while their loved ones died. Dimitri Vargos said as much on his way both to and from the cemetery by Tomasod Lake, where he had just buried his wife.

"Be patient," Chill said. "Give it time."

Powell undid his splint, shook out his thumb, then rewrapped it. "I'm alone here, Chill. I don't want to give it time. I just want to go home."

"I won't pretend to understand what this is like for you, Marcus, but feeling lost has a lot less to do with geography than knowing who you really are...and being okay with it." Chill bit down on the thin end of his pipe, lit the other. "You see the elements as being separate. They're not. You feel disconnected from others because you're disconnected from you. You see yourself as being inside or out, above or below. But you're as much a part of the Universe as everyone and everything else. The top of the caves we live in shares the air we breathe, just as the edge of the shoreline shares a bond with the river. It is not simply liquid and soil. Not one or the other. They are not separate elements, but a continuum. The sky and space above are not emptiness, but a vast sea of infinite energy. When a bird takes flight, it is not merely making its way from one point to another, but streaming through that sea of energy—communing with all the life that ever was, is, or will ever be—every fiber connected to every other.

"The same is true when your ship flies through space. Your feet do not need to physically touch the soil for you to be connected to it. If you can allow yourself to embrace that the air and sea and land and space are all of one ocean, of one energy…of one spirit…then you will always feel connected. You will always have a center."

It took Powell every grain of fortitude to stay composed, from feeling like the victim he swore as a child he would never be again. "Come on," he said finally, trying to reject Chill outright, hearing Chandra and Feather's words spoken from another man's voice. "You really believe that?"

Chill puffed on his pipe. He blew out a cloud of smoke. He offered a half smile. "I didn't always, but I do now. That you are standing here before me is all the evidence I need. Because if it turns out I'm wrong, then I would be left to believe that in the wilderness of time and space…I'm alone. And if I really thought that, I would wander into the hills…and never come back."

CHAPTER THIRTY-EIGHT

SEAN WAS SITTING at a cave console with three computer terminals built into it. He offered Powell a seat, which he was thankful to take, even if he didn't entirely trust that Sean wouldn't yank it out from underneath him.

"I'm trying to piece it together," Sean said. "I've cobbled footage together from different cameras. It's been coming in all day. Just different versions of the same story. I'm looking to fill in the gaps, but so far...I can't find it."

"Marcus," Chill said. "Perhaps you can help."

"I can try. How?"

"Just sit back and breathe. Try to remember that night. Let it come. Let it come..."

When Powell closed his eyes, he thought he could see Terry and Faye in the banquet hall...somewhere. But when and for how long? There were so many faces. *They were there with Dr. Doug for a while, drinking from goblets and then talking to... someone. And then...where? Where? By the...yes! The fiddlers. By the musicians! They were dancing and laughing, although... no, not laughing exactly,* but then he saw Faye whisper to Terry, who drew serious and nodded, and then Chill brought Powell up front with Olivia.

As Powell searched the recess of his mind, he remembered an immense white flash, and then soundlessness, followed by an eruption of fire and smoke and blood. The more he focused, the clearer he could see Terry and Faye, the shock and fight in their faces. But did he witness their abduction or flee for survival? Did he see them at all? Powell couldn't be sure if the images he recalled were real memories or ones his mind invented to match the stories he heard.

"I'm sorry, I can't tell. They were there, for sure. I just don't know…"

Sean zoomed in on video footage outside the banquet hall. "They're not on video, which is odd. But I've gotten multiple reports that they got swept up during the panic. Angie Waters said two men shoved them into the ravine, but Gary Roma was pretty sure they had their mouths gagged and tossed into a jeep. A few others said Faye got shot in the belly. Or the shoulder. Or she was dead. Or not. Either way, nobody's seem them since."

Chill leaned in. "Were there others? Across the region?"

"Yes. We've heard of at least a dozen other abductions in Preno, Tarsus, and Ingram, and another twenty or so failed attempts, from as far west as Lerna, and south down to Djoza. Same deal as here. Bombs went off during the St. Brewer's Day speech, followed by a series of grab-and-runs. I can't find any connection among the targets. It seems totally random."

"I've seen this before. This was coordinated. They were ready…and we weren't." Chill turned away, as if something important occurred to him. "Sean. What else? There's more."

"You know Charles and Audrey Ross? Their necks were broken. And Betty Uston? With the freckles? Her skirt was torn off, but no evidence of rape. Thing is…"

Powell saw Chill brace himself.

"I didn't want to say unless I was sure, but look here. I know it's grainy and hard to see…but I think it's him, Chill. It's Carlos Guerra. It's Riva."

Powell's eye went wide. "You mean the face-slicing guy? The madman?"

"I checked it four times. It's him." Sean said that Riva was the most bloodthirsty monster of their time, and the unofficial enforcer of Eric Osgood, the CEO of Prado City, the Scrapers' center of operations. "They say Osgood made a deal with the Devil. To enforce his corporate rule. And if that's true, then Osgood's more of a monster than Riva himself. Monsters act to their nature. But siding with one? That's vicious and diabolical.

Premeditated. Evil. And if Osgood sent him here, then the Scrapers are up to something."

Sean turned to Chill. "Hey, Chill. You okay? I know this is hard for y..."

But Chill was gone.

Powell scanned the room. "Where'd he go?"

"Nowhere. It's nothing, he had to leave."

Don't toy with me now. Not about this. His father's voice was suddenly loud in his mind. *Never trust a man who dangles the truth. He's playing you.* Powell knew his father was right. But he just had to know.

"No. I don't think so. Chill knows that kid, doesn't he? It's personal."

"Listen, Powell. Chill never talks about it. We all know, and he knows we know, so we let it be." Sean paused the video screen on an image of the banquet hall just seconds before the blast. Chill was giving his speech. The crowd listened with joyful respect. "He was an okay guy before the Battle of Lightwind. I just knew him from around. But his wife and kids were killed in the bombing. Mortars tore them to pieces. Chill found their bodies. Guerra's family died then, too. Before he was Riva. Or so we're told. But you know what? I think *he* killed them. His own family. When the explosions went off, I think Riva saw the terror in their eyes, felt the fear in their hearts. And then he smiled. I think he slit their throats and smiled, and then buried them in rubble. And I think maybe he killed Chill's family, too. And I think Chill knows it."

"Jesus. Everybody think that?"

"Some. People talk. Around the same time, there were bandits, like a pack of dogs. They would raid us time to time. After the bombing, Chill goes out, disappears into the mountains. We heard screams in the distance...and then never again. There are rumors about a river of blood. Their blood. Was it Chill? I really don't know. I just think he had a decision to make. Come back a bitter, violent man, or be a conduit for peace. But you ask me, deep down, buried beneath his smoke, and visions, and talk of the inner chill, I think there's rage in him—and he's ready to blow."

Learning about the abductions and murderous sociopath plunged Powell into a stupefying panic. He had a vision of Jesse just then, when she was still small enough to hold in one hand. He would live lifetimes when she took his finger in her tiny digits, and squeeze. And then in his mind's eye he saw Jesse and Chandra, kidnapped by an amorphous shadow, literally snatched from him as they called out for help.

His heart pounded. Trembling, Powell felt pathetic, the kind of weak, impotent fool his father despised. Maybe his family felt that helplessness on the day of the launch. One minute he was on the world's stage, and then *poof!* He vanished. Just thinking about his girls thinking about *him* made Powell nauseous all over again, a man's worst fears reflected back—that his family would be lost to him, perhaps realizing that he'd never really had them at all.

Civil war or not, he had to get home. He just absolutely had to.

CHAPTER THIRTY-NINE

DOLORES' BAKERY REMINDED Powell of Tim's Place, a roadside diner off Route 4 in Albany that his parents took him to as a kid. The bakery counter was out front, but in her spacious kitchen, in back, four red rock ovens were on full heat. Sitting on a stool at the center island, Powell polished off his fifth slice of warm pumpernickel, which he used to dab up the gravy from a turkey pot pie Dolores made for him special. He was so full that another bite would have made his eye sockets overflow. He went for it anyway. Blueberry pies baked in ovens. The sugar fumes practically soaked into his skin.

"Chill was right. I totally needed this."

"Why, thank you, dear. I'm glad." Dolores put a hand on Powell's shoulder, then cleared his plate. "I've got some warm peaches for you with vanilla ice cream. My husband says I fatten everybody up...but I just can't help myself. Ice cream makes it all better."

Dolores was short but not quite plump, with a round face, large, inviting eyes, and a layer of freckles. Her sandy hair was starting to gray, and her hips, quite understandably, had rounded out. Yet as Grinroad's most prolific baker, she was more like the town's grandmother, as if they were all her brood, and could do no wrong.

Powell didn't normally have a sweet tooth, but he scooped some dessert into his mouth. "*Mmm.* So good."

"When you cook for eight children, you must soothe many appetites."

"Eight?! Good, god. I mean, you're too young and you look so..." He shook his head in disbelief. Powell was more into the lithe, athletic type, but Dolores was gentle and fluffy in all the right places and clearly enjoyed a roll in the hay. "Eight? Really?" Dolores blushed, then wiped her hands on an apron. "You're very sweet. I had my Angie when I was nineteen. She's full grown now. I've been in diapers for as long as I can remember." A distant crash drew their attention to swinging doors. "I hear the triplets now."

Powell choked on the ice cream. "Triplets?"

In they ran, Andre, Sean, and Wendy, their little feet trundling along in unison. "Hi, Mom. Hi, Mom. Hi, Mom." Each grabbed an oatmeal cookie off the counter, running off just as fast as they entered. "Bye, Mom. Bye, Mom. Bye, Mom."

"Oh, yes. Eight little angels. Well...they're not always so angelic, but they're my joy of joys. Five girls, three boys. My husband thinks we've more than enough, the sweetheart, but I'm hoping for two more boys."

"You want more?"

"I know. It seems a bit much. But I just can't imagine my kitchen without the little ones running through. I know that day will come, but I'm not ready yet. My husband, my children...they're my everything. Pardon my asking. But, do you have a family?"

Powell reached into his front pocket. He handed Dolores the picture he had on *Crossline*'s dash. "Jesse's five. She's amazing. She's always two steps ahead of me. And then she giggles when I figure it out. One time I left my security pass on the nightstand, and just as I was about to head back in, Jesse rode her tricycle up to my truck, rang her little bell, and handed it off to me through the window. But first she said I had to pay the toll—a kiss on the cheek. She knew I left it behind. She's got my number."

Dolores the baker stared at him with those great big eyes. She smiled again. "You know...you're just like him."

Powell looked at Dolores with a suspicious smile. "Like who?"

"Like Mitri, dear. Of course. You're a little taller, perhaps, and your hair isn't quite so dark, but you remind Keela of him. You remind us all. You're like long-lost brothers."

Long-lost brothers. The words held him in place.

"Really?...How so?"

"Oh, dear. I thought you knew. No one's told you?"

"Told me what?" Powell's heart pounded—an inner siren, an early warning system.

Dolores wiped the counter. "It's not my place, dear. I really shouldn't."

"No. Please." Pounding and pounding. "What?"

Dolores let out a sigh. "Well...I suppose it's all right. When Mitri was just a boy, he had a younger brother who died from illness. It was very sad."

"But I don't—"

"His name was Mierkos." Dolores approached, put a hand on his cheek. "It means, *The Open Traveler. He Who Soars.*"

Powell leaned against the island. He fell into a moment, drawn to his own little brother gone so long. He'd always felt that there was more to Petey's death than he knew, that his parents had held back to protect him. Or them. Or maybe he'd never really forgiven himself for living while he failed to save his brother. It didn't matter that leukemia was the enemy. Helplessness is a splinter that upsets the soul. Petey was just five years old then. *Who would you be now, Pete? Who would I?*

The front door jingled. Olivia came barreling in, made a beeline for Powell. She wrapped her arms around his midsection, jolting him back to high alert. Suddenly Powell was fearful that she might be armed with a freshly sharpened hunting knife, to gut him like a trout. It took a moment to appreciate that she was hugging him, expressing appreciation, when previously he'd only known her angst. Longing for a child's embrace so far from Jesse, Powell finally patted her back, acknowledging the gesture. But Olivia let go almost instantly, as if he'd approached a physical threshold he was barred from crossing. Without a sound, she offered him a slight smile, which drooped back into her customary frown.

"Here you go, dear." Dolores gave Olivia a stuffed towel. "The usual. Two dozen rolls." Olivia nodded to Dolores, and left.

"What was that about?"

"Oh, you poor thing. You took a blow to the head." Though lost from his memory, before passing out during the St. Brewer's Day attack, Powell crawled over to Olivia and draped himself over her torso, shielding her from the blasts. Dr. Doug said the debris would have killed her had he not intervened. "You saved her life. And now this awful business with her brother and that girl. Well...you can understand why she's attached to you."

Since he first awoke in the hospital, Powell had had a... sense...a feeling...which now began to register. "Can I...can I ask you something?"

"Go ahead, dear. It's all right."

"When I was, you know, out of it, did...?" Powell walked to the other side of the island, staring at the oven, knowing the flames beyond that wall were high. Deadly. "Did Keela visit me? I'm not sure, but...I think she wiped sweat from my forehead." He chuckled uneasily. "It was probably the concussion. Or the morphine." He blinked purposefully. "But seriously. Did she?"

"Oh, I'm sorry, dear. I really don't know. But I wouldn't be surprised. She's quite grateful to you. We all are." The front bell jingled again. A familiar voice called out. "Ah, that's Keela now. You can ask her yourself."

That inner siren went off inside Powell's head again, warning him to evacuate. Evacuate now. He headed for the back door, fleeing more so than leaving. He was embarrassed and ashamed, feeling a little bit vulnerable for revealing a piece of himself that even he hadn't realized was lurking within him. "No," he said. "I gotta go."

CHAPTER FORTY

GRINROAD HOUSED THE strongest, most seasoned fighter squadron in the Westie fleet. Not including the experimental models under construction, Grinroad had twenty-eight battle-ready ships. But only Keela's ship—the *Simona*—was armed with a fully operational wormhole device.

There was urgent talk of counterstrike against the Scrapers, and rescuing their abducted comrades. But the seven Council Leaders—one from each Westie town—decided that other than sending daily patrols within a five-mile radius to search for the missing, restraint was their best recourse. Counterstrike *was* inevitable, but when, where, and how had yet to be ironed out, or at the very least, made public.

In Hangar B, several ships were undergoing routine maintenance, inspections, and minor repairs. Preparations were under way for the next phase of operations.

Toward the back, *Crossline* had dozens of tubes and wires sticking out of it. In one way the ship was bold and proud, with its blast scars streaked across the nose and side, and in another it was weak, damaged, and weary—a battered soldier—with its guts hanging out. Exposed.

The crew chief, Desmond Bachra, was on his back with a soldering iron, tinkering away at *Crossline*'s dangling innards. It was the first time Powell had seen his ship since he landed. Covered in grease and sweat, Desmond rolled out on the mechanic's creeper, sat up, then lifted his goggles. "She took a heckuva beating, but she's a tough ole girl. Don't worry. Another week and bingo-bango-bongo…she'll be ready."

Powell never considered himself an introspective man, but the longer he remained on Aretha the less he recognized his own reflection. Removed so thoroughly from the life he thought he knew, he could see that he'd never given much thought to what it actually meant to *be* the man called Marcus Powell. And now that he wanted to secure his identity, it was slipping farther and farther away. Just being near *Crossline* reunited him with an essential part of himself, as if he'd left a little bit of his soul in the cockpit, and was now absorbing his energies back.

Like petting the belly of a whale, Powell dragged his palm against the siding. He smiled. The joy came from someplace deep within, from decades past, when he was just a boy, imagining what it would be like someday to have the grandest ship of them all. "What's the problem?"

Desmond rolled his neck. "Where do I start? The warp drive has solid engineering, but...*eee*-yikes. It's so inefficient. I had to make a few modifications, especially given the damage it took. I'm almost done there. But the computer system's a *biiiit* more troubling." He shook his head. "It's got fragments of what we use, but other parts are just...*pfff*...they don't match. It's like somebody broke our system into teeny tiny pieces, then put it back together with junked-out scraps. The engineer who worked on it is either a crafty son of a binka-dink and made the most of what he had...or he's kind of an idiot. Still..."

Powell used to love hanging out with the gang in engineering, Ilya and Dana and Ted, but now he couldn't help but think of them all as bastards, thieves and liars, just pretending to be his friends, when all along he was the stupid ape they dropped into the cockpit. "Why don't you just swap out the old stuff for what you got now?"

"As an engineer, nothing would please me more. Your people butchered the design. But unless it's absolutely necessary...no offense...we're not sending you back with anything more than you came with. We'll get you back in flight, absolutely bingo-bango-bongo, but it'll be with your unholy mechanics."

Unholy, Powell thought. *You said it.*

"Oh. One more thing." Desmond handed Powell a mechanical

cylinder the size of his index finger. "I don't think they like you very much."

Powell chuckled. "Oh, yeah. Why's that?"

"It's an explosive. It was wired into your fuel system with a long-range activation trigger. If they wanted to, they could have blown you to bits."

Powell spoke with forced nonchalance. "Just a precaution." But he plummeted into a gaping pit in his soul, humiliated yet again to grasp that from the moment he set foot inside *Crossline*, his safety had been in a more precarious state than he ever thought. Which was saying something. Buddy Rheams really was an evil scumwad. *They were going to kill me.* It was clear to him now. *They...were going...to KILL me.* "You know. In case of capture."

Desmond shrugged. "If you say so. But you can see right here it was activated. There's a manual destruct sequence on the side of the—"

A heavy-footed gait echoed throughout the hangar. Another technician came running full bore. He was out of breath. "Yo, Des. Come on. Code Red, man. Code Red."

Instincts kicking in, Powell wanted to jump into *Crossline*'s cockpit and haul ass back to Earth. He stared wide-eyed and anxious, ready to go. "Code Red? Are we under attack?"

"No," Desmond said. "It's worse. It's Keela."

CHAPTER FORTY-ONE

Gathered in Keela's cave apartment, Sean and Chill had to physically restrain her, and still she almost broke free. Sean took an elbow to the face.

"Let go of me, you assholes! Let go. I have to get her back! Let me go!"

"Whoa," Powell said. "What's going on?"

Chill nodded to Desmond and his tech, who both assisted Sean in restraining Keela. "It's Olivia. I'm afraid she's missing."

"She not missing, you fucktards! She went after Terry. She's gone!"

As if plugged into a main line, another strobe light went off in Powell's mind. That *flash-flash-flash*.

Crowded park. Soldiers.

Flash-flash-flash.

Gunfire. Nearby building.

Flash-flash-flash.

Bodies covered in blood.

Flash-flash-flash.

Blazing fire.

Flash-flash-flash.

Olivia.

"She begged us to find him," Keela said. "But we didn't listen. *I* didn't listen. I just…she needed us. She needed me. She *needed* me. But what if they attacked again? What if they hit us worse? We had to plan…"

"She's been gone about a day," Sean said. "They found her gear. The southern trail."

"So let me go, god damn it. Desmond. Fire up my ship. I'm gonna blast their high-rises once and for all. Fuck 'em all to hell."

Powell knew then what he had feared for days. That his strobe light dreams weren't really dreams at all, but visions. He didn't understand how or why he saw the things he did, or how much he could trust what he did see. All he got were fragments. Slices. Threads of a future that wanted to take him farther away from where he most wanted to be. Home. With Chandra in one arm and Jesse in the other. With Grinroad and Aretha nothing more than distant memories. And yet it was clear what he had to do, as much as he didn't want to do it. He reached inside his pocket, and showed the item to Keela.

"What's this crap? Fuck you and your family. What's the poin—?"

"Red! Quiet! Pay attention." Stunned and annoyed, Keela fell silent nonetheless. Powell squared his shoulders, showed her the picture. "My girls...when I think of them...none of you exist for me. You're nothing. You're gone." Like a mongoose, Keela was snapping to break free. "And yet I'm sick in my soul about this. About Olivia. I can't let go."

Keela scowled. "...And?"

Despite the tension, Powell felt a tenderness beneath her rage. "I'll help you find her."

Released from Sean's clutches, Keela gestured, assuring them that she was under control. "What do I care? What the fuck can *you* do?"

In his visions, Powell had gotten close to Olivia, but he didn't know the last few steps. And in a dense sector like Prado City, being close wasn't enough. Either you got it down to the molecule, or you could walk into a room of armed guards ready to blow your brains out. They needed her precise location, and there was only one way to find out. Powell squinted, sighed.

Crap.

"I need Chill to poke me in the eye."

Before they got started, Gregor Deisenhouse barged into Keela's apartment. Gregor was Grinroad's chief engineer.

"Look. Here. Olivia had it." He presented sheet music.

Keela grabbed it. "What? This? Terry's songs? They suck. So what?"

Sean leaned over. "Hold on. Let me see that." He examined it closely. "Wait. Is that the...?"

Gregor nodded. "He had a knack for engineering. He just couldn't focus."

"What?" Keela said. "What?"

Sean took a step back. "No, no, no. Oh, shit. No, no."

Gregor laid the page on the table. "You see here, how the notes rise and fall and then rise again? You see this pattern? How it swoops and swirls?" The others nodded. "And you see these lyrics? The combination and spacing of the letters on the page are juxtaposed with the sequence of the notes. If you translate them into a formula...it's part of the wormhole code. He embedded the code here. Terry. He wrote it down."

Keela's eyes went wide. "He WHAT?"

"It's only a fragment, and without the rest it could take years...or never...before the Scrapers really know what they have or extrapolate the sequence to fully develop the code. But I also don't know if there are more pages. There probably are. He was always too clever for his own good. Always trying to outsmart me, playing dangerous little games. And when he went overboard with the drink, with the drugs. It's why I let him go."

"Damn it, Gregor. It's fucking Faye. That junkie slut. She had him wrapped around her finger. She ruined him!"

Gregor sighed. "I know, I know. But she's my niece. What could I do? She's always been a wild child. And then my sister died. I tried with Faye, but she didn't listen to me. She never did. I thought keeping her close was better than not. She must have snuck into my lab."

"What do you mean *snuck in*. How? Nobody can get in there. It's the most secure bunker we have. It's impenetrable."

"...It is. But..."

Sean turned to Gregor. "You gave her the code?!"

"No, but I wasn't always careful around her. She must have seen—"

"You fucked us! You killed us!"

Chill extended his hand. "Sean. Don't punish the man. It won't solve our problem."

"You're right, Chill. It won't. But now we *have* to go after them. We've got no choice." Sean pointed to Powell, who had been silent. "Time to man up, flyboy. Close your eyes and see what you see. Because if we don't get to them before the Scrapers know what they have, you are *never* going home. You'll be as dead as the rest of us."

Chill led Powell into a separate room. It was dark except for three lit candles. Powell sat back on the chair.

"All right, Chill. I'm ready. Let's go."

Sitting opposite him, Chill lit his pipe, took two puffs. "I hear the words, Marcus, but not the belief. Are you sure you want to do this?"

"Do I want to do *what*? Hallucinate? Lose control? I don't want any of this, Chill. I don't even want to be on this planet, let alone in this room. But if I need to risk my life *here* to get me back home, then that's what I'll do."

"You're taking a step into an unknown world. We all are. It won't be easy."

"Easy? Oh, come on, Chill. I'm not stupid. I get it. But what choice do I have? You guys have my ship. Desmond says it'll be ready in a week. But how do I know that? If I don't at least *try* to find Olivia, if we don't go after the wormhole code…what will it be then? Another month, a year?…Never? Or maybe the repairs are done and you're just not telling me. And you know what? Desmond said my ship would be *ready* in a week. He didn't say I could have it back or that I was free to go."

"Is that what you believe? That you're a prisoner?"

"Of course I am! We all are. Look at this life, Chill. Look where we are. What the hell's the point?"

Chill offered a restrained smile. "The war. It tests us all. To re-evaluate. To wonder how and why. And whether we resolve those answers or not, we can fight the path we're meant to follow...or we can embrace it and move on. We may not always prefer the options before us or believe the endeavor is worth the cost. But your choices have meaning, Marcus. They matter, whether you think they do or not."

"Yeah. My choices. I know you all think I'm 'the man from the sky' or whatever the hell the Cake says I am. But I'm not that guy, Chill. I've tried to tell you. I'm just not."

"Is that what Jesse thinks? She's always with you."

Powell expelled two fluttered breaths. His time on Aretha had seemed like a dream that would suddenly end, that he would suddenly wake in his bed, with his girls smiling at him, his life as it had always been. But now he accepted that he had been linked to Aretha all along, just as Aretha had been linked to him.

"How do you know this, Chill? How can you see?"

"You have your visions...and I have mine. The dream flight is there for us all to see, but only a few open their eyes."

"I hear her voice, Chill. Jesse calls to me. She whispers: 'Daddy-Daddy-Daddy.' Just a voice in the wind. And then sometimes, when I close my eyes, I hear Olivia, too. I see her face. So I search inside. And when I can almost reach them, when I feel them close...there's no one there. They're gone."

Chill tapped out his pipe. He smiled. "Good," he said. "Good."

"Good? How is that good?"

"It means you're ready to see. Now let's find our way. I think it's going to get ugly."

For very different reasons, Sean and Chill insisted on being part of Olivia's rescue team. Powell could live with that. But he knew he had a fight on his hands with this one.

"Well?" Keela said. "Did you see her? Can you find her? Where is she? Can you—?"

Chill took an easy hold of her. "Let him speak."

"Tell me where she is. I'm going with you."

Powell was firm. He anticipated this. "No. You're not."

In just the second it took Keela to respond, Sean and Chill ducked as if anticipating shrapnel from her exploding skull to ricochet across the room. "Piss off, flyboy. You don't tell me anything. I don't know where you get the…"

Taking a cue from Chill, Powell remained silent as Keela ranted herself out. After several spirited minutes that would have made Olivia proud, she circled around with, "so FUCK you very much, DICKHEAD!"

"Listen, Red. If Jesse were gone I'd be out there already. And you're right. I can't tell you what to do. But ask yourself: is your place on a dangerous road to a dangerous land, or here with your people? Do you really want to leave them now, of all times? I can't answer that for you. But leaving Grinroad has brought you nothing but grief. Your husband, now Olivia…"

Powell wasn't exactly sure how, but the pang in his gut alerted him that his words had veered off track. His intention was for Keela to peacefully, calmly, for the love of Aunt Margaret accept that as Grinroad's unofficial leader, the Westies needed her more than ever to be physically present, to help guide them. And if she couldn't be peaceful or calm about it, then for her to simply appreciate their need, and stay with them anyway.

He was also looking out for number one. Powell was no soldier, but even he knew that Keela was so fatigued by the stress, guilt, and shame of war—and hell-bent on revenge—that she was in no condition to lead a small rescue squad deep behind enemy lines when stealth, timing, and finesse were critical. How much would it really take for her to snap, putting them all in jeopardy? Even the fiercest warriors can crumble, and since Olivia's kidnapping, Keela's resolve had grown increasingly fragile—and unpredictable. The others felt the same. They just couldn't bring themselves to say it. They were happy to let Powell take the hit on this one.

Sean and Chill recoiled as Keela went wild with rage. "You're saying this is my fault, asshole? I oughta rip your fucking head off and kick it down the god damn canyon! I'm—"

Oh, god. Think quick, think quick, think quick.

"Look. Make your own decision. But if you leave now, you'll take more than anyone could carry. And everyone you leave behind...they'll wait with a heavy heart." Powell shook his head. "My wife? My daughter?...They're lost to me. They're gone. And for what?"

Keela slightly unclenched her fists, but she still hadn't come all the way. "Don't fuck with me, Powell. I can't hear bullshit about her."

Don't let up.

"It wasn't random and it wasn't an accident. The Scrapers went after Olivia because they knew it would bang you up inside. They knock you off your game, maybe even lure you out in the open...they've got a shot at you. You don't want that. I know you don't." Powell gestured to her comrades. "You're as tough as they come, Keela. No one's saying otherwise. But Grinroad needs you *here*. Trust me," he said. "We'll do everything to find her."

Severe as it was, the tension in Keela's face slowly, slowly eased up. She looked at Chill, and then Sean, and finally, back at Powell.

Yes? Yes?...Yes?

Keela sighed. It was tense. She pointed. "You two are going, right? Every step?" Sean and Chill nodded affirmatively, which seemed to satisfy her, but with Keela, they could never be sure. "All right," she said finally. "Fine."

Powell let out a relieved sigh of his own.

"Hey," Chill said. "Way to bust out the chill."

With a slight smirk, Powell shook his head. "I knew you were going to say that."

But even with Keela accepting the voice of reason, she wasn't finished giving orders. "If I'm staying here then Dolores goes with you. And don't argue with me. You've got two options. Either she goes...or I do."

Sean and Chill took a step back and made the *eeesh* face. Powell was baffled. "Dolores? The baker? Oh, come on. She's a sweet lady. What are you talking about?"

Keela dismissed his concerns. "Dolores will be fine, flyboy. But I'm not so sure about you. You want to stay alive? Follow her lead, keep your mouth shut, and with that maniac Riva on the loose…shoot to fucking kill."

CHAPTER FORTY-TWO

Keela thrust her hip into Sean's groin. She flipped him over her side, practicing the move again and again. Powell cringed every time Sean went down. And though he couldn't be sure, Powell could have sworn that Sean breathed in Keela's long, red hair as his face grazed the back of her neck, in those nanoseconds between contact with her body and impact with the ground. Still, Keela was really chucking him. Hard.

Powell was perched on a boulder overlooking the waterfall, where Keela interrogated him when he first arrived on Aretha. Otherwise surrounded by the slight forest, Powell studied them, from a distance. The last flip winded Sean, who got up slowly, covered in spruce needles and dirt. Chill sat beside Powell, who watched Keela stand in place. Feet apart and fists coiled, she resumed boxing with Sean, in tight bursts:

Left-left, right. Left-left, right.
Left upper cut, right hook.
Left-left, right. Left-left, right.
Left-right, right kick to the kidneys.
Left-left, right. Left-left, right.

Chill slugged water from a pouch, squinted, and then exhaled. He drank more.

"I know he's your friend, Chill, but I don't trust him. The way he looks at Keela. And me. He's always so close. Like he's up to something."

"It's just his way. He's had it better than some, worse than others. But he's saved my life. Yours as well. He dragged you from the bombing."

"I didn't know that."

"It's the way he wants it. He doesn't like attention."

"Doesn't he? Look at them."

"Better he spar with her now than Keela go looking for trouble. That's *her* way. It's just...something we deal with." Chill reached for his jaw, and winced, sympathizing with Sean's pain. "It hurts him now, but it would be far worse later."

"Yeah. Worse.... When do we leave?"

"Early. Sunrise. The quickest route into Scraper territory is through Djoza, across the southern tip of Lake Abandarro. It narrows to a point. But because of its logical access point, the border is heavily fortified on both sides. Impossible to cross."

"So why are we attacking there?"

"A diversion. While our comrades engage in battle to the south—a major offensive—we'll head north, about fifteen hundred miles. Above the canyons, across the tundra. It will be quite cold."

"We? You mean you, me, and Dolores? And Sean does the flying?...Delightful."

"Don't worry. Sean's an excellent pilot." Sean took a right fist from Keela just then. It landed in his stomach. "We're in good hands."

"Yeah, well...sorry if I don't take your word for it. And what about the storm? I still don't get that."

"Gregor is making the final calculations." For several years Grinroad's chief scientist had been triggering winter-type storms, as an experiment, to create the illusion of authentic weather patterns. The frost and weather conditions blocked out all telecommunications for at least four hours. "We will be subtle in our approach into Scraper territory, camouflaged in the storm. But once we arrive, we'll rely on your sight to find Olivia."

"Not Terry?"

"We'll try, but...I have my doubts."

"Why? What did you see? What's there?"

"Just...focus on you, Marcus. There's much to prepare."

The storm would give them cover as far to the east as what Powell knew as Buffalo, New York. From there they would set down and make their way another four hundred miles southeast to Prado City—the Scraper capital—to find Olivia.

Discussing the details put Powell on edge. He was always ready to fly, loved the thrill of anticipation. But their flight was just a means to an end. The real danger was waiting for them on the ground, in enemy camp, and they were headed for its epicenter. "I mean...I'll do my best, but I can't be certain. I've never done this before." He gestured to Keela.

Left-left, right. Left-left, right.

Left-left, right. Left-left, right.

"What if I'm wrong?"

"Keela has been like a mother to Olivia. Protective. Fierce.... Like many women, Keela longs to carry a child, but the gods have not been so kind...or perhaps they are being merciful. I'm not always so sure."

A deep pang of regret kicked up in Powell's gut. It had been more than a month since he saw his girls, since they even knew he was alive. And being out in the forest, isolated, alone with Chill, made him realize that as bizarre as it seemed, he actually trusted Keela more than any of them. At least he knew where he stood with her. "I'm sorry about your family, Chill. Truly."

"Yes. Thank you. I keep them close. They are always with me. At first I wrapped myself in a cloak of agony and self-loathing. The pain. It crippled me. But I came to see my purpose. My wife, my children? They were more than I deserved. And they've been spared the anguish of our struggle. Their final moments were joyful. They were singing a song. In my mind they are joyful now. And when I see them again, we will sing together."

I doubt they were singing, Chill...but I get why you need to think so.

"Keela is a warrior. Loyal. Determined. Her focus is extraordinary. But she is impulsive, as you know. You don't have to embrace the Cake or that the gods have a plan. Simply look at the events which you have experienced yourself. Keela flew off on her own, in search of her husband...and discovered you.

The next day, during our most festive celebration, the Scrapers attacked. You nearly died. Yet here you are. You survived."

True enough. But his bruises were real. "Okay. So...?"

"It was meant to happen."

Powell refrained from rolling his eyes. More molecule talk. "Yeah?...How do you know that?"

"Because it *did* happen. If something else was meant to have occurred, it would have. At all times each and every one of us is exactly where we are supposed to be, doing exactly what are supposed to be doing. We may not always understand the how or why. The variables extend far beyond my knowing. I can only act upon that which is before me. The rest...I try to let go."

Watching Sean with Keela, something occurred to Powell. "What about Gregor? He's your chief engineer. Why didn't they take him?"

Chill shook his head. "We have him secured. But Terry was far more vulnerable. And I suspect that Olivia was right. Gregor's niece. Faye. She has never been one to trust. We have friends inside Prado City. The Scrapers must have had theirs, too. Was it Faye? I really don't know. But we all seem to agree that the Scrapers had assistance. No one wants to believe that we turned on each other, but they knew just how and when to attack us. We must face our reality. It could not have happened otherwise."

"Chill. You're talking about traitors and abductions. And you're still saying this was all meant to happen? That I'm supposed to be here? And you are, too?"

Chill nodded. "Yes."

Powell rubbed his eyes. His paternal instincts swelled. Was Olivia's disappearance his fault? Had he set these events in motion? Was he to blame? And if Olivia went in search of her only surviving family, would Jesse do the same? Was she headed into danger because his own selfishness had done the worst damage of all?

Chill nodded to Keela and Sean, then produced a joint. "We should let them finish up. I'm going to smoke this. You want?"

Powell watched the two of them, still going at it. *Left-left, right. Left-left, right.* *Left upper cut, right hook.* *Left-right, right kick to the kidneys.* *Left-left, right. Left-left, right.* "No," he said. "I need to clear my head."

Powell laced up his boots, wondering if he would ever take them off again under his own power. Keela stood in the doorway, although he wasn't sure why. Sunlight streaked across the floor.

"Never got a chance to say," he said, "but you fly pretty good. You know." He flicked his eyebrows, and smirked. "For a girl."

Keela's eyes went wide. "You really want to fuck with me today? Really?"

He kinda did. It was his way of deflecting tension. He could see the leading in her body language, that she had something significant on her mind. Or was he the nervous, uncomfortable one, projecting his own anxiety onto her? But she *was* there. *She* came to *him.*

"I gotta ask, and before you jump down my throat, *noooo,* I'm not fucking with you. Well.... Maybe a little. But still." He did the one-hand-other-hand thing. "You pat me on the back, you drag me into the woods. You parade me as a savior, you bite my head off. You visit me in the hospital, you tell me to stick it. You're upset, and fair enough. But come on, woman. Do you love me or hate me? I need some guidance here."

Almost despite herself, Keela let out a restrained smile. "I don't...you know...*hate* you. It's just..." She sighed, then walked to the window. Sunlight caught her cheek. The red of her hair radiated across her face. "You remind me of what I lost. You're just like him. Like Mitri."

Powell was drawn to her, too. Maybe too much. She had Chandra's strength. And smooth skin. "So, uh," he said, re-tucking his shirt, distracting himself from his distraction. "He's a good man? Your husband? Quite a guy."

Keela came immediately into focus, looking right at Powell, almost pleading. "Look what he did for us. What he risked."

"And you feel guilty? Like he did it for you?"

The rage swelled in her eyes again, but quickly dissipated. Powell could see in her a shame she just couldn't hide. Keela nodded, lowered her eyes. "Yeah."

"Well you shouldn't. And he didn't. Your husband did what had to be done. He could've left that responsibility on the back porch, but he took it on so nobody else had to. Me…? I'm a jackass. Nobody made me fly out your way. It's what I do. It's what I always do. Push too far, whizzing on the rules when they get thrown in my face." Powell sighed, letting his eyes drop. "Look where it got me." He knew then just how much he longed for Chandra, how she was far more than his wife and the mother of his only child. She was essential to the fabric of his identity. Powell always knew who he was around her, because in her presence, he never tried to be anything else. He then took an easy step toward Keela. Subtle. Slow. "All I'm saying is…if you carry guilt that isn't yours, it can wreck you inside. It kills you."

Hoping he connected with Keela, that she really heard him, Powell backed off, letting the moment fill with silence. As it held, there was an awkward comfort between them. And then, after a time, she wiped her tears. "You know. You might be right."

Powell's eyes widened with cautious curiosity. "…I am?"

Keela straightened up. "Yep," she said. "You really are a jackass."

CHAPTER FORTY-THREE

THE ROAD LINES whisked along the asphalt. Chandra Powell had the truck at 106 mph. Jesse was strapped into the booster seat in back, kicking her legs, smiling, as if on a carnival ride. There wasn't much chance of getting pulled over, as Houston was glued to the *Crossline* launch. But Chandra hadn't even thought about that. She was going on pure impulse. Something was wrong. Something was definitely wrong.

Sponsored commercials had played on the radio since the broadcast was interrupted: *"...so come on down to Taurus Enterprises' new Shop n' Save mega-mart on Route 59 for all your family barbecue needs. We've got Taurus brand grilles, barbecue sauce, steaks, chips, and beer. And now you can enjoy the new Taurus brand Rocket Supreme nachos..."*

Throughout their years together, Chandra had prepared herself for the worst, as much as anyone can for heartbreak. She wasn't just a pilot's wife. She was *this* pilot's wife. It was simply understood that Marcus risked death at his job just a wee bit more than, say, the cable guy. To deal with the stress, Chandra made a pact with herself. She assumed, no matter what crazy chances he took as a pilot, that Marcus would always come back in one piece and with a smile on his face. So far, so good. But this time?

Yet living in the shadow of death helped her embrace every moment the family was together, because each one before a flight was potentially their last.

What would her life be without Marcus if he were killed? How would she deal with the grief? How would she comfort little Jesse, left to grow up without a father? What would Chandra say? Before they died, Chandra's parents loved Marcus, thought

he was a good and decent man. Yet they warned Chandra of
the risks. The path she followed was hers to choose, but was she
truly prepared to accept the consequences if the danger he faced
caught up with them? Chandra fought against that sentiment
as a younger woman. But as a mother with no living parents to
turn to for comfort or guidance, she understood. Nobody wishes
their daughter to become a pilot's wife. And yet that's exactly
what she became.

Racing along Interstate 10 to Tower Command, Chandra had
no idea what she would do or say when she actually got there.
But she didn't care about security leaks or protocols. She wanted
to know what was going on with her husband, and she wanted
to know now. And lest the Tower wonks thought otherwise, she
wasn't taking *no* for an answer.

The Tower Command security guards were expecting them.
Chandra and Jesse had been through the drill before, directed
to a restricted, underground parking garage. You can't make a
scene if there's no audience. Four levels down they were greeted
by Taurus Enterprises communications director Frederick
Churlson, a paunchy, Stanford-educated African-American man
with black-rimmed glasses and a plaid bowtie.

Walking quickly to the elevator, Churlson explained that,
as came across the broadcast, the warp engines were a huge
success, and Chandra's husband had piloted the ship brilliantly. They were, however, dealing with one more issue. "I
understand your concern, Mrs. Powell, but the broadcast was
interrupted due to a minor communications glitch. We're
resolving it now."

When it came to space travel, Chandra was well aware that
nothing constituted as *minor.* "What kind of glitch?"

"Dale Aranuke will speak with you. He can explain everything better than I can."

"You know...for a P.R. guy, you're not so much with the
answers."

"Yes, yes." Churlson pressed the third-floor button. "People in my position often feel that way. It's an old saw that communications professionals can be the worst communicators. But I'm sharing as much as I can." When the elevator door opened again, he brought Chandra and Jesse down several well-lit corridors, dropping them at the visitor's viewing station. There were three rows of seats, two couches, and a table filled with snacks and drinks. Ceiling-to-floor windows provided an unobstructed view of the launch pad. Jesse helped herself to a jumbo chocolate chip cookie. "I'll let Mr. Aranuke know you're here."

Without waiting for a response, Churlson left Chandra and Jesse, closing the door behind him. Chandra reached for the handle. But then there was a *bzzz click*. Locked. Munching away, Jesse had chocolate chip smears on her face.

Chandra fiddled with the door. She surveyed the room, thought a minute. *Not good.* She spotted the house phone, then lifted the receiver. She heard three quick buzzes—*rur-rur-rur.* No answer. It buzzed three more times before someone picked up. It was Churlson.

"This is Chandra Powell. What's going on? Is my husband okay? Why are we lock—?"

"As I said, Mrs. Powell, Mr. Aranuke can answer all of your—"

Click. Chandra hung up. She didn't need to hear his lies. What she needed was to get out of that room. And she had a pretty good idea about how to make it happen.

Collective shock hung over Tower Command. As far as they knew, *Crossline* and its pilot were destroyed. Buddy Rheams gave the order, but Dale Aranuke pressed the button. And now he had Powell's wife and child just two floors below, unaware, waiting for answers. Aside from the hum of computer terminals, the room was silent.

"Dale." After a moment, Chang whispered his name again. Still, nothing. Had his eyes not blinked, there would have been little sign that Aranuke was conscious.

Aranuke turned his head, but inside he felt like he'd taken a bad turn. The Old Man once told Aranuke that if he wanted the authority he claimed he did, he would be faced with making decisions that he might not want to make. It wasn't the first time someone died because of the *Crossline* project. And it wasn't the first time Aranuke had been responsible. Families destroyed. In his mind's eye he saw Gloria Hicks. Had she lived to see it, she would not have approved.

So, yeah, he thought. *I do have the fangs. I'm just not so sure I was supposed to use them.*

Chang called for him again. "Dale! Wake up!"

"Give me a minute."

"I think you need to see this. It's Powell's wife."

"She can wait."

"Dale!…Look!"

"I said," Aranuke repeated as his eyes drifted toward the monitor. "Give me—" He tried to pinpoint what Chandra Powell was up to. He leaned in close, squinted. "…Is she smoking a joint?"

"Actually…I'd say she's smoking a blunt. That sucker's huge."

Chandra had a plan. By the time Aranuke and Churlson made it to the visitor's viewing station, it was very smoky in there. And stinky. Reacting to what they saw, neither executive noticed that she hadn't actually inhaled, and that her tolerance was strong enough to withstand far more than a contact high. *Good*, she thought. *Phase One.*

Aranuke waved a cloud from his face. "Fffff…Mrs. Powell. I know this is an emotional day, but we can't have you—"

Jesse was standing on a seat, staring at the launch pad. Noting Chandra's signal they had agreed to in advance—three scratches to her wrist—Jesse reached inside her shirt and pulled up a quadruple-layered surgeon's mask dangling from her neck. She waddled over to Chandra, who secured it, covering her mouth and nose. "Play hospital, Mommy. Amookie's here. Have to find Meaty. Meaty-Meaty-Meaty!"

"Not now, Jess. Mommy needs to talk with—"

"Meaty, Mommy, Meaty!"

"Mrs. Powell," Churlson started. "We'll have to ask you to put out that…cigarette. It's a matter of policy that—"

"Meaty-Meaty-Meaty!" Jesse jumped down and ran around the room, extending her arms like airplane wings. The surgical masks covered her face. "Fry me like a beagle. Fast like Daddy. Meaty-Meaty!"

Between Jesse working everyone's last nerve and the obvious affects from his own high, Churlson was getting paranoid. "They'll know what we did. They'll know! They'll find out. You can't smoke in here. We're going to get in trouble. Oh no! They'll know!"

"Meaty, Mommy, Meaty!"

"They know, they'll know!"

His own head about to explode, Aranuke broke through the smoke-induced chaos.

"Churlson! Shut it!" He turned to Chandra. "Ma'am! It's your right to talk, but right now, in this very moment, it's your responsibility to *listen.*" Jesse was still zooming about, but he had Chandra's attention. "There's been an accident."

To calm her nerves, Chandra tapped out the blunt on the bottom of her sneaker. Churlson downed cookies by the handful. But with that single word—*accident*—her rational mind started to unspool. "W-what? What kind of…?"

"Please," Aranuke said. "Sit."

"No…I can't, I…" Chandra leaned back in the seat, pressed her hands against her face. With her eyes squeezed shut, all she could see was pulsing darkness. She started to shake, about to vomit. "Is he…?"

Jesse, meanwhile, was unaffected by Aranuke's pronouncement. Instead she scampered to the door, which hadn't closed all the way. "Yay-yay-yay! Daddy's coming home! Yay-yay-yay!"

With her little hands, Jesse managed to open the door and then slip into the hallway. The door closed behind her.

Before Chandra knew what happened, there was a *bzzz click*. Jesse was gone.

CHAPTER FORTY-FOUR

JESSE CAME TO a narrow hallway with a single elevator, which opened before her. Two computer technicians—one skinnier than the next—were about to exit when she barreled past them. Jesse stood on her tip toes, struggling to reach the buttons.

"Preschool is the other building," SkinnyTech said, amused with himself.

"Yeah," SkinnierTech said, who dork-laughed. "Shnar-shnar. Totally preschool."

Jesse removed her surgical masks. "Buttons," she said.

"Yes. There are lots of buttons, little one. Shnar-shnar." SkinnyTech offered up his high-five hand. Not used to getting high-five invites, SkinnierTech responded eagerly, but missed the target, slapping SkinnyTech in the face.

"Buttons-button-buttons," Jesse demanded. "Push buttons."

"Hey," SkinnierTech said. "You're not even supposed to—"

"Up-up-up. Fry me like a beagle. Push buttons!"

Red-faced and with his glasses askew from the high-five mishap, SkinnyTech was getting annoyed. A name-badge key card dangled from his chest pocket. "Listen missy, I don't think—"

Jesse had no more time for their whiny pushback. Instead she inhaled, opened her mouth, and screamed—the kind of soul-piercing, eye-popping shriek that would have brought Genghis Khan to his knees. Both nerds covered their ears and ducked, as if coming under audible machine gun fire.

SkinnierTech was the first to crack. "Oh, my god! How does she do that?!"

Jesse relented—an illusion that the pain was over. The exhausted tech nerds fell against the wall. She then reiterated her demands. "Pick me up. Buttons-buttons-buttons!"

"No way." SkinnierTech's head started to throb. "We're not—"
Jesse encroached, to demonstrate her authority over them.
She could sustain the assault indefinitely—she was a child, after
all; screeching was her biological imperative. To further her point
she hit a new decibel level that almost ruptured their eardrums.
The helpless nerds re-covered their ears and shrank beneath her
incredible power.

"Holy hell!" SkinnyTech said. "Just do what she wants! Then
call security!"

Jesse was in proper position thanks to SkinnierTech's long,
goofy hands, but she was still frustrated, not sure which buttons
to push. So as she was taught to respond to challenges when there
was no clear and immediate solution, she closed her eyes and
listened—she breathed deep and slow, in through her nose, out
through her mouth—until finally before her were open skies and
white, billowy clouds. And then way in the distance she heard a
screech from her grandmother's spirit. Jesse saw the great hawk
in flight and its two warrior talons. Three of its sharp toes curled
into a hunting grip. Jesse contorted her little hands, mimicking
what she saw. She pressed her digits against the elevator panel—
one hand against buttons 2, 3, and 5, the other against 7, 8, and
11. "More hands," she said. "More hands."

"Pull the alarm!" SkinnierTech said. "Now!"

Jesse opened her mouth. A short jolt got them back under
control.

"WHAT?! I CAN'T HEAR Y—" SkinnyTech yelled.

"DUMBASS! Do what she's doing. Put your fingers on the
buttons. I can't hold her!"

"I'm not helping y—"

"Do it, dumbass!"

Matching Jesse's pose, SkinnyTech contorted his hand into
a claw, placing fingers on the buttons for floors 14, 15, and *BRS*,
Buddy Rheams' private suite. Just above the *BRS* button was a
key card slot. Buddy Rheams possessed the only card. What had
been unknown to everyone except Buddy was that the elevator

came equipped with an emergency backup system in case of a retinal scan problem.

"Push-push-push," Jesse said. "Push." Jesse and SkinnyTech simultaneously depressed the nine buttons, which all lit up and then flashed blue four times before returning to white, thus confirming access to Buddy Rheams' private suite. Arms trembling and his face red and blotchy, SkinnierTech let her down. He fumbled for his asthma inhaler and took two quick puffs.

Taking advantage of their pain and confusion, Jesse grabbed their name badge key cards and tossed them in the hallway. SkinnyTech stuck his foot by the automatic door, allowing the nerds to empty from the elevator, reaching for their badges.

Jesse giggled. "Dumbass," she said. "He's funny."

"Wait," SkinnyTech said. "What just happened?"

"She just called you a dumbass."

"Nuh-uh, dumbass. You're the dumbass."

The elevator doors closed, with Jesse inside, leaving the tech nerds behind.

Chandra started toward the door, to follow Jesse. Aranuke put a hand up. "Mrs. Powell. She'll be fine. But you and I need to—"

With little patience for Aranuke's power games, Chandra opted for Phase Two. She stared into his eyes, hinted at a smile. She then started, slowly, to unfasten the top button on her blouse. She didn't expect Aranuke to reach for her boobs, but she wanted him off balance. Control freaks tend to frazzle if they can't impose the rules or regulate the environment. Coupled with her dense cloud of power weed, there was a situation going on. Churlson was curled on the floor, rocking back and forth, his face smeared with Cheez Doodle residue.

Aranuke stutter-stepped in place. "What, uh...what are you doing?"

Chandra exposed the very top of her cleavage, let her fingers wander down the valley. "What does it look like?" She inserted her hand, let it linger, and then slid it underneath the edge of her red bra. She wriggled her fingers, let her tongue graze her lips, and then, real slow, retracted her fingers. Between them was something long, thin, and white. She put it to her lips. "It's a nervous habit. It helps me…," she said, glancing down at her partially exposed breasts, and then back up so that her eyes again met his, "…relax. It keeps me in the moment."

For all his bluster, Aranuke was speechless.

Chandra lit the joint with a blue and yellow lighter she picked up at a novelty store. The weed was powerful for sure, and would knock anyone on their ass unless they already built up a tolerance to it—which she had—and knew how to pace themselves—which she did. But this one was Feather Finkelbaum's primo strand, passed down through the generations. It was not for the faint of heart. Without serious bong training, two puffs and it was cuckoo for Cocoa Puffs.

"You're really not supposed to, uh…you know…do that here…"

"*Shh-shh-shh*," Chandra said. "Relax." She licked her lips so they were supple and shiny. She inserted the joint between them, took a puff. But rather than inhale, Chandra let her mouth fill with smoke, puckered her lips, and blew the cloud in Aranuke's face. Unprepared for the blast, and before he could reclaim rational, compartmentalized thought, he got a lung full of Feather's Master Blaster weed. Aranuke coughed until his chest and throat were like gravel.

Chandra hit him once more, just to be sure. With Aranuke now obsessing over the lifeline on his right palm, she reached into his pocket, took his key card, and left. She locked the door, leaving Aranuke on the floor, deliberating over just how many snack chips he could fit into his mouth in one go.

After doubling back through the narrow hallway, Chandra finally came upon Buddy's elevator. There she found two skinny dorks, who looked awkward and dumbfounded, even for two skinny, easily dumbfounded dorks. "Where's my daughter? Where's Jesse?"

The tech nerds stared at her, confused and more than just

a little bit frightened. Chandra's partially exposed cleavage put them over the edge. They gestured to the elevator.

"Which one of you dumbasses let her do that?"

The tech nerds shrugged, and pointed at each other.

"Where'd she go? Which button?"

The tech nerds blinked repeatedly, as if that would somehow reboot their frazzled brains. "Umm," SkinnierTech started, and then thought about it scientifically. "A lot of 'em?"

CHAPTER FORTY-FIVE

Gregor's Storm Cloud cover was a successful diversion. Deep in Scraper territory, Sean set the ship behind an abandoned barn about two hundred yards from a stretch of deep woods. Powell drew from his trippy dream flight as they trekked through the snow—its pristine, white beauty obscured the very real danger that lay ahead. He closed his eyes, and before long experienced the strobe light sensation in his mind—that *flash-flash-flash*. He then directed them through the snow-covered woods, which followed a slight, downward slope. With the exception of a few animal tracks, the white blanket of snow was untouched. The sky was long and gray.

They finally let out onto a two-lane highway, with more woods on both sides of the road. As Gregor predicted, the snow started falling harder and faster, severely limiting their visibility, but they kept a steady pace for more than an hour despite the brutal conditions. And then Powell, with his face stinging and raw, recognized a deer coming out of the woods.

Strobe light. Blackness. *Flash-flash-flash.* The deer. *Yes. I remember now. The tree with a black lightning scar. The squirrel darting into a stump.* Which meant that up ahead, through the punishing storm, they would know exactly when and where to stop. The reason became obvious. There was a blockade in the road.

Powell whispered. "How do we get past them? I don't like this."

There were knowing smiles. Dolores looped her arm through Powell's, then patted him with her gloved hand. "Don't worry, dear. Leave this to me."

Two armed soldiers stood in the middle of the highway, in formation, pelted with snow. Parked on an angle, their truck cut off access in both directions. Dolores seemed unconcerned. A large knitting bag hung from her shoulder. Her breath came out in a frosty cloud.

"Hello, boys. I must look a fright. We've been having quite a time of it." Her cheeks were red and puffy. Dolores dabbed at her nose, and then pointed through the falling snow to Sean and Chill, who were both shivering, stamping their feet, and blowing on their ungloved hands. Powell blew his nose into a handkerchief with enough force to pop an eye out. "Our jeep broke down. We're lost again. I'm not much of a navigator, I'm afraid."

The brawnier of the two soldiers eyed them suspiciously. The name patch sewed into his uniform said *Stapoyovich*. He squeezed his rifle a bit tighter, grazed the trigger, and then nodded to *Figg*, his taller, thinner partner. "Nobody's come through this way in weeks," Stapoyovich said. "We'll have to call it in."

"As young men should. Very conscientious. I've been up north, in Carlton City, taking care of...," Dolores nodded toward her motley crew, and lowered her voice. 'Well, they're very sweet and all—they really are—and a fine help around the house. But they're also a bit...," she whispered, "...*slow-witted*." She spoke at a normal volume again. 'But my arthritis. It's just too cold for me now." Dolores rolled her fingers, grimaced, then looked up at the soldiers with just the right mix of discomfort, self-reliance, and well-adjusted acquiescence. "Speaking of which, do you mind if I eat? My blood sugar is low."

Stapoyovich exchanged shrugs with his partner, then nodded his approval.

From her knitting bag Dolores produced a large muffin chock full of banana wedges and berries. She tore off the top. The beleaguered guards stared at the muffin like dogs waiting for scraps, following the pieces from Dolores' fingertips to her lips, and watched her chew, swallow, and sigh contentedly.

"My goodness, how rude of me. Would you boys like one? I baked them myself. A happy stomach makes the day just right."
The good little guard doggies nodded, and then accepted their

reward, which they devoured. "Well, good, boys. Good. Now that we're such good friends and all, I just have one small favor to ask."

The military truck motored along the snow-lined highway. With Stapoyovich driving and Figg riding shotgun, Powell and Dolores sat in the first row of rear seats, behind the guards, with Sean and Chill behind them. Powell held his muffin away like a spoiled fish. He spit out the chunk he was about to swallow. Thanks to Gregor's meteorological voodoo, the snow came down in a mad frenzy. "You drugged these?"

Dolores smiled. "Why, of course, dear. But don't worry. Yours is fine."

Powell had finally learned not to be surprised by anything these people did or suggested, but Grinroad's poisoner was offering him food, and he'd already eaten from her hand.

Dolores nodded to the soldiers, who now possessed poised, though slightly blank looks—an intense, highly functioning trance. She tore a muffin in half. "Can you see here, the yellow discoloration? It makes one quite agreeable, as you can tell by those two up front." She held out another muffin. "And these…?"

"The blueberries?"

"Oh, those aren't blueberries, dear. But, yes, they make you very sleepy. And there are a few other ingredients I best not discuss. A girl's got to have her secrets."

Powell eyed the soldiers up front when a single thought hit him hard. "Wait. Did you give me the brainwash food before I volunteered?" Saying the words aloud freaked him out. "You drugged me into this?"

"Marcus. You shouldn't be so suspicious. You'll hurt my feelings." She winked at her obedient guard zombies through the rearview mirror. They smiled with vacant stares in return. "Besides, the ingredients are difficult to come by. It took me almost four years to gather enough just for the batch I've got with me. I can't spare a drop."

"But the muffins are all in the same bag. What if you mixed them up?"

More than a minute went by before Powell accepted that his question, like many others, would go unanswered. So he sat in silence. He just watched the snow, in large flakes, as they continued to fall against the windshield. The wipers swung back and forth, revealing a long road ahead.

CHAPTER FORTY-SIX

THE RESCUE TEAM passed through key military checkpoints on the way to Prado City. As instructed Figg and Stapoyovich explained to each new set of armed guards that they were transporting refugees from Lincolnwood Center, the psychiatric facility up north, relocating them all to the Chapman-Vitoff Health & Recovery Clinic, where they would then join the City Center theatre troupe. As long as the loonies were properly medicated, they sang and danced and baked a mean batch of muffins—which each new set of guards gladly accepted.

Through the windshield Powell could see nothing except more road and the slight woods, and then finally the first glimpse of the Prado River that surrounded Prado City. But when they approached the highway's arch, his anxiety swelled.

The arch felt ominous somehow, deadly, like the mouth of a dragon whose jaws opened wider and wider, not just to swallow them whole—devour them—but also to annihilate the fabric of their very being. Powell couldn't truly know how his voyage through space-time affected his existence in the memory of those back on Earth. He strongly felt that Jesse had maintained a very real connection with him through her unique gift, but how much of that was real and how much had he imagined?

Displaced in the cosmos, Powell feared that Chandra and Jesse wouldn't mourn his loss or fret his return because in their hearts and minds—in their very souls—there would simply be no one to miss. Perhaps an echo of his presence would resonate with them in a passing dream. A glimpse. But otherwise Chandra and Jesse would live out their days as if Powell had simply never been.

The highway then sank below the horizon so that only the

arch's distant peak—the eyes of that asphalt dragon—appeared ahead. It took them down a long road leading to a horrible, endless nowhere, exceedingly farther from his own center of gravity, and closer to the sickening and monstrous tragedies that befell all who dared to enter.

The road continued to sink until it hit bottom. Despite the murky heat of the dragon's belly, Powell felt a chill run through him. Colder than any needle—soulless—it made his very essence quiver. Foreboding doom.

Powell ran his hand over his chest, over his heart. He looked about the truck, and as he saw Chill and Sean, and then Dolores next to him and the two muffined-up zombie guards in front, he felt something beneath his coat. He reached inside. And when he withdrew his hand, he extracted the *Nan'yehi* doll Jesse gave him, to protect him. To remind him, she said, that no matter where he was or how far he traveled, she would always be with him. He would never be alone. Before anyone could see, Powell shook off a tear. Were he not already seated, he would have fallen to his knees.

Sean leaned closer from the seat behind him. The others were asleep. "You up to this? The visions Chill shared?…You trust them?"

Powell shrugged, ran his tongue over his teeth to prove to himself that he was alert and in the moment. He whispered so as not to wake Chill, who was leaning against the side window, dream drooling. "I don't know. I want to. But those stories about him. From the mountains…"

"It wasn't me," Chill said, as always, more attuned to his surroundings than expected. "It was Riva."

The mere mention of Carlos Guerra rendered them silent.

"I did go into the mountains. Without my family, I had nothing to live for. I had a pistol. To use on myself." Chill sat up. "But one night, I heard the screams. I followed them through the darkness. And when I got there…I found Carlos. There was a small fire burning. I don't know how, but he captured the five bandits, tied them to trees. He approached the leader, held a knife to his throat. Their lives meant nothing to me. They were wild dogs. But I called for Carlos. To stop. To have mercy. And then he came to me. He put the knife in my hand. He raised his arms up, exposing his chest, in sacrifice, daring me to strike. And then he recited the sacred oath:

-*Remember the day, remember the night*-
-*Remember the howl…remember the rite*-
-*Remember the dreams, remember the plight*-
-*Remember us all…remember the light.*

"I thought of my children then, my wife. I saw them waiting for me, to purge my soul. Yet I just stood there. In silence. My heart pounded. I couldn't move. How do you kill a demon? How do you extinguish the beast?…I know they did not actually do so, but I saw his eyes glow red in the night. After our silence passed, Carlos took the knife back from me, and smiled. And then he slit their throats. One by one. He bathed in their horror, in their blood, listening to them scream. When he was done, he looked right at me again. I saw the rapture in those eyes. His communion with madness. Without another word, he walked off, beneath the stars, as if gliding through a nightmare.

"War created a monster. And I let him go. Perhaps he would have subdued me. I don't know. But I failed to act. And because of my weakness…dozens, if not hundreds have been murdered since that night. They were delivered by Riva's hand. But the fault? It lies with me."

Powell slid his hand across the seat belt, felt for his sidearm. Even the soldiers remained still, as if Riva himself was hovering like a mist, about to materialize. Prado City was not far off, and despite the dangers that lay ahead, Powell no longer knew who to fear most.

Coming out of the slight dip in the highway, all the team could see at first were the building tips, then the entirety of Prado City's majestic skyline. It rose from the horizon, growing larger with skyscrapers by the dozens, tower after tower. Glass and metal structures jutting up toward the heavens in all manner of height, gleam, and domination.

An open-air man, Powell had been to cities. To Houston, and Denver, and San Francisco that one time for his cousin's bachelor party. But there was something about the city ahead that made him shudder. It reminded him of his few trips to New York, that city that never sleeps. If you could make it there, the saying went, you could make it anywhere, and maybe even if that was true, Powell never understood why anyone would *want* to make it there, even if they could.

Powell had that rush he would get on the road to the launch pad. The pre-flight butterflies that caused his chest to tighten, his face to go flush, and the taste of adrenaline to coat his mouth, down to his teeth and gums. The difference between now and then was just so very small, but even if for just a few seconds, that intense queasiness would make him question in a shameful, shaky handed way if he knew what the hell he was doing, and consider that maybe he'd be better off hauling ass in the opposite direction and skipping out on the whole damn thing.

But then the intensity of the panic subsided—the urgency of the present snapping him back from his fears of a worst possible future, one that would require him to confront the demon at the gates. He steadied himself, because like his father told him: *Nerves only mean you ain't completely stupid. Get over it, boy. There's work to be done.* The clarity and confidence of his father's voice resonated more than ever.

The truck emerged from the final valley, from the belly of the asphalt dragon. Ahead was a sign indicating the onramp for the Uhlmeier Bridge, a suspension bridge supported by massive cables. Long, slotted shadows were thrown along the windshield as they crossed the Prado River. Feeling the road dissolve behind them, Powell, ironically, felt more solid, centered. He was giving himself up to the hands of fate, if there was even such a thing. He then felt a tap on his shoulder.

"Your ship is just one way to fly," Chill said, seeming more like the shaman Powell had come to know. "You've seen that now. Trust the spirit. It knows the way."

Powell chuckled uneasily. "If you say so."

"Your journey is long, my friend. It's far from over."

"Maybe," Powell said. "Maybe." He checked his sidearm again, even though he was loath to use it. "But unless I make it home again, this journey can bite me."

CHAPTER FORTY-SEVEN

ENTERING PRADO CITY was simple enough. Going with the flow of afternoon traffic, the Uhlmeier Bridge deposited the rescue team on a major expressway leading southbound along the western edge of the Prado River. From there they zigged and zagged through the Theatre District, a luxury retail corridor, and then a tree-lined residential community until they finally intersected with Alabaster Avenue, Prado City's main north/south artery.

From there they traveled along its diagonal path toward the southern base of the island, where they came upon a green space, with a large plaque labeled: *Montgomery Park*

Stapoyovich idled the truck next to a small, triangular building on the corner. There was a bistro at street level, with bay-windowed apartments above, and shopping along the half block, including a mystery bookstore, gourmet coffee house, custom framing and poster gallery, and a boutique, second-hand clothing shop. Directly ahead was a through-street running perpendicular to them, and along Montgomery Park. A wide path ran through the middle of the park. There was a fountain in the center.

Beyond Montgomery Park were three short blocks lined with four-story buildings, mostly art studios and residential spaces. Fire escapes were bolted into the brick face. And beyond those streets again was the Lower Financial District. A wall of sky-scrapers lorded over the residents.

Powell leaned forward. The strobe light went off in his head again. "Wait-wait-wait." He pointed to a spot a hundred yards dead ahead and all the way through the park, beyond the south entrance. On the sidewalk, two men—each cradling a white frou-frou dog—were gesticulating. They faced a large, gray door set between a fusion restaurant and a boutique wine shop. "There. With the dogs. Olivia's in there."

Sean's sidearm clacked against the seat belt. "You sure? Don't fuck around." The others looked to Powell for confirmation. He closed his eyes once again, focused. The strobe light was intense. *Flash-flash-flash.*

"Positive," he said. "That's it."

Dolores addressed her obedient muffin zombies. "Did you hear that, boys? You've done a wonderful job. I'm so proud. We just need some assistance getting into that building."

Unable to hold back an aw-shucks grin, Stapoyovich looked at Dolores through the rear view mirror. "That'll be a tough one, ma'am. Security is tight. See how there are twice as many street lights around the park? Those are tracking poles. They create an infrared grid. Unless you can disable the system, there's virtually no way to get through the park undetected in the time you've discussed. And given the configuration of the surrounding streets, there's no other way to get to that building. It's boxed in."

Dolores sat back, smiling. "Don't worry about that, dear. We'll be fine. But we've got a big day ahead and you'll need your strength. Have another muffin."

Watching Figg and Stapoyovich devour their zombie food, Powell sighed. He didn't even want to think about what Dolores had in mind.

Feeling a need to be near him, Powell followed Chill outside the truck. The nearby park had the buzz of an ordinary day when the next few minutes would bring anything but.

"Marcus," Chill said, as he lit his pipe. "What are the tenets of aerial combat?"

Powell saw a bird take flight, with conviction. It leapt from a fence post and then soared above the tree line. Others followed. "Stay calm, know your surroundings," and finally heeding his father, "fire when ready."

"I know you're not a foot soldier, but the same is true now.

Listen to Dolores. Follow her lead. She is cunning in battle."

Powell shook his head. "I still don't get that."

Chill chuckled. "Why?"

"Because she seems so...you know...cuddly. I mean, when she's not poisoning people. Plus, she's got eight kids. What if she's killed? What happens to them?"

"Dolores has defended our lives, time and again. She knows the risks of combat. Her scars run deep. But she can best protect her children by leading us now. If we fail today...their troubles have just begun."

"But what about her husband? He's gotta be sick inside. Doesn't he worry?"

Chill refilled his pipe. "Your thoughts are with Chandra. With Jesse."

Montgomery Park was one hundred thirty-four feet end-to-end—negligible in flight, but on a runway, it was the difference between safety and danger. And at times, between life and death. Assessing his current position, Powell knew that crossing that threshold would either rip him farther away from his wife and daughter, or bring him closer to them.

"I hear them," he said. "Like a whisper."

"There are those who believe we must bury those thoughts. That our love makes us weak. But the bonds we share survive time and space. They endure. Focus on your prayers—to hold your girls again—and the fear will keep you sharp. What lies between here and there," Chill said, nodding to the park, "is the trust you place in your comrades, and in yourself. Things will unfold as they will. Be ready."

There was rustling in the truck. It was time. "Okay," Powell said. "I trust them."

Chill placed his pipe inside his jacket and felt his belt for extra ammo. "Good. It will also help to load your weapon. Trust only goes so far."

CHAPTER FORTY-EIGHT

POWELL WASN'T A locker room guy, never would be, but he took the unavoidable in stride. And yet even all his years of flight training never quite prepared him for the number of swinging penises that flapped about.

When the operation kicked in, Powell saw the following scene unfold:

Following Dolores' instructions, Stapoyovich soldiered his way to Montgomery Park with a satchel, and one grunt to another, offered a mini-muffin to the guard stationed at the east entrance. As had worked on Stapoyovich himself, the muffins successively drew the attention across the park of the dozen other guards, who one by one got their muffin on.

And then: The flutter of scattering pigeons. Honking cars. The traffic light ahead turned from red to green. Like caps at a graduation ceremony, military attire went flying into the trees. Camouflage shirts and pants hung from branches. An old woman gasped. Teenagers giggled, pointed, and stared. And texted their friends. The girls, too. Three cabs collided. Then the screaming began.

Other than combat boots, dog tags, and their fully loaded pulse rifles, thirteen soldiers had gone stark, raving insane. And hear-me-roar naked.

Embracing their inner divas, the bare-assed mini-muffin squad pounced on anyone with a purse, and like getting combat tattoos, smeared the confiscated eyeliner, rouge, and blush on their faces, plumped their lips with all color of lipstick, and went outright bonkers with the eyeliner. Ready for the burlesque ball, the naked soldiers chest-bumped, and swatted their own heads like baboons declaring war.

"HOO! HOO! HOO!"

They squeezed their nipples. They gyrated their hips. And their appendages, in all manner of girth, outreach, and circumcision, swirled like propellers. Powell, Sean, Chill, and Figg awaited further instruction.

"As soon as Stapoyovich gathers up the chorus line, we go in. Although...," Dolores said, tapping her index finger to her lower lip, "...I think maybe a little less diva dust in the next batch. It's a difficult recipe."

Another wave of screams pulled them back to the fleeing crowd. Cabs tried to force themselves through the narrow streets. Near the edge of the park, one mini-muffin soldier with an excessive amount of purple eye shadow offered Stapoyovich one end of a dog's leash, the other end harnessed around his half-erect penis. Dolores cringed. "Oh, my goodness. Definitely too much diva dust. Must make a note of that. Well, by the looks of it, they'll be completely riled in two or three minutes. Once they attack the...wait. What does that say?" She leaned forward, squinting. "The Merry...Berry...Soda Shop? Huh. What a cute name. Anyway, once they start blasting and hit the upper floors, we'll need to move quickly."

Dolores pointed beyond the park, two blocks from Olivia's location. "If everyone follows my instructions, we have a better than even chance of reaching the other side without taking a bullet in the brain."

The next sequence was key: Entice panic, but offer them a concentrated outlet through which to focus that fear—away from Olivia. And how better to orchestrate chaos than by tapping into the vapid lust for fame? Following Dolores' instructions, Figg explained that Stapoyovich was spreading word among his fellow soldiers that television heartthrobs Drago Arroyo and Dana Lorman—whose sweaty, half-naked images were emblazoned on a massive billboard overlooking the park—overdosed on the third floor, above the Merry Berry Soda Shop, and that the paparazzi, who were still up there, orchestrated the overdose as a major story they could break.

"I'm guessing there will be explosions, sirens, and a fair amount of blood," Dolores said. "Take advantage."

In a surreal, out-of-body moment, Powell watched himself watch the scene around him. Dolores and Chill. Figg and Sean. The park. The naked soldiers. The buildings. The traffic. Sunshine reflecting off the windshield of an idling car. A mailbox with a scratch on the side. Powell wasn't numb, confused, or nervous. He just *was*. The moment before takeoff. And then Dolores took his hand. Amidst the chaos, all he could think was that her clasp was soft. True. His heart raced, settled, and then leveled with an adrenaline high. The team linked hands.

Dolores closed her eyes. "Let our choices have virtue, even though our actions may not. May the gods see our return, forgive our mistakes…and let us find wisdom in our toil." She nodded, breaking the circle. She opened a compact and, staring into the tiny mirror, primped her hair. She then removed a huge, silver-plated handgun and cocked the trigger. She switched off the safety. "Lock and load, boys. They took one of ours. Now make those fuckers *pay*."

Chill, Sean, and Dolores did a weapons count. Figg removed a shotgun from beneath the front seat. He slapped a sidearm in Powell's hand.

Dolores reassured Powell. "It's okay, dear. This isn't my first fellatio."

Eyes a-bulge and mouth open, Powell blinked twice. "Please tell me you mean *rodeo*."

The weapons check ceased. Dolores blushed. "Marcus. My word. I'm a married woman. I have children." She regained her composure, then eyed Powell up and down like a tasty piece of man cake. "But if I wasn't…?" She winked. "You're pretty scrumptious yourself."

They ran. Figg was on point, followed by Dolores, Powell, Sean, and Chill. They came upon the long row of cars gridlocked in front of Montgomery Park, and ducked behind a blue hatchback. A panting dog inside wagged its tail and let out four quick barks.

There was an explosion in the distance, followed by the sound of screams and breaking glass. But they were muffled, so they didn't feel threatening. Didn't feel real. But then came the *fttttt...ftttttt...ftttttt* of automatic gunfire, followed by the hell and fury of erupting violence.

Powell cringed at the persistent screams. He knew then that the ruckus wasn't a random act, but an all-out attack. That the assailants—the very soldiers assigned by the corporate powers to guard the area—were naked, covered in eye-liner and at least temporarily psychotic. And that the blood oozing out of the dead bodies in front of the Merry Berry Soda Shop did not signal the end of the carnage. It had only just begun.

Though an experienced pilot trained to handle high-stress, life-or-death scenarios, Powell nonetheless had never been in live, street-level combat. For just the first few breaths he had that dream-like sensation of *running running running* without being in control of his body. In the single blink of an eye he picked up scattered images: a cellophane bag; a half-eaten sandwich; a decapitated woman; a smart phone with its keyboard open; a pepperoni pizza slice with a boot print in the cheese; camouflage clothes strewn about; a cross-hatched garbage can knocked over; the skyline; two disemboweled soldiers; flames spewing from a window; black smoke; and a street sign that read: *Park Closes at Midnight*

The crowds scattered. Stapoyovich's mini-muffin soldiers engaged in battle two blocks down. Clothed soldiers and police descended upon them in response. And then came a hail of gunfire and the crazy howls and ugly chants that only imminent death draws out.

Refocused, alert, Powell coiled his finger around the trigger as the rescue team chugged across the park, around the fountain. But a clothed soldier ran at them full bore and firing his weapon. Less than a yard from Powell, a shotgun—triggered by a hand he never saw—unleashed its fury and *KRA-BLAM! KRA-BLAM!* The soldier's head exploded like a watermelon tossed from a rooftop. He stopped dead, and fell at Powell's feet—blood and brain matter surrounded the torso, smearing the pavement. And then another soldier charged. Powell raised his arm, pointing the gun. He was ready to fire. To kill. But Sean pushed his hand away. "Don't."

The approaching soldier tapped his middle finger to his thumb three times fast—the *all safe* signal. Figg sprinted from the opposite side. He responded in kind. "They're with us, ma'am. Stapoyovich sent them. They ate the muffins. Good to go."

Chill took Powell's outstretched arm. "Ease up, Marcus. Easy. We're through the park now. Remember to breathe. Breathe… breathe…"

Powell understood Chill's words, but he couldn't unclench his fist from the gun. His pilot instincts refused to relinquish the stick in a tailspin.

Hold on. Never let go.

"Just breathe, Marcus. Like we talked about. Feel your inner chill. Remember…we're here to find Olivia. Just breathe and—"

Crack! Dolores' slap struck Powell on the face. "Marcus! Get your shit together."

Startled at first, Powell's eyes snapped open. He shook his head, then let out three quick breaths. His arm relaxed. Rational Powell was back. "Okay," he said. "I'm okay."

Dolores gently patted his face. She offered an understanding smile. "Sorry, dear. I know it's your first gunplay, but we just don't have time for this. It's war."

CHAPTER FORTY-NINE

WITH AN UNDERSTATED *bing*, the elevator doors opened into Buddy's private suite. Jesse surveyed the landscape—the couches; the coffee table; the wall-mounted TVs; the long corridors on either side of her; the recessed lighting; the paintings. But what drew her attention was a white t-shirt sticking out from the bottom of a closet door to the side of the TV wall and opposite the viewing station. She waddled over, picked up the shirt. It smelled funny. Like candles. She then reached up, and though she struggled at first, got the closet door open.

Rather than finding shelves, storage, or clothes, the closet opened into a dim, cool space with arched red rock walls. Nooks were carved into the walls. In the nooks were wood carvings, leather pelts, and various candles. Many were lit.

The first thing Jesse noticed was her immediate sense of calm. It was the same feeling she had back home, out in the yard, staring off at the rolling hills. Fascinated at how the sky and the land—the upper blue and the lower green—were not separate elements, but layers of the same picture that stretched on and on and on.

Jesse went to a nook. The wood carvings were mostly elongated warrior faces with white, horizontal paint marks. Grandma Feather had many like them. Jesse took one. She unzipped her hoody pocket and produced a *Nan'yehi* doll, like the one she gave to her Daddy. And when she held it against the wood carving, it was as she thought. They were the same.

A cool breeze crept through the closet cave. The candles flickered. Jesse closed her eyes, letting herself settle. She breathed in deeply. Then out, and she turned to catch the breeze. When she opened her eyes, she found herself facing the cave wall. On it was a sketch. She ran her fingers across, and smiled. "Daddy," she said.

Jesse scanned the wall again. She found other sketches and symbols—a hawk, a snake, a red mountain with a white peak. And while she wasn't exactly sure what they all meant, she was certain who put them there and what she was supposed to do next. As she had done many times before, like her mother, Jesse sat cross-legged on the floor, and closed her eyes. And just seconds later, with her mind adrift, she found that comforting gust of wind to carry her spirit where she most wanted to go, welcomed, as always, by the screech of the great hawk.

"Gremma Fevver," she said. "It's Jesse."

Ordering the frazzled tech nerds to replicate Jesse's three-button talon grip—and subsequently kicking them out of the elevator—Chandra had a peculiar sense that the space between the floor she left and the one she was traveling toward couldn't be measured in distance alone.

The elevator emptied into Buddy's private suite. She immediately spotted the closet door. It was left open just enough for someone to fit through. Someone small. Dim, flickering lights shadowed into the hall. She entered the closet cave. There she found Jesse, almost in a trance, sitting cross-legged on the floor. Chandra's heart thumped slowly.

Jesse opened her eyes. She tapped the floor with her open palm. "Sit, Mommy, sit."

Filled with joy, relief, and a queasy apprehension, Chandra nodded. But as she took in the closet cave—the flickering candles, the wood carvings, the paintings: of the hawk, the snake, the mountains…her husband—she felt a warmth in her heart she'd long forgotten. She nodded and took her place by Jesse's side. They held hands.

"Close your eyes, Mommy. Gremma's here."

Smiling now, Chandra awaited further instruction. She had done her best to teach Jesse a great many things, but as Aranuke had said—right then, in that very moment—while it was her right to talk, it was her responsibility to listen. So she did.

"Feel the wind, Mommy. Fly."

Eyes closed, Chandra was breaking through. Her entire body tingled. Random thoughts flickered with the candles: test papers she hadn't graded; her father's yarmulke; the corner stoplight on her way to work, always stuck on yellow; Aranuke; the rail of her mother's hospital bed; Marcus with a beer, at the grill, overcooking the hamburgers; her place in Temple; a half moon shining at night; Jesse. And slowly, the images started to dissipate, until finally they faded into nothing. Her heartbeat settled down. Her mind was quiet.

In the stillness, there was nothing, until Chandra really did feel a gust of wind through her center. She felt puny, like standing in the deep ravine, with the great mountains and the pull of the Earth, of the spirits. And in her insignificance she felt somehow so truly significant, as if her mere being meant that she really did have a purpose.

Chandra's heart was pounding again, when in that inner distance she heard the screech of a hawk. The feathered warrior soared and rose and descended again until it was right upon her. And then Chandra was with that hawk. Together. The same. They soared through the heavens. The clouds brushed her skin. The wind—maybe even her spirit—flowed through her as easily as she could breathe.

The hawk spread its mighty wings. Together they soared. To a mountaintop. And there, in full Indian gear, was a woman.

Feather spoke. "Welcome, child. I've been expecting you."

Immersed in deep meditation, Chandra extended her arms, to finally and truly embrace her mother—and have her reciprocate. The hawk's screech cried out then, piercing Chandra's soul. Transcending time and space, the screech came from the shared language of consciousness, communicated through the cosmos, beyond words or symbols, expressed in the prehistoric yearning embedded in the fiber of all living beings that intrinsically know, somehow, some way, that they are all one with, and part of, the Universe. A part of God.

Chandra opened her eyes. She blinked repeatedly. Back in the closet cave, on the floor, Jesse was sitting there, smiling. And in a manner she had never done before, Chandra started to cry. Just bawling and bawling. The wail came from someplace long ago and far away. The tears weren't of pain, but relief. At long last, she found her way.

Jesse climbed into Chandra's lap and wrapped her little arms around Chandra's neck. "I knew you'd come. Gremma said you would."

Messy with tears, Chandra sniffed, wiping her face. "Sorry it took so long."

"That's okay, Mommy. Gremma says when you were a baby you used to stick your butt out during the foow moon. That's why you have that name." Jesse giggled. "You have a gohden butt name. Gremma's funny."

Chandra hugged Jesse and held her close. "Yeah, she's a regular riot."

"Maybe. But guess why I'm not laughing." Chandra and Jesse looked up. Aranuke stood in the doorway, tie knotted around his forehead. His shirt was unbuttoned. Orange snack chip crumbs littered his jacket. "Try hallucinating that you're water skiing with your dead girlfriend, and then getting the munchies. I don't even like Doritos."

There was much that needed saying. Chandra planned to say it all. But before she could apologize to Aranuke for nailing him with Feather's brain blaster weed, before she could express to her daughter how they would journey together going forward, across the floor spread a long, distorted shadow. Within its confines, there was a mix of familiarity, dread, and hope.

Buddy Rheams shook his head. His refuge from public isolation, his inner sanctum, had been compromised. "So much for security," the Old Man said. "I gotta change that code."

Jesse sprang from her mother's lap, jumping up and down as she pointed. "Meaty, Mommy, Meaty! Meaty-Meaty-Meaty!"

"Not now, honey. Mommy's tired."

"No, Mommy, look!"

Aranuke was baffled. "What the hell's going on? What is this place? Sir. I don't—"

"See, Mommy? Just like Gremma said. Meaty."

"Honey," Chandra said, "you're killing me with this. Let's take a break."

Buddy Rheams took a step closer. "Actually, Mrs. Powell. I think she means me."

Chandra rolled her eyes. "Uh, no offense there, chief, but she does this a lot. She's talking about her Uncle Pete. He died a long time ago. It's a long story."

Jesse shook her head back and forth, smiling and giddy as she did.

"Mrs. Powell...Chandra. The world knows me as Buddy Rheams Jr. But for my first many years, I was known as *Mitri Amos*. My birth name."

Chandra blinked deliberately. Meeting Buddy Rheams, the Old Man, cemented for her that he was a real person. Yet despite his advanced age, thin white hair, and nest of wrinkles sprawled across his face and hands, his posture and pose were remarkably sound. And still she had no idea what he meant. "...Huh?"

"Another long story."

"Then just give me the highlights. Cut to the chase."

Buddy nodded. Smirked to himself. "The chase. Right. In short...I think your daughter is trying to say my name. I think she's saying *Mitri*."

Aranuke looked at him oddly. "Sir?"

Chandra turned to Jesse, sensing in her soul that Buddy Rheams was speaking the truth. "Is that it, honey? Are you saying *Mitri*?"

Her parent's child indeed, Jesse rolled her eyes. "Oh, for the wuv of Anne Mawet. That's what I said, Mommy. Meaty."

CHAPTER FIFTY

BUDDY RHEAMS JR., who revealed himself as Mitri Amos, pointed to the closet cave wall, and the drawings on them. With crow's feet, sun spots, and puffy fingers of advanced age, he explained his former life on Aretha, how he crashed in the Kinsey desert, and how the technology used to revolutionize life as they knew it on Earth had not, in fact, been invented by Taurus Enterprises' scientists, but retrieved from his demolished ship—the *Kosono*.

Chandra and Aranuke stared blankly.

"I'm not saying what I did was right or just. But when your world is torn apart, you get desperate. You make choices." Mitri went to the wall. He ran his finger over the drawings. Jesse joined him. "When I saw your husband for the first time I almost blacked out. You can't imagine what it was like. After all those years, with no one to talk to about who I really was or what I was up against...at *most* I thought I could replicate the warp drive. Maybe. Once the company came together, that seemed at least remotely plausible. But as driven as I was, I never truly believed—I mean, not *really*—that I could ever make it back to Aretha. It was just a fantasy to keep me going. It gave me a purpose. Gave me hope." Gently, he ran the back of his hand along Jesse's cheek. She smiled back. "But when I saw his face, when I shook the hand of this actual person...I knew that he just *had* to be the one. It's like falling in love. When you know you know. See this painting here? These markings? They're burned in my mind. I re-created them from Aretha. They're special to us. Sacred. Doubt plagued me for decades. But from the second he walked through the door...it vanished. The guilt I carried... was gone. I'm sorry, Dale. I know what you lost. It's one of my deep regrets. But it was always going to be Powell. It had to be.

There was no one else."

Aranuke finally spoke in a low, hazy mumble. "It's all because of you. I blamed him, but it's all because of you."

"I'm not here for forgiveness, Dale. Each one of us wanted something we had no inherent right to claim as our own. But we went for it anyway. I'm telling you because we've got work to do. And we have to do it now."

Finally able to speak again, Chandra shifted her head. "What do you mean *we*?"

"For the past few weeks we picked up some readings out there. They were faint from this distance, but the satellites are impressive. I didn't know for sure, but I had to believe that after all these years, my people, from Aretha, finally came looking for me. I just had to find out. So the night before the launch...I spoke with your husband. We talked about the stars. About our place in history. What warp speed would mean. How our lives would change. I didn't exactly *tell* him to do it, but I...*encouraged* him to explore. To see what was out there." Mitri stepped away from the wall. "But then there were problems. We don't know what happened, but he followed that ship through the wormhole. To Aretha. He's with them now. At least...I assume so. But if I'm still here, I have to believe he's okay, too. I don't know why and I don't know how, but your husband and I...we're in this together. As he goes...so do I."

There was silence except for Aranuke's KATI, which had been buzzing every thirty seconds. Chang was sending 911 codes, with variations including *tool*, *a-hole*, and *jerkwad*.

Chandra blinked over and over. Her hands shook. "N-no," she said. "This can't be..."

Jesse jumped up and down. "True, Mommy, true. Meaty says true."

Believing it, too, because the truth has a texture all its own, Chandra went to the wall, let her fingers graze the drawings. She spoke softly. "You're...from this place?"

Mitri nodded, watching Chandra shut her eyes. And by the

time she opened them again, she seemed to have found something within herself.

"And my husband's there, too? You think he's safe?"

Mitri nodded again. "I hope so. I really do."

Chandra turned just then so that she was facing him direct.
"You're married? Your wife is back there, right?"

Throughout his many years on Earth, no one had ever
inquired about Keela. No one knew to ask. But now that Chandra was asking, Mitri almost wept. "I...I pray every day. But it's
been so long..."

Whether an expression of genuine empathy, shock, or a stall
tactic to plot her next move, Chandra nodded nonetheless. Mitri
found the gesture oddly comforting.

"I guess I don't need *this* anymore." He peeled off his synthetic skin mask. The same with his neck and hands. "I realized after awhile I wasn't aging like everyone else. I don't know
why. Something with the wormhole, I suspect. But you can only
look thirty-five for so long without it ending up on VidTube." He
peeled a long strand from his neck. "I hated wearing this stuff,
but it helped me hide, helped me forget. I could feel that it wasn't
Mitri Amos making those decisions. It was Buddy Rheams Jr. It
was just easier this way."

While Chandra and Aranuke stared in sickening, wide-
eyed disbelief, Jesse clapped and smiled and jumped up and
down. "Do it again, do it again! Mommy-Mommy-Mommy! Do
it again! Meaty pulled his face off! He looks like Daddy. Do it
again," she said. "Do it again!"

Chandra and Aranuke could do nothing but blink repeatedly. Their mouths hung open.

Free from his camouflage, Mitri leaned down and smiled at
Jesse. "No more pretending. It's time for me to go."

Chandra shook her head. "Go? Go where?"

"Don't worry. It'll all work out."

Aranuke had other thoughts. "Work out, my ass. What do
we do now?"

"Focus on Powell."

"...Powell? But we—"

Chandra jumped in, ignoring Jesse as she tugged her shirt. "He's in *another dimension!*" Her knees buckled. "Wow.... I really said those words out loud. Oh, god..."

"Have faith, Mrs. Powell. They're tough. He'll make it."

"How can you know that? You said—"

Jesse tugged even harder on Chandra's shirt. "True, Mommy, true. Daddy's in the spaceship. Meaty says true."

Chandra looked down at Jesse. She leaned over. "Did Grandma tell you?"

Jesse nodded. "Daddy's coming, Mommy. Daddy's coming home."

With those words—*Daddy's coming home*—Mitri saw Chandra close her eyes and weep. Purely on instinct, Mitri took her in his arms, in a unique position in all the cosmos to understand how she felt. He didn't say a word. He just let her be. And after a moment he felt her take a long breath, hold it, and then let it go. And then once more.

Chandra stepped away, and picked up her daughter. "Okay. Good. Let's find Daddy."

Yet always the pragmatist, Aranuke was focused on the immediate. "What do you mean...get Powell back? What are *you* going to do?"

Mitri clarified. "I'm taking my other ship out of here."

There was a slight delay, but Aranuke and Chandra had the same thought. They spoke in unison. "*What* other ship?"

"Did I not mention that?" Mitri unfastened his collar. "My bad."

CHAPTER FIFTY-ONE

THE TWO BLOCKS of buildings between where the rescue team was poised to retrieve Olivia—and the mayhem engulfing the Merry Berry Soda Shop—was more than enough to shield them from immediate danger.

The Sun hung from the southwest, draping the narrow block in shade. From a distance came the *fttttt...fttttt* of automatic gunfire.

With Montgomery Park behind them they came to the building's gray, metal door. There were five buzzers, one for each studio. A fire escape was above their heads, zig-zagging up to the roof. Powell had that *flash-flash-flash*. "Third floor," he said. "Art studio. She's surrounded."

Dolores assessed their position. Just ahead, on the far side of Dominion Avenue, began the dense forest of skyscrapers, the corporate megaliths of Prado City. She led the rescue team through another weapons check, motivating any straggler locals to run like hell, and then instructed the troops Stapoyovich had sent over. "Don't let anyone in. If you get harassed, chase them away. But if necessary...shoot to kill." The nearby screams and gunfire were in full effect. With a firm *clack* Dolores popped a fresh clip into her silver-plated handgun, and with a *chick-chack*, she loaded a single bullet in the top chamber. "How long until your buddies show up?"

"You did a nice job disabling the local patrol, ma'am," the lead soldier said. Like his brethren, he was muffin glazed, focused on pleasing his master. "The rest are at the Merry Berry, as you can hear. But not for long. If you're lucky, you'll have twenty, twenty-five minutes before they realize what you're up to."

Powell asked a question on everyone's minds. "And if we're unlucky?"

Antagonized by Powell's interruption—he followed chain of command, reporting only to Dolores—the soldier answered. "Then you'll have less."

Ever the den mother, Dolores was reassuring. "Don't worry, Marcus. We'll be fine."

"I know, I know. It's not your first fellatio." His comment drew startled, if even some angry stares. "What?…I get what it means."

The lead soldier took a step at Powell. "Yeah. It means *blow job*. What the fuck is wrong with you?" He gripped his weapon. "Show some respect."

The others let out tense laughter. Powell curled his neck, sighed. "I really hate you guys."

Figg busted the lock using a hand-held blowtorch, and then led the team up the narrow staircase. The dimly lit wall was dirty, and covered in graffiti, scribbles, and a large painted arrow pointing up and labeled: *This Way for Good Love.* The wood stairs were warped and cracked. They creaked. On the tight, second floor landing, was an old basketball wedged between a silver mountain bike and a small table with mail on it.

But as they came to the third floor, Powell's strobe light sensors were going full bore—*flash-flash-flash*—then unleashed a searing white light. He nodded at the door.

The words *she's here* were about to pass the threshold of his lips when he suddenly felt a tug—a whisper too loud to be unreal—directing him up another flight. There was something up there waiting for him. Olivia was on the other side of the door before them, yet the strobe light in his mind—that *flash-flash-flash*—pulsed stronger than the gunfire at the Merry Berry Soda Shop. Powell squeezed his eyes, to smother the strobe light. But he was commanded upstairs. For the Universe's intricate chicanery it took to position him at that particular place at that particular instance—the beginning of that moment marking the end of another—he could not hold back from those few extra steps.

Despite their plan—Figg would blowtorch the door open and then lead them in close quarters combat—Powell could not resist the jack-hammering call to the flight above. He wasn't a soldier. Never was. In the recess of his soul he knew that his own fate, as Chill said, had never been to *rescue* Olivia, but to *find* her. He was destined for something else. Something more. With his every fiber Powell felt consumed by a riptide of fate. Without announcing his intentions, he took off for the upper floor.

Sean grabbed his arm. "Powell. What are you doing?"

"I have to." Powell nodded upstairs, held out his gun. "I'm no good with this, anyway."

"What are you talking about? You can't—"

"Sean," Chill said. "He got us here. Now let him go."

Before Sean could argue, Powell pulled away. He took the stairs two at a time. Whatever was up there waiting, it was meant for him alone.

Chill took a meditative breath to assess his options. Dolores directed Sean to go after Powell, and Figg to blowtorch the door. She rechecked her gun clip, popping it back in. *Chack.* But as Figg pressed the concentrated blue flame to the lock, Chill recommended—despite the imminence of their assault—that they change tactics. Rather than bust the door open and attack their enemies, he wanted to peacefully negotiate Olivia's release.

"The chill is most powerful," he said. "Striking another only stirs the fists. A last resort."

Anticipating instructions to jam his inner chill someplace dark and unsavory, Chill took that calculated distraction to suddenly force his way through the door, open thanks to Figg and his blowtorch. With a zip tie he lifted from Stapoyovich during the long drive, Chill secured the inner doorknob to an exposed metal pipe running up the wall. He locked himself inside the studio with Olivia and her captors, while Dolores and Figg were cut off, on the other side of the door, still in the hallway, wondering what in the hell just happened.

During the time it took Figg and Dolores to bust the door open, they heard gunshots, smashing furniture, screeching metal, breaking glass, and all manner of shriek, horror, and gasp. The studio was littered with twisted, mangled corpses. And blood. Lots of blood. On the hardwood floor. On the walls. On the bookcases. On the industrial shelves lined with paints and brushes. On the artist drawing table. On the circular saw and metal sanding apparatus bolted to various workstations.

Figg stepped in a red pool draining from a body with paint brushes jammed into each eye. Dolores found another dead soldier, with a leg severed at the knee, slumped against yet another body with its arms contorted in ways she hadn't thought physically possible. Three other dead soldiers were tossed in a pile, gutted, and riddled with bullets. It was difficult to tell which limb belonged to which body.

Another dead soldier was slumped in front of a workstation with an elbow-sized hole in the back of his head. His buddy was on his back, skull in a vice grip; yellow paint overflowed from his mouth. In back, another bloody soldier was shoved halfway through a broken window. The last of them was face down on the floor, a dozen bullet holes in his back.

Covered in her captor's blood, Olivia stood over the body, smoking gun in hand.

Chill eased back in a wicker chair. He smiled as if watching an old family movie he'd forgotten all about. And as he sat there, quietly, a tangible heft—perhaps his enduring grief—disappeared from his face. He removed a cloth from his pocket, wiped blood splatters from his chin. Finally, he took Olivia in his arms.

The shaman expelled a long breath, bobbed his head ever so slightly, and surveyed the carnage. "Woooo," he said. "I needed that."

CHAPTER FIFTY-TWO

POWELL CAME TO the fourth-floor studio. The door was slightly ajar. He entered slowly. The studio was dark except for stray flitters of daylight peeking through the blinds. There was a faint kerosene odor emanating from the radiators. Paintings were mounted on massive, angled installations. Small lamps shone a faint light above and below each painting—halos in the dark.

Before him was a man with broad shoulders, hands clasped at the midsection. He stepped from shadow, dressed in a dark green suit with a white collared shirt and no tie. He was about forty-five with a round baby face, a bowl haircut, and black-rimmed glasses with thick frames. His shoes were polished. He wore a gold watch on his left wrist.

"Hello, Powell. My name is Eric Osgood. I would say that it's nice to meet you, but that greeting rather undersells the moment, don't you think?"

Shock. There was no other word for it. Powell's head filled with panic, nausea, thunder, and shame. It was like a thousand grenades exploded, blasting skull fragments and sanity into the soft pockets of his brain matter. He saw white snow of a broken TV signal—nothing but static. His insides seized. He nearly doubled over. The room shrank down on Osgood until all Powell could focus on was that face, that impossible face—the curl of the lip, the self-righteous lilt of the eyes, the air of entitlement. The room started to spin. Images snapped in and out of focus like drumsticks on a snare drum.

Tower Control. *Snap. Crossline. Snap.* Taurus Enterprises. *Snap.* Shimmering light. *Snap.*

"This isn't possible," he said. "Not possible."

Though a heftier version than the one he knew from Earth,

Powell had no doubt that the Eric Osgood standing before him—the most dominant Scraper CEO—was Dale Aranuke.

"I was hoping you would say that. It took considerable effort to bring you here."

With that smug Aranuke nod, Powell saw red, unleashing his inner howl. He charged, desperate to dig his thumbs against Osgood's windpipe until his exposed neck just...went...*crr-ack*. He might have killed him, too, would have squeezed the life out of Osgood, would have seen the light drain from his pupils, if Sean hadn't hit Powell on the back of the head with his gun butt. Osgood simultaneously stepped aside with his foot out, which Powell tripped over.

Slumped on the floor, shoulder against the wall, Powell was enraged and humiliated and feeling like he simply had no place left to go in all the Universe. Like he was nowhere.

Osgood pulled up a chair. The two were draped in light and shadow. "It's funny, Powell. I've never been what you'd call a *people person*, yet I'm fascinated by behavior. Stress does funny things."

Powell held a hand to the back of his head. He was breathing heavy. "H-how did you get here?...What are you—?"

"I may look familiar, but whoever you think I am... I'm not. Well..."—Osgood and Sean shared a conspiratorial smile—"...not exactly."

"What does that mean...*not exactly*?"

"Powell. You've been here long enough to figure out that Aretha and Earth—am I saying that right?—and Earth, are... cosmic cousins, I guess you'd say. In the grand scheme of the Universe, your plane of existence is obviously a shadow of ours, or ours is a shadow of yours. Whichever you prefer. And if the mysticism of the Universe is just too much for you...the probes sent to your side of the wormhole sent back nearly identical readings to that from our side. It took time to analyze, but where you're from...and here...are simply too closely related to have any other explanation. Just as all the known species of life share a common, underlying DNA, so, apparently, do planes of the Universe. You can ask me all the whys you want. I don't know why. I just know that it's so."

Powell offered a begrudging nod, unsure what Osgood was leading to. "All right."

"Just as this planet—even this solar system—is a shadow, I very much suspect that...so are we." Osgood gestured to himself. "Me. You. I've got my shadow—"

"Aranuke."

Osgood stopped mid-sentence. "Aranuke." He smiled, put a hand to his face. He left it there, drifting off at the notion that there really was another *him* out there somewhere. "It's really something to know that, let me tell you." He gave a slight nod, smiled, and then shook his head. "But just as I've got my shadow, Sean's got his, Olivia's got hers, and while I'm sure you've been told that you closely *resemble* Mitri Amos..."

Powell had a moment of clarity. "...I *am* Mitri Amos."

"Yes," Osgood said. "It appears that you are."

Powell's connection to Mitri Amos had been increasingly evident during his time on Aretha, and hearing his own words spoken aloud—*I am Mitri Amos*—was, if anything, a tremendous relief. Like a hangnail on his big toe, he never appreciated just how much that infected edge irritated his entire system until he pulled off his shoe and finally cut it loose. If Powell was in fact the living embodiment of his cosmic doppelganger, then so be it. There comes a moment in every man's life when his own truth stares him down, with no point in trying to resist. It feels right to submit.

"Sure," Powell said. "Why not? Maybe I really am the one who's come to save you all. I'm a swell guy. And maybe I'm here to bake you a yummy wummy puddin' cake. With sprinkles. And frosting. And a curly cue design on top. Ha-haaaa...for the love of Aunt Margaret." He shook his head in mock delight. "So...I'm assuming that Sean here's been keeping you up to speed?"

Sean offered a wide-eyed shrug.

"Yeah," Powell said. "I figured."

Osgood chuckled. "I consider myself to be a logical man, and logic said 'the man from the sky' was just a Westie fairy tale to inspire faith. And yet even since childhood, my heart...my spirit, even, if you believe in such a thing...told me something else. That your image wasn't just ink on a wall. That it was...magical somehow...and that one day it would come true. It's silly, I know. Especially being a Scraper. But I guess childhood fantasies stay with you. You see, Powell, I forgot about the fairy tale. With the war rattling back and forth, I thought it would never end—that it could not. I've long needed to retrieve the warp drive—and now, of course, the wormhole code—and thanks to Sean and his friend, Terry, I finally have them. But he also sent word that 'the man from the sky' had arrived, and that once and for all, he would 'set us free.'" Osgood smiled oddly. "As much as I would like to say that I dismissed the rumor...that pull, that feeling, that...childhood fantasy...it roared in me again. It took me off my feet. Me. A grown man. I have responsibilities that, on occasion, make me want to take drastic measures against myself. To relieve the pressure. Yet when I became aware of you...my heart raced. My hands perspired." He offered a slight shake of the head. "Perhaps I'm a fool, and I'll accept that assessment if it is truly accurate, but I had to discover it for myself. I *needed* to see you. Despite almost a year of carefully orchestrated plans for St. Brewer's Day—when we found out who you were—we adjusted in real time, to retrieve you as well. I admit, we had a few more bumps than I anticipated, but you are here nonetheless, standing before me. I must say...I do not impress easy, and yet I'm practically speechless. It's really you."

Powell shook his head. As much as he wanted to protest the absurdity of his predicament, there was simply no way that Eric Osgood—this second Dale Aranuke, his shadow—was just a coincidence. "Okay. I get it. I'm so *toootally* the man. Woo-hoo. Yay me. One question."

"Of course. Go ahead."

"What do you want from me?"

Osgood smiled. "Yes, of course. First...we've got to get you home."

Powell nodded approvingly. "Oooh. I like that. Time to get my Earth on. Okay. Sounds good. What else?"

"We want Mitri Amos back. And for that to happen, we need your help."

CHAPTER FIFTY-THREE

POWELL HAD BEEN asked to accept quite a bit more than he originally anticipated since he first sat inside *Crossline*, back when there was only one plane of the Universe he needed to deal with. When, as far as he knew, there was only one *him* to deal with. But now that Osgood was negotiating on behalf of Mitri Amos—not only his supposed enemy but also someone who had been mislaid in time and space—Powell was legitimately stumped.

"Wow. I don't even know where to start. How do *you* know what Mitri needs? How do you know he's alive?"

"Your friend. Chill. He is a guide to you, correct? He helps you…see things…for lack of a better word?"

Powell nodded. "Yeah. I guess."

"I've learned to assess the people around me and envision how one event might set others in motion—reading the tea leaves, as they say. But at no point did I ever have premonitions, dreams or…visions. And then, like you, I met a…man, of sorts. A guide." Osgood visibly shuddered. "I have damned myself to hell for what I've done, but it was a decision made of necessity. I am loath to speak his name, but it is far too late for me to be shy about it now."

There was no need. Powell already knew. "Riva? The madman? *He's* your guide?"

Even Sean was stunned. "*What?* You had visions with him? He's been in your mind? Eric. What the fuck?"

"I know, Sean. I'm sorry. You can only imagine what he's done. The murders. The torture. Burning people alive. The kerosene. It's nearly driven me insane. But for reasons I can't explain, he is connected with Chill. And as Chill has had visions of Mitri, on Earth, Riva has seen pieces, snapshots, of what Chill sees. But never the whole. Riva tells me things, reveals himself to me. I suffer through the visions of horror to glimpse the ones of value." Osgood removed his glasses, pinched the corners of his eyes. "But you, Powell...*you* I've seen in flashes. For the longest time I thought it was the stress of my life. That my mind created a living version of that painting on the cave wall. That I invented you somehow. Obviously...I didn't."

Powell had heard enough. He'd come a long way to find Olivia, and now it was time for him to go. His own girls were on the other side of his life and he wasn't prepared to wait any longer to see them again. So he got back on his feet and dusted himself off. As he held his gun out, Sean took a step forward, but stopped when Powell slid the firearm into the back of his waist band. Osgood stood up to match him. Powell straightened his jacket.

"Maybe you haven't connected all the dots there, chief, but I'm gonna need a team of super shrinks and intravenous Jack Daniel's to get me over my little trip across the Universe. So let me get this straight. You, Eric Osgood, are the spitting image of the very ass wipe executive I know from Earth...who tried to have me killed. Meanwhile, way out here, on Aretha, you've been attacking the Westies to steal their wormhole technology so that you can hop the Universe as well. But to do so, you've been mind-melding with a lunatic, have seen across the cosmos to spy on my other self, and now *you* want to help *me* get back home so that a man you should want dead can make it back alive. That about right?"

Osgood replaced his glasses. "Yes. I think you got it."

"Huh. Okay, then. Just one more question."

"Which is?"

"Why? You already have the codes. What do you need Mitri for?"

"Because I want to speak with this man. I want to know exactly what he's seen, how he did what's been done, and how it's transformed him. Don't confuse me with my fellow CEOs, Powell.

I would like nothing more than to settle in peace. If we keep up our aggressions, none of us will survive. I would much rather see the Westies as trading partners than enemies. And if not partners, than distant neighbors we can simply ignore. But my counterparts in Torent and New Belcie don't agree. They're young and greedy and want the Westies dead forever. But mostly…they are envious, as the entitled mostly are. No matter how clever I may be in keeping the war at bay—convincing them that full-scale attack serves no one—they are relentless. They will never concede. Their influence in total balances my own—a triumvirate structure by design—and for good reason. But because I don't acquiesce to their demands they think I see myself as emperor supreme. Perhaps, from a distance, it appears that I am. I have stature. I have power. I have women and wine. Prado City is our dominant region. But what I really want, Powell…is to explore the Universe. To soar as you have. To see what else is out there. If Mitri Amos can speak about his journey, then I want to hear every last word, every detail. I want to know that we have only just begun, because if this life we have is all there really is…then I am truly left to wonder—why did the gods bother with me at all?"

Powell's father told him to judge a man by his deeds. *Flappin' lips don't mean a thing, son. It's the steps he takes that matter.* Osgood could have killed him easily. And his words felt true. But it still wasn't enough. "Why would I help you? What would be the point? Even if Mitri makes it back to Aretha, the Westies own the skies. They'll never turn him over. Ever."

Osgood smiled. "Because, Powell…I have nothing else to hold on to. So I am putting my faith in you. You are the key, but I'm betting that the miracle of his return will finally bring us together. And if the Westies can't be convinced, nor my people either, then obtaining Mitri Amos will be the least of my worries. We'll develop a wormhole emitter anyway, sooner or later, and then we'll see how it plays out. I am giving you a path to see your family again. To be where you belong. To go home. The choice is yours, Powell. The future is up to you."

Pacing helped him think. Powell surveyed the room, for an escape route devoid of Sean and his automatic weapon. Powell eased along a canvass with mounted, black-and-white photographs. In each, children ran through an open fire hydrant flowing onto a city street. Long shadows stretched behind them. Osgood and Sean eyed his movements.

"Okay," Powell said. "For argument's sake, let's say I believe you. Let's say Mitri is still alive. Unlikely, but fine. How do I even find him? How do I get him back?"

"Give him your ship."

"My ship. Naturally. And if by some miracle I actually get my ass home—I mean, yeah, right—but even if I do, how do you think he'll even get that ship off the ground? It doesn't take off like yours. It needs a transport through the atmosphere. A rocket. The only person who can arrange another launch—hell, who can even authorize one—is Buddy Rheams. And that old fucker isn't going to do me any favors. Trust me on that. Especially not for my…," and he broke out the jazz hands, "…shadow."

Osgood held firm. "I think he would."

"Oh, yeah? And why's that?"

"Ask yourself, Powell. If Mitri Amos is still alive, where'd he end up?"

Powell rejected the idea on principle, but answered anyway. "Buddy Rheams locked him in a cage somewhere."

"Maybe. Or what else?"

"What else? I don't know. Maybe he's got Fantastic Four radiation powers. Like…maybe he's invisible, or Fire Dude. Ooh. Maybe the Stretchy Dude. Although," Powell said, and thought for a moment, "…I suppose he could have survived the crash and went into hiding…"

"Or…?"

"*Or*? I don't know *or*? There is no *or*."

"Or," Osgood said, "he's hiding in plain sight."

"Plain sight. Like where? It's not like he's in Tower Command at the control desk."

"Think higher."

"What do you mean *think higher*? There's only—" The nausea roared back. Hot flashes. Throat like gravel. Powell tried to speak, but no words came out. The strobe light went off in his mind again. That *flash-flash-flash*. Suddenly he saw before him the Tower Command consoles. The technicians and Chang and Aranuke and the Taurus Enterprises logo— the head of a bull, with horns and a nose ring, encased in a crest. And then he saw one man in that glassed-in office over-looking them all.

He's saying Mitri Amos is Buddy Rheams. He's saying Mitri… Amos…is Buddy Rheams.

"But he's an old man! There's no way. He must have—"

"Crashed on Earth, some time in your past. It probably took years, maybe decades, but he replicated the technology and rebuilt his ship."

Though armed with an Olivian rebuttal along the lines of "go fuck yourself, dickbag," Powell quite literally choked on his own breath. He was in such a hurry to spit the words out that air caught in his throat, causing him to gag and cough. He clenched his fists, then pointed.

"No way. *Noooo* way. Mitri and Buddy Rheams are *not* the same guy. So drop it." Powell exhaled with such force he saw black spots before his eyes. His heart beat fast. Hard. He shook his head. "And even if they are—which they are so *not*—how do you even know that?"

"Like I said, Chill has visions. He knows what we don't. You've seen it yourself."

"But…" Powell exhaled heavier, in long, shaky breaths. "I mean…how can…?"

Did Mitri Amos just change his name? Did he become Buddy Rheams? Did he build that company from scraps?

"Nobody knew? That's what you're saying? He just falls from the sky and…?"

It then occurred to Powell that on Aretha *he* just showed up one day. That *he* fell from the sky. *If I'm Mitri Amos and Mitri Amos is the Old Man, then...*

Powell looked at Osgood. At Sean. They looked at him. Their stoic faces were mirrors, reflecting back the certainty he desperately clung to as it dissolved like sand through his fingers.

No-no-no. Not again. He blinked hard once more. The threads were stringing together. *Mitri. Buddy. Me.*

Mitri...Buddy...Me.

A equals B equals C.

"You mean *I'm* Buddy Rheams?"

Osgood nodded. "Correct. And he's trying to come home."

Powell couldn't take any more. He knew he'd made some outrageous mistakes, and he was paying for them dearly. But he refused to accept that he was Buddy Rheams Jr., the man responsible for Earth's distortion and his own displacement in time and space. Instead, he started in with Sean, who stood there silently, with his gun pointed.

"I figured something with you. But this? Really?" Powell shook his head in disgust. "You can't get Keela, so you turn on your friends? You plot with the Scrapers?"

Osgood defended Sean. "You judge too quickly. He's been a friend to them. More than you know."

"Yeah. What a pal."

Sean kept his gun pointed. "You just don't get it, Powell. Do you? Yeah, okay. I love her. And she'll never love me back. Not the way I want. It breaks my heart every day. But so what? Westies. Scrapers. Somebody had to unite us. Someone had to try. The warp drive? The wormhole emitter? It makes us even. It balances us out. If we have it and *they* have it, there's no reason to fight. No reason for war. You think I *want* this? You think I'm a traitor? Well FUCK YOU, THEN! I'VE GOT BLOOD ON MY SOUL! You're not a soldier, Powell. But I am. And a soldier defends his people. No matter what. I took risks, I know. Friends of mine died, and it's my fault. The gods will be merciless with me, in this life and the next. But you see where we are. Maybe Mitri Amos comes home, maybe not. But if the price for peace is to join with my enemy...then so be it. It was the only way. It was this...or die for nothing."

CHAPTER FIFTY-FOUR

THere was a flick of a lighter. It drew their attention to the door.

"Well, well, well. What the fuck happened here?"

Gun in hand, Olivia dashed around the pile of dead bodies and jumped into her brother's arms. She squeezed Terry with all her might, and then lifted her head, staring at him. She choked on salty tears. "Cool rescue, huh?"

Terry studied his fellow Grinroadians and in just those few seconds he could tell they saw the look in his eyes, one that said this family reunion would not have a happy ending. He eased Olivia back, took her hand, and then shook his head with bittersweet disappointment. "Oh, Liv. I don't need rescuing. We're already home."

Perplexed, Olivia blinked several, and then a few times more.

There was a change in the air, a flattening of energy. Terry stepped away from Olivia. He lit a cigarette, and then offered a strange, half smile. And in that sad, petulant manner he had, he straightened his back, forced out a fake, righteous laugh, and blew smoke through his nostrils. It was his way of pushing back, of layering a poisoned cloud between himself and everyone else.

"Olivia. Look at your buddies. I see you've got Dolores and Chill and this soldier dude with you. Even they see it." He took another drag. "I wasn't kidnapped. I defected." He exhaled the smoke. "I *escaped*."

Olivia gagged like she'd been force-fed sea water. "What? W-why? I don't—"

"What did you think, Liv? That you and your little hands were going to save me from the clutches of doom? That this 'top secret' squad was going to trek behind enemy lines, undetected, unharmed? And then for all the ages you'd sing in the pub about glory and honor and dying for the cause?" He pulled a tobacco strand from his tongue. "Come on. Knock it off. There's no epic tale here. It's just life. And it blows."

Terry leaned against the door frame. "Ask Sean. He knows. He set up the whole thing. I think he's here somewhere. Faye's across town shooting up. You were supposed to come, too. But then Chill Master Chill brought you up front with Powell, and before I could pull you out, it was too late. It was an accident you got hurt. I'm so sorry about that, Liv. But I made them leave a patrol behind to get you."

"What the fuck are you talking about? Are you insane?!"

Terry nodded. "Could be. And yet I just don't care. These Scraper fuckheads might rape the land, consume 'til they puke and smother their souls with bad TV. Well fuckin' A for them. They're anesthetized by distraction. *I* want to be anesthetized! *I* want to be distracted! I want to be a drone with no search for meaning. There *is* no meaning! I want to be asleep, even when I'm awake. I don't want to think about war and rebellion and the quest for a new beginning. I don't want to think at all."

Olivia was an empty sack. This wasn't her brother. No. Fucking. Way. "That's bullshit bullshit bullshit and you know it! They killed mom and dad. Geoff and Amy and...and...the others. Thousands. Millions. They killed them all! What the fuck are you saying? This is—"

"Go ahead, Chill. Tell her. Give her some holy ding-dong wisdom about the spirit song chillin' in the bunker of my left asshole. No matter who wins the war, Liv...we all lose. *He* knows that. We all do. Mitri Amos can travel a hundred billion trillion miles and then ten times over again...and so what? You blame these men," Terry said, pointing to the litter of bloody corpses around them, "but it's *man*, Olivia. Man*kind*, although I don't see much kindness here. Whether it happens today or tomorrow, quick or slow, we're going to destroy every mole-cule of this life. We're violent, we're greedy, and dumb as fuck. We suck, Olivia. We're just not worth the effort. And one day, hopefully soon, we'll be gone in a flash. Each and every one of us. And then there will be no more need for distraction. There will be no need for anything."

"But you're all I've got left. They're the enemy! The ENEMY!"

"Enemy? WE'RE the enemy. *We* have warp drive. *We* can open wormholes. They want it, too. So let 'em! Who cares? We're no better, and they're no worse. They wanted code and I wanted out. They said luxury living for the rest of my life, although this isn't quite what I had in mind. You smell that? Fucking reeks of kerosene. It'll be nicer when my condo's done."

Olivia wasn't satisfied. Even with her first glimmers of resignation, she still hoped that her brother would conclude the obvious—that he was full of crap and, as was often the case, just needed to get over himself. "But...don't you want me?...Don't you care?"

Terry kneeled down, wiped her tears. "Listen, piglet. I don't want you to suffer, but we're goners no matter what. I'd rather laugh to my grave than dream of a glory that will never come. There's no way out." He took a look around. "Dolores is right, Liv. You belong with them. I'm sorry I dragged you into this. I should've let you be."

Dolores spoke softly to Olivia. "The gods can be cruel sometimes." She then looked above, drawn to the corner of the ceiling. It began to ripple. "Hold on...."

Figg stepped forward. "Ma'am? What is it?"

"It's fire," Dolores said. "We need to go."

Before Powell could decide if he was quick enough to draw his weapon in time or take Sean with a punch, the studio erupted in flame. Fire shimmied along the ceiling from back to front, down the walls, and then across the floor. It devoured the paintings, driving Powell, Sean, and Osgood for the door. They dashed into the hallway, which was also catching fire. One floor below, the rescue team was on its way down. Powell called for Olivia.

Dolores yelled back. "She's here! Go-go-go!"

As if a thin trail of kerosene had been strategically poured along the walls and banisters—to direct the fire in a specific direction—the roaring flames chased them toward the lower floors, which disintegrated behind them. Breaking back into daylight they all spilled out onto the street. Black smoke rose into the sky, the air ripe with soot and fire.

At the end of the block, Stapoyovich had the engine running. A second escape vehicle—a telephone repair van—was on the opposite side of the street. And by the escalating noise from the park, they knew the Scraper soldiers were closing in.

Despite the imminent danger, Powell had questions. "Chill. You knew along? Why didn't you tell me? Why didn't you say...?"

"...You were healing, Marcus. The burden would have been enormous."

"What do you call this?!"

"Fair enough. But the distraction could have gotten you killed. And us. You needed to learn this on your own. In a very short time you have suffered many deaths, and had many new beginnings. Today brought another. And there's more to come."

Powell was about to reach out to Chill when the buildings on both sides of the studio also caught fire. The flames jumped across the rooftops and down the columns. And yet Powell had an intense sensation, as if the destruction of the physical structure from which they just escaped also incinerated his past, freeing him to advance toward the rest of his life. The strobe light went off in his mind. That *flash-flash-flash*. Space flight. Earth. Chill on his back, laying face up, projecting an odd smile. *Flash-flash-flash*. Powell looked to the shaman, whose eyes went wide at the roaring cascade of fire.

"The flames will encircle us," Chill said. "Quickly. Run."

Their boots scrapped along the asphalt, closing in on their truck, when abruptly Powell stopped them. He saw two soldiers on the sidewalk. Their throats were slit. A crescent moon was carved into the underside of their chins. Powell turned to Chill, as if he knew what awaited him. And despite the incredible heat radiating from the flames, the air around them all suddenly went cold. Powell then heard the croak of a voice—the sound of a demon before it claims a soul.

Standing before them was a man of conviction.

"Hello, Chill. I've been waiting." Riva spoke with both an apprentice's pride and the smug, self-satisfaction of inevitability. "Do you remember the mountains? Do you remember the night? Do you remember the howl? Do you remember the rite? You've come with the one, from your dreams, from our wall. He will fulfill his destiny. As will we all. You and I began this journey together. Here, today, is where it ends." He looked at Osgood. "Eric…I will miss your mind. But will you miss mine?"

Riva fired his gun. Two shots.

Soldiers are often denied the time or perspective to grieve in the moment. But Powell felt a desperation—a tinge in his gut. Confronted by death there is a tenacity to live, a terrified reflex. From the cruel savagery of evolution that propels the metamorphosis from mere possibility to sentient being, it is embedded in all living beings through time and space, back to the primordial ooze. They thrash with incalculable terror to propagate their own survival, a violent instinct, battling for their very place against extinction.

Powell's desperation was heightened then by the shame of impudence, the torment of helplessness. Before him—with a gun in one hand and his pipe in the other—Chill was sprawled on the pavement, on his back. There were two bullet holes in him, one in his forehead, and the other under his left eye. A pool of blood settled beneath his skull. His eyes were open. His smile was odd. Even in death, Chill seemed to know something significant not immediately obvious to anyone else.

CHAPTER FIFTY-FIVE

POWELL HAD NO sense of pulling the trigger, could barely feel the kick. In a hazy, surreal state, the bullets were retribution, spewing like tornado debris—reckless, merciless, consuming. He expelled the cartridges until finally the chamber was empty.

Shock focused Powell's mind on random fragments: the frayed nub of Olivia's shoelace; the number 36 above a nearby door; the back of Dolores' pierced earlobe.

Exhausted weapon in hand, Marcus Powell—father, husband, reluctant solider—killed a man. Killed a monster.

Littered with bullets, Carlos Guerra was now just a bloody shell. And yet he still looked as terrifying as Powell had imagined, his flesh conformed to the ruthless certainty of a deranged mind. The flames rose behind them. The entire block was an inferno. Riva's final act.

Nearly in tears, Dolores leaned over Chill. She removed his pipe. "Damn you, Sean. How could you? How could you…?" If Sean had anything to say, he didn't share it.

Osgood looked upon his own fallen cohort, who set the building ablaze to bring them all together, and then tear them all apart. "Come," the CEO said, and shook his head. "I'll show you the way."

Powell nodded to Figg, who took Chill by the arm, and hoisted him over his shoulder. They all followed Osgood, leaving Riva's dead body to burn.

Stapoyovich was waiting at the corner, with the engine running. Powell turned to Olivia, who was slumped and speechless, staring at Chill. Powell thought of Jesse just then, knowing his only purpose going forward was to do all he could to ensure that his daughter would never have to face such harrowing decisions, that her path would be far different. And yet he understood with a depth and clarity he had never had before that if Jesse's fate was to be confronted by cruelty and danger, then he could never truly prevent it. He could only offer his guidance, wisdom, and love, and hope it would be enough to prepare her for the obstacles that lay ahead.

"Okay," Powell said to Osgood, acknowledging his Mitri Amos proposal. "Fine. I'll do it. I'll help. Just get us out of here."

Sean cocked his weapon, then pointed at Figg and Stapoyovich. "He's right. We've got no time. You two. Take them."

Powell grabbed Sean's arm. "Wait. You can't—"

Sean held his position. "I'll draw their fire. There's a helicopter on standby. Fully armed. I'll buy you time." He looked to Osgood, who nodded affirmatively. "Get to his private airport. It's a few miles away. He'll get you out to the southern tip of Lake Abandarro. It narrows to a point. There's an access way. You can get to Grinroad from there."

"What are you talking about? That's suic—"

Sean's look of resigned commitment made it clear that they weren't negotiating.

"You have to go," Osgood said. "They're coming."

Terry looked down at Chill, then stepped toward Sean. "I'm going, too."

Olivia's voice was strained. "What? No. You can't..."

"I have to, piglet."

"No..."

The flames roared behind them. Black smoke billowed. "I can't go back..." Terry's face was covered in shame. "At least I can do this. I have to. You're not losing me. Maybe this way... you're getting me back."

Sean took one last look at Dolores and Olivia, and then turned to Powell. "Please. Tell Keela I tried to...that I just..." He shook his head. "Forget it. Just go."

Powell hadn't considered Sean's plight—enduring loneliness, torment, and sacrifice—the abominations of war. With Chill's body lying before him, Powell thought of Sean and wondered what it would be like to sleep alone every night, longing for a companion, even as death loomed. How easy it would be to find obsession in a savior. To desperately feel that just a single person had the power to redeem his soul. And that the object of his desire was either choosing to save him, or not.

"Okay," Powell said. "I will."

Olivia reached down for Chill. She put her hand on his cheek.

"You can leave him," Osgood said. "We'll take care of it."

"Go fuck yourself, dickbag. We're taking him."

"I don't think you have time to—"

"I said," Olivia snarled, and then pointed her gun in Osgood's face, "go...*fuck* yourself."

Osgood backed away, but toward Riva.

Powell took Olivia in his arms—she sunk into him—and watched Terry and Sean double-time it to the repair truck. The side door slid open, revealing armed soldiers inside. Within thirty seconds they were speeding toward the park, drawing a wrath upon them, and, Powell saw all too clearly, orphaning Olivia once and for all—a young girl's remaining blood relative severed from her waking life. The father in Powell shuddered with grief.

With the inferno encroaching, the remaining rescue team piled into the truck. A fleet of fire engines roared from a distance. Their wailing sirens grew louder. Powell helped a distraught Olivia inside, but before he took his own seat, he felt a tap on the shoulder. He turned to find Eric Osgood—Dale Aranuke's spitting image—facing him.

"...*What?*"

Osgood smirked, winked. "Take care," he said, closing the door so that he and Powell were separated by more than just opposite sides of glass. "And, Powell...?" Osgood lit a cigar, and shook out the match. "I'll see you soon."

As planned, Figg used the chaos as cover, driving the survivors undetected through the southern streets until they finally crossed the Craig Nass River, leaving Prado City behind. But with those three words echoing in his mind—*see you soon*—Powell felt as if he was plummeting into a chasm.

Did Osgood mean that his own shadow—Dale Aranuke—would be waiting for Powell on Earth? Or that Powell and Osgood would see each other again? If so, did Osgood have a way to Earth? Was his wormhole capability farther along than he suggested? Or did he mean that Powell wouldn't make it back at all? Or if he did, would fate find a way to yank him back to Aretha? Would Powell even make it out of Scraper territory? Or was Osgood just screwing with him? Whatever it was, Powell just wanted to get the hell out of there. And fast.

It was only after they were along a back road nearing Osgood's private airport, miles from the erupting violence of Prado City, when they heard a low rumble. They could see through the windows, against the orange dusk, a black cloud between two skyscrapers. Sean and Terry's helicopter plummeted toward them, but from miles away, it appeared as just a dot in the sky.

Powell closed his eyes, took a breath. With the adrenaline starting to fade he could finally feel that his place in the cosmos—even within himself—had changed forever. If he really did have a shadow, then so did Sean. And if Sean was dead, was his shadow dead, too? And as much as it made Powell queasy to think it, if Mitri Amos—disguised behind the visage and personality of Buddy Rheams Jr.—was his shadow, was Powell somehow responsible for changing Earth's history? Was it Powell's stinking lie? Was he twice to blame for his own predicament? For abandoning his wife and child? For the attack on Grinroad? For the deaths that followed? For Chill?

And if he was actually responsible, what punishment fit the crime? He'd seen men killed, had now killed one himself. Had blood on his hands.

Or maybe there was no punishment because there was no crime. Or maybe it was all just bullshit, because the Universe didn't care about him one way or another.

Chill was laid out in back, beneath a soldier's blanket, as black helicopter smoke lingered in the distance. Olivia leaned her head against Powell's shoulder. She didn't say a word. None of them did. They wanted to pause, to remember their fallen comrades and the road they'd traveled together. But Grinroad was many hours away, and danger was still close behind.

CHAPTER FIFTY-SIX

WHAT MITRI AMOS had not shared with the rest of the world was that, while his alter ego had the Taurus Enterprises space program laser-focused on the *Crossline* project to the point of delirium, he'd also been personally overseeing a second, covert project.

"You were closer than you realized, Dale. You were right. There *is* a bunker more than a mile beneath the complex. It took five years just to dig it out and prep so that it was undetectable even by Tower Command. I assigned a special team to it. They report only to me. They've been working on it, off the grid from the beginning. It's a second ship. The *Kosono II*. It's more advanced than *Crossline*. It can take off on its own. It also has advanced electronics, fuel cells, communications, and weaponry. But I needed to confirm the warp engines before I could put the new ship to the test. It's been a long time coming." He exhaled. "I can finally go home."

Chandra had other thoughts. "Slow down there, cowboy. You're not going anywhere. My husband comes first. Then we deal with you."

Aranuke had similar thoughts, although his were focused on the big picture. "I'm thrilled for you, sir, but what now? The company? Life as we know it?…What do we do?"

Mitri went silent before answering. "I've been waiting for this day for decades…and now that it's here, it just doesn't seem real." He smiled, shook his head. "Life? Hell. It's the human condition to keep plugging along. You'll figure it out. As for the company… it's yours. That's why I kept you close. I've tested you pretty hard, Dale. And I'm sorry about that. But I had to know that you could do what needs to be done, when it needs doing. You can. From the top down, you set the tone. You're the new face of Taurus

Enterprises. You run the show."

In a day of surprises, this one caught Aranuke completely off guard. His face revealed a mix of ego-stroking joy and responsibility-induced horror. "Me? I'm...not the guy for this. You even said so."

Looking thirty-five again—and striking a remarkable resemblance to Marcus Powell—Mitri smiled. "Which is why she'll be running it with you."

Chandra was equally baffled. "Um...say what now? I'm doing what with who?"

"You're the brains, Dale, but she's the heart. You'll have joint, equal power. I had papers drawn up long ago naming you as my successor. I was just waiting for your counterpart to show up. And now she's here."

"*No-no-no-no,*" Chandra and Aranuke blurted simultaneously.

"Mrs. Powell. Chandra. I've heard a lot about you. Your principal, Barney Cahill, is an old friend. He's not just an educator. He scouts talent for me. Typically, it's the students, but he's watched you closely, keeping me posted. His father, Larry, worked for me many years ago. He was one of the first people on Earth I entrusted with helping me grow this company. I owe so much to that family..."

Mitri took a moment to compose himself.

"Barney has convinced me that you're a little too extreme for the local level, but here...you'll be the Yin to Dale's Yang. Or vice versa. You need each other. You'll push him to do the right thing, and he'll push you to just get things done. You'll both hate it, but some things are bigger than we are." He smiled at Jesse, winked. She smiled back. "And, Dale...Chang will be taking over Tower Command. I've put that in writing, too. She's good at kicking your ass. You need it. The two of them will keep you in line."

"Wait," Chandra said, as if realizing that the bridge she was being asked to cross could very well collapse at any moment. "You want *me* to partner with *him* to run *this*?"

Mitri nodded, sighed through his nose. "Yep."

"I don't think…I mean…this isn't…"

"Remember," Mitri said, "the space program is only part of what we do. Arts, healthcare, science…education. The company needs a conscience. That's you." He knelt down. "What do you think, Jess? Should your Mommy be in charge?"

All eyes shifted to Jesse, who smiled. "Good, Mommy, good. Amookie can do it."

Aranuke pulled a Doritos crumb from his ear. "Thanks, kid. I think."

"Yeah," Chandra said. "I don't really see how…I mean… you're this guy from…another…planet? And he's…you know…," she was trying to be delicate. "…him."

Aranuke rolled his eyes.

"And I'm supposed to just…you know…be his partner and… kinda…run the biggest company in the world?"

Mitri nodded again. "Pretty much."

Chandra thought a moment. "Uh…huh."

"Go-go-go, Mommy. Meaty says true. Daddy's coming, too."

In the suite, Mitri removed papers from a drawer. Once signed by all, he submitted them to the Taurus Enterprises board of directors. He forwarded e-copies to Chandra and Aranuke.

"It's done. Effective immediately, as in right now, you two run Taurus Enterprises. Tell people I have pancreatic cancer and wanted to go out with a bang. Because it's me, they'll believe it. I've got medical records in the drawer. Circulate as appropriate." As Mitri leaned forward, he took a whiff, and looked oddly at Aranuke. "Dale? Are you…are you stoned?"

Aranuke shrugged.

"Huh. Good for you."

Aranuke grabbed Mitri's arm. "As my first official act as CEO, I can't let you leave, sir. You've got a lot to answer for. I'm sorry."

"Dale. You blame me for Hicks. And I'll accept whatever responsibility is legitimately mine. But you could've disqualified her from the program a hundred times over, and you didn't. If you feel guilty for not doing more, then that guilt is yours. But it wasn't your place to protect her from herself. We are who we are. We make choices. One after the other. Sometimes they're good, sometimes they're wrong, and sometimes they're just downright stupid. Such is life. The only real question is how we handle the outcome. After Hicks died, you could've resigned, but you stayed. And I'm glad you did. You've got a company to run."

Aranuke released his grip, though not ready to let go. "What about Doc? Millie? I know what you did."

Mitri froze. His lip quivered. He dropped his head and sighed, showing a moment of true surrender. "Doc was my best friend. More than you'll ever know. But he said that he'd sinned beyond repair, and that God was watching. And then he took refuge with a woman who wanted..." Mitri shook his head, sighed. "...I had a choice to make. It was awful. But I did what needed doing. You can't imagine the cost. Wartime forces impossible decisions. You can't see the battle that rages on Aretha, but the war is very real to me, whether I'm on this side of the wormhole...or the other."

"Spin it how you want, sir. But this can't stand. It can't go down like this."

"Dale. If nothing else, a lifetime here has taught me that you can always and forever do whatever you want, whenever you want, however you want...just so long as you're willing to deal with the consequences. I am. The question is...are you?"

There was silence among them. Aranuke and Chandra knew if they tried to expose Buddy Rheams as Mitri Amos, from the distant planet of Aretha, they would likely get a padded cell for their troubles. Or worse. And even if they convinced enough or even the right people that their information was legitimate, was the world ready to hear it? Much as Chandra struggled to teach her students, she again faced the conundrum of distilling fact from truth. Without context, facts can be more destructive than lies.

"Well," Mitri said. "I've got a flight to catch. Dale...you always said that if you were in charge you'd make a real differ-ence around here. Now's your chance."

CHAPTER FIFTY-SEVEN

GRINROAD HELD a feast to send Powell off. *Crossline* was ready for flight.

The ceremony began at Tilted Heart, where they cremated Chill's body, on a pyre. They chanted his name until it echoed through the canyons. *Chill...Chill...Chill...*Keela then offered a blessing for Sean and Terry—loved ones who had lost their way, and in their final moments, tried to find their way back.

From there they gathered in the repaired banquet hall, the first time since the St. Brewer's Day bombing. Music played. The sweet mist of butter and grilled meat filled the air. There was little doubt among them that a full-scale war was coming, and likely soon, but for one night at least, they allowed themselves to enjoy each other in peace.

The slab of wall with Powell's prophecy did not survive. Although sacred to them, the Grinroadians took its destruction as a good omen, believing that the gods removed Powell's image because the man himself had come to fulfill his destiny.

Dolores kissed his cheek, and hugged him. "You be careful, dear."

Powell nodded. "I will."

"I know," she said, then wiped away her tears. "I just hate to see you go. Oh. Look. I got lipstick on your face." She rubbed it off with her thumb. "Don't punish yourself about Chill. He was waiting for you. You set him free."

Powell turned to the side. Keela sat with Olivia, who could barely raise her head. "Oh," he said. "I don't know about that."

"Well, even if you don't, dear, we do. Oh, wait. I almost forgot." Dolores produced a basket. "I baked muffins for you, in case you get hungry." She offered a smile he couldn't quite decipher. "Just the way you like them."

As much as he appreciated the gesture, Powell decided to save the muffins until after the flight was over.

Early the next morning a gentle layer of sunlight shone throughout the cave apartment. A breeze blew the thin white curtains. Powell stirred when the mattress sank. But before he could get out from under the covers, before he could open his eyes, Keela leaned over on all fours and kissed him, letting her body drape on top of his. He was naked from the waist up.

"It's been so long," she said. "I just needed to connect with him. You know. In case it's the last time. Hope you don't mind."

"Don't, uh…" Powell's voice cracked. He cleared his throat. "It's…" He cleared his throat one more time. "No. I'm…I'm good. I'm fine. I'm…"

Her face as red as her hair, Keela pointed below. "Your landing gear is out."

Powell looked down, then bunched up the blanket to cover his junk. "Yeah. No. It's good, it's good. It's *aaaaaall* good. We're good. It's good. We're good."

Keela gave him a wink, then tossed him a shirt. "I'll say. Now let's get you home."

Powell was fully zipped up in his blue onesy. "So where do we connect with the rocket?"

Desmond, the chief engineer, looked at Powell quizzically. "Rocket?"

"Oh, for the love…A giant metal tube with massive fuel tanks that blasts into space? You know. A rocket."

"Ah. Okay. Got it. But you know that *rocket* means *ba*—?"

Powell put up a hand. "*Ep-peh-peh.* I don't want to know. Let's just get going." But he *did* want to know how the engineering crew modified *Crossline*. Despite their initial skepticism, they now saw Powell as a brother-in-arms, and would do anything to help him. In addition to repairing the damage, they reconfigured the ship's launch thruster mechanics, and as with

Grinroad's more sophisticated models, *Crossline* could now take off like a fighter jet, under its own power.

"Sweet." Powell examined the controls. "What else?"

They also enhanced the warp thruster power source so that *Crossline* could maintain those immense speeds for days on end. As an added bonus, they upgraded the weapons systems, just in case.

Satisfied that his ship was in full repair, perhaps better than ever, Powell set back in the cockpit for the first time since his arrival. His ass print was still embedded in the seat. Yet even as he reclaimed the one position he had dedicated his life to mastering—piloting a ship—he was never so happy to think that his next flight might be his last.

One craft over, Keela secured her helmet. She would guide him into space, to the proper coordinates, and then activate her ship's wormhole emitter, opening a pathway for Powell back to his solar system. Back to Earth. And as he traveled through the gateway of time and space and dimension, she would circle the outer wormhole until it closed again. Maybe the Scrapers would launch a ship of their own out there to intercept, maybe they wouldn't. But either way, she had Powell's back. She owed him that much.

The launch crew hurried around *Crossline*. All systems go. Powell was about to initiate takeoff, to leave them all behind, when he felt a slight bump inside his jumpsuit. He unfurled the zipper and reached for his inside pocket. Jesse's *Nan'yehi* doll. Powell let out a tight-lipped smile. And then he waved Olivia over, raised the canopy, and dropped the doll in her hands. "It's from my daughter."

"I'm not a fucking baby, you dipshit."

"I know. But take it anyway."

Dolores hurried Olivia away. *Crossline*'s canopy sealed. Powell gripped the stick, took a deep breath, and counted to three. He felt a strange sadness to leave these people behind. Chill and Sean. Keela. Olivia. Dolores. But he reminded himself that they'd been nothing but grief to him, especially the man who poked him in the eye, helping him to see things he wished he'd never seen, but needed to see most of all.

Powell flipped the final switches, turning buttons from white to red. And as he blasted from the runway, he again followed Keela into deep space, chasing her through the Universe, toward a ripple with a brilliant blue center. Only this time he knew just where she was leading him, and why—and what he expected to find once he got there.

CHAPTER FIFTY-EIGHT

A small monitor outside the elevator doors switched on. It was Chang, addressing the man she still knew as Buddy Rheams Jr. "I'm sorry to bother you, sir. But Dale's not answering his page. It's Powell. He's back! Look."

On the monitor, the *Crossline* signature reappeared near Saturn, just a quarter mile from where it originally disappeared.

Jesse jumped up and down. "Daddy-Daddy-Daddy! See, Mommy, see? I told you he was coming. Daddy-Daddy-Daddy!"

Chandra took Jesse in her arms. "You sure did, baby. Grandma's pretty smart, huh?"

"She said you'd figger it out."

Following Mitri's nod, Aranuke took the lead—the new man in charge. "We'll be right there, Chang. Stand by. We need to talk."

"Oh. Dale. There you are. Um…okay. Ten-four."

Mitri shuttled them into the elevator, though hung back himself. "I'm going this way." He pointed to his bedroom. "The wormhole's open. I need to get there before it closes."

Aranuke leaned in close. With gritted teeth, he whispered out of respect for Chandra and Jesse so they couldn't hear. "I pressed that god damn button. I thought I killed the man."

The elevator closed. Chandra, Jesse, and Aranuke were on one side of the doors. Mitri Amos—a.k.a. Harlan "Buddy" Rheams Jr.—was on the other. There was an understated *bing*. The elevator gears started to roll.

Tower Command was buzzing with palpable energy. Technicians were relaying information and recording data. Media requests had the console lights near overload, and various arms of the U.S. military—including the President—were demanding immediate updates. Eager to respond, the console technicians waited for guidance. The mission was far from over.

Chang spoke for them. "Where the hell were you? Powell's checking in."

"I know, I know. Keep your panties on. We're under control."

"What the…?" Chang stared into Aranuke's face. Before she could give him some much earned foot-in-the-ass, she saw something that surprised her. His tie was undone. The daggers in his eyes were gone.

"Change of plans there, Changy-babe." Aranuke flipped on the intercom. His voice rose above the fracas. "Listen up, people. As you know, *Crossline* has reappeared on our screens. Powell… is coming home." Tower Command broke into a collective roar, ripe with high-fives, laughter, and hugs. "Okay, okay. Jeez. Don't blow a gasket. Once we confirm his safety, we'll reconnect the broadcast and bring him in." Aranuke turned to Chandra and Jesse, and offered a semi-genuine smile. "I'm sure the world is on edge. But I have something else to say.… " He let Tower Command settle down first. It took a moment. "I apologize for keeping this from you, but it was the wish of a dying old man." The staff went quiet. "If you look on your monitors—or out to the runway—you'll see what I mean."

Deep underground, in a hidden world far beneath Tower Command, Mitri Amos approached the *Kosono II*. The canopy lifted. Suited up, he set his right and then his left leg inside. And as his body settled into the cockpit—his back against the seat, his arms and legs in position, the stick, diagnostics, and control panel before him—his entire body shuddered. His hands trembled. His throat drew tight.

Mitri stared straight ahead, but couldn't focus. He squeezed his eyes shut, and held them there. It had taken him more than fifty years to orchestrate his escape, focused so singularly on his return to Aretha that he wasn't even sure if he could finally go through with it now that the opportunity was finally before him. He thought just then of good ole H.R., out in the Kinsey desert, and how the young gas man's generosity of spirit—as much as his dreams—were what truly kept Mitri going, when for years he had been all but beaten down to the point of just giving up for good. Maybe Mitri cared about the lives he touched on Earth more than he ever wanted to believe. Maybe his time on Earth grounded him, gave him roots. Or maybe he knew that even though he was as close as ever to getting back home, he still had such a long way to go.

Mitri needed a moment to compose himself, even if he didn't have one to spare.

There was a hiss of steam and the *uuurrrlll* of unfolding hydraulic arms. Controlled by a team Tower Command didn't even know existed, a massive Tritanium slab rose slowly from the runway, and then shifted to the side. From underground, a smaller Tritanium slab emerged with another hydraulic *uuurrrlll*. On it was the *Kosono II*. In the cockpit was Mitri Amos, known to everyone else on Earth by another name altogether.

"About five years ago," Aranuke announced to Tower Command, "Buddy Rheams Jr. entrusted me with his dream. He said that because of our unwavering commitment, it was only a matter of time before the warp engines came on line. That together we would all usher in a new era of space travel, and through it, mankind would unite in a way that would otherwise seem impossible. But Buddy's dream was also to witness this new era. And if that were so, he wished to one day sit within the craft he helped create, and have a window seat to the stars."

Aranuke explained Buddy's medical condition, horse hockey that it was. "He knows that it breaks every protocol we have. And he understands if anyone—if everyone—tries to stop him. I, however, will not. What you see before you is the next-generation *Crossline* craft. It does not require a rocket launch. It can reach into space under its own power. And if all goes well, he will greet Marcus Powell a million miles from here, and welcome him home. In my eyes, Buddy Rheams has earned the right to live his final moments seeing his dream come true. I'm stepping away from the controls. If anyone wants to signal a security team, to block his path on the runway, I won't interfere. But you'll also have to live with it."

Tower Command remained still, until Chang whispered. "Dale. Is this for real?"

The newly minted CEO nodded. "It's what he wants."

Chang looked toward Chandra and Jesse. "Yeah, but…what about Powell?"

Aranuke let go an empowered smile. "Oh," he said. "I think he'll be fine."

CHAPTER FIFTY-NINE

SOARING THROUGH THE cosmic ectoplasm, once again there was a flash. In his mind's eye Powell saw Chill, Keela, Olivia, and Dolores perched on a mountaintop. Red rock. Blue skies. From a distance, Sean's helicopter passed through the center of Tilted Heart. They turned to greet him, but as if shot with a poisoned arrow, the helicopter exploded, erupting into black smoke.

Crossline's sensors flickered. Powell did a visual scan. When he entered the wormhole, Aretha's moon was in his sights, and before him now were the unmistakable marks of his rightful place in the Universe—the rings of Saturn. After some trepidation, Powell accepted that he was, at long last, on his way home. To Earth.

A transmission came through the com. It was Chang. "Powell? Is that you? This is Tower Command. Do you copy? Are you all right?"

Powell did a butt-jiggling cockpit dance. "Oh, you bet your sweet ass, hot stuff. I'm back, baby! I'm back!"

"That's great, Powell. That's great. But…where the hell were you?"

The Saturn rings were glorious. "Line up the tequila shooters. It's a long story."

Aranuke broke in. "Powell. You're headed back, right? You're okay?"

At any other moment in time spanning every sphere of existence, Aranuke's voice would have been the last Powell wanted to hear. But fate had seen fit to link them across the cosmos—with the image in his mind of a glossy-eyed Chill laughing, leaning back, and clapping his hands at the wonderful irony of it all.

"You probably won't believe this, but I'm glad it's you."

There was a curious pause from Aranuke. "...Really? Why?"

"You won't believe it."

"Try me."

Powell craned his neck. "I might just do that. As soon as I—"

Chang interrupted. "Powell. Listen. There's something else." Powell could hear muffled voices before she continued. "It's...it's Buddy Rheams. He's—"

"Mitri Amos. I know."

Aranuke jumped back in. "How the fuck do you know that?"

Chang had her own questions. "Who the hell is Mitri Amos? What are you talking about? What's going on...? What happened to you?"

"Like I said, it's a long story."

"Well," Chang said, "he's...in another ship. Like yours. Only... newer. Better."

He really made it, Powell thought. *Sonuvabitch.*

"I'll blow off a few rounds when he passes by. I think we... hold on." A flashing red light appeared on Powell's monitor. From his perspective, the message originated almost two months earlier. But back in his proper sphere, the message had originated only two *hours* earlier, sent to *Crossline* as it originally passed through the wormhole. It finally caught up with him, caught up with them all: *DESTRUCT ACTIVATED FROM TOWER.* Had Desmond not disconnected the explosive in the ship's belly, Powell might have been destroyed then and there.

His vision went white with rage. It ripped through him with such intensity—unleashing the angst and pain and fear and desperation of his time on Aretha—that he didn't give a spit if he and Mitri Amos were shadows, brothers, or cosmic Twinkies squished into the same cellophane package, and that killing Mitri would be like killing himself, rupturing the fibrous tissue of who he was. An interdimensional murder/suicide. All Powell knew was that the son of a bitch who had claimed to be Harlan "Buddy" Rheams Jr. ordered him blasted from space into a billion little pieces, leaving his wife without a husband, his daughter without a dad. Channeling his own father, Powell knew that a man can only be pushed so far before his mind can take no more, before revenge overwhelms his capacity to forgive.

Chang's monitor duplicated Powell's. She saw what he saw. "Powell? It's…" There was a moment of silence, and then surrender in her voice. She sighed. "Get ready. He's coming."

Powell flipped switches, powering his deadly arsenal. He was locked in, finally reaching that inner ferocity his father tried to cultivate in him so many years ago, with a rifle in his hands. "Good," he said. "Good. Because I'm finally gonna kill that motherfucker."

Hundreds of hours of simulator training kept Mitri Amos sharp. The *Kosono II* controls handled perfectly. And yet it had been more than half a century since he flew an actual craft in space, and no matter how sophisticated they were, simulators were not the same as flight. They can replicate the experience down to the tiniest detail, but missing was the fear of death, the adrenaline rush triggering a pilot's survival instincts that simulations simply can't evoke. There's no AAA out in the cosmos. You're on your own.

The *Kosono II* finally left Earth's orbit, preparing for warp. With the advanced fuel cells, Mitri would be at the wormhole within minutes. Tower Command wanted an update. Aranuke had only just been put in charge of the entire company, and still didn't quite feel like it was his show to run. Which, of course, it wasn't.

"Mr. Rheams…Buddy. Sir."

"Easy, Dale. Easy."

Chang clarified their position. "Powell's coming to kick your ass, sir. He's pretty pissed off. He saw the destruct order."

Chandra had her own questions. "*What* destruct order?"

Mitri nodded, smiled to himself. "I figured. The wormhole must have delayed the signal."

"What are you going to do, sir? I mean…about Powell."

Mitri looked through the canopy, took in the Earth. He forgot just how mesmerizing the view could be from space. The overwhelming reach of the cosmos. How bands of color refracted around the planet's perfectly round edges. He had spent twice as much time on Earth as he had on Aretha, and yet Earth never truly felt like home. For as much as he influenced the lives of the planet's citizens, he never allowed himself to be one of them, even during those moments when he thought he did. He was a stranger to all who knew him, and a memory to those he left behind. And now, in the recess of space, he was literally a man without a country. Without a planet. A man with no home. Even if he made it back to Aretha, he had no idea what awaited him.

"That's a good question, Chang. I'll think of something."

A message registered on his console. The warp engines were ready. With the final flip of a switch, he unleashed their mighty power. And without so much as a *goodbye, later dude,* or *nice knowing you*, Mitri Amos…Harlan "Buddy" Rheams Jr.… the Old Man…was gone. He left the planet Earth very much the same way he arrived.

Alone.

For only the second time, Chandra Powell stood inside Tower Command. And while it was loud and frantic and full of crazy energy, all she wanted was to hear her husband's voice. To know he was safe. But when she looked at Jesse, who was swinging her little arms back and forth, smiling with anticipation, Chandra saw herself in a way she never had before.

Chandra spent her adult life trying to keep the family traditions from splintering apart, as if the responsibility were hers alone. And now she found herself at the epicenter of the forces shaping her journey. The embodiment of past, present, and future, she thought just then about something her father used to say: *Don't ask permission. Do as you must.*

And how before that moment she hadn't reconciled her father's advice with her mother's, who taught Chandra the importance of knowing when to remain still and let things come, when to crack some skulls, and the wisdom to know the difference.

As she watched Aranuke stride over to the main console, Chandra shared a smile with her family, the kind of smile Jesse wore so easily. A smile that came from remaining still, as Feather said, from allowing the spirits to come, rather than trying to force an outcome she could never really dictate.

Chandra wanted more than ever to hear her husband's voice. She had much to share. But with those unmistakable words—*destruct order*—she was very much motivated to crack some fucking skulls.

Mitri Amos came out of warp seven hundred sixty-two million miles from Earth, just a meteor's throw from Powell's wormhole—with its outer white edges and brilliant blue center. Groggy from warp haze, it took a moment for his vision to clear. But what Mitri couldn't miss was Saturn and its incredible rings.

Chang was operating on the misinformation Aranuke had offered—about Buddy's blaze-of-glory death wish. Aranuke also failed to mention how the Old Man came to Earth in the first place, and was now seeking the very wormhole Powell disappeared through before they tried to kill him.

"Mr. Rheams. Sir? Are you okay?"

Still disoriented, Mitri removed a syringe from the first aid kit, and then gave himself an adrenaline booster. "Yes, Chang. I'm fine."

"What about Powell? We lost him again." It was a question without an obvious answer. *Crossline* did not appear on Mitri's scanners, and was not within visual range.

"Negative, Tower, negative. I don't see him. There's nothing on my screen tha—" Mitri's scanners started to flash. Three massive ice chunks broke away from Saturn's outer ring, hurtling toward him. "I think I've got something. I can see..." Three more ice chunks broke away. Then two more, then three, and then two more again, triple the size of the others. Just one meteor was large enough to flatten all the silicon breasts in Los Angeles, so there was little doubt what it would do to Mitri and the *Kosono II.*

The sight of those soaring ice rocks caught Mitri off guard, which, he quickly recognized, was exactly the point. Those thoughts were confirmed when, from behind the final cluster of ice, *Crossline* emerged in attack position, at full thrusters.

BLAM-BLAM-BLAM-BLAM-BLAM-BLAM-BLAM-BLAM!

The Tritanium-coated bullets were like explosive, heat-seeking fireflies. None of them hit the *Kosono II,* skewing to all sides, but as Powell unleashed round after round, just hundreds and hundreds of them, Mitri realized that Powell wasn't shooting at *him.* He blasted the ice meteors hurtling his way, breaking them into smaller pieces—like frozen buckshot—and across a much wider berth. The fragmented meteors also gave Powell the perfect cover to attack.

Mitri banked hard right and thrusted, taking him *away* from the wormhole—Powell's plan all along. *He's good,* Mitri thought. *And I'm in trouble.* He opened a line. "Powell. Talk to me. This is Mitri Amos. Please."

Powell's response was predictable.

BLAM-BLAM-BLAM-BLAM-BLAM-BLAM-BLAM-BLAM!

"Powell. Come on. Is my wife okay? Keela? Is she—?"

BLAM-BLAM-BLAM-BLAM-BLAM-BLAM-BLAM-BLAM!

The rounds were getting closer. "Okay. Guess not."

BLAM-BLAM-BLAM-BLAM-BLAM-BLAM-BLAM-BLAM!

"Powell...Powell!.........POWELL!"

It may have been almost a lifetime since Mitri Amos was in aerial combat, but those old instincts kicked in. He didn't want to kill Marcus Powell, if he could avoid it, but if it was Powell or him, well...Powell would have to suck it. Mitri came up behind one of the ice fragments. The maneuver wasn't enough to pull away from Powell, but it positioned Mitri to fire off two back-loaded missiles. He hoped they would distract Powell long enough for him to redirect toward the wormhole.

"Powell. I know you're upset, but I'm not your enemy. I don't want to fight y—"

BLAM-BLAM-BLAM-BLAM-BLAM-BLAM-BLAM-BLAM!

Along with another few dozen rounds, Powell let go two missiles of his own. One struck Mitri's first missile, which exploded. The second missile crashed into an ice chunk, which also exploded. *Crossline* clearly equipped with firepower and response capabilities upgraded from its original design, Mitri wasn't sure if he could outrun Powell long enough to reach the wormhole.

Unless Mitri's private engineers did their jobs as well as he hoped. Despite their hands-on access, unbeknownst to them, they fitted the *Kosono II* with its own wormhole pulse emitter. Separate sub-teams had been charged with developing the individual components, while another sub-team assembled them. Nobody except Mitri knew what they were for. He wasn't even sure if it would work. But he didn't have time to experiment. Powell was closing in. Fast.

Mitri had no choice but to press another button, and hope for the best.

It was now or never.

CHAPTER SIXTY

POWELL'S SENSORS WERE flashing. Chang was calling him over and over, but all he heard was the void of rage-induced silence in the vast nothing of space. He was laser-locked on Mitri Amos or Buddy Rheams or whatever he was choosing to call himself, and all Powell wanted was to *blast. Him. Dead.* His finger squeezed the trigger.

BLAM-BLAM-BLAM-BLAM-BLAM-BLAM-BLAM-BLAM!

He sprayed the area with missiles and bullets, unleashing those heat-seeking fireflies until the mechanism was a part of him. Hunting the ship like an animal, the blasts were an extension of his wrath, funneled through his veins, expelled into space. Powell chased the *Kosono II* first away from the Saturn rings and then toward them. The rings grew massive on approach.

Powell used a meteor as cover and then fired the *Crossline* thrusters so that Mitri Amos...Buddy Rheams...his shadow... was within range. Powell's sensors grabbed hold of the *Kosono II*, centered in his crosshairs. His system read: *WEAPONS LOCKED*

With vengeance in his heart, Powell was about to squeeze the trigger. And then a strange thing happened.

Mitri took a calculated risk. The wormhole emitter required an immense power supply, draining from the weapons, thrusters, and hydraulics. If successful, the tactic would be well worth it—a second wormhole leading back to Aretha. If not, he was an easy kill. *No choice*, he thought. *I'm outmatched.*

Mitri gave the *Kosono II* a quick thrust to pull away from Powell, long enough to focus on a single spot in the distance. To initiate the pulse emitter. Mitri had the faster ship, although not by much, but Powell had the edge as a pilot. Despite simulator training, it had simply been too long between flights for Mitri to perform at optimal levels. He had to hope that experience—and maybe even a miracle—would win out.

More than fifty years of plotting, scheming, scraping, and ingenuity, and it would all come down to *maybe*. He thought of Keela just then, though he could barely remember what she looked like. Her face was just a faded memory, an idea of someone he told himself was still out there somewhere, waiting for him, even if there was no one truly left to remember. But if a ghosted memory was all he had left, it would have to do. He had nothing else.

Here we go, my love. Pray for me.

The coordinates were set. Mitri fired the pulse emitter. The surge built up ahead—like a welder's torch cutting through steel. His eyes widened in disbelief. He knew that firing the untested mechanism could be the equivalent of initiating the self-destruct sequence. Just a matter of time before he went *BOOM*. But it was working. It was really working. Though faint, he saw a ripple appear ahead, with a brilliant blue center. As Powell closed in, a new wormhole emerged. "Oh my god," Mitri said. "This is—"

A vibration. Mitri hoped it was simply the effects of the wormhole emitter, that his ship was reacting to the powerful device. But then a spark told him otherwise.

The mechanism shorted, cutting the pulse. Had there been time to consider his options or soothe his wounded soul, he would have sat there, in the cockpit, staring into the great distance. Sunk. Deflated. But with Powell bearing down on him Mitri immediately thrust into evasive maneuvers. Mostly avoiding gunfire, the left wing caught a few bullets. His only option was to reset the warp engines and try another pulse. Without waiting for the coordinates to configure, he again flipped the switches.

One. *Clack.* Two. *Clack.* Three. *Clack.*

A red warning light appeared. The pulse emitter overloaded.

The *Kosono II* tremored, and then went dark. His systems shut down. The warp engines were dead. And very likely, so was he.

With weapons locked on the *Kosono II*, Powell flashed back to the Albany woods with his father. Early morning. The deer drank from a stream. Then it looked up, stared at him. Dead ahead. Its eyes were black and opened wide, oblivious to the impending violence. To its own mortality.

The rifle, that killing instrument, was in Powell's small hands. There was silence, then his father's voice: *Look through the scope. Find the target. Take a breath. See it…And when you're ready…fire.*

In deep space, Powell took that breath. He thought about the weight that came with pulling the trigger. Not long ago he shot Riva dead, felt the pang of extinguishing a monster. But now he had to decide if he could take a life that was no threat to him. If in cold blood, he could murder.

And then a voice came through his helmet. It was Mitri Amos.

"Powell. I didn't want this. Not for me. Not for you." For two men who had spent little time together, there was more between them than the distance separating their ships and the weaponry that could destroy them both.

Find the target…

"I miss Keela," he said.

Take a breath…

"You know what it's like. To be so close…"

And when you're ready…

Mitri let out a resigned chuckle. "…yet so far away."

Fire.

And then another voice came through. "Baby. You there?"

Powell released his grip. "…Candy?"

"Baby?"

"Oh, my God. Baby! Is it you?"

"Yeah," she said. "It's me."

Powell looked to the picture of his family, only to remember that it was gone. And yet in an odd way he was relieved, more determined than ever to see his wife and daughter again with his own eyes, rather than hold on to their image, lest it fade away.

"Hi, Daddy."

"Jesse!"

"Daddy-Daddy-Daddy. Do you see Meaty?"

Chandra clarified. "She means Mitri...er, Buddy, er, you know. The Old Man."

Powell still had his shadow locked in. "You *know* about that?"

"He told us."

"He *what*?"

"It's complicated. Just...let him go. He only wants to—"

"But he—"

"I know, baby. I know." The reach in Chandra's voice found its way to him, soothed an inner wrath he'd only just discovered. But the consequence of confronting his demons was that they now had a voice—they didn't wash away just because Powell finally acknowledged them. That voice was strong. Unleashed. And it wanted to roar. "Don't do it," she said. "Come home."

"Meaty good, Daddy. Meaty-Meaty good."

Caught between worlds, Powell was on the precipice of one, looking back on another. A single step in either direction would shape the man he would forever become. He reached for his console. He let out a hard sigh, flipped a switch. "Mitri...?"

"Powell...?"

Although his console was clear now, all Powell could see was the message: *DESTRUCT ACTIVATED FROM TOWER.*

He curled his lip, re-gripped the flight stick, considered in a very real way depressing the trigger just one more time. But Powell knew more than ever that his actions had consequences. That his rage was less about Mitri Amos, and more about himself, no matter how closely linked they were. And then those amazing words from his two best girls won him over.

Daddy. Baby. Come home.

It took all of his restraint, but finally, Powell's arm unclenched. "Keela. She—"

"She's alive? She's okay? She's..."

Powell let himself calm down. "She's tough. Shaky, but tough."

"T-thank you..."

Soon to be reunited with his own wife and child, Powell was unsure how much to reveal about what he knew of Aretha. "But you should know. It's bad."

There was a moment of silence. "...How bad?"

Powell clicked his teeth. "The war. It's coming."

Mitri stayed silent, an acknowledgement between these two men—two shadows—when words could only dilute the meaning. "I guess I screwed up."

Powell chuckled uneasily. He didn't have the heart to explain. Mitri would find out soon enough. "You did kinda lie to everyone on Earth and changed the course of history."

"Yeah, well," Mitri said, "...you scared the crap out of your wife."

"So did you!"

There was another long silence, the unspoken words of these two men—two shadows—forgiving each other. And themselves.

Laughter finally crept out, until Mitri called them back to action. "Take it easy, Powell. I haven't seen my wife in a heckuva long time."

Powell stared out at the rings of Saturn, thinking that they had been out there for billions of years, just going round and round and round, serving a grand purpose, and perhaps no purpose at all. And that his life had meaning, like Chill said, even when he couldn't see it himself. "It's been a lot less for her...a lot less...if that means anything. She's just like you remember."

There was a long, long pause before Mitri responded. "It does."

It took all he had to keep from sobbing. For a half century he assumed a persona he told himself was just a disguise, to protect himself, but he wondered now if maybe Buddy Rheams Jr. was the man he was always meant to be, and Mitri Amos—husband of Keela Amos, lost son of Grinroad—was actually the one who had spent his life hiding, denying his true self. Mitri left his people as they faced extinction. But had he run toward the solution or away from the problem? Or both? Was he a hero, a coward, or something else altogether? In the recess of space, there were no answers. After a lifetime that seemed more dreamlike than real, a lump rose in his throat. He would have to look Keela in the eyes again to find out.

Without further contact from Powell, Mitri tightened his gloves, ignited his boosters and then, finally, disappeared through the wormhole. Like his time on Earth, it collapsed behind him.

CHAPTER SIXTY-ONE

WITH POWELL SAFE, Chang figured she should say something. "So, uh, Dale, listen…"

Aranuke chuckled. "Please. Don't ruin this. It's been a long day."

Chang nodded. "Yep. It sure has." She'd been fighting herself about it for months, but if this wasn't the time, it never would be. "We don't have to talk about it, if you don't want to, but…no. Yeah. I guess we should."

"Chang. Seriously. Spit it out. If you're going to run the floor…then run it."

"Wait. What? I'm running what?"

"The Old Man promoted you. I get his job, you get mine. We'll probably need to iron out a few things, process-wise. Chandra Powell, too. It's complicated."

"Huh. Well…that changes a lot." Chang patted her stomach. "You see this here?"

"Yeah?"

She let the moment go still before answering, held her eyes open wide.

Aranuke was growing impatient. "*Aaaaaand…?*"

"It's yours."

Aranuke blinked hard before sighing relief. "Jesus. You scared me. For a minute there I thought you were going to…"

Chang could see his gears start to wind, but he wasn't quite there yet. "At Gloria's wake. You had a lot to drink. You were pretty messed up. Me, too. I figured you were an extra dickhead lately because you didn't want to talk about it. But you really don't remember, do you? It was my first time with a man in eleven years." She shrugged. "Who knew?"

Aranuke was a blank stare. He was a sunken ship. "You mean we...? And that's my...? So we're having a...?"

Chang nodded. "We did. It is. And we are."

Aranuke leaned on the console. Chang reached over; their fingers touched. And as their eyes met in an awkward pause, they couldn't help but notice which button was just above their hands. It was red.

Marcus Powell felt like the most powerful man in the world. And in a way, he was. His wife and child smothered him with hugs and kisses. Walking down a narrow corridor in Tower Command, he had Jesse in his arms, Chandra's hand in his. There was much to discuss with the Tower wonks, but for the moment, it would have to wait. "*Sooooo*," he said. "What'd I miss?"

Chandra looked at Jesse, who giggled. "I got a new job."

"Really...? *When?*"

"Today."

"Um...'kay. I think. Doing what?"

Chandra leaned her shoulder into his so that the three of them were snuggled together as they walked. "I'll fill you in. But we've got a few questions of our own...don't we, Jess?"

Jesse nodded. "*Mm-hmm.*"

Powell knew he had much to answer for. Might as well get started. "Oh, yeah? Shoot."

"Chill, Daddy, Chill. Where's Chill?"

Assuming that his journey through time, space, and dimension was but a glimpse into the pure reach of the cosmos, his daughter found a way to surprise him yet again. "Chill? How do you know about him?"

"Gremma told me."

Chandra nodded. "It's okay. Just go with it."

So he did. "*Okaaaay.* When?"

"When you were kissing the lady with the red hair."

Chandra's eyes broke open. She stood up straight again. "Say what now?"

Wormholes, wall cakes, and cosmic shadows? Powell could deal with them all. The same again with muffin zombies, corporate raids, and a distant world on the brink of annihilation. But confronted with an awkward family moment? Not so much. Looking for a quick escape, he glanced at a giant portrait of Buddy Rheams Jr.—his shadow—hanging on the wall, and in an odd, knowing sort of way, smirking right at him, as if the Old Man somehow knew all along that they would meet this way, sooner or later.

Powell nodded in recognition of his two selves. On both sides of the cosmos, the women in his life pushed him to be more than he would have been otherwise, accepted his passions, and held him accountable when he lost his way. Once again, he knew he was in trouble.

"Uh, nothing, honey, nothing. We'll talk about it later."

ACKNOWLEDGMENTS

THANKS TO ALL who read early drafts of *Crossline*, and offered feedback and encouragement. Special thanks to my editor James Chambers, who turned a jumbled manuscript into a tightly orchestrated adventure, to my copy editor Barney O'Neill, for the fine-tuning, and to Nick Dubois, for helping me with the pilot's perspective, especially since he contributed to breaking my thumb in football practice all those years ago.

Very special thanks to my friend Tom Peters, who was there at the beginning, and helped me see just how big *Crossline* could be, and big thanks to all the guys at Crazy 8 Press, who decided they wanted to collaborate with me, and give Crossline a home.

And, as always, hugs and kisses to my wife and children, who are my greatest inspiration, and stand by me through it all.

ABOUT THE AUTHOR

RUSS COLCHAMIRO IS the author of the rollicking space adventure *Crossline*, the hilarious scifi backpacking comedy *Finders Keepers*, and the outrageous sequels, *Genius de Milo* and *Astropalooza*, all with Crazy 8 Press.

Russ lives in West Orange, NJ, with his wife, two children, and crazy dog, Simon, who may in fact be an alien himself. Russ has also contributed to several Crazy 8 Press anthologies, including *Tales of the Crimson Keep*, *Pangaea*, and *Altered States of the Union*. He is now at work on a top-secret project, and a *Finders Keepers* spin-off.

For more on *Crossline* and Russ' other works, you can visit his website, www.russcolchamiro.com, follow him on Twitter @AuthorDudeRuss, follow him on Goodreads, and 'like' his Facebook author page. Russ encourages you to email him at authorduderuss@gmail.com

BACKPACKING HAS NEVER BEEN FUNNIER!

Two backpackers.
One jar.
The Universe's DNA.
The fate of the Cosmos has never been
in better hands.
Except for that time
they initiated the next Big Bang.
They're working on it.

PICK UP THE HILARIOUS SCIFI COMEDY SERIES FROM RUSS COLCHAMIRO:

CRAZY 8 PRESS
www.crazy8press.com

15 BRILLIANT AUTHORS. 15 AMAZING STORIES.

Superheroes and supervillains. AI, private eyes, off-world, and space cruisers.
Sleep surrogates. Time travel. Aliens and monsters. And one DuckBob.
Love, Murder & Mayhem has never been so much fun.

"An entertaining mix . . . of high-energy and sentimental stories."
—Publishers Weekly

"I was awestruck. Each of them were brilliant. Don't miss it!"
—The Book Elf

"This is the strongest collection of stories I can remember reading in years."
—The Irresponsible Reader

CRAZY 8 PRESS
www.crazy8press.com

READ THE BOOK THE NOOK BLOG CALLED "AN ABSURDLY BRILLIANT ROMP":

DuckBob Spinowitz is just an average, ordinary guy. Except he has the head of a duck. But does that really qualify him to save the universe? Unfortunately, it looks like he's about to find out! Join DuckBob on a riotous adventure across the galaxy as he tries to stop an alien invasion with nothing but his good looks, his wit, and his charm.

We may be doomed.

And don't miss the side-splitting sequels:

TOO SMALL FOR TALL
and
THREE SMALL COINKYDINKS

CRAZY 8 PRESS
www.crazy8press.com

WHO DARES OPPOSE A GOD?

At the age of thirty-eight, Zeno Aristos has quit the NYPD and is trying to figure out what to do with his life. Then someone close to him is kidnapped by dark and cryptic forces. The deeper Zeno digs, the more he realizes he's dealing not with a mere earthly adversary but with an entity steeped in the deepest and most malevolent of ancient mysteries.

In *Fight the Gods*, Michael Jan Friedman takes a major creative step beyond the *Star Trek* novels, comic books, and television scripts with which his name has become synonymous, and braves the sinister rooftops and mystical back alleys of urban fantasy. Whatever you think you know of him or of his work...you ain't seen nothin' yet.

CRAZY 8 PRESS
www.crazy8press.com

WELCOME TO CAMELOT!

You thought you knew about King Arthur and his knights? Guess again!

Learn here, for the first time, the down-and-dirty royal secrets that plagued Camelot as told by someone who was actually there, and adapted by acclaimed *New York Times* bestseller Peter David. Full of sensationalism, startling secrets and astounding revelations, *The Camelot Papers* is to the realm of Arthur what the *Pentagon Papers* is to the military: something that all those concerned would rather you didn't see. What are you waiting for?

www.crazy8press.com

THERE'S A LOT AT STAKE HERE!

Meet Vince Hammond. He has a secret that, if his mother finds out, she will absolutely kill him.

No, he's not dating a girl she'd hate. No, he's not gay.

He's a vampire. And Mom is a vampire hunter. And all of his friends are vampire hunters. And his fiancee is a vampire hunter, and so are his future in-laws.

Need an antidote to every other vampire novel out there? Then you're going to want to be *Pulling Up Stakes*. After putting a silver bullet in werewolves in his classic *Howling Mad*, *New York Times* Bestseller Peter David now sinks his teeth into vampire lore, with bloody good results.

www.crazy8press.com

WHEN AZTECS RULE THE EARTH!

It's 2012. Maxtla Colhua is an Investigator for the Empire–an Aztec Empire that successfully repelled Hernan Cortes in 1603 and now stretches from one end of what we call the Americas to the other. But now it is the Last Sun, and someone has decided to punctuate it with a series of grisly murders reminiscent of the pagan sacrifices of ancient times. Can Maxtla find the killer before his city is ripped apart? Next he has to locate the missing star of a brutal Aztec ball game, the idol of millions. But to do that Maxtla will have to challenge the most powerful men and women in the Empire—or see its streets run red with blood.

Aztlan is a pair of murder mysteries set in an exciting world that never was but could have been!

CRAZY 8 PRESS
www.crazy8press.com

THE GODS HAVE RETURNED. ALL OF THEM.

In 2012 every pantheon of gods and goddesses, from every belief the world over, returned... changing the world forever. As the pantheons settle into their ancestral lands, they vie for worshippers, gaining or losing power along the way. The gods find the world of Man a bewildering, crazy quilt, and wish to remake it in their own image. Meet some of the inhabitants of this strangely familiar world in this anthology series that explores faith, divinity, and humanity. Chronicling this new tomorrow are Robert Greenberger, Paul Kupperberg, Aaron Rosenberg, and many more. Join them and discover a world where everything old is new again—even the gods themselves.

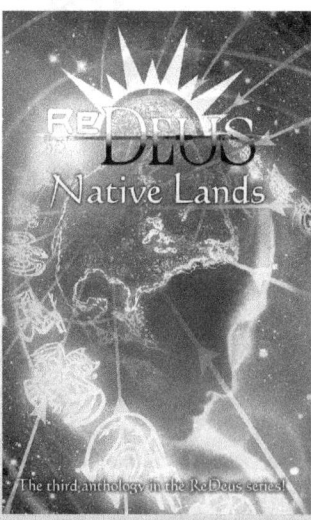

CRAZY 8 PRESS

www.crazy8press.com

GREAT BOOKS BY GREAT AUTHORS
DIRECT TO READERS

WHY?
BECAUSE WE'RE CRAZY!!!

CRAZY 8 PRESS
www.crazy8press.com

www.ingramcontent.com/pod-product-compliance
Lightning Source LLC
Chambersburg PA
CBHW071052250626

47159CB00002B/456